"*Clovis* is a lyrical tale set in the New West, where the interests of oil companies clash with the need to preserve and record the artifacts left by long gone inhabitants of the land. In this novel, Hanna and her archeological compatriots are hired by CanAm Oil Company to assess the impact of an oil line on historical native sites. The complex relationships between her and her co-workers fascinate. The lush descriptions of the natural beauty she encounters are seductive. This is truly a wonderful look into the unique personality of people who choose to make a living doing field work. They are a breed apart. An excellent read that keeps you engaged from the beginning."

—*Big Sky Independent Press*

"*Clovis* is a wonder of a novel that will dazzle you with its impassioned understanding of archeology, Western landscapes, and human connection. Jack Clinton's writing about hiking and climbing and seeking solace in the outdoors is among the best I've ever read. In Hanna, Clinton has created an unconventional heroine for all seasons, a humane and restless seeker who can master every terrain except that of her own heart."

—Alyson Hagy, author of *Boleto*

Clovis *is dedicated to the memory of*
Mary F. Heeran and Helen Heeran Clinton,
who selflessly did what had to be done.

And with love to Dana Wahlquist and
Emma Loulse Clinton.

Clovis

Jack Clinton

Harvard Square Editions
New York
2018

ISBN 978-1-941861-53-0
Printed in the United States of America

Published in the United States by
Harvard Square Editions
www.harvardsquareeditions.org

Prologue

A BARTENDER at a crossroads tavern once passionately argued that this state is not a state at all. It is simply a space one must cross to reach other destinations: a highway; a road; a two-track across a sage and short-grass prairie; a space left by the erosion of wind; a frozen tundra and chalk-dry desert; a land for all that is damned, lonesome and hollow.

This vacuum comforted Hanna as she traversed the spine of a ridge, which she followed to stay away from the mud in the basin. She stopped and stared off across the space that was quickly turning white, as snow collected on sagebrush. She was anxious at the speed and intensity of the storm. "Ten minutes," she said to the falling snow. "What's ten or 20 minutes more?" The horizon appeared vaguely out of the grey sky and ran past her, up to the foothills, and then disappeared into the clouds. The ground was warm enough to melt the May snow; however, snow still collected on the leafy sage, and made the world appear black and white against the descending sky. If she were to die at this point in time, it would be a while before anyone found her. Coyotes and turkey vultures might eat parts of her. She was glad that such a place existed.

This area was at the extreme edge of the survey line, but she came here because she wanted to see if it was still here—where she had hidden it during the preliminary survey last year.

In the windless silence, she could hear the snow pelting her parka. It was odd that there was no wind with the sudden spring squall. There was always wind, but now the large, heavy flakes fell straight and fast from the sky, impossibly heavy, as if no cloud ever could have held them, quarter-sized plates of slush spattering loudly against the hood of her jacket.

She reached the large stack of granite boulders on the shoulder of the ancient moraine out here in the sage prairie, where the glaciers had come to die. The boulders sat upon the ridge, out of place, demanding the credence of geology, stating that megalithic events had occurred, and hundreds of feet of ice had made these ridges and then retreated back to a scanty few acres of dirty, crusty ice hidden deep in the mountains. She walked around to the south side of the moraine and went beneath the overhang of the largest boulder. It was evident that animals sought shelter here from time to time, leaving footprints and scat. They rested here in the warmth of the spring sun as the wind raked its way across the plains. In the center of the alcove's floor there was a flat stone. She turned it over, brushed away some sand, and picked up the Clovis spear point that lay beneath it, remembering Tim's words.

"I'd leave it," he had said, annoyed to have left his survey transit down below, after she had waved and called him up to the site.

"What do you mean you'd leave it? This is huge!"

Tim watched the wind buffet her short blonde hair as she asked him to concur with her blue eyes. He wanted to agree, but settled for the truth. "I know. I'd leave it—and hide it," he said, handing it back with an uneasy awe.

"You're serious?" she asked, staring hard at him.

"Well, you're the archeologist, but I'd bury it right where you found it—either that, or write it up and submit it to be archived on a shelf in a university basement. I'd say it belongs here," he said, before striding back down the hill to collect the transit.

Hanna knew the Clovis would still be there. It wasn't even a matter of faith. It was like swinging one's feet out of bed in the morning, knowing that they would land firmly on the floor. Like the day she found it, when she saw the tiny alcove from the basin floor. She looked up and knew that there was something there, and she needed to see it. She was so certain that it was almost no surprise to find the long,

perfect Clovis point that had waited there for thousands of
years. It occupied the entire palm of her hand and had a
vertical, central flute, which allowed it to be more securely
hafted to the shaft of what was most likely the large arrow-
like dart launched from a an atlatl throwing stick.

When she stooped inside the alcove and saw the
shimmering black obsidian protruding from the sand, she
knew that this was what she had come to see. She knew that
this would make the entire day worthwhile. She knew that
someone had sat here in the sun, or had perhaps come in out
of the spring snow, and left her this beautiful, black obsidian
Clovis. Perhaps it was when the glaciers were still on the
other side of the moraine, plowing south, or when a
theoretical, altithermal period baked the land for a few
millennia. An ancient person had sat here and crafted this
projectile point for her. He, or she, or they, had crafted many
tools, as was evident from the multitude of obsidian and
chert flakes littering the alcove's floor. The material told her
that these people had traveled from far away. The nearest
quarry for black obsidian was hundreds of miles to the
north. Maybe they walked? Maybe they traded?

Hanna imagined two groups of ancient people
meeting on the vast, empty plains, squatting on their heels,
trading pieces of stone, jerked meat, pemmican, perhaps
furs. However, other than the rare stone, there was very little
that each group couldn't obtain on their own. There weren't
even horses in North America yet, and wouldn't be for
several thousand years. The modern bison had not yet
evolved down from the giant, ancient ones; perhaps there
were still a few mammoths left on the continent. There were
not yet pyramids in Egypt, or large cities in Mesopotamia or
in China. Sodom and Gomorrah had not yet been built or
destroyed, nor had the Old Testament God yet created the
Earth.

Hanna held the point in her hand. It was perfect; it was
entire and unbroken. She believed that it had never been
used. Did the ancient one who created it leave it here to be

found at another time? In a world largely without possessions, people didn't simply forget a fine survival tool made from valuable stone. She looked south from beneath the overhang. The storm had intensified so that the exact horizon was uncertain. The worm of fear began to twist in her guts.

The dusty sand of the alcove clung to her wherever her wet hands and clothes came in contact with it. She put the point back in its place, sifted a little sand over it and then returned the flat stone. As she left the overhang she lightly brushed away her footprints from the sand, which was still dry and dusty, below the boulders.

Work was over for the day, and perhaps the next few days, as the storm seemed to promise much more than a quick squall. Outside, the translucent sleet was now sticking to the ground. She hurried along the ridge slipping here and there on large, slush-covered cobbles. She feared that the roads would be turning to gumbo, becoming too slick and muddy to negotiate. They were already in questionable condition after a winter's freezing and a spring's thawing, and it was a good ten miles to the highway.

She sighed with relief once she had started the truck and turned on the heat. After a few miles on the two-track road, she had to get out and physically lock the hubs of the front axle into four-wheel drive. The clay road was deteriorating quickly as it sucked up moisture. Mud clung thickly to the tires, sticking to the inside of the wheel wells and undercarriage. The miles went by slowly and driving demanded her full attention. If she got stuck now, she would be spending the night, or even days, in her truck unless a rancher came along, which was highly unlikely. The snow came in heavy waves like sheets of rain. At times the windshield wipers couldn't keep up with both the snow and the flying mud.

When she reached the paved highway, she gave a celebratory hoot. Weather conditions were nearing whiteout, but now she would be safe. She looked back where she had come from. The foothills, the buttes, and moraines were all gone, except for two muddy ruts crawling out of the whiteness. She sat in the warmth of the truck for a moment before stepping into the swirling storm to unlock the mud-caked hubs out of four-wheel drive. Brown muddy sludge dripped from the truck onto the untracked snow. She walked out into the middle of the road and looked up and down. In one direction the road disappeared at the top of a hill. In the other, it disappeared at an uncertain point on a grey horizon, and she stared down the white, abandoned highway, wondering if there was anyone left on Earth. Snow stacked quickly upon her shoulders. In the quiet, morose beauty of the afternoon, she felt reluctant to drive away. Then she pricked up her ears at the sound of a distant rumble, and returned to her truck. She put on a baseball cap, and slouched down in the seat. A black pickup appeared, speeding out of the storm. She pulled a canister of Mace from between the seats and tucked it under her thigh. The truck roared past, too fast for the slushy road.

Hanna

Hanna spent the night in a hotel room and then returned to the office of High Desert Archeology in Warren the following day. The gale turned out to be a large spring storm, and she knew that it would keep them out of the field for some time. She needed to put in some hours, so she returned to the office where there was always work mapping the archeological sites she found and writing reports. The other field hands knew this also, but she usually arose earlier and nabbed one of the two cubicles before anyone else. Beating the others to one of the computers was no great feat, because bad weather was generally considered 'down time' and a good excuse to eat and drink excessively. Hanna was working for a couple of hours before Karl showed up. His eyes were puffy, and his skin sallow. Dog followed, his hair was in two glossy, black braids—they were a few days old and coming undone. He followed the boss closely. As a slight, boyish woman, without much authority, Hanna was a non-person to Dog, unworthy of his attention.

"Hey Karl, hey Doggie," she said, baiting him.

"Hanna!" Karl said, with admiration, "I was wondering what had happened to you. I thought you might be stuck down to your axels in hell's butthole somewhere!"

Dog snickered obediently.

"From the looks of the Bronco, you had a time down there."

"Yeah, it was kinda close. I left as soon as the weather turned, spent the night in Manton and came back yesterday."

"You been finding much?"

"No, just typical sites and isolates. There is one place that might need to be tested, lots of surface material...a lot of stuff coming up out of the ground, a couple of hearths, fire-cracked rock, some cultural material...hard to tell. Actually, I'd say it should be tested because of the amount of deposition. It's all in the forms."

"Any trouble with the roads?"

"No, but there would have been if I'd left any later. That road's gonna be gumbo until the sun dries it. Send Hugh down there, he'll love it."

Karl laughed, "No, I can't afford anymore of Hugh's four-wheeling."

Dog wandered away as he was excluded from the conversation. He went to the coffee table and poured a cold cup from yesterday, but with a little creamer and a few seconds in the microwave, he was happy with it. He sat at one of the tables and put his feet up. He wasn't upset that Hanna had come in early to claim the workspace; he didn't care for office work. He preferred to sit out a storm, loafing in the office, following Karl and Hugh around, preparing the physical equipment for the field, until it was late enough in the afternoon to resume eating and drinking.

Donna came in at nine in her secretary outfit; pleated skirt, blouse, and jacket. She said hello, and shot Karl a knowing smirk as she sashayed her ample bottom across the office, looking like the well-dressed den mother of a troupe of scruffy hooligans. Hugh came in at ten with doughnuts and a quart of milk. The doughnuts were well received. He grabbed Hanna roughly by the back of the neck and mussed her short hair, as if she was a favorite nephew. "I thought maybe you'd fallen in love with a cowboy or somethin'."

"Well I almost had one," Hanna said dryly, "but he said he already had a sweet thang named Hugh."

Hugh laughed his wheezing, shoulder shrugging laugh. His little Buddha belly bounced joyously.

Dog was visibly relieved that Hugh had arrived. He smiled sullenly and gobbled up glazed doughnuts, gravitating toward Hugh, who was pacing around the office questioning Karl, Donna, and Hanna about the status of different projects. Hugh sucked on his quart of milk and ate doughnuts, consuming each in two bites.

Before lunch, Karl called Hugh and Hanna to one of the

worktables. He was linking together large maps of the CanAm Project, the Canadian–American Gas Line. They reviewed the sections that had been surveyed by CanAm's engineers and then lined out what Karl's company had already walked and flagged. The possible test sites of historic and prehistoric materials had been noted with coordinates, where Hanna, or another archeologist would dig to see what artifacts, if any, lay beneath the surface. Any artifacts or major sites on public lands would then fall under the guidelines of the Federal Antiquities Act and state laws. CanAm had to comply with those laws, and it was up to the crews of High Desert Archeology to be sure they did. The pipeline couldn't advance until the impact on all cultural sites and materials had been considered or mitigated.

Karl pushed his chair away from the table and leaned forward, signaling a change of topic, "We need to get some work done, even if the weather's bad. Let's look at where we might survey and test until it all dries out. I was thinking that it might be drier down South. Maybe we can pick up the line down there and squeak out a week or so along the lower, southern section. It'll be warmer and drier."

"We could check it out first, test the roads.... It's sandy and rockier down there. No gumbo," Hugh trailed off. "Hanna, did you see any CanAm crews?"

"No," she said, "and you could tell from the roads that no one had been in there for a while."

Karl stood back, taking in the whole map. "Hugh, you should go down there with somebody tomorrow and give us a call as soon as you can. We'll send the rest of the crew down if things are dry enough." Karl moved his finger across the map, hundreds of miles to the north, "The crew on this end of the project seems to be moving along well, and we need to match that down here."

"So, we'll be in the Satellite Motel if you need us."

Dog moved closer, fearing he might be left out of the plans, feigning interest in another glazed doughnut.

Hanna watched him from the corner of her eye.

Sometimes she wanted to call him out and use the name she had seen in his file, 'James Edward Medicine Dog'. But she knew that he guarded that name, and it would be a serious affront to use it.

"Yeah, that's fine." Karl scrubbed his face dryly with one hand. "We've got to get going on this. We need to complete more mileage so CanAm can pay me. I need more money before you all get a check. Plus, the rest of the crew members will be showing up soon, and I have to have work for them too."

Hugh looked at Hanna, "What do you think Hanna, you and me all alone in Rocket City?"

Hanna awoke from a daydream, and looked around not understanding the joke for a moment. "No you better take Dog," she smiled. "He'll be better company at the Kitty Lounge."

They laughed for a moment, and Dog wandered away, smug to be traveling with Hugh on the trip down South.

The office was quiet after everyone left for lunch. Hanna knew that the only ones returning to the office would be Karl and Donna. Dog and Hugh would be out at the storage sheds getting the vehicles ready. Hanna snacked on carrots and fruit while the rest of them went down to the Rustler. She longed to eat a huge meal also, to sit at the table laughing and joking, but her vegetarian diet excluded her from these feasts.

Coming in early, and working through lunch, Hanna usually left at three, allowing Karl and Donna to pursue their tawdry tryst. It made Hanna ill to imagine them furtively fornicating on his desk like degenerate teenagers. She had never caught them, but she had returned to find the door locked, or a table's worth of papers strewn across the floor.

"Oh, was that door locked?" Donna would blush, and then, immediately, assume her dignified airs, as if the shabby second-story office was a bank in the city, as if she had no cuckolded husband.

"Did you get caught in that wind? It blew through here

like a hurricane!" Karl roared, laughing at his own joke, knowing that Hanna wasn't fooled for a second.

Hanna returned to her room at the Starlight Motor Hotel at three. She flopped down on her bed and stared around the room. It was a cheap hotel and everything in it was a metal alloy or synthetic composite. She generally brought her own bedding. She often turned the mattress over, put down a thick cotton mattress pad and then her own cotton sheets, sleeping bag, and pillows. The idea of motel patrons performing depraved acts in the same bed she slept upon made her flesh crawl. If she was staying more than one night she left large notes to the maids not to touch the bed. In larger towns, she wrote the instructions out in Spanish also, *"¡Deje la cama como está, por favor!"*

She eyed the TV remote longingly. She wished that it would rain endlessly and she could be in a real house, reading on a real couch. She wished she could go find someone she cared for, like Tim, or Gina, or Paul, and have a beer. Instead, she looked at the corner of the room where her shoes and running clothes waited patiently, and she languidly pulled herself from the mattress and undressed. She looked at herself in the mirror for a moment. She was skinny, with her ribs plainly showing through. Her breasts seemed smaller. She cupped them in her hands for a moment and then pulled on her jogging bra. She stood up straight and found her body to her liking. She looked at her face and saw scratches on the side her cheekbone. Her nose was sunburned and chapped. She needed to eat more. Her cheeks were sunken, making her appear older.

She pulled on her running shorts, laced her shoes, gathered up her pile of sweats and wind-shirts, and set off for the outskirts of town.

She drove out past the wheat fields and the irrigated lands. The winter wheat was well out of the ground, turning the fields a vibrant green. She drove out of the valley and up onto the bench to the waterless desert, where she followed one of the myriad roads that cut back and forth across the

hills. There were deep trenches where the four-wheel drives
had churned their way through the spring mud. There were
steeper slopes that had been used as hill climbs, with tracks
laid neatly side-by-side, quickly eroding into gullies and
arroyos. Hanna continued out, where the subtle hills ended
at a bench. She parked her truck and got out, stretching in
just her T-shirt and shorts to test the air temperature. She
folded her seat forward and took out a small belt that
holstered a canister of Mace, lifted up her shirt, to settle it
next to her skin, and adjusted the belt so that the canister
rested in the small of her back. She tucked in the front of her
shirt but left the back free so she could easily access it. She
hated running in four-wheel drive areas where guys came to
take out their aggressions, destroying the land and their
vehicles, shooting their guns, killing birds, rabbits, coyotes,
prairie dogs, ground squirrels, and each other if they were
drunk enough.

It was breezy and cool, so she put on a nylon wind-shirt,
and headed up a game-and-cattle trail that followed a steep-
sided arroyo. She ran clumsily at first, her breathing labored,
her lungs demanding more air. She plodded ahead with
heavy feet until she shed her lethargy, and suddenly she was
running swiftly down a winding gulley. She frightened
jackrabbits up out of the bottom. They rocketed out in front
of her, too stupid to climb the banks and escape. Grey sage
thrashers flew from bush to bush, eyeing her cautiously.

After a couple of miles, she climbed out of the gulley and
ran across a short plain into the rocky juniper brakes. A good
trail wound through the junipers. The land was not as
trashed up here as it was closer to town. She ran faster,
feeling herself flying down the trails, her legs separated from
her body, her feet hugging the ground, finding their own
way, her freed mind wandering in different directions. The
sun came out briefly, pouring through a hole in the clouds,
heating the ground, filling her lungs with the scent of juniper
and sage. She spooked three does as she came through a
thicket; they bounded away ahead of her, and she sped up in

pursuit. They seemed amused at the odd behavior of the human, letting her pursue them at a distance, then bolting away.

Hanna wanted the 'flying-head feeling'. This is what she called it when she could no longer feel her body, and looking straight ahead, she could no longer see it. When all she was aware of was her mind and her eyes as her consciousness floated down the trail, as if her head was a small alien craft, a space probe, floating above a hostile planet. It would not happen this day, however; the feeling was elusive, like a good orgasm, and she was too far out of shape to force it. Her lungs labored harshly, sounding like they were rattling in the husk of someone else's body. Her legs and feet found their own way, but they felt slow and inefficient. She slowed down and found a pace where she could run more comfortably.

Clouds gathered in the distance, and the temperature dropped. She could tell that it would rain through the evening. She looked at her watch and saw that she had already been running for 40 minutes. Ahead, she saw the junction that would take her back, making the run an hour and 20 minutes. Although out of peak shape, she felt greatly refreshed. She wished that she could run further, or perhaps all day, the way birds flew when they migrated. She could start in Montana and run for a week down to Colorado, run all day, like driving a car; she could float her head across entire states, over mountains, across deserts and prairies, sleeping in the open as the sun set and trotting off again in the dawn's early light.

She knew that she had run far enough and was glad when her truck came into view over the hill, waiting for her like a patient animal. She walked the last quarter mile to cool down. Her legs felt rubbery as if they might collapse. Sweat stung her eyes, and her pulse raged as she struggled to fill her lungs to their maximum capacity. She put her hands high on her hips and stood up straight to help her breathing.

There had been times in her life when all that had mattered was achieving this feeling she had now. Whether there was work or not. Whether school was in session or during summer break. Whether papers were due or it was tax time. Whether or not she had a lover, or was working out of her truck in the middle of the badlands. All that had mattered was running. For years, it had been her drug. It had stood in the way of things she should have pursued and saved her from those that were better left alone. She was mostly over all the anger and angst of accepting her role and life in a world of men. She had outdistanced her haunting bugaboos and lost the voices of doubt and insecurity. Now, she ran because it helped her sleep, and saved her from hours of inane conversations in stifling bars and hotel rooms with unfamiliar and unwelcome crew members.

She returned to her room, showered and prepared a simple meal in the tiny corner kitchenette and sat at the counter watching the news, which only made her loneliness worse. It was all too depressing, but she watched anyway, riots and burning buildings, Middle Easterners running through rubble, firing guns in the air. There were rich, white men, outraged by the demanding gall of the poor and the immigrants. In Bangladesh, the bodies of people and cattle floated lazily in the floodwaters of the Ganges delta, like over-stuffed dolls, bumping rigidly in the lapping waves.

She froze at a knock at the door in the receding light. Hanna set the chain lock and opened the door a crack. Gina was on the other side mocking a scowl. Hanna's heart leapt. She undid the chain and quickly opened the door.

"You can never be too safe!" Gina chided, looking severe with her sharp nose and towheaded curls.

"Well, you haven't seen the swingers around here yet."

Hanna hugged her colleague briefly. "Gina! I haven't even seen you since November! Where did you go?"

"I spent the winter in Salt Lake, just like I told you, at the address you never wrote to."

"Well the mail goes both ways."

"Where would I send it? You don't even know where you went!" Gina laughed, knowing that her statement was true.

"Yeah, yeah," Hanna conceded. "Are you passing through, or are you gonna work?"

"I'm here to work. I went to the office, and Karl said that I could either room with you or Dog."

"So of course, you picked Dog!"

Gina didn't respond. She slid past Hanna and dropped her large athletic bag on the bed that was still made up with hotel bedding.

"You mean you and Dog aren't gonna...?"

"That's really funny Hanna," she said screwing up her eyes and lips. She flopped down on the bed. "D'ya eat yet?"

"Yeah, but I could get a beer while you ate...if you're hungry."

"Hell yes.... I'd eat a skunk's butt!" she said, mocking Hugh. "So what did you eat, two tablespoons of rice, and a cup-o-miso?"

Hanna only smiled at her joke, while looking for her wallet and keys. "Well, let's go eat and look for cowboys."

"You mean cowgirls?"

Hanna pretended not to hear.

"Do you think Karl and Donna are screwing in the office?" Gina asked.

"Do I even have to answer that?"

"Well, it really creeps me out," Gina said, as if she really shouldn't have to deal with something like that.

They stood quietly for a moment, looking at the TV where a wholesome woman was walking through her beautiful garden, telling the audience about the yeast infection she had in her vagina. Gina turned it off. She surprised Hanna by hugging her again. "I really missed you." She spoke into Hanna's shoulder, "You should've called or written."

Gina

Hanna and Gina drove south to the Satellite Motel in Rocket City to meet Dog and Hugh. The engineering firm contracted to CanAm had finished a 45-mile stretch of the line, and the gravel and dirt roads were dry enough to drive. Gina complained the whole way about 'The Rock' as she called Rocket City. "The most beautiful sight on earth is The Rock in your rear-view mirror," she stated. "When I left the job last November, I stopped in The Rock for gas. It was zero degrees and there was a dust storm going on. It was nine at night and I had to put on my sunglasses to protect my eyes from a sand storm!" She looked at Hanna to see if she could even believe it. "I tell ya, when hell freezes over, that's exactly what it'll look like!"

Hanna laughed politely. "Don't worry, we'll leave town early, work long days, and eat in the room. You won't even notice that we're there."

"Yeah, and when I'm dead I won't notice because I'll think I'm just waking up in The Rock." Gina laughed at her own joke.

Hanna looked across at Gina and saw a pampered little girl kept safe and happy with Mom and Dad. Other people in the company referred to her as Whiney Girl.

They came to the outskirts of The Rock, passing trailer houses stuck out on the desert all by themselves where someone had decided to stake their claim in the pounding heat and arctic winds. Some of the trailers were inhabited, while others were abandoned. Now and then, there were ancient sheds, junk, and the shells of pickups outlining where a trailer had been before being hauled to a more inviting patch of desert beside a different four-lane interstate. Sometimes Hanna passed these nomads, with a two-room trailer hooked to the back of an overloaded pickup, followed by a rusting Buick packed with a hefty wife and four children, heading down a desolate patch of highway on a bleak day in December or February. They were like fearless refugees heading out to sea in sinking ships, and any refuge they might find would be better than the world they came from.

The portion of the CanAm gas line that the engineers had surveyed was 25 miles west of The Rock, in the valley of the Blue River, which flowed brown with spring run-off, and stretched a quarter of a mile wide in places. The quickest way to reach this section was to pass through part of the patch. 'The patch', was not really *the* patch, because there were many patches, and they were all simply gas or petroleum-yielding formations under industrial development. Both new and old patches existed where anyone could turn a profit by punching a hole in the ground, or at least convince investors that they could. The patch they were passing through had been under development for some time. There were long rows of petroleum pumps, dipping those huge iron heads like patient pecking roosters, beside pools of toxic wastewater. A grid of flagged ropes crisscrossed just above the surface of the ponds to discourage migrating fowl from making a lethal landing in the poisonous ponds. Older unproductive wells were topped with huge multi-valved caps, appearing as giant versions of what a child might create if left alone with a box of enormous plumbing parts.

Newer gas rigs tapped into gas that used to be considered the dangerous, bothersome by-product of petroleum. There were derricks with flaming towers, burning off noxious waste. The top of one rig appeared to be burning out of control as men watched idly from a distance. There were two emergency vehicles impotently waiting, but no one was moving too fast. A large crew cab pickup full of huge, serious men passed by.

"It's a man's world." Gina said.

"Amen and Hallelujah," Hugh agreed.

"A little tramp like you could probably make some real money out here," Hanna said to Gina, as Gina watched the fire from the window.

"Hugh, could we just leave Hanna right here?" Gina said, as if simply speaking took a huge effort. "She could run the rest of the way."

* * *

Walking the proposed gas line was easy in the sparse vegetation. This was perfect for doing a surface survey of archeological materials. If many cultural artifacts, like worked stone, arrowheads and hearths were found on the surface, then that might validate a need for test pits and then complete excavations if the findings were substantial.

The area was made up of crumbling sedimentary rock. The soil was very light-colored, like dusty snow. Down near the river, floodwaters irrigated and dumped rich sediment on a verdant ribbon of green. Cottonwoods and willows clung to the river bank, a great green slash running through a vast colorless expanse. The land rolled into the distance with occasional lumpy towers of loose rock exposing the stratified layers of petrified mud that had formed half a billion years before.

To Hanna, it seemed that believing in the geology of the area took even greater faith than believing in Adam and Eve, or in the indigenous myth of The Great Turtle rising from the waters. Although she knew the geology was true, she had trouble truly believing that half a continent covered by a shallow sea had risen into a great mountain chain as continental plates collided far away below vast oceans. In her heart, she knew the facts, but in her heart, she did not know if she truly believed that 20-foot crocodiles and car-sized turtles swam through the same geology that she now walked across. She bent down and picked up a black, cylindrical stone from the light soil. This was the fossilized remains of a squid. She held the proof of the sea in her fingers. She could go find clamshells, and tubeworms, and fragments of coral. Yet, it was all too incredible to accept.

Even though she herself found points, and flakes, and
old buffalo horns, she could hardly believe that it was once
wilderness—that there were camps of teepees on the
benches above the rivers, and that tribal children had run
naked, and laughed, and hunted rabbits in the brush beside
the river. Had Indian women really kept camp and rooted
for the tubers of sego lilies, biscuit root, and wild onions
along the hillsides? And did the men really sit upon the high
buttes staring for hours across the unmarred hugeness,
seeking herds of buffalo, bands of migrating elk and deer?
She couldn't believe that grizzlies and wolves prowled and
stalked the human and ungulate migrations, and that the
unregulated, undammed, and un-drained Blue River would
have flooded miles wide in the broad valleys. It was not her
job to believe any of it, all she needed to do was record the
evidence.

Hanna and Gina met Dog and Hugh for lunch down by
the river, in the shade of a cottonwood. They exchanged
artifacts that they had taken and recorded as diagnostic
samples of the area. Most were points, small to minute in
size, with the classic notched base. The size and style
indicated the middle to late prehistoric period. These points
most resembled the classic arrowheads that people think of,
not realizing that the bow and arrow was a relatively late
technology, which occurred only a couple of thousand of
years in the past. The larger spearheads of the atlatl were
utilized for a far greater and older portion of the past.

Hugh produced a beautiful, palm-sized scraper of
translucent white chert. "I found it up on one of the benches.
There were teepee rings up there, and quite a few flakes."

"Did you find anything that you might test?" Hanna
asked.

"Just the whole bench, but that is actually a bit off the
survey line."

"You think we should dig and test any of your sites?"
Hugh asked.

"Na, not really," Gina shrugged.

Dog wandered off behind the trucks, bored with the conversation.

"With all the sediment and wind deposit, it's obvious that there's more cultural material down there," Hugh said kicking the dusty loess.

"Yeah, well if they find it while they're digging, it's their problem," Gina stated curtly. "We're finding an occasional worked flake and a point or two, logic tells us there's more, but we're not actually seeing it."

Hugh nodded in agreement with her.

Hanna took one of Hugh's phony Clovis points from her pocket and dropped it at his feet. "Nice try Hugh."

Hugh laughed and held up his hands, "What. You found a Clovis, out here?"

Hanna was smiling because she did think it was funny, and Gina craned her neck to catch the joke.

"Oh wow, you found a Clovis?" Gina asked uncertainly.

"No, I found the one that Hugh *made* and *planted* for me to find."

Gina took the point and turned it over in her hand. "Wow, Hugh you're really getting good at making these things!"

"How did you know?" he asked, blushing and smiling.

"Well, you really had me for a second, and I did jump for it. But you left it out where even a tourist would find it. And, I don't know, there's just a quality to it that doesn't look like it sat there for ten thousand years. Too crisp."

"Are you ever gonna show me that one Clovis you found?" Hugh asked.

Hanna reacted more than she would have liked to. "How do you know about that?"

"Tim told me."

"Ah, of course he did."

"You never did record it," he said, trying to sound authoritarian.

"And I probably never will."

"Nope, she never will, Hugh," Gina repeated with a huff,

handing the faux Clovis back to Hugh.

Hanna walked over to the Bronco and pulled out their cooler. There was a large log that campers had positioned beside a fire ring, and Hanna sat with her back against it with the cooler at her elbow. She could smell marijuana from the direction where Dog had wandered. Hugh got his cooler and the tiny camp chair he always carried with him, and arranged it so he was facing Hanna and Gina from the other side of the fire ring. He pulled out a quart of milk and lit a cigarette. He smoked his cigarette, sipped his milk and began talking. This was his routine. He was a lecturer by nature and as the field chief he always had a captive audience.

"Where you been, Dog?" Hugh asked belligerently.

"Down at the river," Dog muttered monotonously.

"How come your eyeballs look like they're gonna fall out?" Hugh roared, laughing.

Dog shrugged his shoulders and laughed shyly.

"Both of you looked kinda ragged this morning. You go down to the Kitty Lounge again?" Gina asked.

"Now what do you think?" Hugh asked, peering over the top of his aviator sunglasses.

"Geez you guys, how much do you spend down there every night?" Hanna asked Dog, trying to pull him into the conversation.

"I dunno. What do ya think, 25 or 30?" Dog said, referring the question to Hugh.

"I guess...cover charge...three dollars a beer...tips for the girls," he said, adding it in his head.

"Oh c'mon, you guys spend 50, 60...maybe a hundred dollars down there together every night, stuffing money into their G-strings!" Gina chided.

"It's not a hundred. And besides, I don't stuff their panties. Hugh does that!" Dog laughed.

"Remember when Tim got up on the stage and started jerking his clothes off?" Hugh roared with laughter, spilling his milk.

Dog laughed himself silent. Finally, he croaked, "I

thought those bouncers were gonna beat him to death."

"That guy comes unglued with a little whiskey."

"Is that what happened last year?" Gina asked angrily. "Poor Tim was hurtin' for days. He said he got jumped."

"Well, you can imagine his embarrassment!" Hugh and Dog fell silent with wheezing laughter.

"I can't believe it. You're both certified archeologists. Hugh, you have a master's in field archeology. What the hell are you thinking?" Gina scolded.

Hanna held up her hands. "Listen, how about if you two come to our room with your 60 dollars, and Gina and I will show you our tits!"

"Hanna!" Gina gasped.

"And we'll *give* you all the beer you want."

"Hey you guys, I'm not part of this plan at all," Gina said holding up her hands. "Hanna can go to your room if you want to see her tits!"

Dog and Hugh laughed shyly.

"Well, why not, Gina? It'd be the same rules, no hands and all that." Hanna appealed to Gina. "We'll serve' em a couple of beers and dance around.... They leave us 60 dollars and there ya have it!"

"Come on Hanna, it wouldn't be the same," Hugh said defensively.

"Why not?"

"You guys are too flat," Dog muttered.

"For your information Dog, Gina is not flat!"

"OK, Hanna. OK, we get the point. It is absurd and asinine. We get it," Hugh said, holding up his hands in defeat.

"Well, I am a bit insulted that you didn't jump at the bait," Hanna muttered, as if she was hurt.

"No offense, and thanks," Hugh said, "an offer like that doesn't come along every day."

Dog opened a McDonald's bag and withdrew a stack of yesterday's hamburgers. He ate them one after another, like doughnuts. Gina watched him in disbelief.

"You sure those things are OK, Dog?"

"They don't smell or nothin'."

"You didn't have them in the cooler...?"

"Na, they'll keep."

"That's right," Hugh butted in, "all salt, fat, and soy protein, nothing to rot."

"In ten thousand years they'll be excavating them out of the landfills perfectly preserved, just like hot dogs," Hanna added.

Dog fell silent under the subtle ridicule. He gobbled down the remainder of his last McBurger and walked back to the truck, leaving the McGarbage lying around the fire pit.

"I guess it's that time," Hugh said, rising stiffly to his feet.

Hanna and Gina followed, picking up Dog's McGarbage, stowing their cooler in the Bronco.

Dog was off in the sage, whipping the ground with a stick.

"You got another one Doggie?" Hugh shouted.

Dog laughed and picked up the rattlesnake he had just beaten to death, flipping it toward the road with the stick. He lifted it up, manipulating it with the stick. He used only his good hand. He carried his damaged hand with the thumb casually hitched through his belt loop; he had to arch his back in order to lift the hefty snake.

"Why the hell do you bother, Dog?" Hanna asked.

"I don't want to get bit!"

"You probably step past twice as many as you see."

"Yeah, but they know I'm a snake killer, and they leave me alone," Dog said.

"No, Dog, that's not the way it works," Hanna said. "You're beating your karma to death every time you kill one of those snakes."

"One time my karma ran over my dogma," Gina giggled.

"Somewhere there's an assassin snake waiting for you, to make things even," Hanna warned.

Hugh and Dog stood over the expired serpent. Dog took out his pocketknife and flipped open the blade with his thumb. He stooped over and cut off the rattle.

When he did an awkward procedure like this, it was apparent that his left arm was completely impaired. He never mentioned it, and he was surly when asked about it. All anyone knew was that it was the result of a car accident from when he lived on the reservation in New Mexico.

Everyone looked up as a white truck approached. There was a large CANAM – Petroleum Transports Inc. logo on the door of the truck, followed by their catchphrase: 'Canadian–American partnerships, Pan-American solutions'.

"Shit," Hugh groaned. "Leon Filmore."

"Lyin' Leon Filmore," Dog growled.

"Why don't you guys pick up the line where you left off, and I'll pander to Leon's anxieties." Hugh exhaled a long sigh. "How does he find us?"

"Come on Gina, you got to meet this sweat-ball."

"Hanna, don't!" Hugh said impotently.

"Hugh, five minutes and then we'll go work."

"Who is this?" Gina asked, not understanding.

"He's a project field supervisor for the pipeline," Hugh muttered, "such a putz."

Dog couldn't stomach Leon and wandered off.

The truck came to a stop, and Leon stepped out in his clean, creased, khaki work-shirt with the breast-pocket CanAm patch, impeccable blue jeans, and polished work-boots.

Hanna approached him aggressively. "Hi Leon," she greeted him as he stood pale in the sun. He smiled and blushed, his hungry, grey-blue eyes hunting the faces for a cue. His eyes constantly searched and pecked for scraps of information.

"Uh, hello...."

"Hanna!" Hanna barked, reminding him of her name, just a bit too close, invading his space, reaching out her hand.

"Hanna," he said, nervously trying to back up and take in the scope of her presence. A breeze grabbed a hank of his thin, red comb-over, and he removed his hand from hers, hunting the insurrection on his head to plaster it flat again.

He reached into his truck for his CanAm baseball cap to control the situation.

"Yeah, how are things out here? Are you guys moving right along?" He tried to interpret all three faces at the same time, while watching Dog disappear into the desert. His eyes passed over Gina's body and then returned to inventory what the faces could offer.

"Yes, Leon, we're…" Hugh began.

"Leon, this is Gina!" Hanna said as she pulled Gina uncomfortably close to him. "Gina's just in, but she's a top notch archeologist, who's worked with us before, and can really eat up the miles." Hanna said, searching his nervous eyes doggedly, refusing to let them escape to reap the bounty of Gina's modest curves. "Gina, he's a CanAm field supervisor for the gas pipeline—start to finish. He's everywhere at once, checking up on everything!"

Gina caught the game and took his hand in hers, holding it too long, even though repulsed at its moist, chilly feel. "Oh wow! Hellooo, Leon," she said, sparking him with her eyes. "Imagine never running into you before…?"

"Gina," he said, clinging to her name. "It's not like I could miss you out here." His eyes analyzed her face and then her body.

Gina laughed politely, and then watched, surprised as beads of sweat sprouted from his face. His lips puckered as he considered what to say. His face grew red in apprehension as Hanna also closed in on him.

"Leon," Hugh said with gravity. "Let's talk and look at some maps. The weather has been keeping us away from parts of the line." He was gruff and shot Gina and Hanna a searing glare. "We'll let these women get back at it. We're not getting anywhere, like this," Hugh said, spoon-feeding Leon his retreat.

"Right," Leon agreed eagerly. "Let's get 'er done," he said, laughing pretentiously, mopping his clammy face with a read bandana.

"Hanna, Gina," Hugh said, rearranging his wilted straw

hat.

Gina was warmed up. She stared at Hugh for a moment and gave him a half sneer. Then, she slid her naughtiest eyes at Leon. "Leon," she said, and turned away with Hanna, slinking away as provocatively as she could in dusty, baggy pants and sagging sun-shirt.

"What was that all about?" Gina whispered as they walked away.

"If you don't do that, he starts undressing you with his eyes," Hanna spoke low and fast.

"He's pretty greasy, and he sweats on demand."

"Yeah, he drives Hugh crazy, coming around every second day, fretting over anything that slows things down. He talks nice and smiles to your face, but he'd dump us in a heartbeat if he could get around the antiquities laws." Hanna took a deep breath and relaxed her shoulders, "That was just me being passive-aggressive."

After nine and a half hours in the field the four archaeologists drove back to town. Hugh and Dog showered, in separate rooms, and headed out for dinner, and a dark, cool bar. Hanna wrestled with running or not running, before she surrendered to the temptation of a cold beer in a cool room. Gina and Hanna lay exhausted in the dark of their room, glad to be away from the glare of the sun, lying in their air-conditioned cubicle, staring at the evening news, nursing icy beers from the refrigerator of their kitchenette.

"You know," Hanna said, looking up at the ceiling, "at times I feel really great about the work we do. I love archeology, but then I meet one of the CanAm vampires, and I wonder why I bother. All we're doing is adding another artery to feed the beast."

"I know," Gina said, "I get an icky feeling when I see the people who are running their side of things."

"Right, they can't all be straight up and legit like Dog, can they?"

Gina laughed, "No, not so much. But you know, they're

all such company men. They seem so indoctrinated, so willing to pooh-pooh any environmental consideration."

"Men. All men. White men. Except a few minorities doing the labor."

"I just wish they wouldn't come around, and then I could pretend I was doing meaningful work," Gina said getting up for another beer.

"There'll be no end to Leon Filmore. He'd try to room with Hugh, if he could figure out how to make Karl pay for it."

They lounged in the cool of the room until early evening, and Gina took this time to describe her failing relationship with a perpetual PhD candidate from the University of Utah. Her lover, Dave, had been, and still was, tenuously ensconced at the University, as he had been for years, with a series of grants, assistantships, internships, and stipends. His enduring dream of nearly two decades was to be a tenured professor and live a quiet life close to campus. Gina had known him for one of those decades and supported his dream, emotionally and financially, every winter as she returned from her own pursuits to the smoggy, winter valley of Salt Lake City.

"I think Dave is a Peter Pan," Hanna said.

"I don't think so. He just needs the right research project, and he's done," Gina defended.

"Gina, the guy has a cool little life at a university, and he doesn't want to grow up and move on."

"That's not true! Why would anyone live in poverty for fifteen years if he didn't truly want something?"

Hanna sighed, exasperated, "Poverty isn't that bad if you're in a low rent with a bunch of esoteric, poverty-stricken individuals. It's not like he's been banished to Siberia. He's probably part of a clique of struggling PhD candidates who view themselves as the persecuted intelligentsia."

"Blab, blab, blab," Gina said, getting up, annoyed by the invasive truth.

A chill ran over Hanna as the beer and AC worked its magic. She felt comfortable on her own cotton blankets. She wanted to flip through the channels, but the TV remote was too far away. She listened to the shower, and wished she had gotten there first. Gina was a shower hog, but at least she was tidy and very generous with her shampoos, conditioners and lotions, all the things that never occurred to Hanna.

Gina emerged naked from the shower, holding a towel to her chest. Her legs were tan, as were her arms up to her biceps, and her face down to her neck.

"You have a farmer's tan."

"I know. I'm going to do the rest at a tanning salon as soon as I get a chance," Gina mocked.

Hanna's eyes followed her furtively. Gina's body was lithe and handsome, tiny muscles flexed and bunched in her calves and shoulders as she toweled dry and stuffed away her dirty clothes. Gina's back was long and willowy. Without clothes she was all legs and arms, sprouting from the sinewy whip of her torso. Dog and Hugh would never see or understand the wonder of Gina's body.

Even with all her whining, Hanna still harbored a crush for Gina. She felt like she had always known Gina. From the first day they worked together, from before they met. Hanna loved Gina from her first slumber parties when she shared a bed with her neighbor, Susan, and they secretly practiced kissing, each pretending the other was a boy. Hanna had loved her from her teens when she had made out with boys, but imagined they were Susan or other, curly-haired Ginas. Gina was the incubus of her college days when she dated obligatorily and fornicated ignominiously with apes.

"Hanna, are you looking at me again?"

"Yes, but only in admiration."

"You're not leering are you?"

"No. Men leer. Women admire."

Gina smiled, "Would you really show those guys your tits for money?"

"No, I was just making a point. It'd be too cheap…I'd

probably show 'em to 'em for free if it happened to end up that way."

"Like if we were all on a beach together in Italy or France?" Gina smirked.

Hanna laughed hard at that.

Gina pulled a T-shirt over her head and her breasts disappeared under the soft cotton. "When you say things, people believe them. You've got a good poker face."

"Well," Hanna purred theatrically, "you should call my bluff sometime." She rolled onto her side.

Tim

Tim shouted at the demons of rightist propaganda on the radio, overpowering their railing, fiery voices. He finally spun the dial and tuned in an oldies' station and came to his senses to the voice of Smokey Robinson. He realized he was driving 90 miles an hour, straddling the centerline of the two-lane blacktop. He dove into the right lane, and Aretha Franklin took him all the way down to a safe and sane 65.

"If you want a do-right...all-night woman..."

By the time Bobby Vinton came on, singing, 'Mack the Knife' he was calm again.

Bob, the dog, was less nervous now that Tim had quit screaming. Bob smiled his dog smile as he leaned against the passenger door, his long, fine nose out the window, the wind rippling his silky, black and white coat. Bob smelled the entire high desert as they passed through it, he could smell the distant pines of the mountains, and the Blue River, which was still another hour up the road. Through the general pall of cows and cow shit, Bob could smell the occasional jackrabbit, prairie dog, antelope, and sage grouse. Off the ridges came the scent of aromatic sage, while in the lower swales, the bland scent of rabbitbrush teased his nostrils. He sneezed occasionally. He would pull his head in, and send a fine mist in Tim's direction.

"Goddamn it Bob, you want me to roll up that window? Is that what you want?"

Bob slumped down against the door and laid his chin on the armrest.

"I don't know why you can't just rest your head at the edge of the window, instead of sticking your nose right out in the wind. You know you're gonna sneeze, and then I'm gonna yell at ya. You know the whole scenario as well as I do!"

Bob pretended to be asleep.

"Hey," Tim said, snapping Bob on the butt with two fingers. "You listen to me when I talk to you," he said pointing his finger at Bob.

Bob barked and growled from his side of the truck.

"Yeah, talk back all you want, you damn cur! I'll roll that window up, and then we'll see who suffers."

Bob resumed his position on the armrest.

"You get driven around like a damn debutant, and you get all pissed off if you can't sneeze all over me! Hey! A cow, Bob! A cow! Get that sonofabitch!" Tim swerved his truck over to a Hereford who had wandered to the fence at the edge of the highway berm. He slowed down while Bob hung out the window barking and snapping at the terrified bovine.

Bob spun around on the seat a few times and barked for approval from Tim.

"OK, that was pretty good...just don't blow your nose at me anymore."

Bob lay down next to him on the bench seat, and Tim ran his fingers through the dog's sleek fur.

Tim was on his way to Rocket City. He had held off working for as long as possible. The winter was now months behind him; his funds were running low, and it was too hot to rock climb at most of the areas he had been frequenting. He called Karl to find out if he had a job, and if so, where he might find the crew, or more specifically, where he might find Hanna. It was fundamentally understood that Tim would work with Hanna.

Tim did not have a field archeologist's certificate; he was really not anything very specific, but he practiced a little of everything. He was a damn good carpenter and a licensed electrician. He had done some time roughnecking in the oil fields and spent one dismal winter as an apprentice to a diesel mechanic. Tim had a bachelor's degree in English and had begun a law degree. He had attempted a second bachelor's in engineering, but found it tedious. He completed another bachelor's in biology, and ran out of energy while finishing a master's in anthropology. He liked to sum up his academic career by stating the old saw, "I learned more and more about less and less, until I knew absolutely everything about nothing." Even though Tim was not a certified archeologist, much of the fieldwork he did was not exactly hard science; mostly he drove truck shuttles and walked survey lines looking for artifacts. Lately, Tim had a list of employers for whom he did good work, and spent his years here and there, doing this and that, living out of his tiny camper with Bob the dog.

Tim always liked the particular stretch of highway he was driving down. It was empty. There was an hour of it without towns, houses, or facilities. It was a long, hollow two-lane that passed through a low desert spotted with alkali flats, where the salty ground was white as snow and all that grew was saltbush and greasewood. It was one of the very few roads that he considered long enough, or desolate enough. It made him feel as he had once felt, nervous and uncertain, as he prepared for trips across the West; like shoving off to sea.

The huge treeless expanses had seemed larger when he was a young man, puttering along at 55 miles an hour in an old, green Volkswagen. Roads appeared longer and more vacant then. Time had moved more slowly.

That was when Babe was his dog, the dog of his adolescence, a little old terrier curled up asleep on the passenger seat. He and Babe crossed an ocean of highways and wore out two engines in that Beetle, in searing heat and howling blizzards, through mountains, and deserts, along four-lane highways and two-track dirt roads. They sometimes stopped for work, but that was only for gas money.

He and Babe had traveled down this road before, one vicious winter night. He had stopped and considered the blinking 'Road Closed' gate at the town of Rock Creek. A patchwork of black ice and dry tarmac formed a tenuous surface, and a howling wind ripped across the desert, raking snow and dust into blinding ground blizzards. But that was certainly no reason to close a road, plus he had an alluring date to keep, so he looked both ways and went around the blinking barrier.

He drove on in his little capsule behind the faint glow of his speedometer, behind the weak stab of his headlights, into the blackness. He drove slowly, wondering where he might stay. He knew they would probably never make it to Felicidad. Babe was old by then and shivered on the passenger seat. He tucked his down vest around her and pulled his ski cap tighter around his head, burying his chin down deep in his parka. When the blinding ground blizzards swept across the road, Tim locked the wheel on its path, pushed in the clutch, and took his foot off the gas, coasting with faith, swallowed by a whirling maelstrom. Babe raised her head suspiciously until they passed through the dervish, and Tim accelerated the engine once again. Several times he drifted across the black ice, and again, with faith, he turned slightly into the slide, and straightened out the VW before it hit the dry, sticky blacktop.

Time passed slowly as he drove in and out of range of the fading AM radio stations, the odd stations that travel so distantly in the dark, as if they were nocturnal, a companion of night travelers, a friend to the diaspora and dispossessed. WROK, 'The time-pieces from Tulsa'. KWST, 'The best of the West from Omaha'. 'Have Yourself a Merry Little Christmas' was the favorite of every station. Gaudy lights appeared and disappeared on distant ranch houses; wreathes and bows adorned the occasional mailbox and gateposts, like impotent parodies of hope and joy.

Perhaps it was the eve of Christmas Eve; maybe it was the eve of the eve of Christmas Eve. He couldn't remember. It must have been close, because he was sad and anxious about spending Christmas with an intended lover instead of family. When he had told his mother that he wouldn't be home until New Year's, she replied with silence.

He was nervous about the woman who invited him to Felicidad. She had cajoled and coerced him. He was afraid of realizing that she was merely an ideal whose allure would fade. He was afraid of the lie that he would ardently assume just to lie with her and smell the richness of her skin. He was afraid of being trapped at long, clumsy dinners with her roommates and friends, and long evenings in Christmas houses whose lights burned brightly through the inky arctic nights, seemingly awaiting anyone but him.

Babe stood up and pranced in place in her seat, looking out from under his down vest. She sat up and stared into the shaft of the headlights, the vest slumping to the floor. Tim thought that the moan came at first from the tires as they passed over a different textured surface, but then he heard it next to him; he could see that it came from Babe. The sound grew and elevated in pitch until the radio was drowned and the VW was filled with Babe's mournful lament. He watched her with her eyes closed sweetly, her lips raised and parted delicately, the wail departing her body with the steam of her breath. As her howl continued, Tim feared she would asphyxiate from a lack of air, her life ebbing with one long lugubrious note. She stopped and looked at Tim, and then sat leaning against him.

"What is it, Babe? Are you sick?" He put his hand before her face, and she licked him reassuringly and grumbled softly. "Are you cold, Babe? Is it too cold in here?" Tim reached down and pulled the vest from the floor and tucked it around her. He felt that the heat of her body was warm and strong. He put his arm around her and pulled her snug against the side of his body. She lay down with her head in his lap. Anxiety gnawed at him and he knew that, unless conditions improved, Felicidad was out of range for the night. He could drive it, but there would be little sense in it. It'd be too awkward, standing on the steps, pounding on the door in the middle of the night, a sleeping bag under one arm, and a frigid dog in the other. He thought he might call to see what his date thought of him coming in so late. He hated the idea of staying in a motel, sitting in a room, the pacing, watching TV, waiting for the morning, as if there was something he needed to stay ahead of, something that could close in on him during moments of immobility. Tim craned his neck and looked up at the sky. He saw that a few stars shone brightly. It was only the wind that caused the poor driving conditions. He realized how foolish and paranoid he was.

There were lights on the road ahead, and he felt relief that others also casually traveled on such a night. He noticed that the lights were stationary and wondered if a rancher had gotten stuck at the end of a driveway where the plows had bermed up the snow. As he approached, Tim could see that the headlights were angled off into the sky. Babe whined, retreated to her seat and howled her sad song. Tim's heart sank as a woman appeared, running into his headlights, her red, crazy hair flying wildly, one hand out to halt him, the other clutching at the lapels of her thin woolen jacket.

She ran angrily up to the window as if accusing him, "That's not a deer up there!!! That's not a deer, you know!!!"

The wind leapt through the window, stinging his face with spindrift. "What's not a deer?" he asked rhetorically, but the answer was obvious from the truck on its side with the cab leaning against the bank of the elevated road, its door sprung, hanging back unnaturally.

"She's alive! What are you doing? She's still alive! Hurry!"

Babe wailed woefully.

Tim stepped out into the biting wind. He reached back and grabbed his sleeping bag, which was loose in the back seat. The woman stood halfway between Tim and the shape at the edge of the highway, pleading with her eyes, motioning with her hands for him to change things. She hiccupped huge sobs. "I didn't know…there was no one here…." She choked. "Just the truck…. I ran over…I thought someone hit a deer…." She stood with her mouth agape and silence running out.

Tim saw the figure at the edge of the road, thrown so far from her truck. He knelt down beside the tiny woman there on the pavement, looking like a child. She was unconscious, sprawled and askew on the shoulder of the road, in her dungarees, and waist-length down jacket. Blood made parts of her face appear black in the night. She was hopelessly broken. His tiny first-aid kit was useless against this. He had no training for this. There was nothing he could do. He covered her with his bag. "Turn on the flashers of my car and go for help! Go find a phone! If you pass any plows, have 'em radio!" The redheaded woman nodded obediently, ran off to her car and sped past seconds later, her taillights disappearing into a swirl of spindrift, harried by a vision she couldn't outrun.

He knelt down beside the victim there on the side of the road, spreading the sleeping bag over the woman's body, gently lifting her head into his lap. She was dying. The cold of the pavement sapped the life from her body. There was nothing to be done—moving her would kill her and waiting would kill her. There was no bandage or pill that would save her. She needed heat, and oxygen, and doctors.

She breathed in fits and gasps. There was fluid in her lungs. Tim could hear it rasp as she breathed. He pulled the bag tightly around her and around his own legs as he sat with her. Streamers of snow snaked across the road and a small drift began to build on the lee side of the woman's body. When the wind faltered, he could smell her cologne. He could also smell the beery bar smell. She had been drinking with her friends, laughing, flipping back her shoulder-length hair, full of holiday cheer, perhaps eluding a hopeful suitor. But, then she slid on the ice and rolled her truck when her tires stuck on a dry patch of blacktop, and here she was, in the darkness, on the shoulder of a highway, with her head on the lap of a stranger.

Tim heard voices now and then. They carried across the prairie, back behind the din of the VW's engine. They called and whistled, and fell into rhythmic chants. The breeze came to him just so, and he realized that the woman's radio was still on, singing happily as her life was drawn away by the winter wind.

"Jingle bell time, is a swell time, to dance the night away."

Tim sat cross-legged at the edge of the road with the
woman's head in his lap until his legs went numb. Babe
watched him from the car, barking now and then. He
thought of Felicidad, and of sitting on a couch in a warm
house. He imagined that the woman with her head in his lap
was the woman who invited him to Felicidad. He would sit
on the couch and stroke her hair after her guests left, and her
roommates had gone to bed. He stroked the broken
woman's hair and whispered loving words to her, as she
shivered uncontrollably. At one point the wind lulled, and
the radio became acutely clear. It was Johnny Mathis. He
sang, 'Chestnuts Roasting on an Open Fire'. The young
woman gasped and sighed softly as if it might be her favorite
song. Tim sang along and stroked her hair until she stopped
shivering and her head was cool in his lap.

The highway patrol came late and lifted him to his feet,
warmed him in the cruiser, and gave him coffee from a
thermos. They drove him and Babe to the next town and
arranged to have his Bug left at his motel room. The redhead
never did return.

The next morning, he sat in his car at the junction. It was
cloudy but calm. A skiff of snow lay quietly on the ground
and formed cresting, corniced drifts at the tops of the ridges.
He scanned the horizon for the winds that had raged the
night before, but they had moved on, or maybe he had left
them up North where they perpetually raged.

He sat at the junction undecided. South would take him
to Felicidad. East would take him home. His car was facing
east, and Babe looked straight ahead, whining anxiously. Tim
reluctantly turned his car south and rolled ahead a few yards,
and Babe whined desperately. He stopped again and
reconsidered. He felt intoxicated from the lack of food and
sleep. Felicidad now seemed less attractive. Down there, he
would either have a huge, unpleasant tale to tell to endless
strangers, or a deep secret to keep. He would have
unwelcome sympathy, or he would have to cover his
suppressed distraction. At home, he could quietly relate the

accident to his mother, and then share simple rituals.

Felicidad was little more than an hour away, while Lincoln would be most of the day. He did a U-turn, drove to the highway ramp heading east toward Lincoln with Babe barking and dancing in her seat.

Now, whenever he drove this highway, it seemed to be under the hot, summer sun, and he tried to pinpoint the place where it all occurred. He wondered what her name had been. He thought that he would brave the cold and go back there and sit with her again, if he could have Babe in his car, a girl in Felicidad, and family in Lincoln. But this time he would save her and drive her to safety across an ocean of short grass prairie.

Bob knew. He could smell the whole fateful scene, the arctic air, the highway patrol, and the volunteer fire department. He could still scent the entire tale from a decade ago. He could feel Tim's searching eyes and smell Tim's confused sorrow.

The radio signal faded, and Tim spun the dial, looking for a sweet female voice.

Flight

Hanna was antsy because she hadn't run in three days. With Tim's arrival, she was obliged to spend time with him and Gina and catch up on where they had all been and what they'd done during the winter. Tim was the same maniac he had always been—rumpled clothes; uncombed, stiff, auburn hair; dark brown eyes roving hungrily, as he rambled nervously. With a long slender nose and strong chin, 'he was not hard to look at,' as Gina said. Presently, he was pacing, and lecturing Dog and Hugh as they worked on one of the Broncos that had a failing battery. He was handing them tools, gesturing at a large electrical part he held up in his hand.

"He adores you Hanna, he worships the ground you walk on," Gina said.

"You're crazy, we're friends, and climbing partners. We're gonna climb together."

"Oh climbing, shmyming! Even all dusty and crusty, he looks pretty damn good!" Gina said in a lascivious hiss. "Like an insane knot of bone and muscle."

"Maybe he has a crush on me, but it's nothing more than that."

They watched him through the shades of their room, pacing in the sun outside their window. To Hanna, Tim looked like a marionette, as if his body was solid, but fluidly jointed, and manipulated by a master from far, far away.

"He's obviously an alien," Gina said.

"We're lucky he comes in peace."

"You're lucky he comes for a piece."

Hanna elbowed her in the ribs, "I've seen the way you look at him, maybe you're the one looking for a piece."

"You're so full of it Hanna!" Gina giggled nervously.

"Look at you, you're red as a cherry. You like Tim! You looovve him!" Hanna laughed. "Tim, Gina looooves yoouuu," Hanna called softly.

Gina pounded Hanna's back with clenched fists, laughing wildly.

"I'm going to tell him right now!" Hanna said, motioning for the door.

Gina jumped her from behind and wrestled her to the floor. Hanna was taller and stronger, but she fought back weakly, allowing Gina to win. Gina sat on Hanna's chest. Hanna rested her hands on Gina's knees, and she held one hand to her ear as if she were on the phone. "Hello, Dave?" Hanna said seriously, "It is me, Hanna, I'm out here in Rocket City, and I need to tell you that Gina is in love with an alien maniac."

Gina pinned her hands to the floor and smiled cruelly, her sky-blue eyes cutting deep into Hanna's. "Hello, Dave? I'm here in Rocket City, rooming with a maniac lesbian who's in love with me."

Hanna looked away, pierced by Gina's cruelty. Hanna's strength yielded and melted.

* * *

Hanna's only true recourse to Gina's acerbic tongue was to run. And she ran far and hard, her head floating above the prairie. The soft, sandy road was the only blemish from horizon to horizon. The air was still, and thin clouds darkened the evening. The basin was dry and flat, with little vegetation; she could have run in any direction unimpeded. Her anger drove her on, setting the pace, eating up mile after mile of the open desert. Antelope cautiously watched her approach before barking and running off. Some ran parallel to her for a time before angling off to watch her from a safe distance. Horned larks flew before her on the road, refusing to leave its parameters. She ran even faster, until she was no longer there, until she detached and her feet led her distantly down a track in the sand, until she remained stationary and she spun the world past her, and the wind rushed by her

ears. She metamorphosed as she ran, her short, dirty blonde
hair turned black, she shrank in stature, her skin darkened,
she traveled back endless scores of centuries, until she was a
nameless aborigine, loping across an empty continent. She
was the first explorer, the first pioneer. She ran across a
desert as vast as the Pacific. She called across an echoless
plain and saw the limitless curve of the Earth. She felt the
wind move across her body and smelled the sage that had
baked a whole day in the sun. She ran without shoes. She ran
naked. She ran upon a trail pounded by giant bison, and
mammoths. She ran upon a trail that was paced patiently by
dire wolves and padded nocturnally by the dreadful short-
faced bear. Her life was insignificant; her death would be
inconsequential. She was, momentarily just one more soul
crossing the desert.

Fatigue brought her back, and she was Hanna, Homo
sapiens sapiens once more, drenched in sweat. The terrain
was familiar. Her watch told her that she was approximately
five miles out. It was time to go back. Hanna looked around
curiously. She felt as if something had roused her. Her senses
tingled, and anxiety dampened her euphoria. There was a
chickadee on a sage thicket. She stopped in her tracks.
"What are you doing here?" she asked, as if expecting a
spoken response. There were no mountains or thickets of
evergreens. It wasn't even a mountain chickadee; it was a
black-capped chickadee. It flew a few feet into the air, came
down to its roost and called out.

"Are you migrating?"

In response, it flew off quickly, straight north. Her scalp
crawled and she looked around for danger. She felt that there
were men out here. She turned and started back to her truck,
running quickly, trying to outdistance her fear, as if speed
could prove it wrong. In the flat sandy basin, speed was all
that could outdistance fear. Hanna had only returned a half
mile when an old, black pickup climbed out of a shallow
arroyo, onto the basin floor. Her step faltered, but she ran
with confidence, looking straight ahead, trying to remember

any rugged or rocky country where she might be able to lose a vehicle, but it was a basin, a flat, sandy basin. "Shit," she muttered. As the truck loomed closer, she reached behind her and pulled the Mace from its holster and stowed it in the elastic waistband of her running shorts. Both men watched her as they approached and finally passed her: she never made eye contact; she looked at the ground. Avoid eye contact with dangerous animals! Eye contact is a challenge! Do not deviate your pace or demeanor! She heard the vehicle stop once it had passed, the gears ground as they turned the vehicle around. Hanna left the two-track to give them a wide berth, but continued at a swift, confident pace.

As they pulled alongside her, the man in the passenger seat spoke.

"Hey, you want a ride?"

Hanna ran parallel to the road without responding.

"Hey lady, you want a ride or what?"

She refused to respond. From the corner of her eye, she could see two scruffy faces with baseball caps, riding in an old truck, which rolled along on oversized tires. She stopped, put her hands on her hips and brushed the tube of pepper spray with her thumb to make sure it was where she needed it. She glanced over to estimate the danger. "I don't want a ride."

The driver revved the engine and shifted to a lower gear, "Whall, we ain't gonna jus' leave ya out here."

"Tha's right!" the driver said leaning over to see past the passenger. "We ain't leavin' ya here.... Ya know what I'm sayin'?" he said with an edge of finality.

Hanna stopped and looked at the men. She turned from side to side and calculated all angles of escape. "You telling me I have to go with you?"

"I don't see nowhere to run to," the passenger said, tilting his head, as if it were regrettable.

"So," Hanna said, kicking her toe in the dirt, "if I don't go, you'll make me go with you?"

"Tha's right," the driver nodded.

"You guys practice those accents?"

"What?!" the passenger asked, confused. He opened his door suspiciously as Hanna walked toward him. She ran her hand up her hip and took the pepper spray from the waistband of her shorts. As he moved to get out of the truck, putting his boot on the ground, she leapt, and kicked the door shut on his shin, took a deep breath and sprayed him squarely in the face. She aimed the tiny stream into the cab at the driver and kept spraying as the men gasped, and screamed, and choked. She quit spraying and jumped several paces away before daring to breathe. The passenger lay in the dirt where he had melted from the pickup, retching and shrieking. The driver lay across the seat screaming, and then gasping silently, spasmodically.

Hanna stared down the road both ways, paced around the truck, and evaluated the situation. There was still 30 minutes left to her run, and she wondered if they could recover in that amount of time and come run her down. She considered killing them, in self defense, but there was no easy way to do that, and she had no way of knowing if anyone had seen the Bronco, which she had left parked in plain sight, within view of the highway. She looked in the back of the truck, at an assortment of greasy tools. Hanna grabbed a shovel and focused on the valve stem of the rear wheel. She aimed her blow so that the shovel would come cleaving along the arch of the rim and clip the valve stem at its base. After three tries, the stem spun past her and air whistled from the huge tire.

She went around to the passenger's side and deftly sent the other valve stem tumbling to the sand. Air whistled out, and the tire collapsed until the rim rested on the ground.

"You fucking bitch!" the passenger croaked, trying to right himself. Squinting up through red swollen eyes, sand stuck to the tears and snot that streamed down his face.

Hanna considered him curiously. She had never heard anyone so pathetic say anything so stupid. She wondered if she could use the shovel to cleave off his head as easily as she had the valve stems, or how many swings it would take to crush his skull. She wound up to kick him in the head but he raised an arm in defense and she redirected her foot to his stomach. Air whooshed from his mouth, and his lips moved like the mouth of a huge goldfish.

"Asshole," she retorted calmly, looking down at him, at his filthy jeans, and cheap dress-shirt with the sleeves cut off. She tried to see him as he saw himself, and wondered what effect he was trying to achieve. His shirt had ridden up and she could see the swelling of a budding beer belly, white and fleshy, flecked with curly, black hair. Perhaps it would be more humane to kill him.

The truck's motor was still running, which annoyed Hanna. It was too loud. It muddled her thoughts.

The incapacitated driver moaned and hiccupped for air, he stretched across the bench seat of the truck. Hanna jerked the driver's door open and jumped back, pointing the shovel forward like a spear. He made no move and lay toward the passenger's side, which allowed Hanna to stretch her arm in, kill the engine and take the keys. Her eyes stung with the residual vapors of the spray. She stepped back where she could safely breathe, free of the noxious fumes. She observed the driver. He was older and fatter than his friend and had an enormous ass. She peered around for a gun. There is always a gun.

The driver looked like a chubby kid who'd fallen asleep in his dad's truck. He hiccupped for air in hallucinations of drowning. Hanna looked at the keys in her hand; they were adorned with a tiny brass figurine of a barefoot, bare-chested woman in cut-off shorts.

She used the shovel to scoop a hole in the sand and bury the keys. The sun was lower now, the overcast horizon glowed a beautiful salmon pink. She threw the shovel off into the desert and ran away, running backward from time to time to make sure she was still safe from the men; she thought she could see the passenger moving, and the truck sat sadly with its flat rear wheels, its doors open, painfully quiet, motorless in the labyrinth of emptiness.

She frisked herself and found the pepper spray in the waistband of her shorts, and returned it to the holster, promising herself to ditch it once in view of her truck. She felt momentarily joyful, running into the sunset, even though her eyes stung slightly and her nose ran from the miniscule amounts of the chemical defense she had waged.

Hanna had been gone for two days before the police showed up. A passing fish and game field biologist, found two men staggering down a dirt road, and radioed the sheriff. They claimed that a woman had flagged them down and assaulted them.

Hugh had been through the story with Hanna, and he knew where and how it happened. "And how does that involve us?" Hugh asked the deputy gruffly, crossing his arms, leaning against the truck.

"Well, a Bronco with an archeology logo was parked a few miles from the incident." The deputy studied Hugh's face as he relayed the information.

"Well yeah, we got work goin' on all over the place, we're always out in the field," Hugh answered coolly.

"Between six and eight in the evening?" The deputy eyed Dog, who sulked blackly around the door of his room.

"Well, yeah, sure, these are contracts. They say 'do it', and it's done!"

"Any of your employees workin' on the Vincent road, on Wednesday night, with one of the Broncos?"

"I'm sorry, now which one is the Vincent road?"

"It's a maintained gravel road that heads east, 20 miles north of town."

"Oh, yeah that was me. Wednesday night?" Hugh asked sincerely. "Yeah, I was just makin' sure that my maps were right. We do a lot of work down here, and a lot of information accumulates. Now and then I take a drive, and check it out myself, get it straight in my head and get it on the maps, you know?"

"Well did you see any vehicles, or a woman on foot?"

"Boy I can't tell ya about a vehicle, but I think I'd remember a woman on foot."

"You got that map you were checkin' on?"

"I'll have to get it," Hugh said instantly, "you got a minute?"

"Oh yeah, I'm on the clock."

Hugh walked over and took a tube of maps from the blue Bronco. Dog paced suspiciously under the hotel's covered walkway. Hugh returned and spread the maps across the hood of the deputy's vehicle.

Hugh thumbed through the quadrants, pulled the correct one and spread it out. "Now," he said officially, slicking back his red hair and tugging on his ponytail.

"I was probably parked somewhere around here." He pointed with a large flat finger. "And our old line is that long blue marker line you see. Where did the, uh, incident take place?"

"I can't tell ya exactly, jus' out that road a bit.... Well, we want to find this woman to check the story. It's an odd story if you know what I mean?" He watched Hugh closely.

"Yeah I hear ya. And if it included a crazy Indian, I'd say there's your man!" He laughed, and they both looked over at Dog, who slouched back into his room.

"Sounds like those boys just messed with the wrong gal." Hugh laughed.

"If it's true, she messed 'em up pretty good." The deputy smiled and stretched. He ran his fingers around the inside of his utility belt. "If you ever see anything out there or hear anything you let me know," the deputy said, handing Hugh his card.

* * *

Hanna had found enough work to keep her busy back at the office, and Karl beamed proudly at her story. He stopped her time and again, pressing for details. "So how did you begin your attack?"

"It really wasn't an attack. It was more of a preemptive strike."

"But tell me how?" Karl was almost squirming in his seat.

"Well I acted submissively and approached the truck, and I waited until the passenger put one foot on the ground, and then I jumped and kicked the door shut on his leg!"

"Ohhh!" Karl said, curling his fists inwardly toward his chest. "That had to hurt."

"Then I jumped up and sprayed him in the face while he was still yelling."

"What about the other guy?"

Hanna sighed, "Karl, I told you three times. Donna didn't even ask this many questions. OK, he was already sprayed more or less, just from being so close. But I hosed him down anyway."

"Ohhhhh, man! Those poor bastards! Then you kicked them in the face?"

"It was the stomach, the stomach! And it was only once. The one fat driver was a total mess. I think maybe he was having a reaction."

"Hanna, it was Mace. A reaction is the whole point."

"Then you chopped off the valve stems and flattened their tires?"

"Yes, I flattened their tires! Jesus, Karl! Get over it!" Hanna paused for a moment, "You know the strangest part? Now that it's all over, I feel a bit sorry for them. They were so pathetic."

"Ha, they would have paid more of a price from me."

"Sorry to bust your bubble, but they never would have tried to rape you. You guys would have stopped and had a beer together."

Karl laughed. Then he pleaded with her again to call the police, but she vehemently refused. "They're all men, and they'll all side with the men."

"That is such crap Hanna. They're gonna nail those guys for screwin' with a woman."

"That's what you think. What if you were black and two white guys jumped you, and you beat 'em up, would you report it to a white police force, and go before a white judge?"

"No, but that's entirely different. It's all hypothetical!"

"It's not. It's all real! You have no idea what it's like to be a woman in these little towns; you have no idea at all! Men with power are like gods out here! If it ever went to trial, I'd probably be judged by a Bible-thumping fundamentalist, who'd see all this as a radical, feminist's war on Western traditions!"

"Hanna, you're just going off. This isn't Saudi Arabia. If these guys tried to assault you then they should be arrested so they don't do it again."

"Well I can't prove they were gonna do anything. All they did was follow me and tell me to get in the truck, but they had me trapped, so I let "em have it. For all I know it might have been wrong for me to Mace those guys. They might have been trying to be funny. But I'm not raped and dead, and that's all that matters."

"That's exactly what matters. And it's not funny at all. They tried to make you get in their vehicle against your will, and nobody would ever dispute that it was at least attempted kidnapping."

"They'd lie, they already lied to the police. Hugh said that they told the cops that I flagged them down and sprayed them for no reason."

"Hugh also said that it was obvious that the cop didn't believe 'em." Karl muttered.

"Whatever, I'm not going to the cops, and that's it!"

"Well they know it was one of our Broncos." Karl's voice trailed off.

"Well let them know. Those guys probably left town by now anyway."

"I don't feel right letting it go like this," Karl said, shaking his head.

"You'll get over it. I already am."

* * *

Karl sent Hanna to meet the other half of the crew up on

the northern section of the line. They both thought the farther away from the sheriff, the better. It wasn't ideal, and she pined for Gina and Tim, but at least she'd be far away from the patch.

Up North, they made a camp by the Belle Flue River, in the shade of some cottonwoods. The camp was on private land belonging to Karl's distant relatives. Karl was reimbursing them handsomely with CanAm dollars. "All this energy money is about waste. And you should always ask for the highest price you can say without laughing," Karl explained to her, "If you're not trying to screw 'em they get suspicious. If you don't use it, you lose it."

To the contrary, the crew was living meagerly in the camp, saving the exorbitant per-diem money that they had been allotted for hotel and restaurant expenditures. The owner of the land had furnished picnic tables and some port-a-potties as his part of the arrangement, and crew members often made a ten-mile commute to a KOA campground for hot showers. Every few days they ate meals of Romanesque magnitude at Gluttons Grill, on the highway to Covet.

Although the idea was theoretically sound, chaos reigned supreme. The food situation was dire, because food rotted in iceless coolers, and people begrudgingly cooked hasty meals while stooping over tiny, smoky fires or sputtering camp stoves, and dishes went unwashed. Some members would often forgo the evening meal and drink beer instead, getting staggering drunk by early in the evening, and passing out before the sun had even set.

Hanna was sleeping in the tiny shell on the back of her truck, and this was deluxe compared to the sorry dwellings the others slept in. She had a thick pad and some shelves arranged to keep things off her bed. She also had a tiny camp stove she could use inside the shell for her first cup of coffee, or more if it was raining.

The other accommodations were not so clever. There were cheap department-store tents and large construction tarps, with small construction tarp additions. A tall guy named Ed simply slept in the back seat of his tiny sedan. Hanna was tempted to peak in there to see what position he chose.

The social structure was even worse. Alise, a chunky redhead with no sense of self, was the queen bee. She earned her esteem by the numbers of those she could draw around her and manipulate. She was a continual pain in the ass, a born agitator and conspired with great élan. She hated women as she hated herself and guarded her lovers as jealously as a bitch guards her pups. She fornicated for position and generally pursued alpha males. Hanna came into direct conflict with Alise because Karl had placed Hanna in charge of the camp and the entire northern end of the survey.

Hanna thought it was sad to see Alise's hostile reaction to his decision. Hanna was not one to seek responsibility and would relinquish it to Karl at the first opportunity. She often wished she could simply explain to Alise what a child she was and illustrate how shallow her endeavors were. It was also sad because Alise had a basic instinct and drive that Hanna lacked, the will to associate and bond, the drive to instill fidelity and social position. Alise cared about her image and Hanna simply didn't give a shit. They were natural born enemies, one was a laissez faire lesbian, the other a heterosexual slut who fornicated to meet her needs; one was an apathetic introvert, the other a manipulative extrovert. Hanna trusted in herself and was comfortable as a pariah; Alise was filled with self-loathing and tortured by her failures. It was a match made in hell.

Although not in charge, Alise was also a crew chief, and she gathered her crew around her, which consisted mostly of women with equally low self-esteem, and young men who thought it'd be nice to have sex with her, even if she was a crazy bitch. Poor Sarah was her most faithful cohort. She was an overweight, ex-ballet dancer, a slow learner, and an easy crier. She had a beautiful face, rheumy eyes and lovely skin, but was cursed with an acute capacity to store fat in her buttocks. 'Steatopygia,' Hanna recited to herself from memory, 'the capacity that sub-Saharan populations have for storing fat in their buttocks.' Poor Sarah relied heavily on Alise for guidance. Alise guided and bullied her and made her cry now and then, whenever a foul mood came upon her.

Alise and her adherents had polarized one side of the camp, worked as a unit and shared one of the company vehicles. They dragged their feet and grumbled at every change of plan. Both crews had to confer every evening and map what areas had been surveyed. Alise and her crew were taking the survey south to eventually link-up with the line coming north from Rocket City, while Hanna and her crew were taking the survey north, where the pipeline would meet existing lines and bring gas to the northern refineries, gas distribution centers and railway lines—new arteries to feed the beast.

The evening meetings were generally civil, though perfunctory. Alise took any opportunity to make corrections, or reiterate any statements Karl made, while Hanna nodded politely. Alise's primary concern was bigger, faster mileage, and following 'the line', the arbitrary line on the map. Hanna was more thorough, and though concerned with the line, she was also committed to the preservation of both historical and prehistoric sites. Hanna was more willing to move the line, and stubborn in defending important sites and her decisions.

Schism

Hanna felt as if she had been exiled to squat among the barbarians, battling divided clans involved in acrimonious power struggles. As the head crew chief, Hanna had to spur the ragged, muttering, mutinous band into action every day. Some days, members who were late in dragging themselves up out of the dust, were forced to leave camp before they had eaten or packed a lunch. They assailed Hanna endlessly with arguments of 'better' schedules and more 'democratic' decision-making. She would listen and politely decline their suggestions until their statements took on a malicious edge, to which she would reply flatly, "Do your job, or quit." Finally, after two weeks of this type of abuse she called Karl and told him, "If you're not here to clean house by Friday, I'm leaving."

When Karl promised that Hugh was on his way, Hanna refused this and demanded that he come himself. "Oh, that's all we need, Hugh and Dog organizing things. No Karl, this is your company, and you need to be here for this."

"Hugh's a good man."

"I know, I know that, but he's a pushover. He'll give everyone a break. He and Alise'll go out to dinner one night, and then we'll have to ask her permission to take the crews out in the morning. These people are a bunch of drunken, fornicating buffoons. We need structure here, Karl. We need a goddamn cook and real structure. These idiots can't even take care of themselves. We sent one guy to the hospital in Covet with food poisoning. The sanitation situation is completely Third World. The camp actually stinks—we're talking about squalor, Karl, you hear what I'm saying? I doubt if some of them have even camped out before. A lot of them aren't even archeologists! They don't have any idea how to do the paperwork! What did you hire these clowns for?"

"You don't have to be so harsh. They're supposed to be

drivers and go-fers."

"Yeah, well, your drivers and go-fers are trying to run the show, and if you don't get up here, Alise will make them crew chiefs by Friday!"

"Hanna, you really don't need to go off like this."

"Karl, we have a situation up here and if word gets out, or if CanAm comes around and sees any of the paperwork these guys are doing, you can kiss this bid good-bye. When Alise isn't directly supervising, they randomly chose what artifacts they'll record and what ones they won't. The line passed right through an early homestead that they didn't record it because they said it wasn't very *interesting*! Some of the forms don't list the correct quadrant map. One set of forms wasn't even in the right county!"

"Hanna I really don't need this right now. You can blame yourself for where you are. You wouldn't be up there if you went to the police. The deputy has been over to the hotel to talk to Hugh, and then he called me here at the office. We're covering your tracks, and meanwhile we're way behind on paperwork, and everything else because of the weather. That goddamn Leon Filmore is hunting me down every place I go. Also...we're on the verge of having our next scheduled payment postponed due to lack of survey mileage, and I'm about to freak out, so BACK OFF!!!"

Silence echoed between the phones.

Hanna saw his point and guilt weighed in her heart. "I'm sorry Karl, I'm just trying to do what I am supposed to be doing."

"I know. That's why I sent you up there. Listen, you just fire any, and I mean ANY sonofabitch that looks at you cross-eyed, and we'll be up as soon as possible, no later than Monday."

"You'll get a cook?"

"Yeah, I'll have my uncle find somebody, but the money's comin' out of the crew's per-diem. I'm not gonna feed a bunch of drunks."

Hanna avoided working with the conspirators and spent

most of her days with Paul Zotti. She trusted Paul. He was a substantial person, honest and hardworking. Hanna liked him as a partner because he wanted to work, and not deal with any drama. He was thorough and knowledgeable in all aspects of the Plains Indians, and pioneers, an encyclopedia of small facts. Karl had approached him many times to be a crew chief, but he always declined, insisting on working only as a surveyor or excavator. Paul was small in stature, his face was effeminate, angelic, and he had fine, brown curls that made him appear delicate, but under the soft exterior, was a very powerful and driven individual. He could work ten- and 12-hour days under the desert sun and never complain. His strength was astounding. He often lifted huge stones out of excavation pits and tossed them aside with hardly a grunt.

Aside from his admirable aspects, Paul was weird as hell. He had a great fear of being touched by other people. 'Haphephobia,' Hanna said to herself, 'the specific phobia of touching or being touched.' He would often ride in the back seat of the Bronco even if it was just himself and the driver. Hanna had tried to hug him hello or good-bye once or twice and found him rigid as a post and scared to death.

She wondered if he might be a virgin, a thought that irked her, and she always thought of him as 'the virgin— Paul, the virgin'. What bothered her the most was her own inability to let it go. Though she didn't consider herself a lascivious person, it drove her insane that he could be a virgin. It seemed that for one to have abstained for a brief lifetime was either the substance of dysfunction or sainthood. She felt compelled to excuse her own orientation and lie with him herself, if he would have her, just to fix it, if successfully sleeping with one woman would then help him sleep with others.

Paul told stories when he worked. He told the stories as if they were his own, always stating them as fact, and never implying they were fictitious. His stories were often long and rambling yarns that were nearly impossible, but he had explanations for the difficult parts, which lay within the realm of possibility. Hanna could tell when he was ready to resume his tales. He would look at a rock, or a flying bird, or a moving vista. He would look over each shoulder to be sure that no one would hear, and say, "You know...it was a rock like this...it was a bird just like that...it was in a place like this...." He would break off his stories when anyone not privy to them approached, which was everyone except Gina and Hanna. Hanna knew that after weeks or months without an acceptable audience, he was bursting to relate the next saga or continue an unfinished episode.

The day after speaking with Karl, Hanna and Paul left camp early to look at a historic site they had come upon at the end of the previous day. They mapped it out all morning, finding shards of cream-colored crockery, two silver spoons, some bottles that were broken but identifiable, blue and purple glass with bubbles of trapped gas, some badly rusted buckles and one broken bit. They found two brass buttons, and three lead balls from a muzzleloader, which was an odd find because the balls were there among more domestic looking articles.

"It's obvious," Paul said. "There's no wagon wreckage, no wheel rims, no nails, or bolts, nothing very heavy, yet we're right next to the Bozeman Trail. It's obvious that the glass and pottery is from the mid 1800s. These people were on horses." He looked out on the plains. "They were probably fleeing Red Cloud. Just horses and packhorses, and one or two fighting men, guiding and guarding a small group, trying to sneak swiftly across the route."

Hanna snorted a disapproving laugh and looked at Paul; she was surprised. She had never considered this. She looked across the prairie and mulled over the validity of the conjecture. She shrugged her shoulders. "Maybe," she said. Paul's theory cast a pall over the otherwise exciting find. She imagined them ascending the expansive slope, surprised as they neared the crest of the ridge, looking up to see a wave of mounted Oglala Sioux sweeping through the tiny party but once. Hanna envisioned the white guards too

dumbstruck to even raise a gun, falling to the ground like
October leaves, leaving nothing but the screaming whinny of
terrified horses.

The travelers lay there upon their backs, looking at a
cloudless sky, still numb, lanced and pierced by stone and
lead, not fully understanding what had happened, expiring in
an ocean of grass in what they believed to be a savage
wilderness.

The Sioux grabbed the horses, guns and useful loot and
rode away, crossing the familiar hills of their home.

Hanna shrugged her shoulders and felt a pang of sadness.
She watched some advancing thunderheads and spun
around. It could have happened, she thought. It was an odd
enough place to find a handful of artifacts and a few chalky
horse vertebrae so far from a road, or homestead, stuck on
the side of a hill.

Paul sat cross-legged, quickly mapping and cataloging the
artifacts, dropping them in various sized plastic bags. His
hands trembled as he handled a small knife. "This would be
in a lot better condition if it were down in the desert," he
muttered.

They sat at the top of the hill during lunch. They were
quiet. Paul munched handfuls of corn chips as he fondled his
bags of artifacts, obviously excited over the find. He opened
one bag and extracted a large, ornate silver pin. The head of
the pin was a tooled wreath of olive leaves. He held it up to
the sun and tried to polish it on the arm of his shirt.

"You're gonna compromise that thing if you keep
rubbing the crust off it," Hanna said, thinking of the point
she had found in the desert, noticing that Paul had his own
artifacts that he doted on. She was jealous because he had so
many surrounding clues that were real, that could assign a
decade, a race, and a political era.

"I can't help it. This is probably very old. This is not a
common item for these types of people to have. It's not a
hatpin. It's for a shawl or cloak. It fastened the, uh...garment
at the shoulder." He illustrated with his hands how it would

have functioned.

"Maybe there weren't women here at all. Maybe they were a couple of bushwhackers with a couple of sacks of loot who came face-to-face with their karma?"

Paul raised his head with wild eyes. "I like that. I never thought of it, like the end of *Sierra Madre*. Greed repaid with violence."

"Something like that."

"They had been looting along the Oregon Trail and planned on using the Bozeman Trail as a getaway, knowing that no one would follow them up here."

"If that's the story you like."

"I like that story; I like it a lot. They got what they deserved, and the Indians made off with the loot and a string of horses."

"That would explain why all we have here are odds and ends, it's the stuff that hit the ground during the melee."

Paul Zotti thought about this and looked down the long slope. He could see the shabby scoundrels climb the hill, talking over the whoring they planned on doing in Bozeman. He looked back down at the pin in his hand and said, "You know...I found a pin something like this on a dig in North Dakota, along the Missouri River. It was an odd find because I found it in a layer that was late prehistoric, which is impossible, and everyone dismissed it as sloppy work on our part, or a quirky anomaly, you know, the site had been previously disturbed, blah, blah, blah."

"I knew what it was though, because I had seen a pin just like it when I did my field training in Nova Scotia. It was an artifact from the Norse explorations. It was the type of pin that the Norse adopted from the Irish."

"Paul, you're so full of it! You mean to say that that pin is a pre-colonial Irish artifact?"

"No, no, not at all. That pin's no older than three hundred years. The one in North Dakota was completely different, and when I told everyone what I thought, they laughed all night. It was a difficult story to believe, but I knew what it was, and I begged them to have it tested, which they declined because the man in charge was a megalomaniac. I even kept it for some time, so I could have it tested myself."

"So you're telling me that there were Vikings rowing their boats up the Missouri hundreds of years previous to Lewis and Clark?"

"No, not at all, what I'm saying is that it was an Irish artifact carried by the Vikings and then traded among the Indians sometime between the years 900 and 1200. The Vikings were here, and they traded actively. It wasn't just Leif Ericson you know. It wasn't one or two small fleets. It was probably several expeditions of many boats over more than a hundred years. It was every non-landowning Icelander and every timber-starved community from the Faeroes to Labrador. I'm not just talking. You should see what they have found back there—entire communities and trading centers—L'Anse aux Meadows. Just because they failed to conquer or build cities and ended up going back home, people dismiss them in the history of North America. That's not so. They were the wave of colonists that the Native Americans successfully repelled."

"The Indians should have learned their lesson and done the same at Jamestown and Plymouth," Hanna said.

"It really is funny what a few hundred years will do isn't it?"

"So, what do you suppose the difference was?"

"Gun powder, cholera, small pox, other technologies, and an endless, desperate, pox-riddled, lice-infested population. But for the Norse it was all so different. It's all right there in the Sagas. It's all recorded from the oral histories. The Vikings were hardly more than iron-age people—and there were women as well as men. They were incredibly warlike and thought themselves invincible in their long, fast, open boats. They failed to realize that they were greatly outnumbered, fighting a very advanced, and equally fierce, stone-age people in their native lands. It was disastrous!" Paul said, shaking his head as if it was too horrible to mention. "After the Norse slaughtered a few Skierlings, that's what they called the indigenous, pre-Iroquoian people, they themselves were likewise slaughtered at every opportunity."

"OK, if it was so disastrous, how did the pin get to the Missouri River?"

Paul Zotti smiled, as if she might never ask. He looked around at the plains and moved closer so the tale shouldn't be carried off by the wind. "Well, it was *largely* disastrous, but some people met with limited success, you know...think about how many Vikings were trading and traveling the water courses of the East Coast. Some of them had to have been successful and maybe peacefully traded with the Skierlings instead of killing everyone they came across.

"They were a seafaring people. Think of all the water they could access! Hudson Bay, the Miramichi River in New Brunswick, the Bay of Fundy, the Kennebec River in Maine, the Saint Lawrence River and every tributary, lake, bay, river and channel connected to it. Just as the Great Lakes and Saint Lawrence were roads to the French voyageurs, they were also the same to the Norse, taking them as far south as Indiana and as far west as Minnesota. Christ, you could walk to the Dakotas in a few weeks from there."

"I don't know, I think this is just another story of yours. I've never heard of any Norse sites west of the Canadian coast. I think you're full of it, Paul."

"I don't think so, because it's all written in their epics, and sagas. A young man by the name of Herjolfsson, the son of one of the Icelanders, who first saw the western lands, was said to have sailed and rowed up the Saint Lawrence. There he engaged large communities of Skierlings in trading negotiations. Learning from past mistakes, he used tact and diplomacy instead of violence, and he kept his iron weapons hidden and traded only fabrics and cookery. Herjolfsson moved slowly up the 'seaway' that flows from the inland seas, or Great Lakes. Tribe introduced him to tribe, and messengers and interpreters traveled with him, until he came to Lake Eire where he came into contact with the great cultures. These tribes were most likely the predecessors of the Huron and Iroquois. It was in the region of the Great Lakes that Herjolfsson and his men found what the basis of their trade would be. Copper."

"We need to get back to work," Hanna said, pretending not to be amazed at the flowing diatribe. She took the pin from Paul and he gave it up the way a child might concede a toy.

"I'm sorry," Paul said, suddenly insecure. "Am I boring you?"

"No, it's just that we've used up a lot of time. We can stay here for the rest of the day, and you can talk, but we need to have this site done today."

They worked diligently for a while, trying to make up some time. Hanna had to subtly goad the story out of Paul. Her interruption had broken his cadence, and she could see him recreating the story as he worked. Finally, when the site was done and they were walking back to the vehicle, he looked over each shoulder and said, "Well, this was the Great Lakes region and there was copper and other minerals in great abundance. The Norse recognized the aqua-colored ore immediately as copper, which they could smelt and smith deftly. It wasn't long before they were turning out trinkets, armbands and arrowheads."

"So what? The Great Lakes tribes knew about copper!" Hanna cut in. She was working with a trowel, testing a few inches deep, but everything seemed to lie upon the surface.

"But they didn't have Norse metallurgy and they couldn't make it harder, like bronze."

"So now you're saying they were trading bronze?"

"No, I am saying they were trading hardened copper." Paul defended himself unemotionally, like a seasoned debater, continuing, "So they gave their trinkets away freely at first and waited until the Indians offered goods for the special gifts they desired. As the demand went up, so did the price of their commissions. It wasn't until the Indians were completely enamored with the new art form that the Norse began to charge for everything.

"They worked the magic of their metallurgy in great secrecy to safeguard their future income. Smoke and stench rose from their tiny compound, and some of the Indians moved their long houses farther from the stink of the alchemy. The Norsemen were chided and goaded at great length to divulge their secrets, but they diplomatically declined. Wise men and shamans were sent to them, men who said they could be trusted with their secrets, but the Vikings held out, opting instead to make a gift of some beads or plates and send the malcontents away happy with their trivial victories." Paul stopped for a moment and shot in the coordinates with a compass and map, then registered the exact spot on a site location form.

When he was done, he continued. "Not all the Norsemen worked in the smelter. Some explored the width and lengths of Lake Ontario, and Lake Erie. They traveled with the tribesmen of Lake Erie and hunted and fished along the way. The tribes from Erie were impressed with the skill of the Norsemen with their wooden boats, and with the bow and the spear. Marginal allies of the Erie men challenged their expeditions, stating that they owed no allegiance to the hulking white barbarians. The challenges were accepted and crushed by the unleashed madness of Viking warfare. The Erie men pleaded with the Norse not to kill so many, because these men were valuable allies against greater enemies. They made peace with the survivors, exchanged oaths of honor, and sent them home with beautifully tooled armbands of coiling copper serpents.

"The Vikings were soon looking beyond Lake Erie, to the greater freshwater seas that they had heard rumors of. As you can imagine, the native Erie men wanted to keep their newfound wealth and the secrets of their magic. They had already begun to act as middlemen, trading their trinkets for double the price they had been purchased for. The Norse taught them how to swing copper-studded clubs, as they themselves might swing their broadswords and battleaxes. The men of the Erie region had prestige and honor among the other tribes as they adorned themselves with fine copper, or forced their will with the ferocity of white warfare. The men of the first lakes begged and pleaded with the Norse not to go to the northern and western seas, and warned of hideous people and beasts that could swallow a whole canoe."

Hanna walked one last circle of the site, searching of any further artifacts. She found one last small piece of rusting iron, but it was unidentifiable in its compromised state. Satisfied, they put away their clipboards and loaded their daypacks for the long walk back.

Paul continued as he walked beside her, "The Erie men promised misery for venturing to the other freshwater seas, but the Norse would have none of it. The Indians could not keep the secret of where the next inland sea would be, the Norse were seafaring adventurers in light craft. All they had to do was paddle on and look for large rivers.

"Once the leaves dropped in the Lake area, and the winters set in, the Indians hoped that the savage winter would make the white people weak and dependent. That was not so, and they were surprised at how hardy and unaffected the bearded men were by the severe climate. The Norse ventured forth to explore the region by canoe even as the edges of the lakes were freezing, and heavy chop threatened to sink their vessels.

"They hibernated for a while under the heavy snow that accumulated deeply on the roofs of the long houses. They were accustomed to the long communal winters. Their own people lived in long houses made of timber, stone, and sod. They exchanged crafts with their hosts and fashioned snowshoes, bows and arrows, and pounded ingots of smelted copper into arrowheads, which were heavier, but superior to the indigenous points of stone. They gave up small pieces of their metallurgy, but didn't worry, because it was really the smelting that they needed to protect.

"They carved skis out of young ash trees, and ventured out with their hosts, who favored the slower, but more stable, snowshoes. They were visited frequently in the long nights by the curious women who fathomed the prowess of the white warriors. The lake men, who certainly knew of the midnight liaisons, seemed indifferent, and joked in rudimentary language of blue-eyed, dark babies who could fight like bears and run like wolves. The Norse grew restless and their hosts told them to be patient and await the heavy ice; they would travel more quickly by ice than they would in the forests.

"By the solstice, the ice was thick and covered with hard snow, so they set out and headed west, pulling sleds laden with hides and birch-bark shelters, dried meat and dried fish. The Norse were happy to be moving through an icy wilderness that reminded them so much of home. Traveling across the lakes would have been much easier here than in the barren glaciation and mountains of Iceland or the jumbled, crusty sea ice along the shores of Greenland. They could make many miles a day, unless they came to open water near the river channels, or when leads of moving ice yawned before them. The Indians asked why they needed to move west. They asked them why they needed to move in the middle of winter when warmth, fresh fish, meat, and women awaited them at home. The Norse could not explain in signs and the broken phrases of the two languages. They could only raise two upturned hands of curled fingers, the sign for 'want'."

The sun was low in the sky when Hanna and Paul reached their vehicle. Paul had extinguished the fuel of his tale, and he seemed empty. Hanna knew that he would need a day or two to nurture it along. The facts were muddled now, and needed to be restructured and rekindled. She left him alone to sit in peace in the backseat. He watched out the window, sitting on his hands, as if it might be chilly back there.

The morning before Hugh, Dog and Karl were to arrive,

in the face of a final rebellion, Hanna fired anyone that she considered dead weight. Alise came unglued because Hanna had cleared out most of her toadies. "You're a crew chief, and you can do whatever you want," Hanna said calmly, "but if their cars are still here when we're done at the end of the day, the sheriff will be here to clear 'em out." This was Hanna's final statement, stopping just short of firing Alise, who was a pain in the ass, but knew the pipeline and regulations as well as Hugh and Karl. Hanna knew she would be on very thin ice with Karl if she were to fire Alise.

"You can't do that. You don't have the right," Alise argued.

"If you want to keep them, go ahead. You can explain it all to Karl tomorrow. They're not working today, and they still need to be gone by dark."

Hanna and Paul went to one end of the survey line and Alise and Sarah went to the other. Hanna noticed that Alise must have been in an ugly mood and taking it out on poor Sarah, because she was sobbing weakly as they left.

A women being fired gave Hanna one last jab. "What, you're firing me because I don't do a good enough job for a fucking pipeline?" She stared at Hanna incredulously. "You do know that this project isn't about gas, it's about opening the door for that Tar Sands ooze to come from down from Canada. You should think about that! All my slow shitty work was actually doing the rest of the world a favor!"

Hanna had no response to that. She had heard the Tar Sands rumor among the grumbling conspiracy theorists of the crew. But she dismissed it as one of scores of circulating rumors.

Karl shut the job down for a day when he arrived. The camp was a mess. There were scattered fire pits, garbage, and makeshift latrines hidden among the bushes. In the afternoon, he took Alise for a walk down to the river. When they returned, her eyes were swollen from crying and filled with hatred for Hanna. Karl gave her a shovel and made her scatter the fire pits and bury the privies.

Hanna and Karl reviewed and corrected the site location

forms, and drove the survey lines. Dog followed behind
them dutifully, gloating with pride as he watched his boss
exert his authority, handing out punishments, firing the
freakish white people. In situations like this, Dog
automatically became Karl's aide-de-camp. Dog wouldn't
talk to anyone, because the offending persons were below
him. Hugh chickened out altogether, as Hanna knew he
would. In a diversion from the dirty work, he took Paul Zotti
and Sarah and went to hire a cook in Covet and buy some
lumber for tables and benches.

"It's not too bad," Karl confided in Hanna as they drove
back from the line.

"What do you mean by that?" she asked.

"I mean, it could have been worse. We'll just put the
camp back together, get a few people up here—Tim and
Gina, and we're back in business."

"So, was I out of line by firing all of those people?"

"No, not a bit. Five is not so many, and they were the
worst. I fired the rest. I should have made the hierarchy and
protocol much clearer from the beginning."

"I'm here to work. That's what I want to do."

"I know, and you've already done your work really well."

"Well thanks," she said awkwardly.

Detente

Hanna immediately sensed that something was different when Tim and Gina arrived from Rocket City. When together they seemed slow witted and graceless one moment, and then harmonized the next. They avoided Hanna when together, and each other when in her presence.

Hanna knew that they had slept together, but she'd let them squirm for a while before she brought it up. She was jealous and let down, but it was endearing to her that they fretted over her feelings. She couldn't tell who she was more jealous over, Tim or Gina. She rationalized that it was probably Tim, as she had grown disillusioned with Gina.

Hanna continued to work with Paul. A new sub-contracted crew of state-permitted archeologists arrived two days later and they worked with Alise. Hanna wondered where they all came from. "You get a dozen for a dollar," she muttered. Hanna isolated herself through Paul. He would do anything she said, within reason, and would work in the field until late in the evening, and leave early in the morning. He never asked questions. He just worked. He told stories, did his job, and allowed her to drive him around as he sat on his hands in the back seat.

Sometimes, at the end of the day, Hanna would leave a half hour before Paul and run back to the camp from far out in the field. She would run for more than an hour before Paul and the Bronco bounced along behind her on the poor roads. She made him her liaison and avoided any other substantial contact for a few days. It seemed too difficult to deal with people after all the politics with Alise—and then Tim and Gina were probably having sex all night like a couple of monkeys.

Hanna didn't understand how all this wearisome baggage had accumulated. She didn't go looking for it. She didn't want it. She couldn't care less about the politics of work. She would prefer to let everything and everyone go their own way. "For instant shit, just add people," she muttered. "You ever get tired of people, Paul?"

"Sometimes I think I was born tired of them," he said.

"Do you get tired of me?"

"No, not really; you don't complain, or talk about drivel, and you like to work hard."

"I guess I feel the same way about you."

"That doesn't mean were going steady, does it?"

Hanna laughed at his bold joke. "Will you tell me what became of those Norsemen today?"

"You mean the history of the Norse explorers?" he asked, pushing his dark glasses up his nose with his index finger.

"Yes," she smiled. "The history of the Norse explorers."

"Not today."

"Why not?"

"I'm having some trouble piecing all of the events together. I don't want to give them to you falsely," he said earnestly.

"And I wouldn't want you to do that," Hanna smiled.

"One day I'll show you the evidence, and you won't be so smug."

"What do you mean?" Hanna asked.

"Just what I said."

* * *

With newly-permitted archeologists and a few of the old drivers and go-fers, Karl had the survey back on track in a few days, and he was happy to be out of the office, walking the line, assessing the cultural value of the historic and prehistoric materials they found. Hugh and Karl gathered their minions round the fire and pontificated until well into the night on the meaning of the day's finds. Karl even slept out in the open, under a cottonwood.

Karl came with several new improvements, including a

trailer for the cook, although it still would be a few days
before she arrived. There was an enormous bundle of
canvas, which promised to be a large mess tent, as soon as
the cook arrived. There were several new picnic tables, two
50-gallon garbage cans with locking lids. An additional port-
a-potty was added, as were two canvas shower stalls with
wooden pallet floors. The showers had black rubber shower
bags that had to be filled with water and hung in the sun all
day to warm them. A hose connected the bags to a
showerhead inside the stall.

Camp was far from the highway, in an oasis of forested
hills and meadow valleys. It was a nice camp, on a peninsula
formed by a meander of the river. There was ample shade
from cottonwoods, and the grass was thick and lush. Wild
turkeys called from the ridges in the morning, redheaded
woodpeckers and kingbirds nested overhead. White-tailed
deer appeared and disappeared like ghosts in the late
evenings and early mornings. The sun came up slowly
through the morning mists of the river and descended slowly
through the red hazy sky of the northern plains as hatches of
insects rose from the river.

Hugh brought his teepee and set it up on the edge of the
river. It stood taut and erect, gleaming white in the sun. The
tips of the poles were adorned with bright yarn and Tibetan
prayer flags. Hugh arranged a number of cottonwood
stumps around an ample fire ring, placing his tepee at the
center of beer drinking and nocturnal activities. In the
evenings, he often sat in front of it with a piece of thick
leather across his left thigh, chipping away at a nice piece of
chert or obsidian with a collection of hammer stones or elk
antlers, forming arrow heads or larger spear points of his
own. He would hide these from time to time in digs that
were underway to perplex the new field archeologists. He
would hide a historical-style point in an archaic dig or visa-
versa, which would stymie the crew until they saw Dog and
Hugh sniggering from afar.

Ironically, Dog rejected the culturally fitting teepee idea, claiming his people never lived in them, but he offered no clarification. He chose instead a Sears baker tent, which stood limply 20 yards away. It sagged and hung dejectedly in the shadow of a cottonwood. There were large stains of unknown origin on the walls of the tent. Some of the poles were missing or broken, and Dog tried to make up for that with an elaborate system of guy lines and cords tied from the tent to surrounding trees, which made it look like there was some cosmic significance to their positions. It usually blew down every few days, and in the mornings Dog would be passed out on top of it, guarding it like a bear on its kill. Gina and Tim had a clever arrangement, with her tent just outside his truck, close enough that she could slip into his camper in the middle of the night and be out by morning.

After purging his camp, Karl took the remainder of his crew to dinner at Gluttons. Everyone was going, and Paul told Hanna that she had to go. She made Paul promise to keep her separated from Alise and Sarah. Hanna had been to these events before, and they bored the hell out of her. They would pick a particular restaurant with some particular quirk, like all-you-can-eat buffets, or barbeque joints with names like Porky's, or pathetically mundane steak houses called, The Silver Spur, The Silver Dollar, The Cowboy, The Ranger, The Out Rider, The Calvary Man—same place, different location. They purposely chose these places for the irony of a group of educated individuals eating at such a tacky establishment, imagining that they should be above it somehow.

Everyone would drink too much and complain about the service and talk about other archeology companies and what terrible work they did. They would question each other on what universities they had attended and what degrees they had received, and how they had come to be 'archeologists' as if it were a holy transformation, a birth by fire. The more arrogant members of the crew would dominate the conversation and try to demonstrate how big and powerful their brains were by reciting monotonous facts and answering questions with witty quips.

"You know, Paul, I'd gnaw my leg off to get out of this one."

"I know," he said, "but your absence would be too obvious. I think Karl is trying to bury the hatchet and create a more amiable environment."

"Well, I'm plenty amiable. You think I'm amiable don't you?"

"Oh yeah."

"There'll be nothing for me to eat there. I have better food in my cooler."

"You have to go. You're a crew chief. Just get a potato and a salad."

"Yeah, you just get a potato and a salad," Hanna barked. "They know I can't eat there."

Paul pretended he didn't hear her.

* * *

The catchy quirk of Gluttons, other than the name, was the fact that everything they served was enormous, and all they served was meat. Potatoes and vegetables were merely garnish. The steaks they served overhung their platters on all sides. Beer and refreshments came in quart-sized glass buckets. The mashed potatoes came in troughs swimming in gravy, and the silverware was modeled after little pitchforks and shovels. Hanna swooned with the odor of the place, knowing there would be no food for her. The scent of meat and grease and stale beer attacked her as a noxious haze. She could feel the mist of burning fat settle on her skin and clothes. The inside of Gluttons was adorned with notorious gourmands, like Henry VIII, Nero, Viking figures, and Attila the Hun, holding gigantic hams in one hand and captured maidens in the other. High on one wall was a huge mural of a Roman table, spilling over with fruit and burnt pigs, loaves of bread and tall, clay pitchers of wine. Across the room, a medieval scene of kings and knights mirrored the Roman festivities. There was one picture of three vaqueros eating large lumps of mutton from the points of their long daggers. Behind all this were all the trappings of western architecture, with exposed wooden beams and odds and ends from wagons and saddles.

The waitress appeared in a loud, red and white gingham dress that hugged her ample waist tightly and festooned out in hundreds of pleats over her wide hips. Her make-up was surreal; her tight, blonde curls appeared to spring directly from her brain. She balanced a large tray weighted evenly with buckets of beer. As she set each beer down on the table, its absence threatened to topple the rest, and all eyes followed the tottering platter, accompanied by the 'whoas' and 'ooohhhs' of the mesmerized patrons. As she set the last bucket down, they gave her a round of applause and she blushed under her rouge. Her nametag said 'Jackie'. She was bubbly, and made flirtatious jokes with the men. Jackie and the restaurant were supposed to reflect an ideal of a Western culture, the happiness and plenty enjoyed by the local folk during some time in recent history, when every person was a friend and every friend a neighbor.

The crew ordered their dinners of steaks and prime rib, and appetizers of chicken wings and stuffed mushrooms. Hanna searched the menu for something edible and settled for a baked potato and a dinner salad. She accepted her fate and drank deeply from her bucket of beer. No one held back, Tim and Gina, and even Paul ordered slabs of beef. Hanna felt betrayed but choked it back. She had worked hard that day and had even run afterward. She was starving, but all she could order was garnish. Instead of sulking, she decided to prove her bonhomie, standing with her glass bucket out in a toast, "Here's to Karl, our benevolent employer, fearless leader, and unfailing role model."

The crew rose from their seats, toasting and hooting in a merry roar of approval.

"Oh man, I was jus' gonna say that!" Dog grumbled loudly, pretending to be angry.

As the orders were taken, Alise and Sarah shouted out

jibes directed at Hanna, "Just cut off a leg!" or, "Bring in a calf, and we'll take it from there." The appetizers of chicken wings and sausage-stuffed mushrooms were as enormous, as the dinner salad was tiny and wilted. Hanna started on her second bucket of beer. Karl, Dog, and Hugh were in heaven, sucking the meat from the chicken bones, popping whole mushrooms into their mouths and sucking on their greasy fingers, which left visible smears on the large, sweating glass buckets. All that could have made the night more enjoyable for them was if Jackie had dropped that hideous gingham rag and shook her booty while they ate.

"Hanna, mushrooms aren't meat," Sarah said hopefully.

"No," Alise corrected her, "but they came in contact with sausage," she hissed, raising her eyebrows comically.

A bearded driver named Jessie pleaded in phony passion, and trembling hands, "Eaat the meeaat, Hanna! Eeeaat the meeeaaatt!!!

The crew roared with laughter, and Paul pretended not to hear, while Tim opened his mouth to defend her, but lost the moment and let it pass.

It took Jackie and two bus boys to carry the main entrees to the table. Red fluids dripped onto the rubber checkered tablecloth. Troughs containing baked potatoes, mashed potatoes, fried potatoes, and potato salad followed. Whole loaves of bread and tubs of butter appeared out of nowhere. Bowls of green beans accompanied the meal and Hanna eyed them hopefully until she saw that they were prepared with chunks of bacon. The extra food and a plate of gnawed chicken bones were crowded in Hanna's direction since all she had was a tiny saucer holding a lonely potato.

The crew dug in with their miniature trenching tools, cutting through the muscle, dragging the carnage through potatoes and gravy. Dog was gnawing on a long, seared piece of fatty gristle, which he fed into his mouth with his fingers, as if it was a fat licorice whip. Gina was precisely dissecting her portion of filet mignon, holding her little pitchfork upside down in her left hand, and the butcher knife in her right, pinkies stuck out in good manners. Poor Sarah was chowing down with great zeal, stopping now and then, saying daintily, "Oh gosh, this is so much food. I could never eat all this!" Then she fell back to it with fervent zeal.

Alise was dipping her meat in the potatoes and gravy before stuffing it in her mouth. Karl and Hugh shouted encouragement as Dog chugged a half-bucket of beer, to which they all cheered. Jackie returned with the house offer to anyone who finished his or her beef, 'If the customer would like to try to eat a second portion of beef, the second will be on the house, if entirely finished.' All eyes turned to Hugh, but he waved away the offer, and Sarah looked around, obviously tempted.

Hanna lost interest in her second beer, knowing that she was being dishonest with her self just by being there. Why should she sit there drinking? Was she really part of this? All around her gigantic men, women and children were lost in the abandon of eating. One table of 'real' cowboys ate with their hats on, bumping brims and jostling each other with their elbows, stopping now and then for a 'har, har, har'. There was a table with a well-dressed man accompanied by, what Hanna guessed, was a first date. He was a proud, bull-chested man, dressed crisp and tight, tight, tight! His every move beneath the precision of creases was affected with dogmatic machismo. His date, on the other hand was demure and ceded to his will. There was another table with a large family, both in number and measure, which Hanna figured to be Mormon or devoutly Christian. They bowed their heads and prayed as Jackie delivered their feast, so they could partake of the second deadly sin. The mom was as submissive as the first date at the other table. In a flowered print dress, she kept pulling at the material around her waist, to hide her corpulent tummy. Her husband, a hard-faced man of prodigious proportion, wore a stiff western shirt and jeans, keeping his cowboy hat on above his reddened face. The children were impeccably clean and portly, their pug noses acutely porcine. They ate happily and sucked on their buckets of Coca-Cola, giggling nervously under the watchful

gaze of their massive patriarch. The stubby little girl wore a
dress and mimicked her mom, compulsively billowing out the
material around her waist. The boys bore their fat more
comfortably, seeing themselves as 'big' and 'manly'. She
imagined them lobster-red, searing in the sun at a lakeside
recreation area, doing belly flops off a raft, pulling up their
shorts to cover the cracks of their asses as they came ashore
for another round of hotdogs and sodas.

Hanna lost the thread of gossip as the crew ate and
rambled on. She rose from her chair, avoiding eye contact,
making a false pass toward the ladies room. She wove
through the tables full of feasting Homo sapien, Robustus
Americani, passing them carefully so as not to be mistaken
for a succulent cutlet.

She looked back one last time at Paul, so he would know
that she was leaving, but he was listening intently to Sarah.
Hanna looked around for the exit, which was difficult to see
through the packed bodies and dim light.

As she made her way to the door, it opened and a new
group of gargantuan Robutus Americani entered. She pushed
past them, amazed at the feel of the sheer mass of their
bodies, like pushing her way past livestock.

Back at the Bronco, she opened the rear door and drank
deeply from the five-gallon water jug. It was insulated so the
water was still cool. The smell of burning meat clung to her
hair and clothes. She filled her hands, scrubbed her face, and
felt better. Hanna had drunk too much to drive. There was
nothing to do but wait, so she walked up and down the road
until she felt better, and then reclined in the passenger seat.

She was asleep by the time Tim and Gina found her.
Believing she drank too much, they gave her a hard time,
calling her an 'ole booze hound'. Gina hung over from the
back seat, chattering away at Hanna. Tim, on the other hand,
was as lucid as ever. He pulled Hanna against him for an
awkward, sympathetic hug before he started the car. Hanna
ceded to his will politely, but then retracted. Gina prattled on
drunkenly, jealous of their connection.

On the way home, Tim snapped on the radio to a country station. The songs were generally sad and full of self-pity by men and women who had done someone wrong and lost their way. Hanna and Gina sang along with the refrains, and Tim howled like a coyote to the slower ones. They stopped to take in the night on the long dirt road back to camp. The moon was out, and the pastures and rolling hills shone brightly.

Tim turned off the engine, and they sat on the hood for a few minutes, listening to the silence, talking quietly. Gina tried to talk Hanna into running the rest of the way back to camp. Finally, Gina convinced only herself, and took off running, shouting, "Come on, come on."

Tim and Hanna let her go.

"She'll be back," Tim said. "She's not gonna get anywhere." He paused and then spoke again. "That wasn't too fun for you back there?"

"No, I can't even pretend to be apart of that anymore."

"And then they have to make an issue of it," Tim sighed.

"I know. It's like your not part of the clan if you're not eating meat. It's an insult not to eat it.

"You would have been burned for a witch two hundred years ago."

"No lie," she said dismissively. "But it's no big deal, let's just drop it." With Gina gone Hanna asked him, "So what's going on with you and Gina?"

Tim shifted around uncomfortably, "Oh, you know."

"No, I don't, that's why I'm asking."

"I really can't say. We're sleeping together, not all the time though. And she still calls that Dave guy a lot. Is that his name? I guess I really can't define it."

"Well, lucky you. All the sex and none of the commitment."

"It seems that way doesn't it?"

He put his head on her shoulder, and she shrugged it off. "What, you want both of us now?"

He put his arm around her shoulder to pull her close, "Come on, Hanna you know it's not like that!"

"I know," she said. "I just don't want to have to feel weird around you guys."

"Why would you feel weird around us?"

She leaned back into him and sighed, "I don't know, I really don't. I just thought that it'd be awkward if you were a couple."

"Well, don't worry, we're not a couple. I think we're just 'experimenting' a little bit."

Hanna laughed at his words. "So, you're a couple of scientists, huh?—Vell dis kint ov verk 'asss to be done."

They laughed.

"So, would you 'experiment' with any filly who raised her skirt to you? I hope you guys are safe. Even scientists use rubber gloves."

"No, it's not like that! I've known Gina a long time, and we were working together all the time. We were spending the evenings together, and one thing led to another. That's all."

"Yeah, I could see that happening."

Tim smelled her hair. "She made me do it Hanna. I really didn't want to!"

Hanna pushed away from him laughing.

"It was terrible!" he sobbed. "She was groping me and grabbing me all the time. I thought that if I gave in she would stop...but...but, she didn't," he whispered burying his face in his hands.

Hanna pushed him away, "Don't be an ass."

They sat quiet for a moment, and she asked, "So when will we climb?"

"I know, I thought we would go right away, but then all that crap happened, and you left town."

"So, you still want to go?"

"Oh, c'mon! Of course I want to go. That's all I want to do. We'll go first chance!"

Gina reappeared out of the moonlight, "Hey where did you guys go?"

Tim laughed, "We didn't go anywhere. Where did you go?"

Meg

After her ten-day work stint, Hanna headed south. The crews generally worked for ten days and then took five days off, but Tim and Gina had started their work rotation later so they stayed to work for another two days. Hanna wanted to be with them but thought it best to leave on her own, so she headed south to Felicidad. She needed to be away from the field, and from Alise and the crew. She wanted to be in a larger town. She wanted to have a good meal and a good cup of coffee. She wanted to see her old friend Meg.

She drove for a whole day to be in a town that wasn't economically shackled to beef, beets or petroleum. For four hours she didn't pass a town larger than a thousand people. She drove across empty alkali deserts and traveled over timbered passes. On the drive south, Hanna kept an eye on the mountains to the west. Paul had left two days before her to backpack into those mountains. The weather looked good there, but she could see a wall of clouds building up on the prevailing side of the summits, and she was hoping he would use good sense. Later, when she stopped to stretch her legs, the mountains were still just barely visible and the clouds had stacked higher and darker, and she wondered where Paul might be.

She parked her truck and walked up to sit for a while on the top of a low desert butte of grey mudstone. When not working, Hanna purposely tried to keep her eyes straight ahead so she wouldn't look for artifacts. It was intensely hot in the basin, and the sun seared right through her. It felt cleansing to be away from all the anxiety generated by other people. She felt happy to sit with the desert all to herself and not have to accommodate the feelings and wishes of others. She thought that it was too bad Meg couldn't be here, but Hanna knew that negotiating a dense urban environment was the fire she had to walk through to reach Meg. She sat quietly for a while, and watched the cars pass on the highway, psyching herself up for the drive into the city.

Hanna actually loved this routine of empty roads that led her to Meg, and the day progressed nicely, the sun followed its arc across the earth as she reached the interstate. Once on the interstate, all her anticipation for Meg turned to highway anxiety. She feared the traffic, and the cultivated land, and the condos, which sprang from the earth as quickly as corn. She could see its northward progression. Much of the area she had travelled in the past was now unrecognizable to her. The highway was crowded with factory liquidation centers and one-stop travel malls. The western landscape was mottled and twisted where corn grew and cattle grazed below skeletal broadcasting towers, and John Deere tractors wove their way between the Flying J Super Station and the Conoco Gas and Go. An obsolete cowhand on a motorcycle pushed a small herd of Herefords from one pasture to another below a spider web of power lines, and a horizon lost in a pall of gas and diesel exhaust. This was the new West, a suburb of ranchettes, sprawling subdivisions, and trailer parks, spotted here and there with populations dense enough to be called cities. She had once thought that the West was unique and above this type of sprawling expansion, but it was obvious that this was not the case. This was America, and land was only a commodity as it would be in Detroit, New York, or Newark.

"I have seen the future, and it makes no sense," Hanna said to no one in particular. As she drew closer to the city, she felt as if she had made a grave error. She wanted to flee. She didn't want to see the future. She had almost forgotten what she was hiding from. She thought that she must have been out of her mind to think that she wanted to come down here to 'get away from it all'. What comforts and civilities could possibly make up for the ugliness and crush of humanity that awaited her here? She began to panic as the traffic pressed tighter around the far right lane that she had claimed as her own.

She took her rehearsed path of exits, intersections and traffic lights and finally came to Meg's house, although Meg was gone. Hanna stood nervously knocking on the door of the two-bedroom cottage, five blocks from downtown. She took the key from under a ceramic toad and let herself in. Once inside she relaxed. Meg's house was cool and dark. It was cluttered in a tidy way. All shelves and counters packed with books, trinkets and bills, postcards and nonsense. Headlines were randomly stuck to the refrigerator and corkboards. MAN TELLS NEIGHBOR, I JUST SHOT MYSELF IN THE HEAD! STAMPEDING ELEPHANTS DESTROY WEDDING PARTY. SUPERMODEL EATEN BY CROCODILE! Meg thought that there was great irony in the headlines of daily papers. She made poetry out of it. She thought it would sell, but was finally depressed when she realized she would never be published.

BANK TELLER FENDS OFF THIEVES
WHALES BEACHED IN SYDNEY
BEHAVIORISTS PROVES THAT HOUSE PETS GRIEVE
ROCK STAR DONATES KIDNEY

THE GOP ADMITS DEFEAT
ASIAN MARKET CRASHES
THE WHITE HOUSE IS IN RETREAT
CIVILIANS DIE IN WEEKEND CLASHES

Hanna never understood, but Meg cut them out dutifully and arranged them on heavy poster board. She wanted to make magnetic headlines to arrange on one's refrigerator.

"I think something like that has already been done, Meg."

"Yes I know," Meg had said, "but this is different."

Hanna felt strange in Meg's house. She hadn't been invited. She hadn't called to inform Meg she was coming. She just showed up. Meg was used to it, or maybe she was tired of it. Hanna loved Meg. Meg was her rock. And Meg loved her too, but she was a well-settled person. She owned a house and a small business and didn't move around. She had a cat. She was what Hanna was not.

Hanna felt guilty being here, and she would feel guilty when she left. Meg always cried when they said good-bye. She felt like the bearer of bad news, the portent of impending pain. Hanna wondered if it was unfair to come, or if it would be evil to stay away. Maybe it was egotistical to even consider what pain she might inflict. After all, who was she? What power did she have to disrupt someone's life? She was only a person. It was not like she was a sorceress or bruja. She was actually submissive to Meg's wishes and let her run the show. The only point that Hanna refused to capitulate was her need to move.

Meg lived on a quiet street shaded by tall cottonwoods. It was hard to believe that her house was only a few blocks from the downtown area of a minor city. There was no looming skyline or apartment complexes, just a street of tidy little houses. Hanna could hear the buzz of traffic just beyond the rows of hedges and the façade of trees. This was where Meg lived and where she belonged. She had lived in this house for years and would probably live here for many more. It was what she wanted.

Since Hanna was not officially invited, she left Meg a note on the table, locked the door and walked downtown. She ate at a health food store with a sandwich counter. There was so much to choose from that it confused her. Everything looked excellent, rice and pasta salads, thick heavy bread, and huge choices of cheese, fresh juice, and excellent coffee. Hanna felt replenished. She drank more coffee and watched the patrons come and go. They seemed excessively polite, carrying their non-consuming cotton shopping bags. Their clothes bore the statements of their lifestyles; sandals, loose-fitting cotton clothing, peasant blouses, lengthy gauzy skirts, shorts and tank tops to tastefully expose the definition of their bodies.

Hanna realized these people were probably in disguise.

They were doctors, lawyers, investment bankers, bonus babies working on their fourth degree at the university. Their clothes bore messages of their beliefs and feats of athletic prowess: TELLURIDE BLUEGRASS FEST, BOLDER BOULDER 10K, SUNSHINE CANYON SHIATSU CLINIC, 10TH ANNUAL IRONMAN. This seemed more comforting than the messages she had seen up north: KILL 'EM ALL, LET GOD SORT 'EM OUT! OIL FIELD TRASH AND PROUD OF IT! MY DRINKING TEAM HAS A RODEO PROBLEM. IF YOU AIN'T A DRILLER, YOU AIN'T SHIT!

She left the sandwich counter and bought good food for the house, small gifts for Meg. She wandered around the plaza, which had been closed to traffic and listened to the musicians who played with their instrument cases open for money. She watched the jugglers and magicians performing for free. Panhandlers asked for money; a lunatic was making his flea-bitten mutt sit-up and speak. After each bark, he swept his arms theatrically toward the dog, awaiting applause, as if it were the main attraction. Message boards advertised music and events of political, metaphysical, environmental, heterosexual, homosexual, and existential significance. She went into a bookstore and sat on a velvet couch, reading the first leftist rag she laid her hands on.

She wandered back up the hill as evening settled and the crowds of people began to fill the plaza. It was cool, and she crossed the street to walk in the last rays of the sun. The jagged foothills were visible from that side of the street. They loomed shadowed and craggy over the peaceful little city. They were the kind of mountains people want nowadays, convenient little mountains right outside of town.

The door of Meg's house was open, and the screen door was ajar as Hanna came up the walk. She shouted hello, and Meg appeared in an instant. Hanna was relieved to see the joy in Meg's eyes. Meg held the door open, and hugged Hanna clumsily, kissing her cheek as she passed with her bag of groceries. Hanna dropped the bag on the couch and held

Meg's compact body in her arms. She was so much shorter that Hanna rested her cheek on top of Meg's head.

"Look what the cat dragged in," Meg said, pushing away, eyeing Hanna up and down.

"I feel like I've been dragged by a cat," Hanna said.

"You look good, all tan and lean."

"You look wonderful yourself."

"Oh please," she said dramatically, shaking out her full head of sleek brown hair. "But really, I've been working too much. I'm pale and pasty."

"You're crazy, but you're not pale and pasty."

Hanna could see that Meg was still buxom and rounded, in her strong, robust way; anything but pasty.

"I am so. All I do anymore is work."

"Well, fine then, let's go out right now! We'll go running in the foothills."

"Yeah, we'll run a marathon and then go to the gym," Meg said, her large brown eyes wide with impish sarcasm. "You go ahead, I'll stay here and work on my pallor." Meg pinched Hanna's arm. "What brings you into town? I haven't seen you since Christmas."

"Oh, it's just been a hard couple of sessions. I needed a break from the field. I needed to see how civilized people live. I wanted to see you."

Meg's brows shot up, "Oh, hey do you want me to hook you up with a climbing partner? A bunch of climbers work at the burrito joint across the street from my store. I know them."

"No, no, I want to spend some time with you. Maybe we can run in the mornings."

Meg blushed slightly, "How funny you are here. I had a feeling you might come find me."

"Why did you think that?"

"I don't know, my radar was just picking up a bit of…Hanna on the horizon," Meg said bashfully. "I have a new friend, and she just left for Chicago, to train for a new job. And I thought, 'this is the time Hanna would show up'."

Hanna was unable to cover her surprise. "Wow, if I had…could you imagine my embarrassment, if I uhhhhhh..."

"Oh, I'd have loved to see it, but as always, your timing is impeccable," Meg said as she picked up the groceries, taking them to the kitchen.

"Well it's not like that! I mean I didn't come down here just to...you know," Hanna countered weakly, following her.

"Disrupt my life? Have a roll in bed with honey?"

"No, it's not like that at all!" Hanna said, even though she knew she couldn't lie to Meg. Meg had a surgical method of articulating the reality of any situation.

"Yes, it's exactly like that, no matter how you see it. That's how it is, but don't worry about it. I think I know you by now. I think that it's probably OK."

"You know how I feel about you!" Hanna said, too urgently.

"Don't be defensive. I'm teasing you. Remember, that's what I do," Meg said coming forward a step, rubbing Hanna's arms. "Hanna, I'm 30 years old. We've been, or you've been doing this for at least four years now, so there must be something in it for me. For a gnarly girl you're pretty sensitive."

Even safely in Meg's house, with Meg there before her, Hanna felt anxious for how swiftly the time would pass, because five days was not that long a time to spend with a loved one. One day was spent in travel, even if it was a short trip, travel was a substantial disruption. In reality, this left only three days, because one day remained for the journey home. The second day was spent in cumbersome civilities and complimentary accommodations. The third day was the only day for real connection. The third day was the enjoyably long day. It was the good day, no matter what happened. It was the day of telepathy, of synchronicity, the day where the second finished the sentence of the first. The third day was comfortable because it was padded by the second day and the fourth day. The fourth day was not so good because the third day could not be recaptured, and there was the great anxiety of the departure on the fifth day. The fourth day was uncomfortably long. It was the day of evident truths, annoying disagreements, and visitations and ruminations of the past. The fifth day was gone before it had begun. It was the day that regrettable statements and actions occurred. It was the day that divided the future from the past. It was the day that decided if there was a future, or if all was not already behind them.

The night that Hanna arrived, Meg had to attend a merchants' meeting, and went to work the following morning. Hanna ran and read most of the day, then prepared dinner for Meg, like a dutiful spouse, awaiting her return. Hanna paced when dinner was ready, and Meg failed to appear. She wanted to please Meg. She wanted to reveal her affection, confirm her adoration. When Meg came in and shouted, "Something smells good!" Hanna jumped.

Hanna ran to meet her at the door, and Meg held her arms wide, a bottle of wine in one hand and a baguette in the other, "Honey, I'm home!"

Hanna embraced her, kissed her, and led her anxiously to the kitchen.

"Oh, Hanna. This looks so good. Salad, pasta, cheese and olives...am I late? I'm sorry."

"No, no, no, it's still hot sit down, sit down, and we can eat!"

Meg squeezed Hanna's hand and looked beaming into her eyes. They ate all there was and drank the bottle of wine. Meg told Hanna all about her frame and art-supply store, and how her business was finally strong enough that she had quit lecturing economics classes at the university. Meg was excited for the new businesses coming in around her, lifting her block out of the urban decline it had been experiencing.

Hanna told Meg about life in the field. She had many tales to tell, and felt odd, dominating the conversation. She didn't like this role much and tried many times to relinquish it to Meg, but Meg would have none of it. She grilled Hanna for an hour, extricating the facts of the attempted abduction.

She wanted to buy a gun and go back to The Rock and, "hunt those bastards down like dogs." Her eyes flashed angrily at Hanna when Hanna refused to have anything to do with it.

"Jesus Christ, Meg, I Maced them, kicked one in the stomach, and flattened their tires. Then they had to walk back and tell the authorities that they had been assaulted by a woman."

"That's not enough. I would have cut their balls off."

"Well maybe that's the difference between you and me."

Meg mocked her silently and stuffed another forkful of pasta in her mouth. "And people wonder why there are lesbians in the world." Meg looked around in astonishment. "And we're the bad ones right? I mean, lesbians are always driving around like a bunch of hateful predators, waiting for a lone male to rape to death and leave in a shallow grave!"

"Nobody left anybody in a shallow grave."

"That's only because you didn't give them a chance!" Meg said slapping the table.

"Come on Meg, don't be militant. I've been through this with everyone else. Those guys lost and I won. So, talk about something else."

"I know. You're right, but you'd be angry too if you were me."

Hanna winked at Meg, reached across the table and took her hand.

They cleared away the dishes and cleaned the kitchen together, and then Hanna went up to shower. As she toweled dry, she could hear Meg in the guest room where Hanna was sleeping. Hanna wrapped herself in a towel and quietly stepped across the hall and peered through door, which was slightly ajar. The guest room glowed with candlelight, and Meg was folding back the sheets, and then she turned to look back to the door, sensing Hanna there. Hanna stood wrapped in a towel, watching through the chink, Meg dropped her robe in the yellow light, and got into Hanna's bed, leaving Hanna behind the door chilled and wet.

"You're assuming a lot," Hanna said, pushing the door

open.

"There's no assumption to it. It's my house…and you look silly and cold standing there like that."

On the third day, Saturday, Hanna awoke with Meg beside her. Hanna looked around from the bed. The candles had burned down to nothing in the night, and wax had run over the tiny saucers. Meg would be angry. She took good care of her furniture; she called her furniture 'pieces'. Meg slept on her side, and breathed in steady cadence beside her. Hanna could see the freckles on her back and shoulders. Her skin was pale and young looking. Meg didn't have the hard looking skin that Hanna and Gina had from spending too much time in the sun. Meg's thick, brown hair spread across the sheets. Hanna slowly peeled the sheets away from her, down to her waist. Meg's body was round. Even when lying down, her body and limbs were like the trunk and branches of a tree. She wasn't fat, but she was round, her waist, and even her hips were round. Her butt and breasts were absolute hemispheres. The circumference of her thigh was a perfect circle. Hanna slid her hand around Meg's waist and pulled her into the cup of her own body. She buried her face in her hair and slid her hands up to hold Meg's breasts.

"Hanna, I'm still sleeping. You're so bad."

"Go back to sleep I just wanted you next to me."

Waylaid

That same morning was not as cozy for Paul. Those distant clouds Hanna had watched from the highway two days before, had accurately forecast that Paul would be caught out in a summer snowstorm; as he neared the farthest point on a three-day backpacking loop, he was nailed with a storm that came in on a massive cold front. It came in the night, and he awoke that morning with his tarp sagging in his face from wet, heavy snow. At first it didn't seem so bad, but as he packed up and got moving, the sodden snow soaked him quickly through to the skin, and his light, hiking boots offered little defense against the shin-deep slush. The only thing left to do was to retreat the way he came. In deep snow, he was lucky to find his way. On the swirling frozen plateau, he could only follow his compass through a whiteout, back over an 11-thousand-foot pass, with ten inches of snow on top of unstable talus. Crossing the pass the previous day had taken an hour, while re-crossing it in the storm took four.

Once he was finished with the pass, he still had to deal with his sodden state and the remaining distance to his car, while the precipitation continued to fall as hail and icy sleet. Paul walked for the rest of the day and was forced to camp once more because of darkness and exhaustion. This last night out was miserable because his clothes were soaked through, and the little food remaining didn't pack the calories he needed to fend off hypothermia. As the storm abated at lower elevations the temperature fell beneath clearing skies. He spent most of the night sitting up shivering, wrapped in his wet sleeping bag, drinking hot water he heated on his stove.

Idyll

After a light breakfast and too much coffee, Hanna and Meg ran in the foothills, which were steep and networked with trails. Meg knew the trails well and often came up here after work. She was strong, and though not a disciplined runner, she was doggedly tough. Hanna joked that if she ever wanted to kill Meg, she would simply run her to death, because Meg would die before she would give up. After the initial climb, the terrain followed drainages and the trail sometimes leveled out across brief plateaus. There were huge ponderosa pines, which stood aloof, and broadly spaced, while short grasses, yucca and dwarf prickly pear covered the ground. Clark's nutcrackers and Steller's jays swooped from tree to tree, and ravens rose on the thermals of the east-facing hills.

They didn't speak or pass any other runners. It was still early. The sun was warm but not yet punishing. Hanna had hit her stride and found her breath after the first hills out of the parking lot. As the trail climbed the drainage, she began sweating freely. She checked often to see if Meg was with her, always ten paces back. She slowed to accommodate Meg and let her body move up the steep trail, through shallow gullies where stones had been fashioned to steps.

It was cooler up high as the trail leveled out, and Hanna maintained an easy trot, enjoying the beautiful views high above town, and the coolness of mid-morning. They passed stony crags of red rock, and intercepted a herd of mule deer coming up the hill after a night foraging on manicured lawns and gardens. They were fat and sleek like pedigree farm animals.

"Venison," Meg joked.

"Yum!"

"This would be a six-mile loop if we took this junction," Meg pointed to a trail sign up ahead.

"What are the options if we don't take this?"

"There's another junction further on that would make it about eight."

Hanna stopped and used her T-shirt to wipe the sweat from her eyes. "What do you want to do? I'd do either. Have you been running enough to do eight miles?"

Meg rested her hands on her knees and breathed for a moment. "Oh, yeah, that's OK. Actually, I like the farther junction because the next trail descends on a lower angle, and it's easier on my knees."

"OK, you sure?"

Meg nodded, and they continued down, losing elevation gradually then speeding up as the sandy sloping trail pulled them from the hills.

Hanna felt exhilarated, running down the gentle incline at a good pace. Meg was right behind her. "I'm out runnin' with my gal," Hanna said joyfully to herself. The trail paralleled an exclusive neighborhood perched on a high bench. The houses were expansive and the grounds were well maintained.

"Those deer ate here last night!" Meg shouted. "Once in a while one of these houses burns up in a brush fire," she added after a few steps. "And the mountain lions and coyotes eat their pets," she panted.

Hanna held her hands above her head to illustrate the headlines, "RICH IDIOTS BUILD STUPID HOUSES, KARMA TAKES CARE OF THE REST."

Meg laughed and stumbled down the trail. Two hikers appeared around a corner as the parking lot came into view. Meg couldn't believe how long they had run, while Hanna was surprised that they were back so soon. The parking lot had filled since they left. Meg collapsed in the grass at the edge of the parking lot, her body and clothes slick with sweat. Hanna unlocked the car and pulled out two, quart water bottles; "I added some ice."

Meg sat up and drank without speaking, then ran the bottle over her arms. Goose bumps appeared where the cold bottle had crossed her skin. She walked around kicking her legs and stretching.

"You OK?" Hanna asked, holding the cold bottle to the back of Meg's neck.

"I'm fine. Let's go eat twice the calories that we just burned."

"Only if it's all sugar and fat."

"Sounds like a job for a bakery," Meg finished the rest of her water. "How long did we run for?"

"An hour and 15."

"So what's that?"

"About eight-minute miles."

"That's OK?"

"We're incredible."

"Why don't you move down here, and we'll run marathons," Meg said.

"You're too lazy. I'd have to push you too much, and you'd resent it."

They spent the rest of the day eating and resting and went out in the evening. Meg made a point of showing Hanna off to all her friends, mentioning that they had run eight miles that morning. Some of them seemed uneasy. Hanna noticed that they worded their questions carefully when talking to her.

Walking down the street with Meg, Hanna asked, "Why am I picking up strange vibes from your friends?"

"They're probably wondering about you and me, as opposed to Barb and me."

"Is that something that you're worried about?"

"No. It'll give 'em something to talk about."

"What about Barb?"

"Oh, I'll tell her. We're not really a unit, yet. We're still testing the waters. Anyway, she's in Chicago for a whole month, and God only knows what she's up to."

"You mean you're both seeing other people?" Hanna hissed.

"You should talk," Meg said, taking her hand. "You travel around like some Doña Juana, loving a chain of women up and down the Rockies."

Hanna laughed and put Meg in a gentle headlock. "No, you're the only stop on my circuit."

"Oh, please Juana, don't even try to feed me that. What about your 'friend' Gina who you're always talking about."

"She's straight!"

"She won't be for long! Not if...Juana has her way," she said, raising her eyebrows, speaking as if she were a voice on an old soap opera.

Sunday morning was also nice, waking with Meg once again. The weather was threatening, which blissfully suppressed Hanna's frenetic need to exercise. As the day progressed a light rain fouled their outdoor plans, but Hanna was exhausted from life in general, so sitting on the couch with Meg seemed idyllic. Meg was efficiently dissecting a binder of paperwork from her store, and Hanna read from a stack of Meg's feminist magazines.

Hanna's mind wandered from her reading for a moment and she thought of Paul and she hoped that the rain wasn't causing him trouble in the mountains.

Just as Meg and Hanna were leaving for lunch the phone rang, and Meg spoke for a long time, peering out through the kitchen door now and then, catching Hanna's eye.

When Meg returned Hanna immediately read the situation. She knew it was Barb, and she knew it would make things awkward.

"She said she missed me. I couldn't say the same. That would be a lie."

"Sorry, I had no idea," Hanna said, sliding up next to her.

"No, it's not your fault. I just thought that she would be...looking after herself out there."

"I didn't think I would be interrupting anything."

"It's nothing. No, let's go eat."

Small mishaps and a bad restaurant blundered their secondary plans. The call had cast a pall, and their connection seemed to misfire, and hang out of reach. Hanna spent a lengthy night with Meg in a mood that couldn't be shaken. Meg tried to apologize in the morning, but Hanna told her there was no need. "We're beyond that," she said. "I can understand all of it, and at least part if it is my fault. Can I come back?" Hanna said hugging her, smelling her hair.

"You better. Let's do that day over again."

"It's always the last day...isn't it?"

Hanna drove away with Meg standing in the cool morning in the beautiful shade of the trees on her street. She stood there in a plain blue dress, with her arms folded across her chest, and she took one more step into the street to prove to Hanna that she watched until she was gone. As Hanna dropped over the hill, she saw Meg raise one hand over her head.

Retreat

There was no joyful hiking for Paul on the last day of his full
retreat; he kept his head down and slogged as fast as he
could back to his car, not even trifling with the small creeks
which were now bank-full, deep and cold. He guessed at the
spots most clear of debris and walked straight through the
middle of them. Though much clearer, the final day never
warmed, pushing him to the edge of hypothermia. Even
hiking as fast as he could, he could not raise his body
temperature enough to bring color back to his white, waxy
fingers. He knew there couldn't be another night out, not in
his present condition. After a day and a half without much
food or sleep, Paul staggered into the parking lot, where the
ground was completely free of snow, and nearly dry, and the
sun came blazing out for the first time in 48 hours. He
located the key he had hidden in his wheel well, threw the
pack in the trunk and began the long drive back to the work
camp, with the heat on high all the way to the highway,
deeply embarrassed to have fallen victim to his own 'fast and
light' philosophy.

Home

Hanna pulled into camp as the sun set. The guys were sitting like gnomes upon their stumps over at Hugh's teepee. There was a large fire burning, glowing orange in the darkness. Bob the dog ran beside Hanna's truck as she pulled in, and greeted her as if she had been gone for years. It was evident that the guys were having a time. They laughed and spoke loudly. There was a mountain of empty beer cans. Hugh called her over, and she pretended not to hear, then they all began chanting, "Hanna, Hanna," followed by peals of laughter. She gave them a few minutes while she arranged and cleaned up the back of her truck for sleeping, and then wandered over.

Hugh sat on a stump, higher than the rest, and Dog sat beside him. Tim sat next to Dog in his deluxe, handmade camp-chair. He was plucking his guitar and singing theatrically. *"There was a young cowboy all decked out in silk."*

Dog's squinting red eyes rolled around in his head as he giggled.

Tim played on, *"The rouge on his cheeks gave me a clue to his ilk."*

Hugh and Dog wheezed with laughter, and Paul pretended that it was totally unacceptable in Hanna's presence; he half hid his can of beer between his knees.

Tim plucked a few more cords, *"His spurs were a jingling, as his feet took a pass...But then Hanna walked by and he checked out her...face!"* Tim looked up, smiled and winked at Hanna and then improvised a dramatically strummed prelude to her arrival.

Fat-Assed Brad sat next to Paul. He was patiently waiting for a minute to speak. He looked as dark and simian as ever, with a single Neanderthal brow across his forehead. He had a massive, black-bearded, prognathic jaw, and large shovel teeth that looked like they could bite the husk off a coconut.

His boulder of a head sat on top of an ever-widening body, balanced on top of a butt the size of Nebraska, which he covered with crisp khakis.

"Hello Brad, when did you get in?"

"Just showed up today. I was surveying a big water project in Utah, but it ended last week. He spoke in a suave, head-bobbing manner, as if he sensed that she was sexually attracted to him. "Karl called me. I'm gonna start the next session with you guys tomorrow."

"Well that's great, Hugh and Dog need some leadership."

"Hanna, where you been?!" Hugh blurted out aggressively.

"Oh, just wanted to get away from here for a few days, you know," she said, too casually.

"So where did you go?" Hugh asked, pressing her, imagining that he was funny. Dog's eyes flashed, sensing a conflict.

"Down to Felicidad."

"Oh Felicidad," he said sagely. "You know some people down there?"

Hanna surveyed the situation for a moment. Hugh was ankle-deep in beer cans. There were chicken bones smoldering on the edge of the fire. A bottle of Jose Cuervo stood half empty beside Tim, awaiting its next orbit around the fire. She realized it didn't matter what she said. Innuendo clung like flies to every word. "Oh yeah, a few. I used to know a lot more."

"So what did you do down there?" Hugh pressed, and Tim nervously plucked his guitar, Paul studied his feet, uneasy with Hugh's belligerence.

Hanna smiled confidently and looked around at the faces in the light. "I spent the entire time with a unique, intelligent, and beautiful woman.... What did you guys do?"

Tim twanged a loud, coarse note on the strings, and an involuntary, "Hah," left his mouth, followed by his wolf-howl, which was joined immediately by Bob the dog.

Paul's face beamed in admiration, and he clapped his

hands together with glee; Hanna gave him a wink.

Hugh and Dog sat with their mouths agape, and Hanna walked off to go to bed. Bob followed her and curled up on the tailgate of her truck.

They were quieter after that, and Hanna lay awake for a while. The firelight danced inside the tiny topper of her pickup bed. Because the guys were drunk, she shooed Bob off the tailgate and latched the tiny dead-bolt on the inside of the door. Hanna felt safe in enemy territory. Still, she had her pepper spray within reach, in case any delirious drunks came groping around. She fell asleep hugging one of her pillows, imagining that it was Meg, believing that she could smell her hair, and feel her skin.

Paul

In their drunken blather, the guys had not told Hanna about Paul's near-death experience. Just as Hanna had predicted, Paul had been caught out in a huge summer storm, only returning to camp hours before Hanna.

In the morning, Hanna passed Paul's tidy tent and saw his gear and clothes hanging from a line he had strung between two trees. His stuff was sodden, and she saw how everything was grubby with mud and pine needles, which was so unlike Paul.

She found him in the cook tent, chowing down a huge plate of pancakes, eggs and bacon.

Paul looked up, catching her inquisitive glare, and resettled his eyes on his plate.

"Looks like you had a time."

"Yeah, I got pretty wet out there," Paul said, making light of it.

"Nearly fatal," Tim said as he came to Paul's table with a plate of food.

"Paul?" Hanna said, raising her eyebrows.

"It wasn't nearly fatal. Let's not exaggerate, Tim."

"Well, if it wasn't nearly fatal, then it's only because you were lucky."

"Paul," Hanna said, trying to keep her voice even. "Why should a backpacking trip be harrowing at all?"

Hugh was filling his bucket-sized cup with coffee. "He won't listen to you Hanna. He says it was only the storm—which was forecasted," Hugh said, with a harrumph.

"Listen, I'm sorry I ever said anything to anybody. I got caught out..." Paul said defensively.

"And you didn't have enough equipment," Tim added, rubbing his face with his rough, dry hand.

"All more gear would have done is prolonged the whole situation," Paul sighed.

"That's the whole point of having a good tent—so you can just sit tight if you have to," Tim replied, much to Paul's humiliation.

Hanna was surprised at Tim's accusation. It was out of character, which made Hanna realize the gravity of the situation. Tim was generally indifferent to the tenets of life, love, religion and morality, but apparently, he was a strict adherent to the rules of the mountains.

Paul smiled his Paul smile, and said dryly, "Tim, if anyone on the entire Earth is lucky to be alive, it's you. So let's not try being the safety police."

"Well, that's true, but even so, you should pull your head out of your ass and listen to some simple advice…Paul," Hugh said smiling and winking over the top of his bucket of coffee.

For all his huff and puff, Paul was visibly shaken by the incident, and offended that something like this had happened to him, for he was methodical, and this simply didn't fit into what the outcome of his planning should have been. He was sulky, and Hanna had to pander to his moping. She saw to it that she worked alone with him that day. Hugh caught all the signs and sent Hanna and Paul out to dig some test pits.

Hugh had wanted them out there as his most experienced archeologists. The land they were surveying and testing was in a place where the pipeline crossed the very corner of the Crow Indian Reservation. Although it was technically on the reservation, the pipeline mostly passed through private, white inholdings that excluded it from a lot of the Bureau of Indian Affairs' regulations. Even so, Hugh wanted their most thorough work done, in case anything was scrutinized later.

Hanna was patient as they worked and allowed Paul his sullenness. They both got a jolt when they found where Hugh had planted another fabricated Clovis point. They had a good laugh once they caught the joke, and it lightened Paul's mood.

They each worked alone digging and mapping pits what

lay beneath the surface. Hanna recorded two pits that yielded nothing, the third turned up some carbonized bone fragments, and fire-cracked rock. It wasn't much, but it did indicate human occupation. After finding little more in her third pit, Hanna wandered over to Paul and could immediately see that he was having much better luck. Hanna saw multiple plastic bags ranked in careful rows, full of charred bone and fire-cracked rock, a lot of worked stone, and a few simple blades.

"I can hardly take a shovelful without turning up something here," Paul said cheerfully.

"Better than I did over there."

"That's funny, it seems like your ground was the more likely situation, flatter," Paul said in his analytical tone.

"Exactly."

"Are you mocking me?"

"No, not at all." Hanna smiled. "That's why I started digging over there. I thought it looked better."

"You think it was a winter camp?"

"I don't know. It seems to have a lot of deposition. It was a camp for multiple years, or even decades."

Hanna dropped down into his empty pit and looked at the stratified layers of fire-charred earth. She took a small trowel from her back pocket and probed at one of the dark, grey, black layers with unburned organic materials and bone fragments. "Rich," she said. "If it's this rich here, we could find hundreds of years of material the deeper we go."

"Yeah," said Paul. "Life was probably pretty good here." He stood and looked at the flood plain, a broad valley of cottonwoods surrounded by low, pine-covered hills. "It's easy to see why Red Cloud and the Oglala fought so intensely for this."

"But this is all too early for the Sioux," Hanna said absently, working a long sliver of flint out of the side of the pit.

"Well, yeah. Of course, but still, you can see…" Paul walked around in a patch of tall grass and dragged his feet through the leaf litter. He walked backward, dragging his toes. He kept his arms out to his sides for balance. He was feeling what was below the thick grasses. Hanna could see when he found something. He abruptly changed his direction until he understood what he was feeling. "This is a ring," he said, and walked forward slowly in a circle. "Come follow me. You can feel the stones."

Hanna grabbed a bundle of small, yellow flags from a bucket and walked a pace or two behind Paul as he scuffed out a circumference. Hanna pressed a wire flag into the earth at every third stone. Then, they moved five paces toward more level-looking ground and began to walk backward again, dragging their feet through the deep grass.

"Aaah, here," said Hanna. "I have three...four...a big one...five. It's a teepee ring for sure."

"It is," said Paul.

Hanna marked the teepee ring in four places. "Well, what should we do?" she asked, looking around at the possible enormity of the camp.

"Let's test the first ring, and then assume that the rest will be the same.... We'll let Hugh and Karl figure it out from there. This is going to change the whole survey."

During a break, they sat under a cottonwood drinking water, and Hanna asked casually, "So will you try to do that hike again?"

"I don't know yet."

"Is it marked on the map?"

"Yeah, the way is obvious. The route is marked, and there are trails. They're just vague. And then with all the snow and poor visibility, it was almost impossible to find my way."

"But would you let me go?"

"If you wanted...you could come." Paul lifted his head, surprised and pleased with her offer.

"The snow pack is so deep this year," she said. It'll take another month."

"Maybe, maybe sooner. But listen, there's nothing

different about where I went. It was just a bad spot to be in with such an unusual storm."

"But I would want a tent, instead of your stupid tarp."

Paul wrinkled his nose.

"What, a tent isn't good enough for you?" Hanna asked.

"I know. It's me. I just don't want to carry a *house* around with me. I don't want a huge bundle of crap on my back just to walk around in the mountains."

"Ah, well, maybe I'll see if they have tents for anal minimalists."

Paul paused for a long moment. "You're ignoring the main problem. The more stuff we carry up there, the more stuff we carry out."

"This sounds like one of those logic conundrums," Hanna said, weighing the contents of two empty hands. "Should we bear the burden of useful equipment, or suffer like wet, miserable dogs?"

"We'll figure it out. Maybe we could run in with very little gear…do the whole route super light and fast."

"And die in a simple summer storm. Let's think about it for a while. I just want you to be safe when you're out there by yourself."

"What about you and Tim when you guys are climbing?" Paul was holding her gaze longer than he usually did. He was speaking with ease and without his normal timidity. "That's not exactly like staying at home and watching a ball game."

"I know the idea that you guys have about climbing. But Tim and I are as safe as we can be."

Paul laughed. "That's about the silliest thing I have ever heard you say. Of course, you're as safe as you can be, but the entire situation is fundamentally unsafe."

Hanna laughed and conceded to the precision of Paul's argument. She wanted this day with Paul to continue. She wanted to be alone with Paul a while longer, to have him closer than she could at camp. She didn't want to lose him to the chatter in the cook tent, or around the fire. She wanted him to herself. She felt that she filled a need in him. He was such a cautious and careful person, not quite a man. He was a boy. He was a 30-year-old boy. She longed to take his hand, or walk with an arm hooked through his, but he would freeze like stone. She would make the exception and sleep with him, and mean it, if he would have it, if it would change anything in him. She would do that for him.

They were silent as they cleaned up the site and put their tools in the back of the Bronco. Hanna got into the driver's seat, and Paul climbed in beside her. She stared across the seat at him.

"What?" he asked, looking around.

"You're sitting up front with me?"

Paul blushed, "OK, Hanna, let's not do this. I just want to sit up front and not make a deal about it."

She had the pepper spray pointed at his face, "If you try to grope me, I'll Mace you!"

Paul stared at her in disbelief, and Hanna held his gaze until Paul started to giggle and then laugh until he couldn't breathe, and his shoulders shrugged in silent hilarity.

"What, you don't believe me?" Hanna said snorting a guffaw.

When the laughing finally died down, Hanna put the Bronco in gear and drove away. They still giggled every few minutes.

After a while Paul choked out, "So…" he guffawed, "this dyke and…this virgin are driving down the road…."

Hanna's laughter dropped away, and she asked, "You're a virgin…?"

"No, I'm not," Paul said.

* * *

But Paul had never consummated a relationship with anyone either. But, there was an incident that haunted every moment of every day and skulked in the alleys of his consciousness. There was a knot in the pit of his stomach and a cold sweat on his palms that could not be wiped away.

It was the monkey on his back and the harpy in his ear. It was the thing that couldn't be killed or put to sleep, doped, or drunk to death, or exorcised. It was his own personal beast.

But it hadn't always lived where it lived. It was something he picked up in high school, like a terminal case of the clap. Life was changing then, and it was a crazy time to be an adolescent. At that point, he was a good baseball player. He could play second base, third base and was fast enough for center field. He had a car that he bought with his own money from his work on the family farm, and a part-time job at the town grocery store. And there were girls who appeared to enjoy his company. He had no special set group of friends, but he did have friends, and he moved easily from one group to another.

He was an only child, and he had a stay-at-home mom and a dad who tinkered at growing potatoes and sugar beets. But he wasn't one of those farmers who'd die working in the field. Paul imagined that there must have been some money somewhere, because life was always good no matter what the market prices. Whenever there was ever any serious labor, Dad would engage Paul and hire one of the hands that were always available around town. His dad and mom were there, and home was always home.

At that point in time, the outer-world seemed to have gone insane. When *Deep Throat* began playing at the Cineplex, Paul thought that his mom would need sedatives. "Is it too much to ask not to have to see what double-X pornography is playing next to *The Swiss Family Robinson*. Is that too much to ask? Do I have to read that…title…every time I drive by? What kind of a title is that? Can someone explain what that title is meant to…invoke?" And it only got worse when *Flesh Gordon* came to town.

Paul knew she was right. What kind of a movie was that? He had been invited to go see it with some guys, but it really seemed too smutty. Even though he was a teenager and could think of nothing but sex, he could see that this was an assault on common decency.

He was no prude at this point in time, and he knew that sex was right around the corner for him. Also, he had a contact for small amounts of marijuana, that he sold to pad his wallet, cover his car expenses, and have money to spend when out with friends. And he just enjoyed being the one who could deliver something in such demand. Girls would call to meet him at the Tasty Freeze on Saturday night. He knew that it was only the service that made him so popular, but it was better than sitting at home watching *The Love Boat*.

Paul smoked very little pot himself, and it was only through working with Tony at the town supermarket that he had entered into the enterprise. He felt it was a good business move. It was small, low key, and only on the strict terms that Paul set himself. While running the cash register, or stocking shelves, trusted acquaintances would come through. They would buy a Coke, make small talk, mutter a coded order and Paul would meet them after work at a certain location. It was perfect. Flawless, until he got a flat one evening.

His right front tire blew out, and he momentarily lost control of his car, minimally sideswiping an oncoming pickup. It was a close call, but understandable, and all parties were congenial, there was no citation issued. Paul was shaken but relieved that it would end so well, until the deputy sheriff found a dime bag in the trunk of Paul's car while helping him with the spare tire. That was how it all came apart. That was the thread that Paul had left dangling out there. That was how it all came unraveled, over ten dollars' worth of marijuana. That was the tattered cord the beast used to climb into his soul.

Dad was a firm believer in consequences, and he thought that it would do Paul some good to spend a night in jail to see what comes from this type of behavior. The deputy had no idea that the dime bag was the second transaction of the night, and that it was intended for Sandy, the chemistry teacher's daughter. The deputy disagreed with Paul's dad.

Certainly, ten dollars' worth of marijuana was not a hanging offense. Given the persuasion of the current judge, and the quality of available lawyers, the entire issue was likely to never see the light of day. But that was not the point. Dad thought that the point was to teach Paul a lesson now, before things spiraled into less controllable circumstances, and given the fact that there was pornography at the Cineplex, Mom agreed.

Against the sheriff's wishes, Paul was taken in and held overnight in a cell with Phil and Antoine, a couple of drifters taken in from out on the interstate.

In the morning, he was mostly unrecognizable. His eyes were swollen shut and he was bleeding. He was gagged and suffocating on his own shirt, and his arms and stomach were covered with cigarette burns. He was rushed to the county hospital and then transferred to a more capable one to treat his concussion.

The drifters cynically claimed self-defense against a drug-induced rampage. However, it was a small town, before computerized record keeping, so the deputies destroyed the drifters' records, and their IDs, drove them out to the old gypsum mine, beat them half to death, then dumped them on the edge of the interstate outside of two separate towns a hundred miles apart.

Paul sometimes wished he had a photograph of himself from that day or from that week, before it all came undone, before his car was blemished and never repaired, before he had to live with his parents' guilt.

They could never forgive themselves, and he could never forgive them enough. He wanted to be back to where he was before. He wanted to see that person, to be that person who had lived that life. But mostly, he wanted to see that person who had not been repeatedly raped and tortured. He wanted to see that person that had not begged and pleaded and cried and succumbed to spare himself further torture.

By the time he came back to town, it was his senior year. He dropped out of everything but his studies, avoided his old acquaintances, avoided the therapists that his parents sought out, and avoided the school counselors, except when it came to applying to distant universities with lots of money in endowments. He studied intensely for his SAT and ACT, and filled out endless applications for colleges and scholarships. By June, he had been accepted into a college in California that came with excellent funding.

Leaving it all behind, fleeing was not so difficult. Once he was gone, he thought that what he suffered was not so bad. When he thought that things were bad, he compared himself to people who had really suffered, like the Native Americans, American slaves, the Jews, or Palestinians, or the Aztecs, or the enemies-of-the-state in almost every other country in the entire world. At least his attackers only had cigarettes and their fists. "I didn't have it so bad," he told himself. "It was only one night," he said to himself. "It's not like they had sophisticated machinery for doing all that. It wasn't so bad." That was the lie he chose to carry with him for the rest of his life.

Feat

The summer was moving swiftly, and Hanna began to press Tim for a climbing trip. There had been two breaks with no climbing, or mountains, and this made Hanna anxious. It was partially due to Gina, who was no climber, and whose distaste for climbing made planning a trip or discussing one difficult in her presence. Tim knew he had bungled things by sleeping with her, because she could never be invited on a mountain trip. She was way too whiney for that. When Gina said that she was leaving for Salt Lake a day early, Tim and Hanna locked eyes and raised their eyebrows. "Maybe you two could go climb some mountain," Gina said with a sneer.

They made plans while out one day with Paul, and they invited him along. He was nervous, but excited and agreed to go and hike while they climbed, until Hanna picked the route, which would entail crossing two lakes and ascending a river in a canoe. Paul didn't like water, and he hated canoes. "No, I don't do canoes," he said with a finality that made them laugh. They promised to be safe, no standing in the canoe, and life jackets for all, but he would have no part of it and pretended not to hear them.

"You know," Tim said, "It's not just the canoe. This is a really huge route."

"Well. We'll be alright." Hanna nodded to herself. "We'll just climb as fast as we can."

"There are other routes."

"Let's do this one. I want to do something huge. Spectacular!"

"As long as you realize that this is probably way bigger than anything you've been on before." Tim said seriously.

"OK, but this is still the one. I can feel it."

Hanna changed the subject. "I feel good inviting Paul though. I think he is really happy that we offered."

Once Gina was gone, they packed Hanna's truck and

pulled out two hours later.

* * *

The water was gin-clear and the glare of the sun, merciless. For Tim, fishing was meditative. It calmed him to hunt circles on the water. They watched for signs, as if a perfect stalk and a perfect presentation might win approval and tilt things in their favor. Stalk, cast, acceptance, it often took ten rises for it to work that way.

Hanna knew what fish Tim wanted, but it was hard to keep the correct distance between the fish and the canoe. She had been through this routine before. She read his body language for directions, as he dropped a shoulder in frustration or sighed and stood up straight when out of casting range, and finally crouched in approval when he located a fish.

He stood in the front of the canoe, even though their packs would sink like stones if they flipped. The trout that fed on the surface film were wild, hefty, two-pounders. They were cleaning up after an earlier hatch. Tim called them 'gulpers'. These rainbows sucked dead mayflies from the lazy foam lines that the breeze had pushed to this lee side of the lake. The trout reminded Hanna of killer whales, slowly porpoising, head, dorsal, tail. Tim tracked them with intensity, watching one, two, three rises. His line was in the air, his rod snapping like a metronome. He guessed the location of the next rise and let the line fly. It was looping and floppy at first, but gained speed, righting itself, straightening to a horizontal line just above the water, landing lightly. There was a head, dorsal, tail and the line snaked across the water. Tim raised the rod and set the hook, which was followed by a huge whooshing swirl.

Tim dropped his shoulders with satisfaction. He relaxed. Bob the dog watched the water and knew there was a fish on.

"Nice," Hanna said. "Daddy has a fish, Bob."

Bob's tail thumped the bottom of the canoe.

Tim let the fish go, stowed his rod, and sat down to paddle in earnest. They entered the river, and it was hard to paddle up the swift current. In no time, they were sweating, and Bob hopped out to follow and hunt mice along the grassy banks. Tim and Hanna both jumped out to push and long-line the boat through shallow rapids. The river steepened for a hundred yards of swift riffles just below the second lake. They both got out into the knee-deep current, pushing and pulling the canoe past this section.

They beached the canoe at the lake and called for Bob. It was hot and mosquitoes buzzed. The second lake was smaller and prettier than the first, and it felt more remote here. The forested mountains came down almost to the shore. There were trout rising at the mouth in the slick current where the lake was drawn into the river.

Bob emerged from a stand of aspens, bounding to see above the flowering tufts of potentilla.

He was covered with dust and stickers and his mouth was frothy from so much hunting and running. He drank deeply at the lake, and Tim watched Hanna admire him. A smile spread across her face. "You bad dog," she accused him, pushing him with her toe. "Hey, you listen to me."

Bob grumbled good-naturedly, annoyed to have his drink interrupted.

Tim had the canoe pointed out into the lake and sat patiently as Hanna picked the burrs and stickers from Bob's coat, helping him into the boat. He was afraid of canoes, only truly comfortable jumping out of them.

"You gonna fish those?" Hanna nodded her head at the fish rising on the slick current.

"No, we better go."

Stronger, Tim sat in the front and paddled fast, deep strokes. Hanna paddled with his cadence and corrected their direction with the angle of her strokes. The west face of Square Top loomed above them and Hanna could feel Tim's dread. She had to crane her neck to see the mountain in its entirety. She knew that Tim was scared, but there was nothing to be said to dispel it. She wanted to enjoy this and guarded herself from his fear. She told herself that they would move confidently, and would be composed on the vertical, alpine wall. She knew that in the hyperboles of his skittish mind, Tim was considering the route a death sentence. He could never just block out the scenarios of chaos and disaster. He imagined rockfall, leader falls, steep run-outs with no protection, wide steep cracks, thunderstorms, soaking wet bivouacs, ad nauseam.

Hanna tried to counter his dread, telling him her visions of hot, pounding sunshine, perfect pitches of white granite, hundreds and hundreds of feet of it, an entire day of swift, challenging climbing. She wanted to pull herself, sweaty and winded after an astounding pitch, onto belay ledges and look ahead to the next equally intriguing expanse of rock; a grade five. She wanted a grade five.

She couldn't see their route yet. It was still out of sight, deep in the canyon. At the base of the mountain, they looked for a suitable stand of timber to stow the canoe and crossed a hundred yards of meadow and sage to reach a patch of Douglas fir. Dragging the canoe together in tandem, it slid easily across the slick, green grass. In the forest, they left it out of sight and hid the paddles even further away. Tim rigged a convoluted line to hang the cooler in the towering firs, and grunted, dissatisfied with the job he had done, certain that the reported grizzlies and black bears could easily knock it down to eat their food and drink their beer.

Hanna didn't like the idea of the bears but knew that they were even more annoying to Tim. She imagined these bugaboos stalking Tim along the trails and haunting his fitful dreams. Hanna holstered her pepper spray in her waist belt, and swiftly hid two cans of beer deep in Tim's pack as he retraced his path to the paddles, marking it with broken branches.

They shouldered the heavy packs, and harnessed Bob into his dog packs, one on each side, like horse packs, and

then set out toward the roar of the creek. They picked up
vague game trails that led to larger ones until they found the
main trail that followed the line of least resistance up the
draw. The work up through the forest was hard and sweaty.
There were fresh deer and elk droppings and more than one
pile of bear scat. "Do you think that's grizzly bear or black
bear shit?" Tim asked, standing over what appeared to be an
enormous hairy dog turd.

"You should taste it," Hanna smiled, "the proof is in the
pudding."

Tim snorted a brief laugh and Bob came forward to
investigate. His hackles were up, and he walked on stiff, wary
legs. "Heyyyy," Hanna growled, "what's that Bob?"

Bob leaned forward, sniffing suspiciously. "Look out!"
she hissed, flipping the turd at him with the toe of her shoe.
Bob leapt away, snapping at the turd as if it were a striking
snake.

"Easy Bob," Tim growled at him.

Hanna laughed and stomped a foot, and Bob sprang
away.

Bob caught the joke and pushed past them, loping boldly
up the trail. The forest and soft pine-needle path yielded to a
stony trail and finally to house- and car-sized boulders. The
creek roared, appeared and disappeared as it wound and fell
stone by stone. The way was slow and tedious, and they
often cliffed out on huge boulders and had to scramble back
the way they'd come. Bob struggled, and Tim relieved him of
his dog packs, adding them to his own huge load.

Exhausted, they topped out on the boulder slope and
entered a small, level glen to find themselves at the base of
the route they'd come to attempt. It was sobering, and they
stood for a moment struck by the scale and angle of it. It
hurt Hanna's neck to look at it. Hanna had hoped that she
would swing leads with Tim on the entire route. She wanted
to lead, to go first on half the pitches, but she suddenly felt
that this wouldn't happen.

It was not the beautiful, friendly white, granite wall she

had hoped for. It was a large, dark dihedral, which divided
the main buttress of the mountain; bisected by bands of dark
granite and diorite, and pegmatite, it was not an elegant line.
It was an enormous corner that was filled with cracks and
flakes. There were roofs and baffling, blank sections. Hanna
felt the worm of fear start to writhe in her guts.

"Well," Tim said, smirking, "how do you like your 'alpine
wall' now?"

Hanna tried to cover her surprise. "Oh, we can climb
that," she said weakly, and then laughed as Tim saw through
her bravado. "Holy shit! I didn't think it was that big!" she
conceded.

"Well, I tried to tell you. What did you think a grade five
wall looked like?" Tim opened his hands in the direction of
their route.

Hanna smiled sheepishly, "Well, now I see."

"A grade two is a nice little route. A grade three lasts part
of the day. A grade four takes most of the day. And a grade
five...you should think about maybe sleeping on."

"And this is a grade five?"

"It looks like one to me."

The sun was well west now, and they set up their tent on
the first level spot. The sweat evaporated off their bodies
and it seemed chilly in the early shade of the mountain. The
sky was flawlessly blue, with no wind. Hanna observed this
and said, "I guess it won't rain tomorrow and let us back out
with dignity, will it?"

Tim looked around, "We can only hope," he said, lazily
waving his hand at a few mosquitoes that had found them.

Hanna's hands felt cold, and she wanted to shake her
anxiety. "So we gonna do it?" she asked with empty bluster.

"That's the plan."

"What's the plan?" she demanded

"To climb that thing and be back here by three."

"We'll be back here by noon."

"By 10:30," Tim boasted.

"We'll be back for coffee." Hanna laughed.

In the evening, Tim found the beer in his pack. "I should drink both of them and make you watch!" he scolded her, opening one and taking a few sips before he tossed her the other.

Limber pines towered over them, silver-barked and lanky. The creek was slow and lazy here, enjoying a brief respite before it tumbled a thousand feet to the river valley. All around them were fins and towers of granite. Slick, carved faces and smooth domes told a tale of glaciation. Along the creek, the grass was tall and rich. A mosaic of meadows claimed any portion of earth not shaded by the pines or excluded by slabs of granite.

Tim allowed Hanna to arrange her things in the tent and crawl into her bag before he followed her in. She was not crazy about sharing a tent with him, but it was better than carrying her own, or sleeping out on the ground. He was hypersensitive about her space and avoided any contact with her. Hanna had to force her bunched bag against her mouth to keep from laughing.

* * *

Tim was outside the tent with his headlamp, and Hanna heard the purring of the camp stove. She could see the steam from Tim's breath in the beam of his headlight. She didn't welcome the idea of being cold. At such an early hour, the thought of food was repulsive, and even coffee made her gag. Tim kept passing her a water bottle of Tang, telling her, "Camel up, camel up." She took sips and passed it back, but he said, "Drink more." After coffee, half a bagel, and a liter of Tang she felt ready to move. As Tim finished his second cup of coffee, Hanna re-hung the food to protect it from the bears, and gave Bob his cup of food.

"Five-thirty," Tim said, flipping away the dregs from his cup.

"What do you think?"

Tim leaned his head back, and the beam of his headlamp

shot off into the starry sky. "Well, I don't think it's gonna rain, so we better go."

They shouldered their packs, and Bob jumped and leapt to be going. Tim told him to stay, and he dropped as if he's been shot.

"Ohh, poor Bob," Hanna whined.

"Bob'll be a lot better off than us."

They each patted Bob on the head and walked out of camp, following the glow of their headlamps through the forest.

They put on their harnesses and roped up in grey-blue light. Tim led off across low-angle slabs, from ledge to ledge, and tree to tree, always to the left, toward the base of the dihedral. Hanna followed, immediately surprised at the difficulty of the climbing. On a ledge, as they exchanged gear, Tim said, "The climbing is bitchy." He was irritated by how hard the 'easy' slabs were. Past two more slab pitches, and it was fully light as they reached their route. "It's seven," he said, trying to be casual. "I thought we'd be two pitches up the dihedral by now."

"The route-finding on those pitches was confusing. These will be more straightforward. We'll be alright." Hanna was glad when he took the rack with all their gear. He didn't make an issue of her leading.

He moved easily up the first 20 feet of the dihedral. "We'll just go on, and if it takes too long, we'll back off."

Hanna knew that he was lying. He'd never back off, unless it rained. He'd keep climbing until they reached the top or it was too dark to continue. After another 30 feet he slowed down and his feet moved from hold to hold and back again. He was breathing hard as he jerked up in swift lurches, and then stopped on tiny rests to place protection. "This is hard," he spoke to himself. He put in another piece of gear, clipped it. "That's better," he sighed, as if he was reassuring a child. He shook out one limb at a time and then lunged forward to the next rest and moved on. When the rope was almost gone, she heard him shout down, "Off belay!" and she followed the pitch. She found things immediately vertical and unnerving. She choked down her initial fear, trying to move as fast as she could. Hanna wanted to be a good partner and follow as fast as he led. The distance slipped by—30, 60, a hundred feet—and he was still 20 feet higher. Hanna reached the belay ledge, sweaty and winded. "Jesus Christ, where the hell did that come from?"

"You thought so too?" Tim asked. "I thought I was just being a baby.... It looked like I was on route." Tim started taking gear from Hanna's harness, and she re-stacked the rope.

"Oh, yeah, that was the only way to go. Maybe this next pitch isn't so hard."

Tim snorted a guffaw, "It only looks ten degrees steeper."

"You're on belay," Hanna said, as Tim nervously looked ahead, and took stock of where things were on his gear sling.

To belay well, Hanna had to hang off the anchor that Tim rigged. She took a wide-legged stance on a tiny ledge, then a deep breath and leaned against the anchor, half expecting it to fail.

Tim climbed, and the corner grew darker and more broken as they passed a band of diorite. The corner was acute, and Tim shuffled his hands up the crack and stemmed out with his feet. His legs shook and trembled, and he grunted from time to time. As he ascended higher, she heard his hoarse whispers, "Oh, goddamn it.... Shit!" A few tiny rocks whizzed past, and one dinged her helmet, filling her with dread. "It's loose and steep up here." Hanna knew that voice, and knew that all was not well with Tim. Still, he moved up, and the rope rarely halted for more than a minute. Then, it stopped. "Off belay," he croaked.

Hanna found Tim sitting uncomfortably in a tiny hole in the wall. He had his helmet and pack off, and his hair was matted with sweat. Hanna pulled herself onto the ledge, and remained on her hands and knees, breathing for a moment before she could talk. "This is way harder than the guide book rates it."

"Holy shit," he said. "That was too much."

Hanna rolled over and sat next to him. The tiny hole forced her against his sweaty body; his breath was rank with fear. "What do you think?" She hoped he would suggest retreat.

"We'll do two more pitches. It looks easier up ahead. We'll look at the time and talk it over."

She knew they were in it to the end. He arranged the gear on the rack, fumbled a carabiner and it fell free a long way before it touched the wall and ricocheted wildly away. It was nauseating to watch. It gave her vertigo, but her eyes followed it until it was gone.

At the end of pitch six, there was a good ledge. They could sit comfortably, hang their packs and drink Tang. They drained the liter-and-a-half bottle in two long draughts. Tim was wired from all the leading, going first, and making sure they were on route. He looked up and down and said several times that it was only 10:30. His voice was hard to read. "That's one third of the route," he calculated. "If we continue like this, we'll be off by three." Tim spun his head around. "The weather looks good.... Doesn't the rock look better ahead?"

Hanna said nothing. He was out of touch. All he could do was climb, transformed into a machine, a climbing monster. Hanna looked down and considered a descent—six steep, full-rope lengths past horns and flakes and some loose rock that would certainly hang up the ropes. She was glad when he climbed on, taking his exhausting panic with him. She looked around at how beautiful the tiny canyon was so far below them. She wanted to enjoy where she was. The vegetation so verdant, bordered with sinuous, grey slabs of granite rising everywhere in wonderful spires and domes. The cobalt sky was cloudless, and the sun was just now creeping into their megalithic corner. They were already much higher than the surrounding peaks. They had always planned on doing a 'big' peak, and this sure seemed like one to Hanna.

On the second half of the climb, the beautiful, benevolent sun seared them senseless, and the rest of the water was gone by pitch 12. The hardest pitch was an off-width chimney, and Tim had no gear big enough. The sun pounded directly into the crack, and he squirmed, panted and cursed his way up it, ten, 20, 30 feet with nothing to protect a fall. He slipped several times, muttering, but caught himself. Hanna watched, resigned to the fact that he'd fall past and pull her off, and together they would plummet 12 rope lengths to the talus below. Tim reached a narrower section and placed good gear, and clipped it to his rope. He sighed so deeply that it sounded as if he'd sob.

Hanna followed, but she had hit the wall, and gravity sucked like a current on her feet, her arms weak and rubbery, her pack was useless and filled with lead. Every section looked so impossible, but then she pulled herself onto a ledge.

"There are only two pitches left! We're there!" he shouted, almost assaulting her. "Look," he shouted ecstatically. "No more vertical."

She lay there panting from the struggle of the horrendous chimney and wished he would stop talking; she wished that they could stop climbing for 20 minutes, and that they had water, and that there was shade. They both had bloody knees and elbows from the chimney. Hanna had even skinned her chin.

Two pitches passed with no summit in sight. The climbing, though no longer steep, was still demanding as they passed false summit towers and gendarmes that impeded their progress. Several times they had to climb minor towers, only to rappel off the backside. With every disappointment, Tim struggled to suppress his rage. "Sonofabitch," he muttered. His voice carried an edge of panic. "We should be there!"

"Let's just stop," she said, and he spun immediately to try to stop the words.

"Let's just stop," she repeated the words, and his face immediately softened.

"No, not now, not here. It's one more rope. Two more ropes. That's all. If that isn't it, we'll stop. And if it is it— then it's over!"

She considered his words for a few minutes, so tired that it took time to comprehend them. She knew that if they stopped, and if it grew dark, they would have to use their headlamps, and would never find the right descent in the dark. They would have to bivouac and hug each other against the long, cold night. They would suffer, and Bob would worry himself sick, but they would probably survive and come down in the morning. "That's fine Tim. You just climb and climb, and I'll follow and follow."

"Well, it's not like we can go back now. We'd never be lucky enough to make all the rappels before dark. Up is the way down."

"I guess that ironically explains it all."

"It's not like you couldn't have known."

"I know now. Let's go. It doesn't matter now. All we can do is go."

At four, at the end of pitch 20 they stood on the flat summit massif, a quarter mile wide, and topped with beautiful meadows of alpine mosses and flowering sedges. It was still cloudless, and a strong, cool breeze blew. They tottered with exhaustion as they stripped away their harnesses and gear. Hanna's swollen feet screamed as she peeled away the tight-fitting climbing shoes, and blood surged back into her crimped toes.

Tim paced around barefoot and took off his shirt, he laughed and raged. "Holy shit, we did it! Man, I'd like some water. Maybe we'll find some pools up here." He straightened up and looked around and then continued, "Fifteen pitches my ass! Try 20! I wonder if those guide-book people even know where the hell these mountains are?" He paced, not knowing what to do with himself now that the climbing was over.

Hanna watched Tim wandering around the summit, hunting for water in the granite basins. He looked like a person capable of very little, so skinny and disproportionate, muscle, bone, and sinew. His hair, out from under the helmet, stuck out at odd angles. He was giddy to be alive, yet sad to be on level ground.

She felt jealous to see him lost in euphoria. She was angry with him because the route was too much. She wanted to blame him for pushing them too far, placing them at too great a risk, but she knew that it was her idea. She'd pulled this genie from his bottle, coaxing him past his cowardice. He never would have done this, had she not nearly demanded it. She wanted to hate him for not backing off, for being confident, for leading 20 hard pitches, for having a secret switch that transformed him. She too wanted to be transformed.

The wind blew, and she looked at where she was, her anger extinguished. She knew how lucky they were to be here. They were lucky to have been piss-your-pants scared, and dehydrated, and exhausted, and they would be lucky to stagger back to camp by dark.

They down-climbed into two dead-end gullies and had to re-ascend hundreds of feet back to the massif before they finally found the correct descent. After four hours of descending, and stumbling over loose rubble, they were on level ground, although now completely in the dark. They moved and groped along slowly. The ground was finally damp and soft and they knew they were in the glen where they had camped. Tim was in front and moved like a ghost. Hanna could only see parts of him, the white skin of his arms, his white calves. She was hot and sweaty, but the air was remarkably cool. It was quiet as they crossed from tree to tree, across the moist earth, and it seemed as if it wasn't happening. Then Bob barked, and Tim shouted for him.

Tim sat by the blue glow of the stove, in front of the tent preparing a pot of soup, eating a little of everything. Bob wolfed his obligatory evening scoop of chow and caught the tidbits that Tim flipped to him.

Hanna sat wet and naked on a warm boulder after washing off in the pool. The canyon was pitch black, and Hanna peered into the darkness for grizzlies. Up high, on the route they'd climbed, there was still an alpine glow, and she wondered how well they would be able to see if they were still on the summit plateau.

Hanna studied their route, now just a dark scar; she wondered where they were at different points of the day. She felt a sick dread pass over her as she imagined them up there in serious trouble. She chased the thought from her mind and focused on the sputter of the stove and the warmth of the boulder. She was glad that they were not more competent, or jaded by all this. She knew that this climb could be measured only against themselves, and though minor in the context of the world, she knew it was still quite a feat.

Recovery

In the weeks since Karl had weeded through the work camp and ironed out the rough edges, work returned to the long, long, day-to-day routines. The ten-day stints came and went as the summer picked up speed. Hanna again began to feel the anxiety of something passing. It had taken the entire ten days to recover from their route in the mountains. She daydreamed of the climb as she worked, and it filled her equally with elation and deep dread. Climbing was not the type of thing that she wanted to live with day-to-day. It seemed it would be like living with a dark secret. She worried too much, and sometimes just remembering the most harrowing parts of the route with Tim could make her heart pound and her palms sweat.

Tim was in no mood for the mountains when the next break came along. Once past the euphoria of the route, he felt guilty for pushing them too far. He hinted that Hanna should have listened, and she jumped at the accusation.

"Don't even try that with me, Tim. You were the one on the sharp end. Just because you're too crazy to stop and turn around has nothing to do with my idea—I had no idea..."

"Exactly; you had no idea. I tried to tell you, but you had no idea. And when I tried to tell you, you just pooh-poohed me, like I didn't know what I was talking about."

"No, that's not the point. You—we—could have turned around at any point. That's all we had to do."

"You can't just turn around, Hanna. Retreating is just as dangerous. There is the cost of all the gear we would have abandoned in the rappels—if we even had enough to get to the ground. And there was all the money for food and gas, and then there was all the time, sweat and effort it took to haul it all up there."

Tim was lit up now, but he relaxed his shoulders and dropped his gesturing hands. "You have to honor your commitment. We couldn't just stop because it was too big, because it wasn't too big, and I knew that, and you knew that. It wasn't too hard either, because we were doing it. We were moving well. But maybe the effort was too much, and the danger was too much. We were one screw-up from total disaster." He looked at Hanna, "I can't blame you, and I shouldn't. You know, it's like facing that thing that you don't want to face. But then you face it, and survive it, and feel the pleasure and accomplishment. But more than anything, what I feel is that I never want to go through that again." He stood with that thought for a moment and then smiled wryly. "It was the best, hardest thing I've ever done though."

"Well, I am sorry if I made you face your demons," Hanna looked at him. "I never thought a guy like you would have any. And you did try to tell me, but I wasn't hearing you. Was I?" She let the words hang, looking away across the river. "But you know what I always say...?"

"What?"

"What, what?"

"What do you always say?"

She grabbed him by the ears and pulled him toward her and kissed him hard on the mouth, then pushed him away violently, pointing her two pistol fingers at him, pulling the trigger, "I say...hunt your demons down like wounded animals."

He reached for her, but she turned away, he watched her go and understood how clear life can be at certain points, how you see it now and then, when it rises to the muddled surface, like those pink dolphins in the muddy Amazon. It isn't much, but you see it, and you know what it is, and you understand.

After dinner with the rest of the crew, Hanna went down by the river and looked out across the shallow valley and up into the pine-covered hills. Mule deer were venturing out to feed on the greener grass beside the water. A northern shrike was casually drifting from fencepost to fencepost, hunting grasshoppers and mice in the tall grass and prickly pear. The sky had threatened a hard rain earlier but it only sprinkled lightly. The little rain that fell was enough to settle the dust, and now the sky shone with intense clarity, an unbelievable blue against grey, pink and rose-colored clouds. 'This is good,' she thought, 'this is enough.' She was sated.

She knew that Tim was right in feeling the way he did. But often that was the only way she could reach these highs. She wanted to recognize this and sit on this plateau. The sense of fulfillment that had eluded her earlier was now coursing through her body. She could smell it and taste it and feel it in every nerve. The climb was such a useless, futile, and contrived thing to have done, and just as equally, precious. Hanna wandered back to her truck, and Bob was waiting faithfully for her in the quickening darkness.

A male bluebird clung to the door of her truck, fighting himself in her rear-view mirror. Hanna spoke for him in a squeaky macho voice. "You sonofabitch, I thought I'd run you off. Weelllll.... You ain't had enough, eh? Here then, take that and that, ohh you want some more do you?" The self-embattled bluebird caught a glimpse of Hanna, glared one last time into the mirror and flew off for the night.

Bob rose to meet Hanna, escorted her into the territory of her truck, and lay back down on the small square of carpet remnant that she kept out on the ground to keep her feet out of the dirt.

Hugh sat alone in the ring of light from the fire outside his teepee. He appeared calm and sage-like, unmoving in the depths of the comfort of his camp chair in the dancing firelight. Hanna could hear him chipping away at a rock, forming another point, to prank one of the newbies.

Dog was in his leaning tent just a few yards off. No one knew what he did when he disappeared into his tent so early in the evening, and no one ever ventured to ask.

Alise and Sarah had driven off for showers and drinks some hours earlier and returned nicely buzzed. Much to Alise's chagrin, Sarah had chosen to smuggle a man back to her tent with her. Alise had stomped off so she couldn't hear the soft, "Oh, oh, oh," as Sarah rutted wildly with the 'man' who was actually a mature-looking 17-year-old, with his older brother's expired driver's license. Alise finally brushed her teeth, and crawled into her own tent, sulking and tossing fitfully in a mixture of jealousy and disgust.

Tim watched from the window of his camper as Hanna readied herself for sleeping in her cramped truck shell. She was moving about on her hands and knees in cotton shorts and a tank top, fluffing up pillows and arranging sleeping bags. He could see her in the weak glow of the battery lantern. He admired how she was content in her truck even when closer to towns and hotels. He would have liked for her to come over and have a drink with him, and maybe spend the night. But if she wanted to, that is what she would have done. He was glad that Gina was still gone. He didn't love her, and she was escalating the whole affair beyond the release of occasional physical needs. He shook his head and thought, 'Between me and her boyfriend in Utah, the little minx sure must be getting some action!' With all the campers' windows open, Tim could hear Bob, whimpering and running his legs in his sleep, dreaming that he had a coyote locked in the death grip of his massive jaws. Tim could hear an odd, faint, wistful, "Oh, oh, oooh," which he thought was a fledgling owl calling to its mother in the night.

Meadows

With a new break upon them and Gina still gone, Tim invited Hanna to Averoso to visit with some old friends and maybe do some moderate climbs that, as Tim said, 'we definitely won't die on'. Hanna felt odd going with Tim. It was becoming a regular thing, and she knew that Gina would be intensely jealous, no matter how platonic the relationship remained. Hanna had to admit that their relationship was sprouting legs. Tim was obviously in love with her, and she could not say that she didn't love him in some ways and at some level. She knew that she could trust Tim, and that there was no one more fun or interesting to spend a break with. So, they left in his truck, with Tim at the wheel, Bob the dog riding shotgun, and Hanna in the breeze of the passenger's window, letting her hand windsurf behind the side-view mirror. The ride was long and empty. Tim didn't have much to say. Hanna saw how his relationship with Gina had been cramping her relationship with Tim. Hanna felt that she was the one who had the actual relationship, and that Gina was just screwing him, and becoming a real drag.

Tim had skillfully coaxed a water bottle out from behind his seat and steered with his knee as he unscrewed the cap and then lifted the quart bottle to his lips. It was exactly as he drank, that Hanna said, "You know, I really don't even want to have sex with Gina anymore!" Tim choked for some time as water streamed from his nose and tears ran from his eyes. When he could breathe again, he croaked, "Well, you never really did, did you?"

"No, but now I don't really want to anyway. Do you?"

"Thanks for telling me, but...I don't know if we should be talking about who wants to have sex with Gina. Would you want people talking about who wants to have sex with Hanna?"

"Well, just a minute...I know that you guys, as in the

male crew members, talk about this all the time. I have personally heard you with my own ears, during your late-night sessions with Dr. Hugh, discussing the quality of our bodies." Hanna looked sideways at him with her eyebrow raised.

"Ok, but I don't know if you and I should be having this discussion about Gina; it seems really weird."

"As if you would ever turn down a chance at something really weird!"

"I wouldn't do anything weird with Alise and Sarah."

"Don't be mean. Sarah is perfectly nice."

"Is it wrong to respect Gina's privacy and not have this conversation?"

"There is nothing wrong with us having this conversation, Tim. I'm just telling you that I don't think that I feel sexually attracted to Gina anymore, and I am asking you if you still feel sexually attracted to your lover, Gina, anymore. Is that really so bizarre?"

"In many circles that would be extremely bizarre!"

"But between us it isn't. You just don't want to answer it because you know that the answer is 'no'."

"Yes, the answer is 'no'! OK? I thought it was going to be a brief…"

"Experiment, remember?"

"Yes, it just happened, I never really gave it any forethought." Tim glanced across at her a couple of times, "What, so you've never made a mistake and had an affair with someone you shouldn't have?"

As an experienced collector of failed relationships, this question stopped Hanna in her tracks. Bob looked at her and put one paw on her lap.

Hanna and Tim arrived late in the evening to the small community of Blue Fields, or, the Meadows, as they were known, which lie just outside of Averoso. They took a roundabout, scenic route to the Meadows, totally avoiding Averoso. As night fell, they drove up to a small cabin and a huge outbuilding. Lights came on in the cabin, and a few minutes later, a small, bearded man appeared in the door and shouted at Tim, "I didn't tell you to come in the middle of the goddamn night!"

They hugged briefly and stood in that awkward masculine silence for a moment. Tim turned to Hanna as a distraction. He reached out to her to bring her closer, "Fred, this is Hanna, Hanna, Fred," he said, almost shouting with excitement. Fred grabbed Hanna in a strong hug and then pushed her back to look into her eyes, his eyes were clear and blue and impish. "Well, if you're bringing good-looking women with you, I guess I don't care if you come so late." Fred squeezed her arms and then released her.

"Oh, I wouldn't have shown up without a woman for you to leer at."

Hanna blushed and Fred turned quickly toward Tim. "Don't be crude Tim, you're making her uncomfortable."

"Not likely."

"I can honestly say that I have never known a Fred before," Hanna said, beaming at him.

"Yeah, well Dad was one of those arrogant Krauts and named me Fritz, but Mom changed it to Fred when they divorced."

Hanna blinked at the logic involved and smiled.

Fred made them sit on the porch and came out with a small cooler of beer. "You can rummage through and take what you like—had a party a while ago, and everyone brought that micro-brew crap. I can't stand it; smells like someone fermented a fart. But take what you like." Fred chose a Bud and held it in his hand for a moment. "Ice cold," he said, his eyes twinkling in anticipation.

"It doesn't get any better than that," Hanna quipped.

"Amen!" Tim roared religiously.

"Tell it to the mountain!" Fred joined in, suddenly looking like a preacher, just by tilting his head and raising his chin. He caught Hanna in his headlights and winked at her.

Against all her will, she found herself blushing.

Tim broke their moment. "Tell us the news from the

Meadows, Fred."

"Oh, hell, you wouldn't believe the hooey going on around here." He paused for a moment, taking a long swallow from his Bud. "First, there is all the normal life with people pissed off at each other, etcetera. But the big news is that we all found out that Dean has cancer, in his prostate; if that that isn't ironic…I don't know what is. And now he's gone through several epiphanies, given up the bottle, and become a holy man. He even has these Zen masters and patchouli-oiled Buddhist princesses visiting his place." Fred put down his beer and smiled. "Just a minute," he said and disappeared into his cabin.

"OK, he's getting ready to tell us a story."

"I sensed that," Hanna said. "I think I can tell what's coming next."

Fred emerged from his cabin with three small glasses of amber whiskey, and passed them around.

"Bingo!" Hanna laughed, "I guessed whiskey!"

Fred looked at her as if he didn't understand, "If you like, but suit yourself," he said with great satisfaction, returning to his seat, taking up his Bud. "Everybody good?" he asked. "So, where was I? All this would just be life, right? But Dean takes up smoking weed because it helps with the nausea, and his appetite and all that, which, I don't know if it does, or if it doesn't, but it certainly makes him more pleasant than he used to be. And then he gives up almost all his other medicine. Because his insurance won't cover the half of it with the pathetic program he bought into. So, his lawyers are 'advising' him to put up the ranch land as collateral against his future medical bills."

"Wow, that's really harsh."

Fred looked at him, reproachfully, "Harsh? You have no idea. Just wait. Am I boring you?"

"Not at all," Hanna said, "Just the opposite, now I have to know the rest."

Fred smiled with huge satisfaction. "Well, Tim, you know that Big Wally always had his home industry down in the basement, and of course he was taking care of Dean as best he could. And he starts to make a name for himself as a 'herbalist' and I mean he starts giving the shit away. He has people with all kinds of ailments coming all the way out from town to pick up their medicine. And of course, this would all just be life, right?"

"Well, in some circles."

"Anyway..." Fred said, raising an eyebrow at Tim, "Ted Bundy up on the hill…."

"Ted Bundy? Who? Ted Bundy?" Hanna shouted.

Yeah the guy's name is Theodore Bundy, and you can't hold his name against him...."

"But we will anyway," Tim added quickly.

Fred touched Hanna's arm and then pointed to a huge house overlooking the valley. It was nearly dark now, but the house stood out well in its enormity. "Doesn't that place just look like where an asshole would live? He calls himself 'Theo' but that makes him even more arrogant, and everyone calls him Ted."

"To his face?"

"When they feel like needling him," Tim snorted.

"Anyway…" Fred said with a long pause, glaring at Tim, "Ted gets wind of everything going on in the valley—how, we will never know, but he does, and he starts narking to the authorities about Big Wally's weed production. And they really couldn't care less, because we're so far out of town. But Ted, who thinks he's important, has his people, or somebody, start pressuring the county guys pretty hard."

Fred took a pull from his whiskey and then his beer and continued. "So, now it's a total mess. But a lot of the guys and gals from around here are old Forest Service workers, and some of them went over to work for the county for a change, so we're all dialed into what goes on at the sheriff's office. One of the deputies came out—of course everyone knew when he was coming. He talked and looked around. Really pathetic showing, I must say, even though they were on our side. But they gave Wally the word that things can't continue as they have been."

"All it takes is one rich asshole," Tim said shaking his head.

"But why would Theodore be such an asshole?" Hanna asked.

"Well, because he is one for starters; and then he had some kind of wicked Dutch guard dogs, and Dean shot them when they were killing his pigs. Plus, Tim and his buddy were riding his ex-girlfriend."

Hanna turned and looked at Tim with raised eyebrows.

"That was Andy!" Tim growled defensively.

"Very Western," Hanna nodded, turning back to Fred.

"The gurus have convinced Dean to quit eating pigs though."

"Too late for his health, or the dogs, but it will count toward his karma," Tim agreed.

"Not that the whole event really mattered that much, but it fanned the flames." Fred stroked his beard for a moment. "Really, the lawyers want Dean in debt so he loses the land, and puts it on the market. The realtors want to fill up the center of the Meadows with McMansions. That is what the whole mess comes down to."

Fred finished the corner of his glass and suddenly seemed bereft of words. He looked around as if searching for more words in the air. It was fully dark now, and cold, heavy breaths of mountain air swirled down into the valley.

"Well, that's it for me," Fred said, pushing down on his knees as he rose. "I got work in the morning. You guys can have the gear room beside the shop, but I'll be working in there early."

"That's fine, we'll probably leave before you get going." Tim drained Hanna's untouched glass of whiskey.

"Yeah, yeah, crack of dawn, bla, bla, bla." He held up Hanna's empty whiskey glass, "If you let him do that enough, he'll expect it." Fred winked at her, and let his hand slide down the back of her head. "Goodnight, but Wally and the rest of the crew haven't seen you for a while, and they're gonna want to have a to-do tomorrow evening, so try to be back by sevenish."

"There's not gonna be whiskey is there?" Tim smiled.

"'Fraid so, Son, 'fraid so!"

Hanna and Tim spread out bags in their room, which was, as Fred stated, a gear room for all the equipment from a lifetime of bachelorhood and adventuring. There was fly-fishing gear, and gear for river trips. There were long, heavy, wooden oars, a few guns on a rack, some mountaineering gear, a pyramid of coiled ropes, camp stoves and Dutch ovens, skis too numerous to count, tents and large puffy sleeping bags hung carefully from a long rod. There was a bookshelf of guidebooks and maps to different wildernesses in America, Canada, and various locations in the world. Only a narrow aisle remained in the center of the room where Tim pulled down thick foam pads from a shelf and laid them three-deep. With such little room, Hanna had to lay down her pad and bag beside Tim. She felt uncomfortable with the assumption that they would sleep so close, but happy with his nearness. She could see his discomfort, and it amused her—how they stayed so quiet over the most obvious. Tim was awkward and quiet and only said a few words before they slept.

Lure

Paul was no stranger to wandering alone, so when Hanna left camp with Tim, he also left and drove to the mountains to be away for a while. He was planning to invite both Hanna and Gina to go with him, but Gina never came back for the last session, which was fine with Paul. There was no love lost between him and Gina, and he suspected that she would have probably whined too much anyway. All he really wanted was for Hanna to be there, but perhaps not one-on-one. He had no idea what it would be like to be with a woman for so many days. And Hanna could see into him, and he felt that she might see things that she didn't want to, things he didn't want to revisit. He had wanted to be with her, but he had waited a day too long to ask, and she made plans to go off with Tim.

He wanted to walk through the mountains and tell her the rest of the story of how a Gaelic brooch made it to North Dakota. He wanted to tell her the facts; he had the evidence. He could show her. And he had done more research and found other clues throughout the Midwest, an iron spear point in Minnesota. But the theory was what he was trying to prove. Because what physical evidence did Lewis and Clark leave behind in two years of traveling across the same path? And even if it wasn't the Scandinavians, how could it not have been the Gaelic, Celts, or Phoenicians?

He imagined boat loads of swarthy Phoenicians landing on the shores of Virginia, asking themselves, 'Where the hell is this place?' And the indigenous people on the Virginian shore wondering, 'Whoa, who the hell are those guys?' Paul laughed at the scene, not because it was so odd, but because he knew that it really happened.

The same scenario had happened to Columbus, to Cortez and Pizarro. It had happened in Jamestown, and at Plymouth. It was common knowledge that the Basque and

Portuguese were secretly fishing, whaling, and trading along the shores of North America long before Columbus arrived. It was accepted as fact that pox-riddled European trade goods rubbed out many of the East Coast tribes before the Mayflower ever landed. The Phoenicians were sailing from modern-day Lebanon, all the way to the British Isles to trade for tin before the birth of Rome. How many times had life-rafts without any means of propulsion, and with living people in them, successfully crossed the Pacific and Atlantic Oceans? Homer told how early Mediterranean civilizations plied the waters of that sea as if it were an inland lake. And the Polynesians crossed every inch of the Pacific in little more than canoes. Yet, to academically propose the idea of Iron Age Europeans exploring the interior of the Americas was blasphemous. That was the point he was trying to make.

It only took a few hours for him to arrive the east side of the mountains, but then it took another hour to reach the parking lot because the mountain roads were steep and poorly maintained. Paul drove an old Toyota sedan and the going was very slow. He had been hoping that Hanna would have insisted they take her truck when she considered where they were going.

There were two other vehicles at the trailhead and a few lumps of dirty snow marked where there had once been tall winter drifts. It was deeply cool when Paul got out of the car, which reminded him of the altitude of the parking lot. There were a few spots where hikers could spend the night, and Paul considered it, but there were three or four good hours of light, and he knew that he could put four to six miles behind him before dusk.

Paul was a minimalist backpacker who favored speed over security, and his backpack was really just a large daypack. He carried a stove inside a cooking pan with a cup and spoon. He had a short sleeping pad, a tarp for sleeping on in good weather, and under in bad.

He had the clothes he wore, a set of light long johns, a fleece jacket, a storm coat, a knife, a headlamp, and a few other items. In the daylight, he was moving fast and this kept him warm. At night, he was sleeping and needed nothing but a pad, a bag and the tarp. It was a great philosophy, but this notion of Paul's had landed him in a lot of trouble more than once. Trouble came from large storms that trapped him with nothing but a piece of nylon between himself and very ugly conditions. Still, he thought that this was better than carrying huge amounts of weight.

His pack was completely ready in the trunk, and he double-checked for details like a lighter, headlamp, and pocketknife. When he was satisfied, he shouldered the pack, locked the door, stashed the key in the wheel well of the front tire, and started walking down the trail.

A mile from the car, Paul was watching his feet on the stony trail, when he looked up and was surprised to see a couple stopped before him. He could tell from their packs that they were climbers. Skinny, little people with huge packs were usually climbers. The woman was a redhead with large, white teeth, and gnarly, veiny legs sticking out of her shorts, and muscular arms sticking out of her T-shirt.

The guy whined, smiling sarcastically at Paul, "Hoowww much faaaarther?"

"Just a mile," Paul answered.

"What? A miiiiillllle?" the gnarly redhead chimed in.

Paul let the joke die and asked about conditions.

"Normal...what you'd expect, more snow the higher you go. But the trail is good and there are good boot tracks through the snowy sections. No bugs yet," the dark haired guy added.

"It's amazing not to have bugs," the woman almost shouted. "The last time we were here it was just miserable."

"The creeks are kind of a drag. Deep and cold." The guy looked around at the afternoon shadows. "How far are you going tonight?"

Paul re-adjusted his pack. "Oh, you know, just a few miles, to get away from the parking lot."

The woman nodded her head. "There are good sites in

the big timber up a few miles. We would have camped there ourselves if we weren't heading out. Big trees and flat ground, and a good creek."

"Good," Paul said. "I'll look for it."

"Can't miss it. Be safe, have fun," the guy said, as he passed Paul and continued down the trail.

The woman looked at Paul for a moment, and there was something around her eyes that reminded him of a girl from his high school. "Watch the creeks," she said.

Paul put his head down and walked hard. He was sure that there would be no more interruptions, just the meditation of walking and breathing and sweating. The country beyond the parking lot was healthy forests of huge Douglas firs, and spruce, and the terrain was not difficult. It climbed slowly for a while and then flattened out. He crossed a few small creeks, but there were always stones arranged, or a convenient crossing log, and he kept his feet dry.

He entered a thick creek-side forest, and he knew that this must be what the climbers were talking about. It would be just the place to stay for the night. He could string the tarp between two trees and be comfortable on the soft pine needles. In a few weeks, it would be a very buggy place to avoid, but for now, after four miles of walking in the late afternoon, it was perfect. In the sand at the creek he found bear tracks, and convinced himself that they were black bear rather than grizzly. He preferred bear tracks to the signs of men. All a bear would do was steal your food or kill you. It wouldn't torture and sodomize you first.

Paul knew that this idea would start him tugging at the thread. He tried to put it out of his mind. To stop unweaving that webby fabric—the indiscretion in Idaho, the teen tribulation, the regrettable ruination, the sick jail-cell rape scene, common as pigs in a ditch. He tried to busy himself with camp. He tried to pump some water, but he ended up staring blankly at the creek, with the movie behind his eyes. He searched for a way to re-sew the weave, if only he hadn't laughed at Antoine's name. Of course, Antoine's offense was only a ruse, but if he had tactfully given no offense, perhaps it all could have been avoided. They seemed friendly at first. They asked Paul if he had any matches. They had cigarettes but only a few matches. When they lit up they offered Paul one, and he politely declined.

"Suit yourself," said the tall one. He smiled and looked boyish in a tall, gawky way. "What're you in for?"

"I had some pot in my car," Paul said, watching for their response.

"How much?" asked the shorter, swarthy one.

"A dime bag."

The two looked at each other and laughed deeply. "And they threw you in jail?"

"Your dad comin' to get cha?"

"Na," said Paul, as if it didn't matter. "Dad says I have to spend the night."

The two men laughed again, raising their eyebrows at each other. "Oh, he's a hard-ass!" said the tall blonde man.

"He wants to be."

"All dads want to be the dick," said the shorter man, who seemed angry with the hard-assed dads of the world. "I hope he don't end up regrettin' treatin' ya this way."

Paul didn't understand, but he agreed with the possibility.

They seemed more at ease with Paul once they learned of his criminal activity, talking to him casually, but in a dominant, questioning way. Each of them took one of the bench beds and left Paul to pace or sit on the floor. There was a steel toilet and sink, and Paul considered sitting on the toilet, but it seemed improper.

"What's your name?" the tall blonde one asked.

"Paul."

"Paul," he said listening to the word. "St Paul, the big man!"

"Well Paul, I'm Phil, glad to meet cha," he said, shaking his hand.

"Glad to meet you, Phil."

The shorter, darker man stepped forward. "Antoine," he said without a French effect.

"Antoine?" Paul asked with a slight laugh.

Antoine gripped Paul's hand, pulling him closer.

"Antoine, Antoine LaFavre," he said to Paul. "You think that name is funny?"

"No," he said casually. "No, I just never knew anyone with that name. I like it. It sounds French."

"That's because my dad's from Canada. That all right, Paul?" He slowly released Paul's hand.

"Awe. Now you've hurt An-twan's feelings," Phil said with a smiling leer.

It was after lights out, and several hours of awkward needling, that Phil first hit him. Paul saw shadowed movement from Phil's direction but he never saw what hit him. He can remember Phil kneeling over him, asking him, "How you gonna make that up to An-twan?"

'What can you say to this?' he asked himself. 'Is there a correct response?' he wondered. Then he saw Antoine squat down and unload a punch to the side of his head. Antoine stood, shook his hand for a moment and lit a cigarette. Puffed on it a few times and then blew on the tip as Phil unloaded another haymaker to Paul's face and then covered his mouth so he couldn't scream.

By the time the scene replayed, his camp was ready and he was sitting in front of his cook stove with his mouth open, staring at the water about to boil.

"Maybe I should tell that story," he shouted. "Do you all want to hear that story? Are you listening?" he screamed. He stood and held his hand to his mouth to silence himself, but then kicked the pot of boiling water off the stove, a cloud of hot steam filling the grove of trees, droplets stinging his face. "Could you listen to that one? Will you share that with Tim and Gina?" His voice was now just a croak, and there was a sob deep in his throat, that he refused to let escape. The stove was still erect and sputtering at his feet, promising fidelity in his moment of madness. The pot lay five yards away, its round mouth now an oval.

A camp jay flew off nervously and alighted on the brushy platform of a spruce branch.

Paul bent the pan back into shape, re-boiled the water and poured it into the plastic and aluminum envelope of freeze-dried spaghetti, and let it sit for a moment. He was calm again by the time he ate his meal, but had the exhausted empty feeling, that he knew he could never fill. Afterward, he swished the foil packet with water and hung it upside down on a branch to dry overnight a hundred yards from his camp. He didn't like the idea of bears and he kept his camp clean and hung his food bag properly. It was dark by the time he finished a cup of tea and lay down on top of his bag. The evening was perfectly clear but he had set up the tarp between two trees to keep the dew off him in the morning. Sleep came quickly, and he awoke cold in the dark and sat up surprised. He took off his clothes and put on his long johns, stuffed everything else into his pack to form a pillow, and burrowed deep in his bag.

Acknowledgement

Hanna awoke to Tim nudging her with his foot and waving a cup of coffee in her face. "We'll have to go soon if we want to get back in time." Hanna could see through the flyspecked windows that it was still far from sunrise.

"What the hell Tim! It's four o'clock!"

"I know, but this is just what we have to do, if you want to go…"

"And be back in time for your bachelor party."

"And miss the thunderstorms. And get in front of the slower parties."

"Ok, just shut up for a while."

"No problem."

They drove away in dim light and breaths of steam. The light from Fred's kitchen glowed yellow. Hanna had a second cup of coffee in her hand and a bowl of oatmeal on the dashboard.

When Hanna and Tim left the truck, they passed some sorry-looking climbers, who had obviously slept in the parking lot, standing in the cold at the back of an SUV stirring a pot of breakfast. Hanna set the pace because they hadn't spoken much, and she was still huffy over the four o'clock wake-up. She knew that it was petty to hold a grudge over nothing, but Tim seemed indifferent to her mood anyway. She set off to do some pissed-off-walking. It would have been a perfect time to run, with the air cool and the light soft.

Tim gave her space, and she quickened her pace, crossing the last of the valley flats and low bogs. There were interesting birds as the forest and understory were well established. She saw lazuli buntings, a blue grouse and what she guessed was a solitary vireo.

She could hear the brrzzzing of wrens, but never saw them. Black-capped chickadees and rust-bellied nuthatches continuously gleaned the mature Douglas firs as she passed. The trail slowly rose into the forested hills at the foot of the mountains. Her breathing became more rhythmic and deeper as the trails steepened and then became a series of switchbacks that led to a long, ascending ridge. At the end of this ridge there was a junction. The way was obvious, but she stopped and waited. Tim came ten minutes later and sat in the sun, which was now strong, a few degrees above the horizon.

They drank water at a spring trickling across the trail. There would be no more fresh water until they reached the canyon, so she filled her bottle, drank it down and filled it again. The switchbacks loomed un-shaded above her; some were short zigzags, while others angled around the ridge of the canyon and reappeared high above, heading the opposite direction.

Tim sat with a sheen of sweat on his face, smiling in anticipation of the trail that lay ahead of them. "This is gonna hurt," he beamed.

Hanna handed him the full, cold water bottle and he drained it quickly. He dropped his pack to fill his own bottle and sat looking out across the valley. "There are elk. Watch that first gap in the trees there below us. Look now." And there they were, fast and silent moving swiftly and secretively in single file, there one moment, and then gone, the calves already sly miniature adults. A Canadian jay landed on a boulder above them and waited for food.

"It's still only morning, what, 7:30/8:00?" Hanna said.

"Look at what you would have missed, if we were just getting up now."

Hanna left the statement hanging and went first again, leaving Tim behind, the sweat flowing, the sun pounding. She found pockets of cool air from the night before, but the sun was quickly dissipating them; dust rose up from her feet, and she could feel a film of grit on her teeth. She climbed the switchbacks, one, two, three, how many? At the end of the last, long switchback, she turned the corner, and there she was at the mouth of the canyon, the mountains looming before her; another half mile and she came to a wall of talus with cairns marking the way through car-sized boulders. At

times, the river ran below her feet, ten feet beneath the
rubble. From deep down below, cold air swirled and
caressed her legs as she passed. She waited for Tim again on
the other side of the talus, at a small alluvial plain where the
spur they were to climb touched the canyon floor. There
were tents here, but all the climbers were gone. It was
already growing late to begin any of the longer climbs. High
above them along the dusty trails, climbers moved in single
file weaving through stone and dust en route to the higher
peaks.

Tim and Hanna moved more slowly, threading up gullies
and across slick glaciated slabs, vague ledges and around
towers, until at last they were on top of a prow and could
continue no farther without ropes. Tim emptied his rucksack
and Hanna uncoiled the rope from her pack. Tim's
movements were different now. This was business. The rack
of gear was quickly put in order, carabiners counted, slings
arranged and laid flat. When all was ready, he handed it to
Hanna.

"What?"

"What, what?"'

"You're leading," Hanna said, pushing the rack back at him.

"No, this is you. There'll be some fixed gear and some
pitons at the belay ledges."

Hanna took the gear timidly.

"Go on, this is what you want," he said

She slipped the gear sling over her head and across her
chest. She put long slings across her chest in the other direction,
and clipped short chains of carabiners to her harness.

"Go on, it's getting late already. You'll be glad." Tim took
the end of the rope tied to her harness and ran it through his
belay device, clipping it to his harness. He tugged at the rope
a bit and checked her knot. "You're on belay."

Hanna put her hands in the crack and pulled herself onto
the rock. Edges for her feet appeared as needed, while the
crack and ledges provided everything she wanted for her
hands, she moved up, dropped a chock into the crack and

clipped it to the rope. She moved higher, put in another piece, clipped the rope and moved higher again, and then she was moving, moving over stone, and she wasn't afraid. She was intent and pensive, solving the riddle of the moves in front of her, but all was obvious, and it was like swimming up a ladder. The distance passed quickly, and then she stood on a flat ledge. There was a nest of webbing threaded around a rock horn and an old rusty piton. She clipped them both to her harness with some slings and added another chock to back it up and called down that she was off belay.

She took a breath and looked down at how far she had come. Tim, looking so small, was smiling hugely. He waved to her and took her off belay. She realized that she was breathing hard and sweat ran down from under her helmet.

She pulled up the last few feet of slack until she felt Tim's weight and put him on belay, laughing to herself, looking around at the blazing sun and the black razors of ravens slipping past; she was on a small stance on the long prow of a large mountain: where she wanted to be.

Tim was following swiftly, and she had to work to keep the rope tight. She watched him follow so quickly, doing sequences of moves and then stopping to see where the route went. Then, he was on the ledge, smiling, clipping into the anchor;

"I told you, I told you this was the route. Nice, isn't it? It's even better than I remember." He was already taking the gear from her even as he spoke. He quickly took in the belay and then looked above, already leaving; he was the machine again. She paid out rope and leaned against the wall, feeling the potency of the sun, watching the tiny humans moving so slowly down below. Off to her left, they were ascending switchbacks that led to the higher peaks. Compared to the last route they did, this was a metropolis, a beehive, not a wilderness.

Tim brought her up to a tiny foot ledge where two anchor bolts had been drilled into the wall. He had two slings ready for her, and she clipped in; he immediately began exchanging gear.

Tim was talking and using his hands to demonstrate the way. "This is the best pitch, and the one after is just as good. As the cracks thin out, go to the left of the arête. It's obvious, and the belay is huge. We can drink and eat a bit at that one."

Her pitch was surely the best, and Tim restacked the rope on the ledge, and told her to lead the next one too. Then they were on easier ground and moved together with the rope shortened between them. Hanna pulled over a prow and there was the summit. She was stunned, because there had been other false summits, and there seemed to be no way that they had covered so much ground, but there she was, all alone on a peak with other peaks around her, some above her, some below. She pulled up the slack, but it was obvious that Tim was not waiting for tension to climb. He came over the edge a moment later with loops of rope in his hand. He pulled off his helmet, whooped and took a few deep breaths.

"How was that!!! I never get tired of that route. Imagine if the first five pitches kept going and going?"

"Yes to all of that," she said, amused at his enthusiasm. "Thanks, that was perfect." She reached out and hugged him, awkwardly with all the gear and coiled rope. She leaned away from him. "I felt it, I felt what it's like to move together, to move on rock."

"Yeah, we were getting it…you were great. Climb your ass off, switch gear, climb your ass off, repeat…"

"Well, thanks."

"Thanks nothing, I'd do it every day with you."

Hanna was embarrassed by his honesty. "You would, wouldn't you?" She looked into his eyes and he looked into hers.

"I would." He let his hands drop from her arms, "But come on, getting up is only half. Look out west, rain is on the way, and I don't want to be here at storm-30."

Hanna coiled the rope, and he put the gear in order, twisting it into manageable lumps and stuffing it down hard and deep into the bottom of his pack. Hanna did the same with the rope, and when they were done, they each ate an inadequate energy bar, drank what was left in their water bottles and started down a gulley that divided the west side of the peak. They quickly cliffed out, and rappelled down to a small ledge. Tim pulled the rope, and they followed the ledge to the south where they rappelled once more into a broader, lower angle gulley. "That's it," Tim said. "We can stow the rope and take off our harnesses. Time to put our heads down and walk."

The descent was fast and easy, and soon they were down into the talus that filled the south fork of the canyon. The sky above them azure and the sun searing, Hanna smiled contentedly and sang songs inside her head as she followed the madman's swinging gait down dusty, gravelly tracks and then boulder to boulder as they passed the edges of moraines that bisected the canyons, marking the edges of forgotten glaciers. They gained the ridge of one of the moraines, and Hanna looked down one side to a dusty little patch of crusty ice that had once been a burly glacier plowing thousands of tons of debris before it, and she felt the foreboding of a changing world and a changing climate. "You're not alone," she said, "we're all going the same way." She felt the grasp of reality wend its way into her euphoria, and she tried to dispel it, but as she walked along that moraine, she felt as if she were walking across someone's grave.

She jumped as Tim spoke, "There was glacial ice there the first times I passed here. It wasn't much of a glacier, but it's gone now." He handed her a hard candy from his pocket and fell into tales of past climbs, harrowing escapes and funny things that his partners had done up here. He rekindled her joy, and soon they were laughing as they tripped along down the trail.

"Lies," Hanna laughed, "Lies! That did not happen."

"I swear to God. May the coming lightning strike me!"

"But not me?"

"But not you, princess. Let me go on...so, we wake up in

the middle of the night in the middle of a hellacious rain storm with lightning and thunder—the real thing you know—and there's this soaking wet woman crawling into our tent, who says that she was separated from her partner and put her pack down to look for shelter and then got lost, until she stumbled upon our tent. Anyway, it's freezing, and all we could do is spread our sleeping bags and make one communal sleeping arrangement."

"With her soaking wet?" Hanna said incredulously.

"No, not any more, because Andy talked her into taking off her wet clothes—to avoid hypothermia, of course."

Hanna was laughing at the vision and the logic of Andy's persuasion.

"It gets worse, listen. In the morning I see that the woman is sleeping in Andy's arms…"

"That's a lie; it has to be a lie!"

"Whatever. In the morning, it's clear, and we go out to find her pack and look for her boyfriend, who is totally hypothermic and crying, thinking he has lost his true love forever. So we get his stove going, fill him up with hot tea and oatmeal, and we fish some relatively dry clothes out of his pack. In an hour he's all set, except by then he notices that his true love, Catherine, is now leaning against Andy, and she's wearing his fleece jacket and oversized long johns…. And the guy starts to cry…again."

"Aaawwwe, you guys are so mean."

"Hey, I had nothing to do with it, it was Andy and Catherine I'm the one who had to walk Ted…. You know Ted. I had to walk Ted down until he warmed up and could make it the rest of the way on his own. He stole Catherine's car though…"

"You mean Ted Bundy? Ted the asshole? Well of course he'd be an asshole if you treated him like that! It serves you guys right, and that bitch too! Is that the end of that pack of lies?"

"More or less. Catherine climbed with us for the next two days, and she was an incredible climber. I have no idea what she was doing with Ted. Everyone says he was always such a dick. But I had to move to a cave, because she and Andy were rather shameless. I'm sure Catherine was close to inviting me in, and I just didn't want anything regrettable to happen between Andy and me."

Hanna laughed at the sober assessment of his predicament. "That was noble of you."

Tim laughed, holding up his chin, "I must say."

"That can't be true, though. How could that happen?"

"We're standing where it happened. It happened right here. This is where the tent was, right here behind this wall of rocks."

"Oh, you were here no doubt, and something happened, but not the way you're telling it, it's too crazy."

"You know, I think it was because it was a different time. The world had changed. People were waiting for the other foot to fall, and they wanted to be reinvented, but they were also barely post-adolescents, without any governing ideology."

"Blab, blab blab. Oh shut up! Be reinvented? No governing ideology! What? The world isn't changing now?"

Hanna went first again. She was giddy with the day and Tim's stories. She was sure that they must be partially lies, but he believed them, and she could see that he told them only for her sake; they were the stories that he was giving to her.

At a confusing part of the trail, she stopped to wait. It was hot and she needed water. The clouds hung just out of the reach of the sun, hung up on the lee side of the range. But they were building, and stacking higher.

"This is a good spot. There's drinking water." Tim shouted ahead to her. They filled their bottles at a spring on the edge of a scree field. "Do you want to see the Ice Spa?"

"Is there a story with it?"

"Probably, but none that I know." Tim laughed. "It's right here, down where the creek comes out of the boulders."

They left their packs at the water and moved down into the depths of the canyon, passing a huge keystone that stopped the downward progress of the boulders' tumble. Below the looming plug-of-a-stone, was a pool that came frothing up from underneath, the pool seemingly more air than water.

"Wow, that is really cool, it looks like a Jacuzzi."

"It's deep enough to jump into. But jump lightly," Tim said, suggesting a breaking action with his hands."

"And hot enough. Will you?"

"Only if you go first."

"Would you take off your clothes?"

"Only if you made me."

"You're such an ass. I'm not that little tramp you found in the storm, by the way."

Tim ignored her accusation. "It's about five feet deep."

Hanna pulled off her T-shirt and sports bra, and dropped her shorts. She smiled at Tim and jumped in like a small cannonball. And then she was shooting out, faster than she dropped in, whooping and screaming.

"Whoa that's pretty cold. Aren't you jumping in?"

"No, looks too cold."

"You have to!!"

"I never said I would. I just wanted to see you without your clothes."

Hanna laughed and threw a rock hitting him in the leg.

"OK, OK, be patient!" He took off his shirt and dropped his shorts, covering his crotch with one hand and his chest with the other.

"Don't worry, Tim, there's nothing to see," she laughed.

He leapt into the water and disappeared below the froth. Then, he reappeared with a wheezy, breathless roar, climbing onto the hot stone, dancing with cold.

"Yes, very little to see," Hanna laughed.

Tim moved carefully in bare feet, sighing as he sat on a hot, black rock and stretched out, letting the sun heat his skin. "What else in the world is that much of a rush?"

"Very few things."

"Can people from the trail see us down here?"

"No, we're too deep in the boulders."

"Can we sun for a while to dry off—is there time?"

"The last I looked it was only one. We have some time, and we have a while before the clouds come over. Relax, it's all good." He said, reclining with his shirt over his eyes against the sun. He sensed her moving around, seeking a comfortable spot on the hot rocks. The heat rose up from below, and the sun baked them from above. Hanna could feel the cold chased from her body like a naughty child with nowhere to hide. On the smooth dome of a rock, she closed her eyes and crossed her legs and meditated for a few minutes, as well as she knew how. She recited her mantra, 'This is...enough.' She recited 'this is' while inhaling, and 'enough' while exhaling. She was only a few cycles through, and she could feel wellbeing rise up in her, and felt it spread through her body. 'This is…ennouugh. This is…ennouugh.' She rode out the sensation for some time until the moment had passed, and she became wakeful. She slowly opened her eyes, blinking at the brightness, and the clarity of the world. She felt a tear of joy come to her eyes, and she said aloud, "This is enough."

She looked over at Tim's brown body, with the white lines where he wore his shorts. He was asleep. He easily dropped into sleep during work breaks, and now there he was dozing, in the sun, sprouting a chubby erection. She got her shoes and picked her way across the boulders to him. She sat beside him, gently lifted the shirt from his face, careful to shade his eyes, and they fluttered open. She leaned close and looked into his eyes. "We've been here for a while. I'm dry, should we go?"

"It might be time," he answered.

"Yes, it might be," she kissed him on the lips. "You have a hard-on." She reached down and took it in her hand. "This isn't going to be habitual, I'm just expressing appreciation for this time." She put a shoe on each side of his hips and lowered her knees onto them. Then she reached beneath her and guided him into her. He moaned and she shuddered.

After only a few strokes she said. "You can't…inside me…if you do, we are through in every way."

"Yes, I have very good control."

"Of course, you do. Just tell me when." And she began to ride harder and breathe in gasps. Against her control, she was bucking higher and faster, and then Tim was pushing her off.

He kissed her and then looked into her face, and he saw her clear blue, elfin eyes and the sweat misted on her forehead, and the disarray of her short blonde hair. He saw a child there, and then a woman. She didn't say anything but pulled him close and held him tightly, and he spoke quietly into her ear. "You know, that was just a little bit crazy?"

"Shush," she said, as if he might be waking her. "Ssshhhh."

They plunged into the pool together to clean up. After drying and putting on their clothes Hanna kissed him again. "I am trusting you with this Tim. I'm still committed to women, and now maybe we're just intense friends—can you do that?"

"You're safe with me. I have no expectations."

As they regained the trail, clouds covered the sun, and it was instantly cool enough to make them stop and pull on wind shells. Looking overhead, she watched the Douglas firs sway in the gusts before the squall. She felt tired, and the world had a surreal texture. She knew that this would always be a day by which others would be measured.

By the time they reached the truck, the first few drops of rain came down thick and hard, and as they drove away lightning flashed somewhere behind them, and thunder shook the truck as sheets of water lashed across the windshield. Tim looked at her and smiled an 'I told you so'.

They were silent as they drove. Tim flicked on the stereo. Ironically, it was a song Hanna knew well, and she waited patiently for her favorite lyrics to come around:

The heart has it evenings, it seasons
And songs of its own.

Solitude

In the morning, far to the southeast, Paul was up at the first grey light, putting a pot of water on the stove. He had two cups of tea before he got out of his sleeping bag. There was heavy dew on the ground, which was a good sign that there would be no rain that day. After a quick bowl of oatmeal, he was packed and walking before the sun touched the ground.

The miles passed quickly and he found himself at the edge of the timberline by noon. The sun was brilliant, and he stopped for a long lunch beside a large creek that he would eventually have to cross in order to climb the pass to go over into the next basin. He looked around at how much snow had disappeared in just a few weeks. He ate dried fruit and jerky and brewed up some tea while admiring the canyon.

Paul thought that he might go over the pass that same day, but there was a hanging glacial cirque that he was curious about from his previous trip. So, instead, he moved up the canyon and set his camp there in the shelter of some boulders. When he had his camp the way he liked it, he left everything behind and climbed the steep talus slopes until he reached a low-angle snowfield. It was easier going on the snow, and he followed it to the lip of the hanging canyon. He rested on a huge boulder overlooking his camp far below him. Behind him was the bowl-shaped cirque, scooped out by the ghost of a glacier. It had gouged out a trough until a larger glacier had clipped it off at the end, like a creek into a main river. And here he stood with his feet firmly planted on what thousands of feet of ice, and tens of thousands of years had done, and what another ten thousand years of time could not undo.

From here, he could see two fin-like peaks of solid granite that had not been plowed away by the glacial massif. He scrambled along a crumbling arête to the closer of the two peaks. When he reached solid rock, he found that the way was hard, but it would be regrettable to try to climb back down. He was hoping that he had, by chance, chosen the harder way to the top, and that there would be an easier way off. Passing one more, hard step, he found himself on the summit. The tiny peak was just one of many spurs sticking up from the plateau, all about the same height. He spun around one time and looked in all directions, seeing nothing made by man: no people, no tents, no planes, and there was no sound. Two passing ravens took little notice of him and moved on. There were lakes and tarns tucked in among cirques and canyons. He thought it would be a great future trip to stay up high and climb these higher spires, and camp beside the tiny lakes.

Searching for an easier descent, he found that the opposite ridge was little more than a walk-off; he followed it down to the rim and headed down the spur he had ascended, and back to his camp. When he was a bit more than halfway down, he traversed out onto steeper snow and pointed his feet down the hill, skiing on the soles of his boots, turning back and forth down the slope until he hit a deep hole and went into a tumble. He flipped onto his butt and then slid down to the run-out, eventually slushing to a stop, laughing at the wild ride.

He was wet and chilled from the snow and could see the long shadows creeping east. The day had been full, but it was already ending. It seemed like just a few hours since he had left his camp. A little walking, a little exploring and it was time to eat and go to bed—get up and do it again.

This high camp was a little more difficult than the one the night before. The tarp didn't set up as easily in among the boulders, but he preferred to be here above the timberline, among the rocks and short grasses, sand, snow, and water. With the sun gone, he put on all his clothes, ski cap and light gloves, and went to the creek to get water for dinner. He closed his eyes and pulled out a dehydrated meal for dinner—"Turkey Tetrazzini! A light Chablis would be perfect with this."

The cold deepened, the breeze died, and the silence was so profound that even the purring of the stove seemed like roaring jet engines. Rosy finches came among the boulders, hunting seeds and spiders in the stunted forbs and lichens. They studied him, but paid him little mind, coming in close, even moving under the tarp. A pica randomly appeared and disappeared with mouthfuls of herbs to store for the winter.

When dinner was gone, Paul made water for tea, cleaned out the foil dinner bag and left it to dry. He sat with his eyes closed in a stupor. He wondered what he would do or say if Hanna, or both Hanna and Gina were here. Would it be awkward? If they came, they would all move much more slowly. Hanna would move fast enough, but she would probably want a proper tent, and more leisure time. She would be fastidious with the food, eating like a neurotic Chihuahua, nibbling at a bit of brown rice, while Paul wolfed down meaty, freeze-dried envelopes of chow. Paul couldn't decide if it would be worth it to have her here. "Be careful what you wish for!" he said aloud. What if she wanted some kind of intimacy! His heart raced with dread and anxiety. 'Don't be an ass!' he thought. With her designs on Gina, and Tim's tactful courting, she had more than enough romantic attention. 'But what if it were me for some reason?' His heart raced again.

He drank off the rest of his sweet tea, and got up, searching for a place to put the food bag. In the end, he left it on top of the highest boulder, and crawled into his bag with most of his clothes on, made a pillow of his empty pack, and drifted to sleep almost before he stopped moving.

Saturnalia

After a long, hard climb, Hanna was happy to relax a bit before people started arriving for Tim's party. The guests came in ones and twos, mostly men, but some women also. They came expecting Tim. He was their minor celebrity and naughty prodigal son come home. They shook hands, hugged him and cast a cocked eye upon him as he related what he was currently doing, as if he might really be a spy, or a famous artist just in from Paris. Hanna was given the same treatment, and the men she met hugged her robustly and let their hands linger a moment before they released her. They were mostly older than her and looked deeply into her eyes as they spoke. The women were coy and unassuming as they delved carefully into Hanna's friendship with Tim. They were mostly beyond Hanna's age, but generally fit and healthy, as if they had once been the younger women of these aging men, but now they were the aging women of these older men.

Tim came over with his arm over the shoulder of a handsome man his age, a bit younger than the rest, with a halo of thinning blonde curls. A woman with straight, ginger hair followed a step behind Tim and his friend, but her presence preceded them. She was perhaps a few years older than Hanna and Tim, but untarnished. "Hanna," Tim almost shouted, "this is Andy, and this is Catherine!!!"

Catherine pushed in front of Andy and hugged Hanna warmly, "Yes, it's me, Catherine. Tim said you already heard the whole story. Tim is making me tell you that that is what happened, more or less, the way Tim remembers it."

Tim was smiling smugly.

Andy cut in and shook her hand. He was shy and had little to say, other than speaking of the East Spur, and then Hanna realized he was talking about the route that they had just climbed.

"Andy, don't bore her with climbing!" Catherine said to

Hanna, "He's just excited because we did the first ascent of that route, the day after that fateful rainstorm, when Ted stormed off out of the mountains and stole my car. The climb was Tim's idea. Wasn't it Tim?"

Tim smiled and nodded his head as the guilty party.

Catherine took Hanna by the elbow and walked her to a table of wine and liquor, leaving Tim and Andy in revision of the route. They laughed and pantomimed the moves.

"They are like children, aren't they?" Catherine asked.

"Maybe aliens," Hanna said, "benign aliens."

Catherine poured a hefty plastic glass of white wine, and held up the bottle in offer.

"You know, I'm still feeling a bit dehydrated, I might just go with water."

"Wait, I have just the thing. Let me."

Catherine opened a red and white cooler and prepared a tall concoction with a splash of lime. "It has soda water, ginseng and ginger. No booze, I promise."

Hanna drank it down on Catherine's insistence, and then Catherine prepared another.

"Just let that work its magic and you'll be good to go for the rest of the night. I drink it after I work out. So tell me, you live with Tim out in the field, on archeology digs?"

"Well, I live out in the field, and so does he, but we don't live together. And generally, we survey. We don't usually dig. The digging is hot and tedious."

"And you like it?"

"Oh, yeah, as much as anything else I've done. It's really varied, you know. Sometimes it's just office work."

"Nice."

"This seems like such an odd place, with all these men living out here. Where are the women and children?"

Catherine laughed, "We used to call this the Boy Corral." She smiled wryly, and Hanna could see the girl lost in the mountains in her impish green eyes. "If you ever needed a good shaggin' you just came out here to one of the parties. This is where all the guys from town bought the only land they could afford—and they often had girlfriends and wives who went in as partners, but mostly they left after a few years, or affairs split things up." Catherine waved her hand toward the road. "But it used to be pretty remote out here. In the summer, the road was hard enough, but in the winter you could only get in by snowmobile. Even when everything was going well—it was just plain hard to live here."

"But the guys just had to live on the edge of the wilderness?" Hanna asked.

"More like on the edge of Gomorrah. A little cabin on the edge of Gomorrah."

"Did you ever live here?"

"Oh we took care of a house or two now and then, but it never really appealed to me."

"I told Andy, 'If you want to live out there, be my guest.' They are just old boys—as in children, but this is how they want to live, so what the hell." Catherine looked wistfully at the crowd as she said this.

The men were importantly setting up tables or work benches with plywood tops and the women were right behind them setting down bowls of food. Fred was busy grilling large slabs of elk and deer. He and Tim had been fussing over the meat, flopping it around in a marinade all afternoon. The shadows came down from the forested hills, reached past the party and the darker coolness seemed to calm the guests. There was a loud clanging game of horseshoes behind Fred's shop, and some women were taking turns trying to walk a low slack line.

Catherine pointed out one of the guests, "Look, here comes Dean. He's dying, you know. Cancer."

A couple of women ushered Dean into the party. He was older than most of the people at the party. His hair had gone white, but he had a robust headful. He was slim and still handsome, with a long, fine nose and square chin. Many stopped their conversations to greet him with hugs and warm handshakes. He waved off a beer, and accepted a small plate of food. Bob the dog stood at the edge of the group and was intent on staying close to Dean.

Catherine took Hanna around to meet the guests and get a plate of food. From the selection and quality of the food, she could tell that there were many vegetarians among the crowd. The food was excellent, and a lot of the veggies were obviously fresh from someone's garden. After the climb, Hanna was starving and fell on her food with great relish. She had a hard time talking and stuffing her face at the same time. She accepted a tall white wine from Catherine, but sipped at it carefully. She knew what it would do to her after a day like she'd just had.

As night fell, a large fire sprang up in the center of things. She could still hear the clang of the horseshoes, music was playing, and couples, some of them women, danced on the small lawn beside Fred's cabin. One of the men took her hands and pulled her into the crowd, he led her through a clumsy swing dance, then some reggae came on, and everyone held their hands above their heads like palm trees. The music slowed again and Catherine found her and put her hands on Hanna's waist to dance with her. Hanna could tell that Catherine was feeling fine about herself and had to laugh as Catherine gossiped about Fred's friends. Catherine caught Hanna's eyes in the beam of her own and held them there, and when the music slowed even more, she held Hanna close, and Hanna picked up that gay vibe that heteros give off when they're loaded.

Hanna studied her face and guessed that Tim must have mentioned Hanna's gay preferences to Catherine. As the music stopped, they were standing outside the circles of light. Hanna felt plucky and subtly took Catherine's hand, which Catherine allowed, smiling hugely. She had only meant to punish Catherine's recreational gaiety, but with Catherine's concession, Hanna now felt herself blushing and guffawed in the grand goof of the moment.

Another swing tune came on, and men came to the edge of the light, hunting partners, rescuing Hanna and Catherine from their moment. Catherine would have none of it and she pulled

Hanna out to dance, first slowly, and then leading her through some simple swing moves as the tempo grew. When the music changed once more, no one seemed to notice the two women trapped in the gravity and orbit of the 'Tennessee Waltz'.

As the song ended a tall, handsome man with a large, walrus mustache peeled Hanna away from Catherine. Hanna looked out from the melee for Catherine or Tim. She saw Tim in the company of two women, who had him backed up against the bar table. The mustachioed man saw her gaze and said, "He can't help it."

As the man swung her around, she saw Bob the dog sitting beside Dean, the cancer patient. When the music stopped, she took this as a moment to escape to a safer place, walking over to the furry security of Bob.

"Is Bob bothering you?" she asked the white haired man.

"No, he's good company. He stays close, but keeps his mouth shut."

Hanna looked back at many of the orating buffoons and laughed, "Not everyone can do that."

"The silent fool is halfway to becoming a sage," Dean said with affected authority, winking at her.

"They sure go after it, don't they?" Hanna said, looking back at the swirling, shouting dancers.

"Always have. I remember when most of them got here. I thought they were the definition of debauchery, although I had little room to talk in those days. At night they'd be dancing around a fire like a bunch of Indians. Some nights, the women would be walking around bare-breasted before the sun even when down. 'Course I only know 'cause I was watching with my binoculars. They were crazy hippies in every sense of the word. You should've seen the summer solstice parties."

"That's when you were still ranching out here?"

"Yeah, my dad was pretty old by then, and I was the only one that'd live with him out here. 'Course I was blaming him the whole time from keeping me from being a top bull rider. Little did I know how much pain he saved me. Now all the bull riders I used to know are crippled up, or dead. Hell, my brother hit the ground so hard it popped his goddamn eye out. Never did work right after they put it back."

"Anyway, that's why I stayed out here. Dad wouldn't move to town. Said he'd shoot himself first. And that's what he did once he started to lose control of his, ah, bodily functions. He told me, too. He laid it out. Said he had a good run, and he was just getting off while the existence was still wonderful. And he never used words like that, but that time he did, said it was a 'wonderful existence'. He'd done his chores that day, fed the horses, moved the cows to the pasture away from the calving sheds, even fixed a gate." Dean paused for a moment, trying to remember the original thought. "Oh," he laughed, "I remember now. Anyway, Dad had no idea what all these guys were about." He laughed heartily, "One time he was looking for a calf, and came upon some of the gals sunbathing without a stitch of clothes on. When the gals looked up they just waved, and said 'good morning' and Dad was stumped for days. He asked me several times, 'What kind of people would do that?'"

"Well, I was a little pissed off that they dumbfounded my dad so badly, and I went over to ask them what the hell was going on, and Big Wally—you know him?"

Hanna shook her head.

"He'd be the biggest guy here, with the mustache, you seen him?"

"Oh yeah, I danced with him."

"Good dancer, eh? I've seen him dance at the Stagecoach, the gals like him. Anyway Big Wally, he jus' looks at me and shrugs and says 'Oh yeaahhh. Those girls are visiting, they're from Olympia, Washington.'"

Dean laughed and laughed and Hanna fell in laughing with him too. "He says it like that explained everything—like I should say, 'Oooohhh yeahh, Olyyymmmpia.'" Dean had a good laugh, and Hanna stayed right with him, until they chuckled a few last times and paused in an awkward silence.

"Am I talking too much, honey? The boys got me all doped up, and I just talk on and on and one thing leads to another."

"That's fine, all I can do is listen."

"Well then, there you have it."

Bob moved closer and sat in an alert manner as if he was on guard.

"Not many people live in one place anymore, like you have, you know," Hanna commented, inviting him to continue.

"You're not lying either. They can't, why you couldn't…the social and economic pressures drive them away. If I weren't dying, I couldn't live here much longer without sellin' off." Dean looked at Hanna in an embarrassed fashion. "You know I'm dying, right?"

"Yeah, so I was told. Cancer, right?"

"You got that right. I didn't want to shock you. Sometimes I forget and drop it like a bombshell, and they get all gawky, you know?" Dean chuckled.

"Yes, I would have been really shocked if I hadn't known previously," Hanna snickered. "Should we be giggling about it?"

"Oh hell, there's nothing to it. We're all going there, some of us sooner than others." Dean shook his head, at a loss of words and then recaptured his original tangent.

A crushing wave of sorrow and loss washed over Hanna and she lifted her head and looked to the sky as if a dark shade had suddenly flown past; a spasm gripped her chest, and she felt a tear come to her eye. She looked to Dean but he stared off, ruminating on a thought. She hunted out Tim in the crowd and saw him with his friends, and Bob was at her feet staring at her. As the feeling lifted, she thought the sorrow must be for Dean. How silly was it to mourn for a man she'd just met?

"But I know what you're saying about people moving," Dean said, recovering his thought. "It is like no one is from anywhere anymore, or people are from anywhere other than here. But I moved some too, you know. Our family was part of a large ranching clan, and we summered up here, but in the winter we went to the family's larger holdings down South. That's where our stock came from. We'd unload them down in the canyon and drive them up here where they'd be belly deep in grass by May—and it stayed that way until September or October. Then we drove 'em back down the canyon, to haul 'em down South."

Dean stopped again to try and find the point. "But we moved around a bunch. Dad even took work in California, down around Sacramento. I couldn't believe what some of those desert ranches called range. Hell, if you'd a put one of our Herefords out there they'd be belly up and bloated in three days. We went to the ocean, swam in the Pacific. Yeah, that was a long time ago. It's funny how Dad was at home wherever he went. Just talked to everyone like he'd lived beside them his whole life."

Hanna laughed, "Kinda like you and me."

"Well not quite. We know each other already, wouldn't you say?"

Hanna was unable to respond, and then a woman came forward.

"Dean, have you been eating?" The woman was standing in front of them with a small plate of food and a plastic fork. "You can't be smoking if it's not helping your appetite." She handed Dean the plate and made sure it was secure in his lap before she relinquished her grip. "Look, nothing but healthy choices!" she smiled. "Tabbouleh, a nice salad, a pasta salad, and some fresh bread, and a tiny sliver of Fred's elk for you."

"Now Rhonda, you know that I am not eating the meat."

"It's just a sliver Dean, and there is no carcinogenic crust to it."

"Would you eat red meat?" he asked Hanna, matter-of-fact.

Hanna looked at the woman, Rhonda, trying to read the correct answer in her face. "Well, I can't say, I would...but I know nothing of your...regimen." She smiled, satisfied with her tact.

Rhonda laughed and put her hand on Hanna's shoulder, "Are you in politics, honey?"

"This is my sister-in-law Rhonda, and Rhonda, I have no idea who this woman is."

Hanna blinked, shocked that she had not introduced herself yet. "My name is Hanna."

"Well Hanna, this is my main caregiver, partner, and sister-in-law, Rhonda. We caused quite a stir when we shacked up, but by then the family was in full feud, anyway, wasn't it dear?"

"It wasn't my family, Dean. It did ruin my relationship with my sister. But only because she was jealous." Rhonda smiled as she ruffled Dean's tufted white hair and winked lewdly.

Hanna stood and shook Rhonda's hand and looked into her light brown eyes. She was handsome in a cowgirl way. Her skin was an earthy brown, and she had friendly crow's feet at the corners of her eyes.

"You're a bit younger than the usual crowd out here aren't you, dear?"

"I guess. I'm here with Tim."

"Ah, Tim. Well, careful with that one, and don't let him drink any whiskey!"

"No, I have been watching, and I've only seen him with beer tonight, but I've heard about his whiskey rages."

"He must have some Indian in him...or Native American, I should say. And that's no rage. It's a deep, delusional insanity."

"Well, I grabbed the keys to his truck, and I know how to lock the door to Fred's shop."

"Dean needs to eat, Hanna. Can I trust you to see to it?"

"Please Rhonda, just sit and eat with me. Hanna and I've had a nice visit, but sit and eat with me now. Don't get all dramatic over it."

"Yes, take my seat, Rhonda, I should check on Tim."

"Well then, good-bye and thanks for the conversation. But listen Hanna, I do well in the morning. Would you have coffee with me in the mornin'? I bet you're an early riser, and 'course so am I." Dean caught her eyes, and she could see the young rascal in the spark of his blue eyes above his browned cheekbones.

"Sure, I will." Hanna looked to Rhonda for approval and

was pleased to see her wink.

"Good enough, early as you like. It's the place in the center of the Meadows."

Hanna drifted back into the party and eluded Big Wally's mitts as he reached out for a new dance partner. Andy and Catherine were having an important looking conversation with a sober looking couple dressed in sharp casual wear. Fred appeared and threw his arm around Hanna. His hair was tousled and his eyes bright with merriment.

"Here she is! Here she is! I haven't danced with you even once."

"And that's a good thing," a woman next to him said. "You can't dance to save your life, Fred."

Fred roared with laughter and said, "But I just want to be a little closer to her."

"Fred, you have your arm around me, how can you be any closer?" Hanna asked.

Hanna caught Tim's eye from across the party and gave him the nod.

Hanna used the nod as a pretext to escape Fred's clutches and approached Tim, "Have you been drinking whiskey, Tim?"

"No Ma'am. On my best behavior."

"I don't want to spoil things for you," Hanna said, gauging his sobriety.

"Well you're my guest, and I didn't want to make you uncomfortable. How would it be if I was doing regrettable things, and everyone was looking to you for an explanation?"

"From what I heard, it doesn't sound like anyone would need any explanation if you were being regrettable."

He smiled and looked into her eyes, "Are you thinking that you're done for the night?"

"I think I'll drift away, I've had enough, but it's your party, so you stay up, I'll sneak away to the shop." She watched from the door of the shop as Tim returned to his people, the knot opened to acknowledge him and then closed around him.

Circumstance

Paul was as sore as he had ever been. He groaned as he rolled over to light the stove and put on the pot of water rimmed with fingers of ice. After his morning routine, he was walking long before the sun came into the canyon, and it didn't catch up to him until he had climbed halfway up the pass at the head of the valley beyond the cirque he had explored the day before. He was gingerly negotiating boot tracks frozen in the snow when he first stepped into the sun's rays, and minutes later he dropped his pack to shed a layer of clothes. He sat in its warmth and drank down a long guzzle of water, wishing he had a second bottle.

The pass topped out on the plateau, and Paul could feel the altitude in his shortness of breath and the searing force of the early sun. He wandered around for a while before he found the vague track that left from the main trail, marked with a simple cairn. He followed this south, and in an hour, was looking down into the next drainage. He could see most of the route that would take him back down to his car. He filled his water bottle at the base of some melting snow and ate an energy bar. His food bag was already growing light. He had a dinner, a breakfast, and one more day's worth of lunch foods. This made him nervous when he compared his food against how far he had to go, but that was the trade off with going fast and light.

Maybe next trip he would invite Hanna and Tim. He had no problem with Tim. Paul knew how attracted he was to Hanna, but that didn't bother him. Paul had no romantic designs on her; it was beyond the realm of possibilities. Paul knew how competent Tim would be here, but not in any macho way. He seemed to be competent in just about everything. Next time he would invite them both. If they wanted to climb, that would be great. Maybe he would climb too, but if not, it would give him time to do long hikes from camp without a huge pack weighing him down.

At the base of the pass, Paul took off his shoes and socks and soaked his feet and knees in Carson Creek. The water was like ice, but he knew that it would relieve his fatigue. The sun was high and hot, so he took off the rest of his clothes and splashed and scrubbed the salt from his body and then dried in the sun. He felt rejuvenated and was ready to head down the trail.

Paul had to cross Carson Creek twice. Once here, to avoid steep terrain on the north side of the creek, and then again down lower, to access the next pass, to take him over the saddle back to the north and down to the trailhead. The crossing where he bathed was a challenge, but he found a stout stick and negotiated it without pants, barefoot and with little problem.

The route he followed down the canyon was not maintained. It was unmarked and vague, he lost it from time to time, and it had no bridges. He hiked down the south side of the canyon, across gravel bars and huge slabs of bare rock, but it quickly changed to scruffy, stunted pines. This was a much steeper canyon, and the elevation dropped away quickly. Smaller creeks poured in from both sides. The north side of Carson Creek was steep and craggy, so going back up and re-crossing above would do him no good. He was certain that further off in the forests below he would find some downed trees to take him over.

Carson Creek roared louder with each mile; it was now a frothy, burly river, its cool mist landing on his face and bare arms; its endless din annoyed him. At different points, downed trees extended out into it, but none quite made it over where he needed to be. He found where the steep, scruffy trail switchbacked up through a rocky drainage on the other side of the torrent. He ditched his pack and went to scout for a crossing down the creek for another mile, but saw that things only got worse below.

Paul's final choice was where two logs met in the middle ᶜ the river, one from one side, and one from the other.

They would have made a perfect crossing, except for six inches of water that ran across them for a few feet where they met in the middle. Branches stuck up from both logs, which would both help and hinder his crossing. If he abandoned the route now and went back the way he came, it would cost him three hours and a lot of exertion and humiliation, marking his second retreat from this canyon in just a few weeks. He weighed three hours of work and failure against five minutes of fear.

Paul thought that if Hanna was here she would go back to the pass, but that didn't help him, and he paced back and forth wrestling with his choice. In the end, he chose to cross the creek on the logs. He put his pack back on, took a hiccupped breath of air, and stepped up on the log, and walked across it until it he was standing above the edge of the bank. He took a few more steps and felt the vertigo of the water rushing three feet below him. He traversed out, from branch to branch, his heart racing as he crossed a gap without anything to catch his balance. Just before the point where the logs met in the center, two branches blocked his way. One broke easily, but not the other, and he had to go around it. There was a bit more room to pass on the upstream side. As he shifted his weight and began easing past the branch, his foot slipped on the wet bark. He immediately leaned too far back with the weight of his pack past the balance point, and it pulled him to the water. He put both hands on the branch, but it was not rigid enough to hold his weight, and it flexed with his fall. And then his right foot slipped, and he fell into a sitting position with the crooks of his knees holding him to the log for a moment, but he was not strong enough to extricate himself from this position.

There was a certain mercy in his situation; as the branch came away in his hands, it was so swift, brutal and violent, that he did not truly feel the pain from the blows as he was driven against the boulders in the creek. The speed and violence gave him no time to consider his plight. The first, numbing shock came when Paul entered the glacial river

headfirst and backward, swept away. His pack and boots
took him to the bottom where he was driven against rocks
and logs with the racing force of the river. He felt shock and
dismay, but fear, panic, and sorrow were not among the
things in his mind.

Dean

Dawn came too soon, but Hanna was up with the sun. She pulled on some clothes and a jacket. Tim was sleeping deeply beside her in the side room of Fred's carpentry shop. He smelled beery. She slipped out silently into the dewy morning. It was cold, but still she went and washed up at the spigot. She felt good and sore from the day before. She had carefully nursed two glasses of wine, so eluded a hangover. There was little sign of the night's festivities, a few glasses and bottles hidden in the deep grass but not the wreckage she had imagined. There was an extra car in the drive, and Hanna eyed Fred's cabin, imagining the scenario. Tim had left the camp stove set up on his tailgate, and Hanna boiled some water to brew a strong coffee. She fished some milk from the cooler and pulled one of the lawn chairs into a small patch of sun. She looked into the rising sun and took in the tiny valley, the draw and meadows. It was quiet. Around the small houses and cabins a slight fog hung just over the rooftops. She could see the tint of blue smoke from the night before and hear the echoes of last night's laughter hung up there in those wispy skeins curling into the clouds; some horses grazed lazily in the wet grass. This was better than the party, she thought, as she let the sun bake away the morning's chill.

She could see Dean's cabin, and she wondered if she should go down there. What could he want to say? Why should she spend the morning with him? She knew that she would because he had asked, and he was dying, although he didn't look like it. What did that mean, dying? As he said, we're all dying, but he was just dying sooner. And when would he die, tomorrow? In a month? A year? Wasn't he 60 or 70? Isn't that about time anyway? He was marked as dying, and everyone acknowledged that unfortunate celebrity. 'The dying man'. The title annoyed her and she felt the need to shake it.

Hanna got a sleeping pad out of the back of the truck, spread it in the sun and sat there for a few minutes. She crossed her legs and tried to meditate for a while. She stopped, turned her back to the sun, and had better luck. She began her mantra, caught the edge of nothingness and rode it for a while, but then lost it when bits and pieces of yesterday seeped up through the cracks, the climb, the ice spa, having sex with a man...? Catherine's eyes. BAM, Catherine's eyes, no use pursuing nothingness while your mind was staring into those green pools. Those eyes were no whirling voids, Hanna thought; they were the promise of everything. She wondered why she sucked at meditating. If only her brain would shut the hell up and stop with the minutiae. "Oh well, this is enough!" She stepped into her sandals and walked through the dewy grass in the quiet morning, down to Dean's. Bob followed for a few paces but decided to stay and guard the door to his sleeping master.

She could see Big Wally already hoeing in his garden. He was going quickly down the rows of vegetables like a practiced farmer, and Hanna wondered where he grew his cash crop. Hanna left him to his work and continued quietly down the road. She opened the gate to Dean's place—the little, old cabin beside the small log barn. Swallows flew up from mud puddles with beaks full of mucky debris for their nests. She could see Dean standing in the window as she came to the porch, smiling beatifically, white hair standing on end. He opened the door, and she stepped into the cabin's main room: living room, dining room, and kitchen. It was like stepping into a tiny diorama in a museum, like a replica of what a turn-of-the-century ranch house was like, with the wood cook stove, the ancient gas range, the huge, iron and enamel sink. The logs were shiny and burnished from decades of life, smoke, laughter, fighting, loving, and tragedy. If the logs could talk, what would they say, what could they not say, what could they not know about human existence, what had they not seen? Hanna sensed how the walls had sheltered and protected Dean, the baby, the toddler, the boy, the teen, the young man, the man, the old man, the dying man.

Hanna held out her hand to him, and he took it in his two hands, which seemed too large and strong for a man his age. "I'm glad you could make it," he said sincerely.

Hanna opened her mouth to speak but a small, framed display on the wall caught her eye, and she turned to it involuntarily, rudely, consumed by a large black Clovis wired to the wooden backing. It was perhaps a bit larger than the one she had found, and though not as fine, it could have been made by the same person.

"Ahhh, I should have known, and hid it." He shook his head. "Archeologists," he said. "Now you'll be distracted all morning." Dean smiled at her and took the picture-frame from the wall and handed it to Hanna. He went over to root around in the kitchen while Hanna studied the Clovis.

On closer inspection, she could see that it was broken in half. It was a clean break at the tip of the vertical flute, but the two edges met perfectly.

"I found that with my dad." Dean said. "He was always rooting around when we were moving cows in the desert. He wanted to find Butch Cassidy's gold. Never did, but we found all kinds of other stuff instead." Dean chased a thought around in his head for a moment. "Coffee?"

"Please."

"Toast with that?"

"Yes, please."

"It will be warmer in the sun, let's go out to the corner of the porch. You can bring the point if you like."

"No, maybe I'll look at it again later."

Hanna took an oversized plate with the coffees and toast, and Dean followed her to a rough table outside.

They sat quietly for a few moments. Hanna felt awkward, but she could see Dean was calm. She wondered how many times he'd sat there. Had his mother sat here with him on her lap?

"Where did you find it?" she asked, a bit too impatiently.

"Oh, the spear point? North of Rocket City, out by the buttes."

Hanna was about to pick up her coffee, but she pulled her hand back so she wouldn't spill it, and her heart raced.

Dean had played a lot of poker in his day and he knew that he had just turned over an Ace. "Honey, I'd say you got something to say about that."

"The buttes?"

"Yeah, we used to have a grazing permit down there. And the grazing was hit or miss. We ran the cows down there in the early spring. So tell me, what do you know?"

"I found its twin, along the hills north of there, you can see the buttes from where I found it.

"Sure, that was good grazing. I know those hills well. The whole area is strewn with artifacts. Historic and prehistoric, Dad always said that one was a very old point. He said it was a Folsom."

Well, actually it's a Clovis, but the style is similar, as was the technology used to make it. A Clovis is older, though."

Dean got up and went into his house, when he returned he was carrying an object that appeared to be a large piece of dirty coral. "You know what this is?" he asked.

Once she could see it, she knew immediately, "A mammoth molar. You found that out there? How close were the point and molar?"

"Not far, 20 yards. I told you that place is thick with stuff like this."

"That's close enough, isn't it?"

"Very coincidental," Dean said with a furrowed forehead. Tim says the pipeline runs along the edge of that area?"

"It does," Hanna said, conceding a nod.

"That's a goddamn sin," Dean said with the slightest flush of anger. "To plow all that up...The roads are the worst part. You try to tell people, but all they can see is the money. The money will be gone in a heartbeat, but those goddamn roads will be there forever. People say it's only desert. Like it can't have value because it's desert, but it'll have a lot less value once it's plowed under and torn-up by pickups. They treat it like a playground that can only bring them pleasure when they're destroying it. Sure, I'm as bad as anyone else, moving cows through there, but we always grazed them as fast as we could, and once it was grazed, we moved on, because for us, there was an inherent value to the health of the land. For industry, the land is more valuable once it is ruined, because then there's nothing left to fight over."

Dean's discourse left Hanna feeling guilty of collusion. "I know," she said, "we dug a lot of test pits, and altered the line several times, to whatever was the best alternative. The original route went right through the middle that area. It's rich in cultural material, and we had to go slow through there. The line is now farther to the east.

"Well, I wasn't saying that as any kind of a barb. Not at all. I know that you do all you can do. It's the entirety of the area that I was commenting on. That's what needs to be protected, and our money systems cannot allow that. An expansive, intact environment like that is their boogey man. Even if there were nothing out there of any value at all, they would still be compelled to destroy it." They were quiet for a moment until Dean spoke, his face flushed red. "I shouldn't talk about those things. It disrupts my serenity," he said with a sly wink.

"Don't I know," Hanna said. "I lose entire nights of sleep over it."

"Did you sleep last night?" he asked.

"Yes, all the way through. I snuck away pretty early."

"I noticed," he said. "I was right behind you. They were having fun, but I had visited all I needed to. The rest was going to be nonsense." After a moment he asked, "Where's that dog?"

"Bob? He thinks he's guarding Tim, and Tim's still sleeping, although he's usually pacing before the sun's up." They both looked over at Fred's shop but saw no one stirring.

"Tim's a hungry one, isn't he?"

"Yeah, I don't believe in types much, but he's a hungry one."

"He could make a million, if being hungry and ready was worth something." Dean shook his head, moving his chair a bit further into the sun.

"But he wouldn't know the value of a million, would he?"

Dean laughed, and held up his hands in confusion. "What the hell am I supposed to do with this?" He laughed, imitating Tim. "No, it wouldn't help him at all. He would just go looking for another million, or another woman. No offense, but it would be like him with women, wouldn't it? He suffers and pursues, and then as soon as he catches up, he is off after a new one."

"Why is that?" Hanna asked, "Why do men do that?"

"Why do people do that?" he said, looking into her eyes.

She smiled, "I don't know, I don't know at all…"

"It's a mystery. But without hungry people, nothing much would happen."

"Bad things happen because of hungry people," Hanna said, surprised by his statement.

"And a lot of good things."

"So…Dean…what made you change so much?" Hanna looked him in the eyes, and she could see the deep twinkle that said she had hit the nail on the head. This is what they came to talk about.

Dean spread his hands before him in silence and in great satisfaction for a moment and smiled. "Well, I guess it's the same old story of emptiness and meaninglessness, debauchery. Maybe I was eternally *hungry*. In a word, I was bad, and I knew it for a long time, but I also knew that I wasn't meant to be that way. I mean, many times you can look at a mean, ignorant sonofabitch and know that that is who he or she is supposed be. But I knew I shouldn't be that person. And I hate to say it, but it was drugs that brought me around."

"What, like antidepressants?"

"Oh, hell no!" Dean said looking offended. "Listen, I was about as empty as I could be. I was drinking too much, and it brought me no joy. Womanizing shamelessly, and it brought me no joy. I knew good, caring women, and I discarded them. I was letting my place go, and that is about the worst of it, because I have what very few people in the entire world have, and I was neglecting it. Anyway, one day a friend of Fred's shows up from down South with a load of peyote," Dean sat up and leaned toward Hanna.

"Oh boy, you should have seen the fire dancing in those days, naked, painted bodies leaping 'round the flames, the whole shebang. Big Wally gave me some, to help me from my spiral, and he tried to inform me on how to use it, which I dismissed in the most arrogant way, choosing to stick with my whiskey and bitterness. Then, one day, for whatever reason, I took all he gave me and went for a ride on my favorite horse. Well, of course that was a dumb thing to do, because I thought I was just gonna get a little buzz, like dope or booze, you know? Then, before you know it, I'm puking my guts out, fall off my horse, and bingo! I'm hit with a crashing wall of total unreality. I was crawling through the sagebrush like a spastic reptile, with my horse following along, wondering what the hell I was doing."

Dean finished the last sip of his cold coffee and paused, looking at Hanna as if he was wondering if he should continue. "Well, I asked my horse to stay with me, and he said, in whatever method of communication we were using, 'Of course I am staying with you, you dumbass!'"

And that was it. This act of selfless loyalty made me weep like a baby. His unquestioning, unconditional commitment to me, made me see everything that I was and I was not. I sat up and realized that all I thought, and all I wanted to have, all I hungered for was false, and all I thought I was, was wrong, the reasons why I hated people and things—pure fantasy. I realized that I was not a nice person, and the people I chose to be around were generally not nice people.

But most importantly, I realized that I was meant to be a kinder person. That was the message to me from a whole day on my belly in the sage. Be a nice person. Be compassionate. And so that is what I have tried to be. I'm glad that I learned that before I started dying, because now I know that it was an authentic change and not just something that I clutched at to win some karma on the other side." He looked at Hanna and beamed a huge smile, showing his large irregular yellow teeth. His eyes were glassy from the joy that filled him from telling this truth, and Hanna blushed in the presence of his moment.

Hanna started to giggle and then she started to laugh. At first she could control it, but then she fell into a long silent suffocating laugh at the idea of a misguided cowboy having a soul-shaking revelation while crawling through the sage, and then being enlightened by a horse. Dean was stunned for a moment at what he thought was rudeness, but he fell into laughter with her as the cause of her laughter became apparent.

"Sorry," Hanna choked, "but did he say, 'D-d-e-e-eaan you du-u-u-mb a-a-asss! Bhe-he-e-e ni-i-ice!'?" Hanna imitated the horsey voice and began laughing again silently as tears ran down her cheeks and Bob haw-haw-hawed along with her.

"Well, that was about how it all happened," he said catching his breath. "The sum of what I understand of my time on earth comes down to a brief communication I once had with a horse."

A long pause ensued and both sat looking out at the idyllic morning. "I could see how you could spend a lifetime here," Hanna said.

"It wasn't hard. I had a lot of work, and it wasn't all here, we had cattle everywhere, up in the high country, down in the desert. There were lots of us—cousins and uncles. Granddad. The whole shebang is gone now, all split up; too many mouths to feed. Too many needs and not enough profit." He smiled and caught Hanna with a mirthful glance.

Rhonda came out on the porch and stepped into the sun, rubbing her arms. "You guys aren't having any fun out here are ya?"

"Did we wake you up?" Hanna asked feeling guilty.

"No, I've been up for a while. The bed just felt good this morning." She looked at Dean sternly. "Did you eat Dean?"

"I did, my dear."

"Enough?"

"Probably not."

"How many coffees?"

"One, my dear."

"Meds?"

"No, love," Dean shot Hanna a quick guilty glance. "I better get on that," he said, taking Rhonda's hand.

"I'd say so. Eat something with them."

Dean pushed himself up from his chair, gathered their plates and cups from the table and walked stiffly to the kitchen.

When he was gone, Rhonda pulled back her morning hair. "He'll be OK for a while, but he'll start to fade and then smoke a bit. That makes him better, but he won't be right until this evening." Rhonda looked at Hanna and smiled. "You've actually caught him at his two best times of day. He reads through the worst parts of the day."

"Is it hard on him—is he really uncomfortable?"

"Well, not with pain, but he worked hard all his life, and now he can't; he struggles with that, you know? Look at the stables and barn. It's all overgrown and going to hell. You don't notice it because you never saw it before, but I know it bugs the hell out of him. We can't bale hay anymore. We have to lease all that out, which won't make us enough to pay our taxes. People help a lot, but that kinda sticks in his craw."

"Will he have enough money?"

Rhonda guffawed, "Only if he dies," and then she covered her mouth, embarrassed. "It's still hard to say that word. I know he bandies it around like it's the same as moving to the next town, but it's still hard for me to say it."

"It's a permanent word, but he seems OK with it. Is he really?"

"He is. He's an odd person, and I think that his enlightenment; his change to being a more reasonable person really helped him. He used to be a grouchy, ole hell-raiser. I think if he was still that person he would be very bitter."

"You have to wonder if one would have happened without the other."

"Well, I am not one to wonder about all that. Things are what they are; some are good, some bad. We just deal with it." She looked stern, and then reached across and took Hanna's hand. "He finds people like you, and he knows that you're one of a kind. I think that's how he'd always win some people over in the wink of an eye—and now he's even less inhibited about it." She looked for words for a minute. "Thanks. This time spent with you will do more than any of that smoke or those meds. He'll be right all day." She looked away for a minute and then stood up, as if she had something to do. Hanna looked at her and saw how Dean loved her, how she was short but wiry in that way that some cowgirls aged, her long, brown hair was peppered with grey and pulled back in a who-cares way that set off her hard, intelligent face. "We have to meet with the family lawyers— Dean'll have a little shit storm to weather today. He'll do fine though."

"Should I be going?"

"No hurry, he's on his way out. But I need to go put on my serious clothes."

Hanna stood to offer her hand, but Rhonda stepped past it and hugged her firmly. Rhonda leaned back and caught Hanna in the beam of her brown eyes. "You stop and say hello when you're back!" Then she turned and went back into the cabin.

Hanna leaned against the porch post wondering if she should leave, but then Dean was back, and he had his white hair slicked down and an old cowboy hat in his hands. He was dressed neatly in jeans and a button-down shirt, but he did have on a pair of Birkenstocks.

"Have to go meet with the 'liiiiars' today. The nieces and nephews want a bigger piece of the pie. But that has nothing to do with you. Thanks for the mornin'. I'm glad to have a good talk. And I knew you'd want to see Dad's spear point." His eyes were glassier than they had previously been, and Hanna noticed a tremble in his hands; he seemed ten years older.

"It was my pleasure, Dean. Good luck with everything, I really enjoyed our conversation."

"More like my pontification. I hope I didn't bore you. Sometimes I go off..."

"Not at all. If I was bored, you'd have noticed."

"Well, you're a good listener—here, this is for you. Open it later sometime when you have a few moments." He handed her a tiny box that was taped shut. "It is nothing, and maybe it is foolish. You can disregard it if you want."

"Well, thanks, and I promise to stop when we're back." She hugged him and felt his body, it was as slight as Rhonda's had been.

By the time she got to the bottom of the steps he had gone back into the cool of the cabin and she felt a small panic at his absence, as if his presence could have assured her that mortality wasn't so. Hanna stood there for a moment and felt the potency of the morning sun, and then started back up the road to Fred's.

* * *

Tim and Hanna said good-bye to Fred and left the Meadows by the old road that was now neatly paved. They were soon passing trophy homes in the river valley, they stood empty on verdant lawns with well-bred horses idle in their irrigated pastures. On a steeper hillside were more humble homes where the working people lived, caught in their symbiotic relationship with the wealthy. Tim read

Hanna's mind, "It's a market of vanity and illusion. The only real job that the working people have is propping up the vanity of the wealthy and feeding their illusions. Look, all that was created were empty spaces. Large geometric vacuums."

"With horses."

"Well, yeah, with horses. Where would the trainers be without the horses?"

"On welfare."

"No doubt."

"Where're the horses Bob? Gitt'em Bob!!" Hanna shouted. She leaned back as Bob's head shot out the window, barking viciously, as the horses at the fence spun and ran off, bucking and tossing their heads.

"Good job, Bob," Hanna laughed. "Get Tim, Bob, get Tim! He's getting gloomy about rich people."

Bob shot back beside Tim and licked his face, leaning hard against him.

"Hey now, I'm driving, that's enough."

Bob dropped back down on the seat, claiming as much space as possible.

They passed a Chrysler SUV with a quiver of kayaks on top, and then a tight pack of bicycles ridden by lean young men in racing togs. In Gros Ventre, people sat on the deck of a tiny café and crowded the parking lot of a larger restaurant. The lot was filled with BMWs, Audis, Hummers, and shiny new American pickups as long as chrome locomotives, pulling rafts and river dories, tractors and horses. Mountain bikes and road bikes zipped across the road. Serious looking riders put their heads down and peddled hard. A blonde, slender Athena consorted with a chiseled Adonis in the dust of what was once a small, poor town. A mountain gear shop had wheeled out racks of skis and cold weather clothes on sale from the previous winter. There was 60 percent off all winter gear.

"That's quite a sale."

"I must say," Tim said flatly, establishing the fact that

they wouldn't stop.

Some dreadlocked hippies walked a tightrope and juggled on the lawn of the last modest house left in town. Tim honked and waved to them.

"Kindred spirits?"

"Something like that," Tim said.

"Don't bet on it," Hanna snorted. "Look at the campervan in the driveway. It's not what you're going to be driving anytime soon."

"Where are the poor people?"

"Working, and out of sight."

Hanna was surprised that it only took two hours to leave the mountains and be out in the desert and plains again. The mountains hung behind them like a green façade that ran through the desert. They drove quietly, each in their own thoughts. Hanna could see that Tim was happy. She knew that this was the type of life he wanted, events and action— the kind of life that you could tear the top off of and drink down and have it run off your chin. They had climbed mountains, tramped under the hot sun, shared food, drink and high spirits with people who cared for them. They had made love, and Hanna was still stunned by that. They had journeyed. Hanna felt the deep satisfaction also. And she tried to find something that was wrong such a life, but could not, because perhaps it was enough. "This is enough," she said.

Tim and Hanna had left too late to drive all the way to the survey camp that same day, so they chose to stay in the desert. They had both worked in the area before and decided to drive out where some dunes crept across the long, flat, hardpan. They stopped at a lonely gas station and Hanna went inside to forage, while Tim refueled the truck. She managed to find some milk and cornflakes, but the rest was pretty grim. There were frozen burritos and pizza, little camp tins of beans and franks, jerky, pickled eggs and sodas by the 12-pack, and hardly anything else that even Tim would consider edible.

The large young woman at the counter rang up Hanna's bill while Tim washed up in the restroom. "Where are ya headed?"

"Out to the dunes."

"Oh," the woman said, "there's a hotel just another 40 miles down the road."

"Yeah," Hanna smiled, trying to engage her. "We know, but we both worked around here, and we thought it'd be nice to camp."

The woman raised her eyebrows and straightened her checkered smock. "Well," she smiled, "I'd take sheets over sand any day. Why, you don't even have a real camper. You want me to warm you some pizzas. We have to-go boxes."

Hanna passed on the pizza, but bought Tim a smorgasbord of pickled eggs, jerky, and a bag of chips, with a six-pack for an appetizer and dessert.

"There ya go!"

Hanna drove the truck while Tim munched away with a beer between his knees. She did eat some chips, but couldn't even watch as he ate the pickled eggs.

"You sure you don't want any?"

"No," she smiled. "You go ahead."

"You hit the nail on the head. Gas station food, beer, driving a truck out to the sand dunes."

"A cute, little designated driver at the wheel," she said.

"Bingooo and giddyup! Let's take this fork up here."

They pulled into a hardpan cove between some dunes, shut off the truck, and stepped out into the warm evening. They stretched as they walked around, and Tim let a hand full of sand run between his fingers.

"No wind," he said, holding up his hands.

Hanna dropped the tailgate of the pickup and lifted the door. "Kind of messy back here," she said as she rummaged through the cooler.

"We can just sleep out on a tarp. There's no wind or bugs." Tim listened to the quiet. "Nice temperatures, and the moon'll be half full."

"Yeah, let's do that," she said, pulling out a folded canvas tarp. "This will be so much better than driving all the way tonight. There's no work tomorrow anyway."

As Tim arranged the pads and sleeping bags on the tarp, Hanna was watchful to see how closely he aligned the bags, ready to chastise any assumptions, but he did well and she smiled, "You're a good boy."

After she ate a foil packet of party leftovers from the cooler, they went to the top of one of the higher dunes where they could see across the basin. The dunes only occupied a few square miles, but it was obvious how the wind picked up the sand from the toe of the dune and then deposited it at the head, leaving the hardpan of the basin behind spic and span. The dunes traveled across the basin in this way until they met the foothills where the sand was permanently deposited and eventually vegetated with grasses and sage. Hanna could see all the way to the buttes that marked the foothills where she had found the Clovis point. She felt the silhouettes of the buttes watching her there. Like an indifferent Mordor, spying on her from across the basin, inviting her to come claim her prize.

Then it was dark, and she spun 360 degrees without seeing a light. They sat at the top of a dune, her sitting between Tim's knees. He put his arms around her. She felt content enough to sit there all night.

"I feel anxious to look out at all this, Tim. I used to feel that this desert would always be here like this, and now I feel like it might all be borrowed."

"I know exactly what you're saying. I worry more for the desert than for the mountains."

"Do you believe the rumor that CanAm is only a scam to clear the way for another pipeline to carry Tar Sands oil down out of Canada?"

"I don't know if I believe it, but I have heard that, even from the petro people. I wouldn't doubt it."

"We aren't helping—with our work, are we?"

"We aren't stopping anything, that's for sure," Tim

sighed. "I might not do gas and petroleum jobs anymore."

"Someone else will. And they won't take the care that we do."

They sat in the utter silence without moving, and Hanna hunted for a way to lose the momentary heaviness.

"Have you ever tried meditating, Tim?"

"Not very seriously."

"Did you have much luck?"

"Not really, but I did feel better afterward."

"Yeah, me too. I just can't seem to get to the nothing."

"I know," he said, "I am always too anxious for something to sit and wait for nothing."

"Sure would be nice though—to get there."

"We could try here. It's a very Zen-like place. Two archeologists sitting on a dune...."

"Sounds like the lead to a joke," she said, and something about her statement reminded her of Paul. Her anxiety spiked for a moment and the deep sorrow she felt with Dean swept through her chest again.

"Let's sit for 20 minutes."

"Neither of us has a watch," Tim said.

"Yeah, but look at the moon! It's just peeking over the hills."

"OK, when it's one hand high we'll stop."

"Alright Tim, but you sit over there so I'm not distracted." She moved a few feet to a more level spot in the sand and wriggled her butt down to support her back. She crossed her legs, let her palms fall to her lap, and looked around. She saw the dark and purple land against the night sky. The stars were fully out and the gyre of the luminous, sinuous billow of the Milky Way was clear.

Warm air made her breathing routines easy and natural, and she began her mantra of 'This is enough.' She settled deeper into the sand and let her mind go, drifting from issue to issue, but letting them pass. She didn't fear them, but saw each one as it was and let it pass or linger. And then she

began to catch a moment, or be aware of an empty moment
that was just sand and warm air and stars and darkness. But
then it would be her checking account, her truck, or Gina, or
Catherine's eyes, or Dog killing snakes, or men lurking in the
desert, or Paul. Where could Paul be? But then
there…there…there it was…. What was that? Just there ….
Don't chase…. Be here…. This is enough, this is enough….
She opened her eyes. And there was the moon two hands
high, and bright on her face, Tim's blue silhouette standing
on the crest of the dune, and she smiled at his impatience.

With the moon illuminating their way, they climbed and
descended dunes well into the night, before they returned to
their camp beside the truck to sleep. Hanna drank down a
liter of water, brushed her teeth, and undressed in the warm
desert night, shook the sand from her clothes and folded
them on the tailgate. "No sand," she demanded. She stepped
onto the tarp where Tim had carefully arranged the pads and
bags together.

He waited awkwardly in the night, his farmer-tanned
torso gleaming fish-belly white against his dark face, arms
and legs. She stepped into his arms, and they kissed. She
pressed her body against his and felt the coolness of their
skin as they touched. "I want to think about things Tim. I
don't want to make love to you right now. But we can sleep
together. Can we do that?"

"No, we need to grab at each other like monkeys."

"Maybe in the morning," she said.

They lay naked and still on top of their nest of bags and
pads, with the entire universe above them. After a while she
reached out for his hand, but all she got was a twitchy
response, and she thought that she could hear the rhythm of
sleep in his breathing. A cool breath of air slid across her
body as she pulled a sleeping bag over her and arranged a
pillow under her head.

When they hit the highway in the morning, Hanna's hair
was still wet from the shower bag. "So Tim…how are we
going to handle this when we get back to the camp?"

"I don't know. Are you committed to just women?"

"Don't be irrelevant."

"I'm not. I just don't know if you want to continue with me. Are you alright being with me?"

"Of course, I'm alright being with you, but that doesn't mean I took the cure or anything. Can we be OK like this?"

"Well, yeah."

"Well, yeah," she mocked, "So…?"

"So, what are we going to do at camp?"

"Yeah, what are we going to do at camp? What if Gina's there? Are you going to act like nothing happened?"

"No…that won't do."

"So what will you tell her?"

"I haven't thought about it. I have no idea what you want with me."

"Don't play games, Tim! Don't make me say and ask everything! I can't say what I want yet," she said blushing. "But we should have a plan."

"I really don't know, but sleeping with her at this point would be false, and I'll just call it off, which is what she might want, after visiting what's-his-name."

"OK, well, let's cool it for a while. I mean, you're right." She stared out the window a moment and thought she might have caught a glimpse of a pair of sage grouse. "It would be better if we weren't together in camp. That would be awkward, but you can decide if you should be sleeping with Gina or not. I can't have any part in that argument."

"I'm good with however you want it to be, Hanna. I can be your lover, or we can just continue as we have in the past…But you're who I want to be with, that's all."

Hanna couldn't speak for a second, and had to stare out her window. "I feel the same. Let's just be normal and see what we have to deal with when we get there."

Search

Hanna was the first one up at camp on Monday morning. She was awakened by the 'feee, feeee' call of chickadees in the trees outside her truck, hopping around on the topper above her head. When she got up, she saw Bob sitting beside Paul's camp tent. He came over immediately and leaned against her leg. It seemed to her that something was missing as she looked around, but all appeared normal. She noticed that the new kitchen tent had been moved closer to the trees. That was different. She saw the beer cans around Hugh's fire pit and knew that the boys had taken a few moments to reaffirm their friendships and tell some lies about the weekend's conquests and defeats. She thought that if Tim even hinted at any intimacies of their weekend then they were through.

She sat in her chair beside the tailgate as she boiled water for coffee and waited for the kitchen tent to open up. The cook Karl hired came with a huge tent, gas camp stoves, tables, everything. She did a great job, Hugh had said as he patted his stomach.

Hanna sat in a heavy fleece jacket with her coffee. The ground was dewy, and the sky was painfully blue. Chickadees were hanging around in the hawthorn bushes beside her. They weren't feeding. They were just hopping back and forth calling out their 'chicka-dee-dee-dee'. Hanna looked at them. The one closest to her turned its head so that its eye looked hard into Hanna's eyes. It didn't move. It just sat and looked at her with its black, bird eye.

"What's your problem?"

Bob made a gruff pass at the bird, and it flew to the top of the hawthorn and chica-dee-dee-deed, a bit more. The others flew away, but that one stayed.

It's a black-capped, Hanna thought. Where have all the mountain chickadees gone?

Bob sat beside her, and Hanna caressed him. He wasn't usually so affectionate. He had his pride and was generally not a lap dog.

The cook opened the door flap and rolled up the sunny side of the tent half way.

Hanna took this as her cue, and she walked over with her coffee.

She ducked into the tent, "You open for business?"

"You hungry?" the woman smiled a good-natured smile. "Name's Martha, and you?"

"Hanna."

"Look's like I got my work cut out for me if I'm gonna put any meat on your bones!"

"Well," Hanna said dumbstruck, "I look heavier in winter clothing."

"No doubt, no doubt. But sit down. It'll be a few minutes. I got eggs, toast, bacon and pancakes. Of course, there's cereal and oatmeal. There's a bit of fruit, but it's too damn expensive and doesn't last in the heat—just give me five more minutes."

Hanna sat, breathing in rich lungfuls of frying food and the deep, musty smell of canvas.

Hugh came in without his hat on and his hair all here and there. "Hanna...Tim said you guys had a good trip!"

She looked at Hugh and saw that his smile was benevolent. "Yeah, it was a fantastic trip. We got up a stellar route on a peak, and visited some fun people."

"I've been over there to the Meadows. Some kind of community, eh? Great people." Hugh shook his head. "Too bad about ole Dean. You know, my uncle used to run some cows down south of there, and I remember running into Dean out in the desert. I was a lot younger than him, and more of a pickup driver than a cowboy, but he was always a friendly and sincere kind of guy." Hugh stared off for a moment. "That was a long time ago." He turned to the cook. "Martha, you got any asphalt in the coffee urn?"

"About a half mile."

"That's all I need," Hugh laughed, and his belly bounced beneath his bulging T-shirt. "What's to eat?"

"Same as yesterday and the day before, and the day before that."

"Well, that's fine as long as there's bacon." Hugh looked over at Hanna. "Gina's not coming back, you know?"

Hanna covered her shock as best she could. "I didn't—I thought something was up when she missed the last session."

"Yeah, well some gal had to leave a curator position to have a kid, and Gina's taking it over for good—a small archive of historic and prehistoric stuff on campus. She's gonna move in with what's-his-name."

"You know, I couldn't remember his name even when I was looking at him!"

Hugh laughed, and Martha joined in.

"And his face is as common as his name," Hanna added.

Martha lifted the lid on the warming pans, and Hanna and Hugh picked up a plate each and went down the line. Alise and Sarah came in, followed by Dog. Hugh filled up his bucket-sized cup with coffee and sat down at the table. Hanna sat with him and Dog; Alise and Sarah sat at a different table. Hanna was hungry and tucked into her scrambled eggs and toast and a small bowl of oatmeal. Dog and Hugh went heavy on the eggs and bacon.

"Paul's not back," Dog said, looking at Hanna.

Hanna jolted her head back. That's what's missing, she thought, his car. "Wow, Paul's always here. Did he call Karl?" Hanna asked, looking at Hugh.

"This is the first I've heard of it," Hugh said looking at Dog.

"Well his car's not here," Dog said as if it were obvious. "And he'd be moving around by now if he was here. He's always about the first."

Hanna stepped out the door of the cook's tent and looked at Paul's tent and where his car should be.

"This is no good, no good at all," she said.

"Don't worry, I'll call Karl as soon as the office opens. Paul's car's pretty old…it could be anything. He's probably holed up in a hotel somewhere, waitin' for a mechanic."

"It's nothing, Hanna. I'll call the office." Hugh repeated. "He might even be there with Karl."

"Yeah, no problem," Dog shook his head, dismissing it.

Tim came in holding an empty coffee cup, going straight to the urn. "Did you guys notice that Paul's car isn't here?"

Hanna spent the day with Tim, Alise and Sarah. They returned to the last place she had worked with Paul. With so many artifacts on the surface and below ground, they were now digging deeper test pits. Almost every hole turned up something. At noon, they quit digging and wrote-up forms in the shade of the large cottonwoods. Alise had gotten over her insurrection and was more pleasant to work with now, and Sarah was as sunny as ever. She had kept her young lover for a week or so, but she let him go when she found out his age. She crowed, "He might have been young, but he was talented!"

Alise rolled her eyes and growled in disgust. "Wait till his mom and the sheriff come after you."

Sarah looked up, shocked, as if she had heard a loud noise.

Alise took advantage of her astonishment. "Yeah, it's serious business to mess with a minor."

Hanna came to Sarah's defense. "Don't worry, Sarah, the sheriff would be patting him on the back and buying him beers to press him for details."

Alise conceded, "Isn't that the way it works."

Tim was out measuring off the edges of the sites with a compass and a hundred-foot tape.

"CanAm isn't gonna like this at all," Alise said, looking at Tim.

"Leon Filmore already caught wind of it," Hugh said.

"He was here the day before yesterday, pacing and wringing his sweaty hands," Alise said. "Sarah calmed him down and invited him to eat at the tent, which was way worse than just having him drive away in a funk."

"Oh, the poor guy's just doing his job," Sarah sighed.

"Well from now on you can help him do it. He'd probably like that, the way he was staring at you," Alise waved her hands at Sarah. "You can have him! He is too slithery for me."

By the end of the day, it was obvious that most of the artifacts were confined to the immediate floor of the tiny valley or the benches above the river.

"They were camped on the benches away from the bugs in the summer, and down in the valley all winter," Alise concluded.

"There's room for the pipeline, but it won't go the easiest way."

"Never does, that's why Karl gets all the money. Imagine what a no-win situation he's in? They pay him to go survey and find stuff, but they're really paying him not to find stuff, so when he does find stuff they don't want to hear about it." Tim shook his head.

Hanna held up her arms to the valley, "Imagine what every extra working day costs them."

"See," Tim said. "They'll have to comply here, because this area is relatively populated, and even though this is a private inholding, we're technically on the reservation. If this were out in the desert, they'd just plow right on through. Once Karl, Hugh and I drove way out to start a survey line, and they already had the whole thing dug."

Alise blinked incredulously, "What did he do?"

"He couldn't do a thing. He just wrote them a bill. If he'd complained, no one would've done anything, and plus he'd lose the next bid if he pushed it." Tim looked at them and spoke seriously. "There's nothing regulatory about what we are doing. We're really just facilitators."

"So did they get away with it?" Alise asked.

"No, they had to pay up, but the fines are figured right into the bid." Tim smirked.

"I know," Alise said, "I met some BLM guys who have

seen pipelines and drilling fields progressing on satellite imagery that have never even been proposed yet. When they raise a stink about these activities, someone from Washington, DC calls and tells them to shut the hell up!"

As they came down the road back to camp, Hanna was expecting to see Paul's car. Her heart raced a bit, and she went immediately to Hugh's teepee. He looked at her and said, "There's no word. He never called. We don't even know where he went. We called the sheriff, and he said that technically he's not even missing yet, and he won't be until tomorrow morning."

Hanna had to choke back her panic. She knew that this was desperate. She paced for a moment, Paul had told her where he was going. She tried to remember. Of course to the mountains, but where, where specifically? He was going to.... She couldn't remember. "Dickenson Park," she shouted, "he was going to Dickenson Park. That's where he was going in!" Hanna clapped her hands. "He was worried about his car making it."

Hugh and Hanna went out to call Karl, and Hanna spoke because Hugh was too passive. It was late, and Hanna was half surprised when someone answered the phone, but she knew what was happening when Donna picked up. "Hello," she said curtly.

"Hello, Donna, this is Hanna, I need to talk to Karl—it's important."

"Of course it is," she sighed, and then a moment later Karl was on the phone.

"Karl, I know where Paul went in. It's Dickenson Park. That's the northeast access to the mountains, but before the pass on Highway 70."

"OK," Karl said casually, "I'll call first thing in the morning."

"Can't you call tonight?"

"No, I can't. He is not even missing until tomorrow."

"Listen, there's a Forest Service work station just a mile from there. They could go over to check on the car in like ten minutes. Have the sheriff radio the Forest Service. It would take someone over an hour from the highway, and you know that they won't drive up there."

"OK, Hanna, if you don't call by eight and tell me he's with you, I'll call. I know some people in that office, and I'll get the message out. That's all we can do for now. He'll show up. Don't worry. He is a cautious guy."

Hanna knew that 'a cautious guy' was code for 'pussy'. She wrestled with her rage for a moment. "Karl, be at the office at lunch time, and we'll call you then."

"No problem, I'm up to my armpits in work. I'll be here." There was a pause. "What the hell did you guys tell Leon Filmore? He was here wheedling all afternoon."

"Jesus, he's back to you already? Well, what can we do? We can't just make the whole site go away."

"That's what he wants. I'll talk to you tomorrow."

Hugh stopped for a six-pack on the way back to camp, and he and Hanna each opened one once they turned onto the long dirt driveway to the camp. Hanna could see that Hugh was worried too, but he predictably told her not to be. "For all his weirdness, Paul does not go looking for trouble."

"I know, I know, but he also never misses a day of work, and he's always where he should be when he should be. Has he ever screwed up anything as long as you've known him?"

"No…nothing."

"If it was Tim, or Gina—Gina didn't show up for a whole session—I wouldn't think twice. I'd say, 'Oh yeah, they'll show up.' But not Paul, he would never not show up."

"I know, I don't like this at all." He took a long pull from his beer.

Dinner was subdued, but Hanna was impressed that Martha kept her in mind when she laid it out and the meat was on the side, not stewed into the meal.

Tim kept a low profile, sitting with Hugh and Dog around the fire ring. Bob moved back and forth restlessly. He stopped often at Paul's tent and sniffed skittishly, then he would come back to Hanna and sit close to her.

"It's not good is it Bob?"

Bob shifted his weight around from foot to foot and tucked his tail around his butt.

Hanna slept very little and was up before light. She couldn't stay in her truck shell another minute. She knew that Paul had not arrived because she would have heard his car in the night. Still, she looked around at all the places he might have parked. She sat bundled in her fleece jacket, brewing her coffee, waiting to call Karl, waiting for anything.

Finally, she took her headlamp and went to Paul's tent, unzipped the door, and stuck her head in like a burglar, afraid to be discovered. Inside, she saw about what she imagined. He had a cot with a small pillow, instead of sleeping on the ground. His clothes were neatly folded into wooden boxes and milk crates. He had a small shelf made of bricks and plywood, with stacks of dog-eared novels and notebooks.

There was a small stack of topographical maps on a shelf. Alone beside the others was one map by itself. She opened it up and could see that it was the topo for the Dickenson Park access. She sat on his cot and spread it out, finding the trail at the end of the road, the one he must have taken. But that led to multiple trails and those trails to other trails, and to other trails. She knew that his time was limited, so she looked at what would be possible in just a few days. The map was annotated with pen markings of Xs and arrows, and Paul's neat script. She knew that Paul would prefer a loop, rather than out and back.

The established trails offered little in terms of a loop, but one of the routes marked with Paul's arrows went up to the main pass and crossed a plateau before dropping into Carson Canyon, the next canyon south, parallel to the canyon that left from the trailhead. She found a lower pass that would have led Paul back to his car. She could see it very clearly; she knew Paul, and she could see him there in the canyon. She knew where he was. She looked up, and Bob was staring at her through the door, but he was not looking hopeful.

Hanna choked down some oatmeal and ate a couple of bananas as soon as the tent opened. She took some toast with her, leaving before anyone came in. She went back to her truck and began packing. She waved down Tim as he went to breakfast.

Hanna was stuffing her sleeping bag down into the bottom of her pack as he came over. "I know where Paul is," she said aggressively, "I have a really good idea."

Tim knew better than to disagree with her when she used that tone. "Let me grab some food—make me some of your coffee, and I'll be back."

Hanna looked at the map again, but all she could see was the route Paul would have taken. Bob was shifting his weight and stepping in place.

Tim came back with a full plate of food, and he looked at the map Hanna had spread across the hood of her truck. He could see the way immediately. All the other trails went off in directions that never circled back. Paul was always talking about good loops he had done. He liked hikes that took him across plateaus and along routes rather than well-traveled trails. "If his car is there at the trailhead, we'll know where he is." Tim agreed. "My pack is still packed. All I really have to do is take out the climbing gear. My truck or yours?"

"We'll take mine," Hanna said. "The roads can't be that bad.

* * *

They were on the highway for three hours before they turned off onto the dirt road to Dickenson Park. Hanna's truck was much smaller than Tim's, and they had to go slowly.

"I have a hard time imagining Paul here with his car," Tim said.

"I know. He's so anal about it."

"It even still smells like a new car inside."

"He won't allow anyone eating inside it."

"That is so freaking weird. What American guy doesn't eat in his car?" Tim shrugged.

"Paul."

"If we get there, and his car isn't there, I am going to be pissed you know."

"Well, stand in line with Hugh and Karl. Karl was so pissed he hung up the phone on me when I told him we were leaving today. He didn't say I was fired, but I wouldn't be surprised if we were."

"We?"

"Well, are you at work, or are you with me?"

It took another hour to reach the workstation. Then, they topped one last hill and came down into a parking lot, and there was Paul's car with two others and a couple of pickups. There was also a ranger's truck with a guy inside doing paperwork and talking on the radio.

Hanna walked over and tried Paul's door, but of course it was locked. She looked in through the window and saw nothing that would lead her in one direction or another.

The tall, lanky ranger came over immediately. "You know that vehicle? You know the owner?"

Hanna stepped forward and reached out her hand. "Hanna," she said and read his nametag, "Ranger Dave," she smiled.

"That's me," he said.

"Just a guess," Hanna smiled again, she was trying to appease him because she wanted no problems with her search.

"So, you know Paul Zotti?"

"Yes, we work with him."

"And you drove all the way here? He's only just been reported missing."

Tim followed Hanna's lead and spoke in a friendly manner. "Well, we know him, and if you knew him the way we do, you would know that something is wrong."

"So to be missing is out of character?"

"Completely," Hanna said, nodding her head.

"He wouldn't just extend his trip, or rest a sore knee?"

"No, he would crawl out with his last breath before he would not fulfill a plan."

"Did he tell you where he was going?"

"No, not really, just here to the Dickenson Park access."

Dave nodded, "He hiked alone a lot?"

"Almost exclusively," Tim added. "Fast and light, you know."

"Any ideas then, where he might have gone?"

Hanna pulled out her map and spread it out on her hood.

* * *

The ranger tried to dissuade them from going to look for Paul, but legally there was nothing he could do. It was early afternoon by the time they left. Without heavy climbing gear and just three days of food, they were able to cover a lot of miles, making it to the timberline by nightfall. Bob the dog seemed to sense the point of the mission and appeared to have Paul's scent from time to time.

Once they had their tent set up they went out and hiked around to see if they could find any sign of him. But in a wilderness where everyone was exhorted to leave no trace, they found no trace. Hanna caught sight of bright yellow, behind a screen of stunted trees, and went charging into a clearing, scaring a couple who were squatting over a small camp stove beside a yellow tent.

"Sorry," she said. "I thought that you were going to be someone else."

The couple had not seen anyone who matched Paul's description nor had they seen any lone hikers at all.

At camp, Hanna and Tim cooked a light meal and got in their bags just at dark, to start out as early as possible the next morning.

Lying in the dark Hanna said, "You know, Paul was hinting around for me to come with him on his trip."

"Don't even start with the guilt and second guessing

Hanna. That's not gonna lead any place good."

"I know, but if only we could read the signs. I kept having these feelings while I was talking to Dean."

"You can't drop everything anytime anyone hints at you to do something. What if Alise and Sarah hinted at you to go manhunting in Rocket City?"

"That's not the same thing."

"No, but if you didn't go with me to Averoso, and I got into some kind of trouble, you'd have no responsibility in that situation. Just don't go there, it isn't healthy and it isn't helpful. You can't spend your life trying to read signs. That's what crazy people do!" Tim put his arm under her head and pulled her close. "Let's just sleep and be refreshed in the morning. I'll light the stove early."

Hanna slept off and on and was only deeply asleep by the time Tim lit the stove just before dawn. They were away in the first few minutes of full light. Up at the end of the canyon Bob sniffed around in some large boulders, and Hanna found a spot where someone had obviously pitched a camp, and there were tracks there that seemed just a few days old. It was a tiny grotto, just enough for a small camp. Bob was interested in the site, sniffing it out. He sat down in the copse of boulders as if he were certain of something.

They consulted the map and then started climbing the pass at the head of the valley. Up on top, the trail continued on for many miles, but one route quickly forked south, down into Carson Creek after just a few hundred yards. Hanna was sure that was where Paul had gone. They let Bob go first, but in the rocky, sandy soils he seemed lost. They found simple cairns and a vague trail that marked the route across the plateau to the next drainage. They stopped before descending, and drank water and ate dried trail food. The canyon below was the twin of the one they just climbed out of, but the snowfields in the cirque at the head of it were much larger and the canyon itself was higher. The sky was clear above them, with a few passing clouds.

"It would be nice to be here in other circumstances," Tim

said.

"I know. It seems so odd not to be here with such a mission."

"Well, let's go find him and kick his ass for scaring the shit out of us!"

"He'll wish he was never born."

With light packs, they moved quickly down the switchbacks and came to the most obvious ford on Carson Creek. Bob was excited again and he began sniffing and barking. He stopped and put up his hackles for a moment and then sat down. At his feet, was a single, black, synthetic glove leaning against a rock.

Hanna's heart leapt. "Look, a glove, it looks like someone just dropped it. The grass is still holding it up off the ground. Bob knows. He knows...."

Bob sat still and made no attempt to retrieve the glove.

"Let's leave that there and look at the map one more time," Tim said. "Let's be sure he didn't go up and over the end of the canyon in any other direction—because we're only guessing at the obvious."

On the map, there was no good reason to go to the head of the canyon. There were some vague possibilities, but mostly dead ends. And none of the possible routes would lead him back to the car.

"I'm certain that he went down the canyon. The route over and back to the main trail is just three miles from here." Hanna looked down the canyon. "You can almost see it from here. It probably goes right over that saddle."

They took care wading the icy, rushing creek and set off downstream. The nature of this canyon was different than the one they had ascended; It was steeper, and more alpine. The bedrock was more extensive and closer to the surface; the floor was tilted, and all the water was forced to this side with the creek. With larger snowfields, there was much more water. Even the side creeks took skillful boulder-hopping to navigate. As the creek began to roar, Hanna was filled with apprehension. She soon noticed that the closer they got to the trail on the other side, the more impossible the creek looked. They passed one last creek and then found themselves at the only conceivable way over. "This was where he would have had to cross," Tim said, and Bob picked up a scent in the grass.

They walked a mile downstream, but the trail completely disappeared into a dog-hair pine forest with blown-down trees. Bob found nothing down there to pique his interest. They came back up to the most logical crossing and settled on the downed trees that met in the middle of the creek. That was also the point that most interested Bob.

Tim stepped up on the log that met another in the center of the frothing current. "This is crazy—would he do this?"

"I don't know. I just don't know. I would say no. But I've never done anything like this with him."

Tim stepped down from the log, dropped his pack and started back across it. As he edged his way out, he could see one of the branches ahead was freshly broken. At the base of it there was a skewered, torn piece of fabric. Tim dropped to his knees and stretched to pick it off the branch. It was the kind of heavy polyester that mountain clothing might be made of.

Hanna was sitting on her pack with her head in her hands. She knew. She could see, because it did look like maybe you could do it, and then there was the vague trail right there on the other side. She suddenly felt so tired; she had thought that this might be one time of incredible luck. She thought that they might find that his car wasn't even there, or that they might find him with a twisted ankle, or broken bone, or they might find someone who had just seen him. None of that was true. She knew that he was in the creek and sighed in defeated exasperation.

Tim came to her and handed her the fabric. She held it and rubbed it between her fingers and thumb. She didn't recognize it, but she knew it was his. As she touched it she could feel that it was Paul's. She showed it to Bob, but he looked away, wanting nothing to do with it.

"Hanna, I am going to walk down the river to try to locate him. I don't know if that's possible, but I should try, so we can tell the rangers when we get back. Maybe you should stay here. Are you good with that?"

"I'm fine. I don't want to find him. Not if he's not alive. I'll wait here."

When Tim was gone, she moved her pack out into the sun and took off her wind shell. It was such nice weather to have such a heavy darkness on her heart. She felt a few sprinkles of water. She looked up and saw that a single cloud was dropping a light shower from a mile away. There were river cobbles all around her, and she bent to arrange them into a cairn. She built a small one and then knocked it over and built a taller one. She knocked that one over and build one that was even taller, that came up to her thigh. "I'm sorry Paul, but that was such a stupid thing for you to do."

Tim came back and Hanna could see in his face that he had found him. He sat next to her and touched her knee. "He's dead Hanna. He's still underwater—but there's no way we can get to him. He's hung up in a log jam."

* * *

Hanna didn't cry over Paul, she missed him and mourned him and looked for him in the morning, and waited for him before she left camp, but she didn't cry. It seemed heartless to her, and she didn't understand it. She sat having breakfast in the mess tent, and there was an odd silence between her and Martha. She knew that Martha would have loved him and fed him well. Hanna could see that Martha missed Paul. She missed the very idea of Paul.

Hanna was surprised at how undone Sarah was by Paul's death. Alise had cried for a bit, but Sarah could not be consoled, and she had cried nonstop for hours. Karl came and checked her into a hotel and sent Alise to look after her. Karl and Hugh offered the rest of the crew a few days off, to get themselves together, but in the end, most chose the distraction of work. Hanna saw Hugh's fire late in the night and caught him with a beer in his hand and tears in his eyes.

"The dumb ass," he said, embarrassed by his tears.

Hanna hugged him awkwardly and kissed his bearded cheek. There was nothing left to say, and Hanna stayed with her hands on his shoulders, the two of them staring into the fire.

Purgatory

The massive site Paul and Hanna discovered at the north end of the survey halted any further progress there, as all the digging and testing completely blocked the right-of-way. Alise and Sarah stayed up north for a while to finish digging and writing-up forms, while Hanna and the rest of the crew drove south to continue with the southern portion of the survey north of Rocket City. With dry weather and smooth sailing, the CanAm pipe-laying crews came marching on. The southern end of the pipeline was now within 15 miles of where Hugh and the survey crews had left off before heading up North.

Fat-Assed Brad had been working with Karl in the office for a week, but he came out and joined them to speed up the survey for surface artifacts and any random test pits. Karl had replaced Gina with Christian Chris, who had worked with them the summer before. As his moniker stated, he was a serious Christian, and a very abrasive one. Hanna couldn't work alone with him, and Dog once dealt him a violent, glancing blow with a shovel. Chris had a lurking air about him. Tall and stooped, with lank brown hair, he stayed within a pace or two of whoever he was working with, which annoyed Hanna no end.

After her narrow escape from the two roughnecks in the desert, Hanna hung close to the guys, and Tim made himself available when she needed a good run.

Hanna checked into the same room that she had shared with Gina. She still fretted over the questionable sanitation of a standard hotel room, but ruled out sleeping in her truck. God only knew what kind of deviants and serial sickos patrolled the parking lots in the middle of the night. The population of drillers and pipe crews in the area was too transient. It would be better with a room, even if it used up most of her per diem money to have it to herself every night.

Tim had begged her, and Hugh had forbidden her to run alone down there. Hugh had pounded his thick index finger on the hood of the Bronco. "No more running alone," he said with his most impotent authority.

The crew headed out in a three-vehicle convoy early in the morning to the end of the old survey line. They traveled on the wide gravel roads and then narrower secondary dirt roads. The traffic was heavy, with large tanker trucks and trucks laden with piping and diesel engines, thundering along with general contempt for anyone who tried to share the dusty roads.

Long, king-cab pickups carrying crews of men to the patch passed by. Heading to the sweet spot where the massive geologic anticline brought the porous gas and oil-bearing sandstone within drilling distance of the surface. And though many wells were 15 thousand feet deep it was still close enough to yield massive profits to those who tapped into it—as long as gas and oil prices stayed high.

At first they came to the older, derelict machinery and pumps of the original petroleum booms. Some of the machinery functioned, while the rest of it sat rusting like the huge, broken toys of apocalyptic giants. As they approached the patch they came upon a few newer rigs, and then rig, upon rig, upon rig, forests of rigs with flaming vent stacks, burning off noxious and unusable gasses. Then, the surface was webbed and tangled with the pipelines, hoses and machinery that accompanied the rigs. The desiccated corpse of a wild horse clung to the edge of the road and watched the traffic go by with pitted eyes. Someone had put a beer can in the sorry curl of its bony hoof.

They passed the CanAm pipeline crews; long queues of digging machines and men laying out pipe across the ground that Hanna's crew had previously surveyed. Passing through the patch, the air was filled with dust and the stink of drilling, the sky warped and shimmered with the flaring of toxic gasses. There was the sulfur stink of rotten eggs and burning diesel. Men stood and watched the little convoy pass, like sheep passing wolves. Hanna wondered if Dog had his pistol in his boot. Her hand slid down, and she felt the pepper spray under her work-shirt.

Dog felt her anxiety, "How would an Indian and a white woman do stranded out here?"

"Is this a good day to die?" Hanna asked him with a nervous laugh.

"Don't worry," Dog said, "the white men will protect us," his voice was heavy. "See, you guys yell at me for throwing garbage out the window, but what does it matter with all this going on? Who owns this? It doesn't belong to any of us. This isn't my land or your land. Even though it's public, they just plow it under and stir it around and leave all their broken wreckage around, and spill all their shit everywhere, but if I throw a bottle out the window, then I am one screwed up Indian." He laughed his wicked laugh, and Hugh smiled and looked at him in the mirror.

"That is quite a speech for you, Dog," Hugh said.

"Well, it's the truth isn't it?" he said, appealing to Hanna. "You know everyone talks about pristine blab, blab, blab. But what the hell is all this? This about trashes everything if you ask me. When people talk about hell—this looks about as close as you can get. The things that they mess up here go way, way beyond decency. It's in the air, the water and the soils."

"That about wraps up what I was thinking. We're all responsible for this," Hanna said.

"And if you even mention it might be bad, then you're liable for a serious ass-kickin'," Dog scowled. "Like we all got our rights? Unless you're in opposition to the patch."

"Don't get too dark. I'm not in the mood for that right now," Hugh said. "Let's just survey some miles, do some work, and go back and have a beer."

"And look at some girls?" Dog said, punching him on the shoulder.

Hugh was embarrassed, "Maybe not tonight Doggie."

"Do you guys want to stick some twenties between my

tits?" Hanna asked caustically.

"Come on Hanna, we've had that conversation already," Hugh grumbled.

"No, really, you could stick some fifties in the crack of my ass, and I'd walk around like a rooster," she said, laughing too loudly at the vision in her mind, suddenly feeling angry.

Dog pulled out his wallet, "All I have are tens!"

Everyone laughed for a moment and then fell quiet.

They passed a tanker truck bogged down in sand. It was chained to two monster pickups. All three trucks were throwing sand and dust into the air. The pickups were backing up and lurching forward, backing up and lurching forward. Excited men surrounded the commotion, shouting and running like boys.

"That's enterprising," Hanna harrumphed.

"Undaunted American ingenuity," Hugh added.

At the north end of the patch, they pulled out onto a long flat pan. The heat shimmering up from the ground assaulted them when they got out of the air-conditioned Bronco. Karl and Chris arrived in another Bronco and were walking the line ahead of them with a transit, checking coordinates against what CanAm's engineers had surveyed. They set up blue flagging as the parameters for their part of the survey.

As they were far from water, Hanna guessed that there would be insignificant numbers of artifacts. But in the context of thousands of years, and with changing climates, an archeologist could never really tell what he or she might find. All it takes to change the cultural deposition of a landscape are a few decades of rain. With a good spring here and there, anything was possible. Dog had a snake-stick with him; and the small green prairie rattlers seemed to be everywhere. He wasn't out of the truck ten minutes before he was beating some invisible victim beside a clump of greasewood. Hanna guessed it would be an uneventful day for everyone except Dog.

It felt cleansing to be out in the searing heat, to walk and forget about things for a few hours. There were horned larks, and a few meadowlarks in the open alkali pans, singing away as if this was Gods' own Eden, and they were personally blessed with it. There were small desert sparrows now and then, but Hanna ignored them, because they irked her with their bland sameness. Occasionally, she saw lizards and tiny desert chipmunks zipping along from bush to bush, and horned toads stood like statues, believing themselves invisible as she passed.

The team was far enough from the patch that they could no longer hear the pounding of huge diesels or the roar of tractor-trailers. Occasionally they could see plumes of dust, or they'd catch a sulfurous stench floating on the breeze. They all wore chemical badges that changed color if they were overtaken by a cloud of hydrogen sulfide, which could kill them quickly. Hugh wore an expensive gas detector that would give off a piercing wail, and they had gas masks in their packs, but in reality, if they were overtaken by a large, dense cloud, they would be dead in a moment, their lungs dissolved into foam.

To Hanna it seemed like they were traversing the landscape of a malevolent, alien planet, a desert prowled by heavily armed barbarians in huge machines. And these were the vanguard for another much larger machine that mindlessly carried out its work without regard for a thing that got in the way. These machines were simply part of a crude, and yet sophisticated, titanic, multi-celled colossus that crept inextricably across the steppes. Hanna could see the machine hatching from the ground already formed, magnificently terrible, like Blake's Tyger.

"What dread hand and what dread feet," she said aloud, to hear the words.

The plants, people, animals, and minerals that fell before the beast were churned to sun-baked dust and then left in a pluming track. Huge, leachy, clanging ticks sucked oil and gas from the earth, farting out flaming candles of noxious waste.

When Hanna looked up, she had no idea where she was or how much time had passed. She was out in the middle of an endless pan and had to turn around 360 degrees before she could pick out Karl and Chris with their surveying transit. But were they before her or behind her? She turned again and saw the crew distantly behind her. She knew where she was, but had no idea what they were doing. They were out scurrying around below the feet of financial and mechanical giants politely wielding words like compliance. Should she curtsy and ask, "Do you comply, Sir?"

"This is bullshit," she said. "A bunch of bullshit."

She walked for the rest of the day and saw nothing but her own feet walking across desert hardpan. She forgot about artifacts and flags and the parameters of the survey and searched for Paul.

* * *

Hanna never quit expecting Gina show up at her room— knocking too hard, and then her comic leer on the other side of the gap of the chained door. Hanna wondered what Gina's frame of mind might be. Was she happy, or trapped, or happily trapped? Maybe Gina was ultimately right. Get a soft job at a university. Find a mate and move in. To hell with all this living out of tents and trucks and hotels! Enough was enough. There were other ways to do archeology, other than petro surveys. None of it paid as well, but she didn't have to do contracts for gas and oil companies. The real world wasn't far away. Get a house and move on. She took a shower and flopped on the bed, surfing through the channels with the remote, but it all seemed foreign to her. Somewhere, she had lost the context of it. Even the dead among the wreckage of a war zone on the news could coax no emotion from her.

Hanna turned the TV off and put lotion on her face and hands. Then she arranged her own sheet and sleeping bag on top of the bed. She looked out the window hoping to see

Gina's, or Paul's, car. She knew she would never see Paul's car again. It had been towed off and parked with the other impounded vehicles of unfortunate circumstance.

She needed to run. There was no doubt she could run hard tonight. A bulging bubble pressed against her chest. If it were unleashed, her feet could fly. No one could catch her. Her head would float. That ancient person would possess her. She would travel in time; fly. But Tim was gone, and he had told her to wait, "Don't go! I'll be back. I have to shuttle a truck with Dog."

However, that is exactly what she did. She drove east, and parked on a long, high butte where she could see in all directions. There were no plumes of dust out there, so she drove down and parked in some broken badlands with many gullies and arroyos, where she would have better luck outdistancing a vehicle. All she would have to do was cross and re-cross the drainages, and no truck, or anyone on foot would ever be able to catch her. She ran without mishap. She ran inspired, fast, indefatigable; she chased jackrabbits and mule deer. She ran until she detached from the world, until she changed to that other person; she ran as the small brown girl. She ran at brutal speeds until the copper taste rose in her lungs, until her legs were beyond hurting and sweat blinded her eyes, until she pulled the hills down with her legs and she ran across the tops of the buttes. She ran until she staggered to a stop and all she could muster down to her truck was a very slow jog.

Anti-climatically, she went downtown after her run to look for food, driving through the strip. It was late in the evening, but traffic was heavy as she passed by the convenience stores, gas stations, the Lightening Lube, Tobaccomart, Big Barrel Liquors, Redman's Pawn and Bond, NAPA Auto, Big G's Tires, and Thomson's Salvage Yard, with its acres of wreckage and spirals of razor wire. She drove past the fast food joints for hamburgers, pizza, chicken, tacos, and Chinese. The buildings suited the corporations—come buy our food, or goods and get the hell out!

A weak thunderstorm came through and stirred up dust devils as it rolled along, the rain barely making it to earth. A gust caught her truck and gave it a shudder and then moved on to clap a huge piece of sheet metal clinging to the corner of TJ's Sports Bar. The wind swept on down the street, picking a huge piece of cardboard up out of a ditch and sending it dancing across the crowded five lanes of traffic, only to flap and struggle against a wall of hurricane fencing.

She turned off the strip and went to the historic, old town center. It was just a few blocks long, where the buildings were traditional red brick, and some were wood—mostly bars or saloons. There was an expensive steak house in the old railroad hotel. She knew it was exorbitantly priced to keep out the roughnecks who had simply had a good week. She could get a good salad there, but it would be way too expensive, and there would be nothing to go with it. She circled the few downtown blocks in her search, wondering where was there a real restaurant that served real food, cooked by real people?

In the end, there was only the Don Pancho taco franchise, where she got two bean burritos and a side of rice. She knew that the beans contained lard, but she was starving. There was nothing to drink other than soda, so she went to the largest convenience store on the strip and hunted the soft drink refrigerators for something that contained real fruit juice. She stood in line with her apple juice and a bag of almonds, in front of a rack of magazines and studied the pictures of semi-naked women rubbing themselves against monster trucks and muscle cars from the seventies. There was one entire row dedicated to the gun industry. Most covers boasted handguns and military-style weapons. Women in negligees held large pistols defending their apartments from white-trash methheads, and minority rapists. 'Nobody gets up from a .45.' 'Buy Your Kalashnikov Now, Before They Are Outlawed.' One cover showed a casually dressed, well-groomed white man with a leashed, lunging Rottweiler in one hand and a large black handgun in the other, 'Guns and Dogs, The Total Defense.'

She thought of Tim, singing his version of, 'America the Beautiful', "*Oh bellicose for egregious crimes …*"

The sun was down but the temperature was still warm, and there was a humid texture to the air after the passing squall. She went back to the hotel and ate at the little picnic table out front. Tim came over with a box full of books. "I thought you might get bored without Gina and…" he left Paul's name hanging in the air, setting his books down in front of her.

Hanna picked through them with one hand, the butt end of her burrito in the other.

"Mostly they're pretty trashy, but there are some good ones. Good biographies, histories."

"Genghis Kahn? Hannibal?"

"Well, I am a guy."

"No biography of Jane Austin, or Virginia Woolf?"

"There is a See-mus Heaney."

"I don't know who she is," Hanna smirked.

"I recognize the name…but the guy at the used bookstore acted like she was quite a treasure."

She nudged him roughly, "Thanks. Did you know that *Seamus* was a man?"

"I guess that would explain the guy with the eyebrows on the back cover." Tim looked at her oddly for a moment. "You went running didn't you?"

"I did," she said, knowing she couldn't fool him, "and that's all there is to it."

"All right then, I guess I won't lecture."

"It won't do any good." She said frowning sarcastically. "You want my second burrito?"

"Oh, Don Panchooo!" he said with affected machismo. "Don't mind if I do." He took a bite, "Hey, there's no meat in this!"

Hanna laughed. "That crap they put in there isn't meat either!" She sat for a minute and then said, "You know, I never did a lot of stuff with Paul at night, but this is when I miss him the most. I miss him not being here. I miss not eating with him. I miss not being able to knock on his door."

"I know. We always tried to get him to go to the bars with us. He would blush so hard in the strip bars. Dog would secretly tip the girls to put him on the spot. I think he really liked Paul, even though he'd never show it. Sometimes you could see that Paul just liked being with us. He would still get carded! And we'd tell the barmaids that his IDs were fake." Tim and Hanna smiled quietly for moment.

"Do you miss Gina?" she asked. Tim raised his eyebrows in surprise, and Hanna laughed. "Don't worry, it's not a trick question."

Tim laughed for a moment. "I do. I do. You know, she was difficult sometimes, but she could be so funny, and she really wasn't looking for much from me."

"No, I think that was pretty obvious! But, I miss her too. She was such a pain in the ass, but she was entertaining. I wonder what her guy thinks about her moving in?"

"Wow, that could be a shocker for him."

"You wouldn't like that too much would you?"

Tim raised his eyebrows and shook his head, no. They sat quietly as Hanna looked around and took his hand when she saw no one there. "Thanks for giving me space. I am still struggling a bit."

It was almost dark now but the summer twilight would last for a while yet. "If you don't let anyone see you, and you bring your sleeping bag, you can come sleep in my room tonight."

Tim smiled broadly, "I thought you might have moved on, after everything that happened."

She squeezed his hand, "No, don't be stupid."

* * *

The entire crew drove north the next day, farther away from the patch. There were not going to be wells or transmission stations along this portion of the survey, simply pipe. Without any extraneous activity to survey for, this section would go quickly. They would walk the line, pick up and bag any cultural artifacts, register what they found on the forms with corresponding coordinates, flag the location, and continue on down the line. The desert in this section was healthier and more pristine; perhaps it received a few more inches of rain than down below. The sage was taller and greener than the low black sage down around the patch. There were also tall native bunchgrasses here. Hanna could see the big fuchsia blossoms of the prickly pear cactus as they drove down the road. With more vegetation, there were good numbers of sage grouse and white-tailed jackrabbits, antelope, and birds of prey. She relaxed a bit and enjoyed the ride, looking out at the crumbling, distant buttes, displaying their grey, red and brown layers of geology. Now and then, they passed low-grade coal seams on the hillsides. Hugh liked to point them out. He had written extensive reports on which seams had been mined by homesteaders. One cold day, they started a small fire at lunch and got some of the coal to burn.

There were wild horses up here; and they were very wary of people. The stallions made huge pyramids of manure on the tops of hills, and they seemed to understand the significance of roads because they would also make their dung cones wherever roads intersected. Hugh mentioned that they were often shot.

"Why do they shoot horses?" Chris asked, looming over Tim, a step behind him.

"Because they can," Dog replied.

Fat-Assed Brad and Chris walked the west side of the survey, Dog and Hugh on the east, and Tim and Hanna came up the center. They walked part of the line that passed by fresh springs that bubbled up at the base of the chalky bluffs they had seen from so far away. Even with more vegetation covering the ground, they found much more cultural material within a mile or two around the springs.

They found two nice examples of Eden points. These were not as stylized as a Clovis or Folsom, lacking the central flutes, but they were generally longer and thinner—more modern, at about nine thousand years old.

Hugh and Hanna marked them precisely on the map, confirming their exact position with a compass. They put them into tiny plastic bags and wrote the coordinates where each point was found on the bag. Feigning interest in a flowering patch of prickly pear, Hanna walked off the survey line and pushed one of the points into the earth, it was too perfect to be cataloged upon a shelf.

"It's very easy to believe that this has always been desert." Hugh assumed the role of the sage. "But the climate was always shifting back and forth. In fact, this could have been prairie only a few hundred years ago. It is almost prairie now. It's certainly steppe more than desert. Up in the buttes there are huge, old, dead trees that haven't yet rotted away. What climate did they germinate in?" He looked at them all, as if what he was asking was very important. "Then, the baking temperatures of the altithermal period drove all these people to the very highest environments for at least two thousand years. These points fall into that timeframe."

He stood with a wand of a pencil in one hand and a compass in the other. Everyone took this as the cue to stop and listen. "There are historical accounts of these springs being very important. There was an ephemeral creek that used to flow all the way into the dunes down below the patch. It has disappeared lately, but it ran periodically, even back in the early sixties. They used to drive cows out here in the spring and when they hit the dunes they'd turn 'em east to meet up with the Blue River. We'll pass the old line camp when we move after lunch."

Hanna watched Hugh carefully labeling the plastic bags he was preparing to file away. She knew that Hugh desperately wanted to understand the people who made these points. He wanted to sit with them around a tiny fire in the tall sage as the sun fell, and share dried venison and simple tubers, and then walk for a full day under the arcing sky. They would walk for days and days and days within their home range, maybe they'd run. Perhaps without horses, there was less contact among the tribes. Maybe back then there was less competition and they greeted each other fraternally when bands met in this dry ocean. She knew that Hugh would give anything to be with them.

They reached the cowboy line camp after lunch. It appeared suddenly over a small ridge on a bench, out of the wind. The vegetation was much greener at the camp than in the surrounding sage, and it was clear that water seeped up into the surface soils. Three sickly, stunted cottonwoods barely survived around a crumbled well and a collapsing one-room log cabin. A small log barn, barely large enough for a few horses seemed to be held up only by the power of it own volition. The site was well preserved. It was a camp used by cowboys herding their cows way out here, or an emergency shelter for travelers just passing through.

They poked around and picked up bits of metal, horseshoes, a pulley, nails, the rusting lid of a jar. Hugh went through the garbage pile behind the barn. He arranged the broken glass into different piles and time periods—purple glass, blue glass, glass with bubbles, glass without bubbles, glass with seams, glass without seams, crockery, ceramics, and porcelain. "It's all here in the midden," he said proudly. "All the most telling artifacts come from our garbage heaps." Hugh dug down into a layer of wood and tin roofing and came out with a few pages from a girly magazine.

"That's why I don't worry about my garbage," Dog cut in. "I just want future generations to know what I was up to."

"Look at this! 1962." Hugh looked over the top of his sunglasses at the fine print at the bottom of the page. "*Sir Magazine.*" He carefully turned through the brittle pages. "*Adam Magazine*—it's a man's world." Hugh held up a yellowed, blotchy picture of a well-muscled man standing next to a woman in an evening gown, whose top had all but fallen away, exposing every possible inch of her breasts except her nipples.

"I bet these pages got a lot of traffic."

"I don't even want to think about it," Hanna said.

"Sin is nothing new," Chris added beatifically.

"Women seem to have had bigger tits back then," Dog said thoughtfully.

Everyone turned and looked at him for a moment, even Chris.

"Well, it does seem that way," he said defensively.

"Maybe they just photographed the bigger tits more?" Brad asked.

Dog walked away with his snake-stick, rattling it through the brush.

They left the line camp, and descended into a broad valley where the land had been pushed around by heavy equipment at some point, and then abandoned. Odd pieces of machinery had been left behind. More recently, the local, off-road vehicle crowd had made use of the area. The hills were torn and scarred, and there were racecourses ripped through the sage. Hanna's senses started to tingle as she entered the degraded terrain. She walked with the guys to what must have been the center of the motorized festivities.

There were multiple vehicle tracks. They appeared to have had all types of vehicles. Everywhere, tire tracks spun in circles, and a huge fire ring in the center of the dirt showed that they had burned everything they brought, leaving the debris toasted and melted—bottles, camp chairs—lumps of plastic things twisted into grotesque forms. There were huge bones with meat hanging from them, crusted over like jerky. Bob the dog was wagging his tail, approaching it hopefully.

"Hey, Bob! No!" Tim scolded.

Bob lowered his tail and ears and slunk away grumbling.

"What the hell is that?" Hanna asked.

"Did they kill a cow?" Brad asked, wrinkling his nose.

"Maybe an elk," Dog said. "There's that desert herd."

"So, what the hell?" Hanna asked. "Do we need a police escort just to come out on public lands? Are we going to find murder victims out here?"

The ground was littered with bullet casings of every caliber. Hugh picked one up and peered at it over the tops of his sunglasses. Shattered things that had been shot lay on the ground like battle victims. Shot-up appliances ventilated with a dreadful hail. Washing machines and stoves had stood before a firing squad.

"Did they really hate these things?" Hanna asked naively.

"Of course not," Chris answered in a huff, pushing back a limp hank of hair. Tim snickered behind his back.

"Then why bring appliances out here to shoot them?"

"Because they can," Dog said dryly.

They inspected a row of pallets, set up with targets on them. They walked over and saw the classic circle targets. Then, there were human targets of public enemies, like Muslim terrorists with turbans and bombs, Chinese and Russian soldiers; there were black thugs and Chicano thugs, white-trash thugs.

"What, no Indians?" said Dog holding up his hands in confusion.

"Brad, you're the anthropologist. What do you think of this, it seems pretty ritualized?" Tim asked.

Brad waddled about for a few steps, taking in the carnage; he laughed nervously, more loudly than he should have. "It's almost like art, isn't it? An expressive and frustrated condemnation of the modern world, one fashioned with brazen crudeness."

Dog caught his meaning and nodded knowingly. Chris and Tim stood with their mouths agape, smacked by his insight.

Hanna walked over to the next set of pallets, and the targets on these were pornographic centerfolds. The armed partiers had shot the heads, breasts, and crotches to pieces.

"Do you think they hate their minds or pussies more?"

she asked Hugh, who had just walked over.

"I don't think they hate either," Hugh said gravely, "but they feel they have to destroy what they can't control."

"I'll agree with that," Hanna said.

She turned to Tim, "You should write a song." She started bobbing her head back and forth, punkishly, *"Tits tits tits, pussy pussy pussy, kill kill kill."*

"I think you nailed it all by yourself," he smiled uncertainly.

"It could be their anthem," Brad said, as if struck by the brilliance of it. "The complete enculturation of uninhibited, violent misogyny."

Chris and Hugh shifted about uncomfortably, and then Dog asked, "Nothing about killing Indians? We are the invisible minority," he said, shaking his head.

They walked through the scattered trash and bullet casings, across the wash, and out of the immediate party zone, passing piles of dirt. There was a small foreign sedan behind one of the mounds, shot to pieces, with the windows smashed out.

"Stolen," Hugh said. "I heard they do this. They drive them out here, beat them to pieces, and then strip everything of any value."

Tim looked in through the window. "Even the seats are gone."

"Think we could find them at Thompson's Salvage Yard?" Hanna asked.

"You bet!" Hugh said.

They left the car and climbed a low hill. When they topped the bench they spooked a cloud of ravens and magpies.

"Well, this isn't gonna be good," Dog said.

"Holy shit, why do I feel like I'm going up a jungle river?" Tim asked.

"So are we about to find green lumps of rotting hippo meat over there?" Hanna asked.

"I just hope it isn't the owner of the car."

The sage was tall and it was hard to see. They soon caught the whiff of death, and took a few more steps. They could see a huge, furry white belly and sighed with relief when they knew that it wasn't a person. They took a few more steps and saw that it was a young horse.

"Probably a yearling," Hugh said.

There were holes across its chest and neck. One of the back legs was gone.

Tim raised his hand in the air, "You know, maybe we are going in the wrong direction here."

"I second that," said Hanna. "I think north might be the better choice."

"Well at least we know what the meat and bones in the fire were."

"Indians don't even eat horses," Dog said.

"They must be from the South," Chris said, stooping his lurking frame even further to get a closer look. "I heard they eat horse meat in Louisiana, or maybe it's Florida. It's legal there."

"They eat anything down there," Dog said haughtily.

"No, they eat everything down there," Chris corrected him.

"They don't eat horse meat in Louisiana! OK?" Hugh said, shaking his head.

"I am just telling you what I heard from the mission people."

"They probably ate it when they were all high on Jesus," Hanna laughed and everyone joined in. Chris walked off, sulking at the blasphemy.

They turned away cautiously, expecting a horde of screaming thugs to jump up shooting.

"I just don't want to be eaten by the confederacy of the cannibalistic undead." Tim laughed.

"Yeah, it's time to get the hell out of Zombie Town!" Dog said.

They walked back to the Broncos and drove a few miles north, finding nothing but beautiful sage steppe. The pall of negative vibes lifted as soon as they got out of the Broncos and set off to the north. They topped a rise and Hanna could distantly see the buttes marking the way to the boulders where she had hidden the obsidian Clovis point. She felt like she was becoming a satellite to the buttes. She circled them at a great distance. She thought she would go there someday and try to climb them. There was always a little sneak route to the top of desert buttes.

Granite bedrock came to the surface near the line, and there were potholes in it. "This is where they used to grind the Indian ricegrass into flour," Tim said. "I've heard of this place and looked for it a few times."

Dog picked up a smoothed rock from the grass, "Here's one of the grindstones."

They passed the piece of smooth granite around. It had a polished face on its blunt end for pounding, and one long edge for making long grinding strokes to yield flour. The stone rendered everyone reverent and pensive. As they passed it around, each person could feel exactly how it fit their hand and how it was used. When they were done, Dog kicked a shallow hole with the heel of his boot and partially buried it. It was something a collector would want to have. Hanna and Hugh recorded the site, even though it was off the line.

The afternoon was nice, hot, but not too bad, and they covered a lot of miles. The spring rains had been sufficient to make the desert vegetation healthy, and there had been summer thunderstorms to help things along. Verdant swales of vegetation showed the location of water seeps. There were doe antelope up here and though they had dropped their young long ago, they still kept them hidden in the tall vegetation. Coyote tracks marked the sand, and golden eagles patrolled the sky, searching for tiny, young fawns. The crew never saw any young, but the does barked nervously at them from time to time, or ran close by, trying to lure them away when they neared the hidden babes. A weasel stood proudly on a rock with a mouse in its jaws and considered the crew.

It hid the rodent down a crack and then came back, moving closer to them in fearless curiosity.

Every direction was nothing but rolling hills and sun-dappled ridges, low buttes, and long mesas. Once a little distance obscured the details, even Zombie Town, down below them, appeared beautiful and inviting.

There were junipers and limber pines up at the very top of one of the ridges, and they sat there filling out paperwork and cataloging what they had found. Hugh had discovered a very long, elegant Eden point, and he passed it around before he cataloged it. "Imagine how large and heavy the dart would have to be to accommodate a head this size?" He was talking about the atlatl darts. Hugh had an atlatl himself and he took it out at times to throw the fletched darts at targets set up on hay bales. He was a decent shot with it. At 20 or 30 yards he could hit a paper plate every time. It was nothing amazing, but with a lifetime of accumulated skill and cooperative hunting strategies, it would be a substantial survival tool. "With a hunting party of six or ten hunters doing a group stalk, or a game drive, they must have been pretty successful."

This day had been much better than the previous and Hanna felt energized enough to run a few miles back to get one Bronco and then shuttled Hugh and Dog down for the other two. Chris went back with Brad, and Tim and Hanna took the third.

Hanna got out and ran for eight miles while Tim hung back a hundred yards so she would feel like she was running alone, but he kept an eye out for traffic. Tim hated to have to be so cautious, but that was the world they lived in.

He puttered along, listening to the oldies' station, thankful for plenty of water and a good air conditioner. He watched Hanna run across the flats, and he was impressed with her. He had run at different points of his life, but he had never run like that. He was driving ten miles an hour, so he did the math and figured that she was probably running a mile every seven minutes or so. Nothing too special, but at that speed she would be able to compete with a lot of people. At a race pace, there were not a lot of people who would want to compete with her.

Hanna spooked doe antelope, and they raced her for short distances, trying to draw her away from their young. Hanna would speed up, sprinting, while they comfortably loped along, and then they would rocket off at an angle. She would slow to almost a walk after sprinting, and then set off at a good pace again. Even at this performance level, he could see how poorly evolved humans were. Only with intense knowledge and trickery would she be able to survive out here.

After an hour, she flagged him down, shimmering with sweat, streaked in dust. He handed her a water bottle, and she drank it down. She stretched and walked around, high stepping and kicking herself in the butt with the heel of each shoe. He helped her get the five-gallon igloo cooler up on the hood. She told him to turn around and took a short sponge bath, mostly to cool down. She dried off with her jogging top and shorts, put on a fresh cotton T-shirt, and her long work pants.

"There! Fresh as can be!"

"I'd never even know you ran."

"Do you want to run now?"

"No, I'm good. I'll just drive back."

"Well you should run with me sometime."

"Oh, yeah I will…sometime."

"Tomorrow?"

"Maybe, if it's not too hot."

Calling

Tim left at the beginning of the next break. He had committed to meet a climbing partner in one of the deep canyons down South. Hanna didn't want to intrude, and Tim had hinted that his friend would probably be angry if he showed up with Hanna, expecting to climb as a threesome.

Without Gina and Paul, Hanna found herself with nowhere to go. She called Meg at her store, and Meg told her not to come because her lover was in town. She did make a point of saying, "But that doesn't mean quit calling."

Hanna sensed that Meg's situation was less than ideal. Hanna didn't tell Meg about her current affair with a man. That would take some time to relate. It was something she'd feel out at a later date.

Hanna sat on the tailgate of her truck considering the honesty of the situation. Am I a perverse abomination? What am I doing? Hanna blamed Paul's death for her anxiety. If only he hadn't crossed that creek. She was haunted by the image of him crossing from one log to the next, stooped over, moving from branch to branch. If she had gone with him, or if she had invited him to come with them, if he had chosen any other route, he would be here, and she would be at peace.

Without a better plan, Hanna drove to the northern work camp. She knew that everyone would be gone. Only Karl and Hugh would be there trying to figure out what to do with the cultural material in the valley. The fact that it was private land within the boundaries of the reservation created a bureaucratic limbo. They were trying to get around the existing right-of-way.

She parked her truck in her spot under the trees and went over to talk to Martha who was just packing up to leave for a while. "Well I guess they're gonna shut her down, and I think I'll go home and see the ole man for a bit. I'll be back in about four or five days. Karl and Hugh and the girls will be workin' by then. The guys are up at what they are referring to as Hanna's mess."

"It's not my mess. Paul's the one that found it all."

"Yeah, well it's bad form to blame the dead." She caught Hanna's eye, as she thought her humor might have stepped out of bounds.

Hanna laughed to relieve her apprehension. "Well, I think I'll heap the blame right back on him."

* * *

"The earth doesn't lie does it?" Hanna asked, walking up behind Karl.

He looked up from a trench. "Not even for the sake of an argument." He smiled, "This is fairly massive isn't it?"

"That'd be my guess. Too bad it wasn't just me. My holes kept coming up empty, but then Paul hit the jackpot every time."

"Stupid Paul!" Karl growled in jest. "Oh well, all we can do is give this area a wide buffer and move on. CanAm will have to approach some of the landowners for a different right-of-way. It's all just grazing and sketchy oat and wheat fields. Someone will grant an easement to make pocket money. It's obvious that it can't go this way, or at least not until we mitigate and catalog everything. Really, it's CanAm's problem, not mine."

"What do you think the reservation people will say?" Hanna asked, to put it out in the open.

"That's the great unknown. You just can't tell," Karl said, shrugging his shoulders.

"How so?" Hanna asked.

"Well, because it's private land, they might not choose to fight that battle. I'm sure they know about this already. There has been a car around that looked like the tribal elders, and there were some lawyer-looking guys with them. They never talked to us though," Hugh said holding up his hands.

"It's not like it's Mesa Verde or anything. Sites of this size are still pretty common"

"I get the feeling everyone is just holding their breath," Hanna said. "So what will you tell CanAm?"

"The truth. It's up to them to decide how to move forward," Karl said. "Either move the line or dig and catalog the entire camp. Those are the only choices. That's the way the easement is written."

"But they'll shoot you as the messenger," she winked.

Karl raised his eyebrows and made his mouth into an O. "Not me, I'm gonna send Hugh."

Hugh laughed until his belly shook. "I'd do it just to see the looks on their faces."

Karl changed his tone when he spoke to her again. "Hanna, you can stay if you want, but I'd say it'll be at least five or six days before we come to any kind of decision and put people back to work."

Hanna stayed and helped for a day, since she was there, and then left, as it was obvious that she wasn't needed. She drove south and east to the southern end of the range where Paul had died. She knew It'd be crowded that far south in the range, but cool up high, and she'd have many running and hiking options. At first, she felt lonely traveling by herself, but warmed up to it as the day wore on. She stopped in Lawson, an old cow and mining town that many young people were recently calling home. She got a good cup of coffee and vegetarian lunch at a bakery. There was an outdoor shop next door where she bought some socks, a new headlamp, and some energy bars, and filled her five-gallon water jug at a hose out back. The drive from Lawson to the trailhead was one of her favorites, climbing on the very southern shoulder of the mountains, with their foothills to her right and a sea of sage-covered steppe to her left. The two buttes were out there in the furnace of the sun, aware of her, as if they thought, 'Ah, there she is—where has she been for so long.'

And Hanna replied, silently, 'I should go there, why don't

I go there? I have time—after the mountains, I can go after the mountains.' The road led past a historic gold-mining town and then down into the sage, an expansive gentle slope to the south. As the highway broke onto the sage covered slopes, she caught the dirt road heading north, back toward the peaks. She was comfortable here and drove slowly as the road rose and fell over a shoulder, and wound through a crotch between the hips of two knolls, breasting across a short spine of a plateau.

There were sheep grazing and traditional sheep wagons, now covered in tin rather than canvas. They were Peruvian and Bolivian shepherds, contracted to the huge ranches down around The Rock. Their large dogs ran and barked from afar as she drove past. She took a two-track out to a turnaround where she could see out to the south and sat for a while drinking from her water bottle and looking to the buttes. The ridge where Hanna found the Clovis lay hidden in the hills to the west. The sun was potent, and she let it pound down upon her in the utter silence. A gust of wind found her now and then, but each breeze left a vacuum of silence as it passed, even the clack of grasshopper wings and the chip of horned larks seemed loud out here. She could see the empty, untraveled road all the way to the highway.

She found a camp a mile from the trailhead in a large, open park surrounded by pine forests and tall granite mountains. The informal campground was crowded with all kinds of campers. There were horse people and traditional recreational vehicles, motorcyclists and four-wheelers, fishermen and people just sitting out for an afternoon before returning to a faraway hotel room. Once she found a spot for her truck, she got out her camp chair, a map and a beer and looked at the possible routes she could run in the morning. She felt strong and wanted something difficult with lots of elevation that would take most of the day. It came down to three possibilities, then two, and finally the one was clear to her, a good route that would loop through two canyons, up the Glacier Lake Draw, and out Black Canyon.

She dug around to find the climbers' guide to the area and double-checked the difficulty of a saddle she would have to cross. She felt anxious and excited and cooked rice and veggies to fuel the next day's run; she ate until her stomach hurt and then ate a bit more. She cleaned the dishes in a small cloud of mosquitoes as the sun set, and washed up in the creek; she was ready to sleep as campfires began to flicker in the dark. She had been here many times before and was familiar with this end of the range, often sharing camps with large groups of friends, drinking and making merry the night before arduous hikes or hard approaches to difficult climbs. Tomorrow there would be none of that, just light clothes, running shoes, a fanny pack, and speed.

She jumped quickly into the back of the truck and slammed down the door to escape the bugs. Even so, she spent some time with her headlamp, slapping and clapping them out of the air, before she slipped beneath her sleeping bag against the refreshing chill of high elevation.

* * *

Hanna was catching on to Tim's belief in early, alpine starts, and was awake long before first light; she lit her stove in the back of the truck and drank her first cup of coffee, relaxing in the warmth of her bag. She let the stove run to warm the camper shell and then turned it down low to toast a bagel. Having prepared everything the night before, she was ready before she knew it, and had nothing more to do but drive to the parking lot, chomping on a second bagel, while anxiety gnawed at her guts. To fail on this run halfway and be stranded with nothing would be dismal and dire beyond words.

There were already climbers in the parking lot, moving in the pools of light from their vehicles, standing in light down jackets and ski hats, with steaming cups in hand, above large yawning packs awaiting the burden of even more gear. They eyed Hanna curiously as she stretched behind the tailgate of her truck and jogged and plunge-stepped around the parking loop. Once she was warm, she shed her extra clothes and stuffed her wind shell into her fanny pack, locked up her truck and left at a slow jog. It was still dark enough for her headlamp, but she ran without it, feeling her way along the sandy trial, preferring to go slowly in the magic of the predawn. There would be no people for hours; she would pass their camps unnoticed while they tossed and considered brewing breakfast. It was just her, the cold air upon her legs and face, and the sweat building under her ski cap. She was mindful of every nuanced change in the light, running on the dusty path through the forest beside the roar of the creek, the sky dark, and then silver-grey, at first full of stars, and then with just a few, and then with none. The ghostly blur of an owl flushed from its roost, and then every tree was visible, the branches against the sky as well as the trunks, and then the trail was there in detail, every rock, every root. All at once her eyes could penetrate into the forest. In the grey light, the sky was pink, and the clouds turned purple, and then there was sun on the highest peaks and it was light, truly light, and there was no stopping this day.

Hanna ran faster in the morning chill, knowing that later the heat and sun would punish her. There were mule deer in the meadows along the creek, and they watched her curiously because this was not the hour for humans. The first few miles were flat, but then the terrain steepened and turned rocky as the creek roared louder with its drop. With the rising elevation, the lodgepole pines turned to whitebark and limber pines. The light morning dew evaporated, and dust rose up from the trail. But the air remained still, and the dust hung behind her. She ran on until she came to the first lake, as the sun touched the ground, and she saw tents in the trees back from the shore, but no one stirred. It was marshy, and then rocky, along the northern edge of the lake. There were broad creek crossings, which were shallow but annoying, and she had to cautiously leap from stone to stone to keep her feet dry. And then, she was climbing steep, rocky trails, and the granite bedrock was there at the surface. At first there was an occasional slab, but then the ground was mostly solid, white granite, and trees clung to small islands of soil, or grew from their own collection of needles and bark, and the old middens of cones collected by squirrels.

She reached the second lake as the sun blazed, but the trail remained in the shade as it hugged the western faces of great domes of granite, and she was grateful for the cool chill. From here, she entered the broad canyon and ran on pure granite. The creek had carved its shallow way and dropped pool-by-pool, but the great granite shield yielded little. The mountains were vast sweeping slabs and spines of white geology, which had pushed and bulged and shoved, and thrust upward, only to be ground and scoured by two thousand feet of ice. Trees and vegetation only grew from cracks and fissures or where pine duff had built up behind walls of rubble. She ran past huge, erratic, glacial boulders that thousands of years of melting ice had simply left behind.

Hanna passed a climbing couple lugging their loads to the final lake where it sat in a perfect dish of granite. "Where are you running to?" they shouted after her. And she had to think, stymied for a moment, laughing. "I don't know," she said. And ran off along the vague trail that wound through the rubble of the lake's steep eastern shore. Still, she remained in the shade, climbing up long ramps and grassy goat trails, past cairns and small beat-out platforms where people had stopped and eaten and put on, or stripped away, climbing gear, or fallen asleep, lost in exhaustion and descending darkness. She crossed low-angle slabs of pure stone to reach other ramps of sloping cracks. And then she could run no farther, but had to climb and scramble, and her lungs were scorched with the taste of copper. She went as quickly as she could, scrambling with her hands and feet, leaping from one rock to the next. She passed a seep of water flowing over a ledge, and stopped to drink her fill. It was hard to start her legs moving again, but she could see the col just above her, and this inspired her to move faster. Then she was there, standing in the blast of the sun, in the stiff wind of the notch. She could see down from where she had come from and then down into the next drainage she planned to descend. To her right were towering spires, and to her left, the sweep of the arête of a ridge. How many hours she wondered, how long had this taken? She had purposely left her watch behind. She wanted the sun to be her timepiece, and though high, it was still to the east. She stretched her arms wide, and touched her toes and spun around and saw all that there was to see. She smiled and laughed and wondered where Tim might be, and if he too was sinking his teeth into this life. She looked for Paul and wondered if he was with her.

She picked her way slowly down a trail that followed ledges and cracks, but it was grassier and slicker, and there was more snow; this was the lee side of the prevailing storms, and snow lay trapped on this side. The exposure was to the north on this side, and the sun left these slopes before it reached its snow-melting intensity. This side was barren and bereft of clustered trees. It was more remote, and she could see no tents tucked in among the stunted willows and boulders. She took the greatest care, for if she broke an ankle, there would be no crawling to someone's camp.

She found plenty of water from small springs, and she drank often and filled her small bottle from time to time. When she guessed it was noon, she stopped and ate two energy bars and cooled down by running water through her hair and soaking her feet and splashing her arms. All the uphill work was over, and now she just needed to endure, and not fall or suffer an injury.

She passed a small lake in a deep chasm and had to hop from boulder to boulder along the steep shore for several hundred yards. It was strenuous, and mentally taxing, to pick the safest and quickest path without falling. But then she passed this lake, rounded a bend, and suddenly she was looking up the same drainage that she had ascended so many hours before. The sun had moved well west, and she still had six miles of sustained running ahead of her. She drank all she

could at one last spring and filled her small bottle. There
would be no more drinking water until she reached her
truck.

Back at her truck, in the evening, it was all she could do
to heat a can of soup and drink it down. She bathed in the
river, drove a few yards to a patch of evening shade and
chased the mosquitoes from the back of the truck. She lay
there with climbing ropes as pillows propping her up.
Resting in a blissful stupor of exhaustion, she watched the
evening come and the light fade. Her mind drifted to Meg
and Tim and what they might be doing, but she was glad
neither of them was there, and she prayed for Paul in her
own way.

Entropy

Hanna woke before dawn and sat up expecting an event, or plan, or work, to slap her in the face and make her kick off her bag, but there was nothing. She thought for a moment, but there was nothing. As she lay back down, she felt the ache and fatigue of her body. Even her arms were sore and she slept until there was sun outside the truck and she could wait no longer to pee. It was hard moving inside the shell on the back of the truck. She groaned as she flipped up the door and dropped the tailgate, rolling out into her flip-flops in one smooth motion. The sun felt good but she knew that she would have to find shade before it climbed too high. She sat in her chair drinking coffee, enjoying the luxury of it. She had done all there was to do and now her most pressing issue was staying clear of mosquitoes and avoiding the heat of the middle of the day. She drove to a better camp deeper in the shade of some pines, closer to the creek.

Mid-morning, she was at the creek rinsing out clothes when a woman appeared on the bank above her. Hanna jumped a bit, but was too tired to get to her feet.

"Sorry, didn't mean to scare you," said the woman, coming carefully down the trail. "Actually I was looking for a good spot to do what you're doing."

"This is the spot. You can even pound your clothes on the rocks like they do in South America if you like," Hanna joked.

"Maybe not so much—just rinse the sweat out. Do you mind...?"

"No, no, not at all."

"I don't know why, but I hate doing this kind of stuff where people can see me."

"Doing your dirty laundry?"

"Exactly."

"Well your laundry secrets are safe with me."

She was a tall woman with a kind face. "Claire," she said holding out her hand.

"Hanna." Hanna reached up awkwardly.

"Don't get up."

"Not if I don't have to."

"Did you just come down from the mountains?" the woman asked.

"Well yeah, I went on a long mountain run yesterday."

"How long."

"Looonnng!" Hanna groaned, rolling her eyes.

"I get it," Claire laughed. "I faked a mechanical problem on my bike, so I wouldn't have to go out all day again with my crew."

"Ah, they hit the trail pretty hard?"

"Yeah, and fast."

"Well, there's plenty of shade and cool water, and it appears that the bugs don't come out until sundown."

"And we won't have to talk about mountain biking."

"I don't know anything about it."

Claire washed her clothes and then picked her way down to a deeper pool and washed up, putting on fresh clothes.

Hanna saw bruises on her arm as she towel-dried her long brown hair. "Did you fall off your bike?"

"What?"

"Your arm," Hanna stated.

"Oh yeah," she said with a laugh. "It really hurts to fall off your bike when you're an adult."

"Do *real* adults fall off of bikes?" Hanna asked.

"Will we ever be adults?" Claire asked with a touch of irony, and quickly changed course. "Where are you staying?"

"That was my truck you passed under the trees."

"Ah, the tiny one?"

"Yeah, that one."

"That looks lonely; you should come eat with us tonight...if you'd like."

"Well, sure, if I am still here...give me a shout."

"Well, I will. See you later," she said, climbing the steep

bank, disappearing from sight.

Hanna spent the day stretching, drinking water and tea, trying to rehydrate, reading from the box of books Tim gave her. In the afternoon, it rained in an uncertain way, stopping and starting, fading and then strengthening. The rain went on for an hour, drumming on the tin roof, rumbling in the distance, purring Hanna to sleep.

Hanna was sitting in the evening sun when Claire came over and invited her to their camp for drinks and dinner. When Hanna arrived, she was shocked at the gleaming new trucks, with matching campers riding on top. They had professional-looking, folding aluminum tables and crisp, new camp chairs, and a cooler the size of a small coffin.

"Wow," she said, trying to think of what she could say that wouldn't be rude, or fawning.

"Oh, I know, Wade has to have all the gear. You know how geologists are," Claire said. She opened her mouth as if to explain but then let it go. "So what'll it be? Beer, wine, a drink?"

"Well, I am guessing that the cooler is packed with ice, so I'll go for a beer."

Claire motioned for Hanna to sit down and then seated herself in practiced leisure, crossing her long legs, slouching, pulling her long, brown hair over her shoulder so it didn't snag. She was tall, with a full, robust body, and Hanna guessed that she had been a serious athlete at some point in her life.

"So what did you run?" Claire asked immediately.

"I ran up to Glacier Lake, over the col to the Black Lakes drainage and then back."

Claire sat up with a start, "You did not! You ran over the col?"

"Well, I climbed, and then climbed down the col, but then I ran the rest," Hanna said modestly.

"My God, it took me five hours to backpack into Glacier Lake!"

"Well, yeah, but that's with a pack. If you go with

nothing, you move much faster."

"Sure, but if anything happens and you don't make it, you're screwed." Claire stared at her for a moment and then threw back her head and laughed, stood halfway from her chair, holding her beer forward to clink Hanna's in a toast. "I can't believe it. Doing something like that would never even occur to me." Claire stared in admiration. "That's why you were sleeping all day."

Hanna laughed, uneasy with the attention. "I know, it'll take a few days to get over." There was an awkward moment, and then she asked, "Where's the rest of your crew?"

"That's a good question," Claire said, expressing a little worry. "They should have been back by now. I'm thinking that they either found a spot to sit out the rain or had some mechanical trouble." Claire had a way of speaking that seemed to beg agreement to what she said. "I would go look with the truck, but God only knows where they would be."

"No, that would be silly, and then they would return while you were gone."

"Exactly how it works."

They were on their second beer when two people rode up on mountain bikes, looking dusty and tired. Claire introduced them as Ben and Eve. Although in the mountains, they looked like people from an office. Their faces were sunburned red, rather than tanned brown and the biking clothes they wore were new enough to have creases.

Eve had a short nest of sandy curls, a pixie nose and mirthful face. She laughed lightly even as she introduced herself.

"Where's Wade?" Claire asked quickly.

"He's walking. He hit rock and broke some spokes. Ben said, wiping his glasses.

A shadow crossed Claire's face.

Eve shook her head, laughed unconvincingly and said, "Not happy!"

"We'll go get him," Ben volunteered, taking off his

helmet. His dark, sweaty hair clung to his head, and he seemed too slight to own the truck he was unlocking. "Our camper is empty. He can put his bike right inside."

Claire's mood had changed. She rolled the foil-wrapped potatoes back along the edge of the coals, and hustled efficiently through the cooler, pulling out a large plastic container of salad and a container of what appeared to be meat. Hanna made herself available, cutting tomatoes and onions to add to the salad. Claire talked and joked with her as they worked, but she seemed distracted and ill at ease.

Ben and Eve came back with a large, dark haired, baby-faced guy, who stepped out of the truck and stretched his back. "Well, you dodged a bullet today, Claire," he said with a snort of a laugh.

"Too hard?"

"Way too hard," Ben jumped in.

"Sage brush, rocks, dead-end roads. It was a disaster," the large man said, with an edge to his voice.

Claire had a beer and a chair for him. "Wade. Sit down!" she said, "Have a beer, and then you can wash up."

Wade took the beer, pecked her on the cheek, plopping down in the camp chair. He ended up facing Hanna and raised his eyebrows in surprise. "Who are you?" he asked.

"Hanna...the dinner guest."

He smiled an inscrutable smile, and Clare said, "Wade, this is Hanna. I invited her for dinner."

"Wade moved to raise himself from the chair, but Hanna was quicker. She reached a hand down to him. "Hanna," she said.

"Wade," he said.

"Hanna is a runner, a mountain runner." Claire spoke to the silence.

Wade was drinking deeply from his beer, not listening to her. "What are we eating tonight?" he asked.

"Meat and potatoes."

"And beeeer!" Ben added.

Claire and Eve moved the cooler and table, setting dinner

out and shooing away a few flies. Claire lowered a grill over the fire, scraping away the crust of fats and proteins with an old camp knife.

Wade got up and walked toward the creek, and Hanna watched him go. He was a magnificent specimen of Homo sapien, Robustus Americani: thighs like trees, a broad back, massive, rounded shoulders, with a huge, bullet head sitting on top. Hanna imagined him and Claire in full rut, with the camper rocking violently, bouncing fully off the ground.

Claire tried to hand Hanna a tub of marinated steaks and a barbeque fork, but Hanna failed to hold out her hands for them. "You can put these on the grill." Claire pushed them forward a bit further and Hanna took a step back. "Umm, I am a vegetarian, I don't handle meat."

Claire stared at her for a moment, and her face changed slightly as she understood. "Oh," she said, and turned her head a bit as if looking for an acceptable response. "Well then, you strip the aluminum off the potatoes, and I'll put the steaks on."

Hanna felt less hopeful of the meal, now that her choices were winnowed down, once again, to a potato and salad, which she had helped prepare, like a damn scullery maid, while the men drank beer and washed up. She resented the situation with the food, and apparent machismo. She was dreaming up a polite exit, but the guys wandered off, and she fell back into conversation with Claire and Eve, and decided she would simply eat and run at the first chance. She moved several times as the smoke of the burning meat followed her. Eve had stirred up some gin drinks in large plastic glasses and handed them around giggling, as if it was the naughtiest thing she had done all day.

Ben returned and placed the two tables end-to-end, setting out bright red, enamel plates, and then arranged the chairs.

Hanna ended up across from Wade and she couldn't stop staring at the size of his massive head; it looked like he could drive it through a wall. His thick, black eyebrows overarched his blue eyes, which were at once amused and then perturbed, and contradicted his smooth, childish face. Hanna dished her salad high and took a large potato, mashing it open to cover it with butter, salt and pepper. She was happily flushed with alcohol, and she told herself that this was probably more than she would eat at her truck.

The steaks came around, served from a large frying pan, and the others pulled choice slabs onto their plates. Wade saw that Hanna had no meat and he handed the pan to her.

"No thanks," she smiled to placate the huge Robustus.

"No meat?"

"No thanks, I don't eat meat."

"Ahh," he said. "Don't eat meat."

"Wade," Claire said, "you don't eat vegetables."

Ben and Eve laughed, and Wade stabbed a piece of beef. "Well, that's fine, I'll just eat yours. It always seems funny to me," he said, looking at Hanna with his contradicting eyes, "that many people drink something toxic like alcohol, but do not eat meat."

Sensing the meat conversation on the rise, she looked into his eyes and smiled. "That is funny," she said, conceding genuinely.

She saw his eyes, smiling and then annoyed.

"Hanna, what are you doing around here?" Eve asked.

"I'm taking a break from a survey."

Wade looked up from his meat, "A survey?"

"Yeah, we are working on an archeological survey for one of the pipelines out of the patch."

"Aaah," Wade said with his childish smile. "A surveyor."

Claire's eyebrows peaked for a second, and then she forced a smile, "Wade is a geologist down there."

"No lack of geology down there!" Hanna said congenially.

"No, there's lots of work. We make a lot of work for a lot of people. All the regulatory people lick their chops when they hear about a new petro project."

Hanna smiled, choking back a sarcastic, 'Thank you.'

Ben stirred up the fire as dinner ended in the falling light, and Wade moved to his camp chair. Just as Hanna was ready to make her escape, Eve put another drink in her hand, and so she stayed. She was still starving and she knew that another drink would never do her any good, but she hung with Claire and Eve as they cleaned up dinner, wondering what the hell they were doing, and why they were doing it. She had a burning urge to lecture, but took a swallow from her drink instead.

The boys came around for another drink, and Wade asked Hanna, "What have you been doing way up here by yourself?"

Claire interceded, "Oh, I was telling you, she is a mountain runner."

"A vegetarian mountain runner—seems pretty specialized."

"How about you?" Hanna asked, trying to change the subject.

"Contractors and regulations have us stalled out," he said seriously. "We have rigs that can't come on line until the pipelines are down. The pipe can't be laid until the surveys are done," he said, with accusation in his voice.

"Oh well, if people behaved, there wouldn't be so much regulation," Hanna replied, her face growing red.

"Do you run in the desert, when you're down by the patch?" Eve asked, determined to redirect the conversation.

"I do," Hanna said. "It's my favorite."

"They drive around, run around," Wade grumbled. Claire moved beside him and took his elbow.

"Let's not pretend you're the victim here," Hanna said bluntly. "You guys waste all the time, money and materials you possibly can, and screwing people is the name of the game, so let's not even pretend there are good guys and bad guys."

"You wouldn't be doing your archeology if it wasn't for our projects!" Wade said, his baby-face now red and petulant.

"Well, I guess I would, but it wouldn't be so regrettable."

"You run in the heat of the day down there?" Eve asked, doggedly forcing her distraction.

"No," Hanna replied politely, "I run in the late evenings."

"She ran up to Glacier Lake and then over to the Black Lakes and out," Claire added, speaking to Wade.

"In a day?" Ben asked.

"Back for dinner!" Claire said.

"That's at least 20 miles—really hard miles," Ben said, sizing Hanna up and down.

"It looks like that on a map," Hanna broke in, trying to move with the new angle of the conversation.

Wade raised his eyebrows, his mouth making an O of surprise, his eyes wide in realization. "You're that bitch that Maced my guys!"

Hanna jerked her head toward him.

"You are! You're that bitch—when they asked you what you were doing."

Hanna stood up and measured the distance between herself and her hosts. "When they stopped to rape me!" The ice of fear trickled down her spine.

"They weren't raping anyone."

"That's because I Maced them first!" she said running her hand up to her hip to feel for her Mace.

"You're crazy, those guys are too fat and lazy to force themselves on a skinny runt like you."

"Wade!" Claire said, pulling on his arm.

"So you're defending rapists?" Hanna's voice rose. "You have a bad week, get laid off, break your bike, and your response is to defend rapists?"

"If you're out there running like that, then maybe you deserve whatever you get. Maybe they would like to know where you spend your time," he said, arrogantly taking a step toward her.

Hanna's drink was in the air, hitting him squarely in the face, and he roared as the alcohol and citrus doused his eyes. Hanna saw his big paw sweeping out blindly to her, and she dodged to avoid it, but misjudged and moved directly into its path, the hand that meant to grab her hair landed as a solid blow, sending stars zinging across her vision. She tried to spin away, but he was a massive American male, full of rage and liquor, and he had a full handful of her hair.

"Wade!" Ben leapt forward, but Wade's free hand pushed him away, and Ben stumbled backward over the firewood.

Hanna caught a glimpse of Claire, staring mortified with fear.

Hanna reached out blindly. Her hands fell on the table, but it was just aluminum and offered no leverage.

"You think you can do that to me?" He was shaking her like a doll.

The table was collapsing, bottles and cans, pans and glasses tumbling. Hanna's hand groped across the table, grasping for anything. Wade had forced her head down toward the ground to control her, and they both stumbled to their knees as he stepped on a wine bottle. She saw the barbecue fork next to a smashed bottle and grabbed it, swinging for the first part of him that came into view as he pulled her from the ground. He hollered. She was going to stab him a second time, but the fork was torn from her hand as he leapt away. She was in the air, and then skidding and rolling across the ground. Wade was bellowing, howling, screaming and raging, dancing around with a barbeque fork lodged in his thigh.

Hanna's head spun as she got to her knees.

"You stabbed him? You stabbed him?" Eve asked, as if curious, and wondering if it might be funny.

Claire was running beside him, eager to help, but afraid of being caught by one his huge maulers. Ben was there with a chair. "Sit down, Wade, sit down, we have to see; we have to see!" He shot a glance at Hanna, as if asking her to help.

Hanna was on her feet, and Claire was running at her. Hanna held out her hands, as Claire towered over her.

"I don't want to fight you," Hanna croaked.

"What are you doing?" Claire screamed. "Run! Run!"

Retreat

Hanna was in no condition to drive, but she threw the few armfuls of things she had into the back of the truck. She knew that she missed things in the dark, but dismissed them as she dove behind the wheel and tore off out to the road, driving at the fastest speed she could manage. It was fully dark, and she watched for lights in her rear-view mirror, but none followed.

There was an occasional oncoming vehicle, and she slowed cautiously as they passed so as not to call attention to herself or her truck. It was 40 minutes before she passed the first junction, and still no one followed. Then she was out in the sage, topping a hill before another junction. It was a three-way, and she knew that she was finally safe. She stopped on the far side of the hill, turned off her lights, and ran back to the top and observed that no one had followed. She looked in the back of the truck, grabbed a water bottle and moistened a towel to wash her face. In the cab of her truck she turned on the interior lights and scrubbed the crusty blood from her face. The towel came away filthy with dirt and clotted blood; she could see that her lip was huge and she had some raw scratches on one cheek and her hands. Her eyes welled up to cry, but she choked it back. "You're fine, you're fine," she said. "Just keep driving, you'll be fine."

After a short stretch of highway, Hanna turned south onto the good gravel roads, heading toward the old survey line where she had found the Clovis. She took a dirt spur road that led up into some thick junipers and decided that she could safely camp there. She had to walk around to calm herself. She drank water and took aspirin to counter the blow to the head. "Jesus," she said to the night, "imagine if he had really gotten a hold of me!"

The back of the truck was a mess, but she made it up to

sleep in and took stock of what she had; although she knew she had lost some things, she still had her cooler and the five-gallon water jug, which was all she truly needed for the night.

She was stiff and hung over when she awoke, but her face looked better in the morning light. She didn't want to explain this one to Hugh or Karl, and figured it could easily pass as a bad tumble on a rocky trail. Her stomach felt raunchy, and she chose coffee and apple juice instead of a real breakfast. She drove off timidly down the road, going slowly, taking care to avoid deep looking sand. There were no new tire tracks, and she felt safe, being far enough away from the patch to avoid any unwanted human contact. There were fresh cow turds, but she doubted that she would see any ranch hands. She felt for her new canister of Mace and slid it under a T-shirt on the passenger seat. 'Just be nice and sweet, suck right up to them, and then shoot 'em in the face!' She thought that she might be like a rattlesnake that way, but even they gave a warning.

Hanna wondered if it would be easier to kill the next guy and bury him. But there would be something that gave it all away, like how the deputy found his way to the motel. There's always someone who saw something. And those guys weren't even dead. They were just pissed off and embarrassed. She felt an icy pit in her stomach. What if she ran into those same guys out here? Or what if Wade found her somehow? She would have to run for it.

It would never happen, she told herself. Those guys were a hundred miles away, making money in the patch, and Wade was probably in an emergency room getting a stitch or two, a tetanus shot, and antibiotics to counteract the two greasy, meat-slathered prongs.

Although in pain, Hanna felt oddly buoyant and cut loose, as if things were aligning their own way, and she should just follow them. She headed south where they had surveyed the year before, and then earlier this spring. She wanted to drop down where the desert met the mountains.

She wanted to see the Clovis point and maybe look around to see if there was anything else down there. She wanted to find it again, for Paul, if he could see her. She had always wanted to show him the Clovis and then listen to him create the story of its origin.

After a little more than an hour of circuitous driving, she found the ancient moraines just beyond the base of the foothills. Hanna parked her truck, put some trowels and two quarts of water in her daypack, and walked out to the long ridge. She wound her way through the boulders, sliding now and then in the loose rocks and sand. Flakes and blades appeared here and there, and she noted their location in the context of the largest boulders. All this rubble was granite, gneiss, and basalt. There was no sedimentary rock, meaning that this came from deep in the mountains, pushed out here like the berm of snow in front of a plow. The successions of moraines were obvious. She was on the outermost esker, but toward the mountains she could see, from the waves of frozen moraines rippling out from the hills, where lesser glacial events had left their marks.

The large, white boulder was as she remembered. She came under the south side into the little solar alcove, and took off her pack to drink some water, sitting for a moment looking south to the buttes. And there they stood, like huge lighthouses, guiding the pioneers, and the indigenous populations before them, across the plains. They were visible even in the night when there was a moon. Whenever in view of them, no matter how distant, she felt their presence, the watchfulness and omniscience to all that ventured across the broad basin.

The sun was now directly overhead, so it was shady in the grotto. Hanna moved the stone and was shocked to see that the Clovis sat on top of the sand and gravel, waiting for her, pointing to the buttes, and she felt wary of touching it. She stepped back and saw no tracks coming or going. "Did Tim do that?" she asked aloud.

She held the point in the flat of her palm, gazed at it and

turned it over. It was a bit longer than the width of her palm, and the black obsidian glistened like wet glass. It was perfectly proportioned, and the fluting ran across from side to side, to meet at the deep central channel running vertically from the bottom to the center of the point.

She stared south at the desert and watched for the megafauna that roamed the plains 13 thousand years ago, six thousand years before civilization began to gather in wretched little cities. She wanted to see herds of giant bison grazing belly-deep in sedges and forbs in a landscape that was wetter than the current one. She wanted to be watching with a group of hunters, sitting entranced by the oneness of the world that stretched before them. The reality of these men was no secret. They were much more robust than their women, and they were violent, like the oaf that had roughed her up last night. Their bones bore the injuries of violent human conflicts, not random accidents. There was nothing blissful or magical about them. They were of the same ferocious lot that followed, and were cut from the same cloth as the descendent tribes that raided and warred, even as the annihilating wave of white immigration rushed at them from across the plains.

Still, she wanted to be with them and sit quietly watching and waiting, scratching at lice, moving out into the sun. How long would they sit and watch? Did ravens tell them when the bison were coming? Did animals with symbiotic relationships come and tell them to be ready. How precise were their plans and traps? How did they accommodate the wind? How did they drive a stone point through a thick, pliant hide? How much meat could they carry? How far could they carry it?

Were there long times of peaceful idleness, when they just sat here knapping new tools or touching up old ones? Fathers and uncles sat with sons and cousins; maybe women came for various reasons, such as gathering fresh foods while they awaited a big kill. Maybe the big kills were simply random, and it was really the women who caught and trapped most of the foods. It could have been the idleness that drove the males to such violence. Perhaps there was some inherent madness in the meat. Because if they were regularly killing enormous megafauna, laden with fats and proteins, then why all the violence? Wouldn't they simply pat their engorged tummies, scratch at lice, and engage in post-feast sex with their women?

She wanted to believe that there was something special about these people, but it was highly likely that they were just as crazy as everyone else. Their lineage lived for thousands of years on the plains in some sort of balance, but even that was out of kilter, because the original Clovis people drove mammoths, mastodons, and other megafauna to extinction in only three hundred years. In a nanosecond of geological time they ended 65 million years of evolution, and their perfectly lethal projectile points followed the extinction. Why every last mammoth and giant bison? Couldn't they do the math? Couldn't they foresee the impending extinction, the end of their culture, the end of the feast? "We are so good at math," Hanna sighed. "It's arithmetic that kills us."

Perhaps the only reason that they lived in balance with the later environment was because they had not yet figured out a way to elevate their populations to a point where they could screw it all up again. And their descendants probably died in great numbers when things failed. They had to be nomadic to follow the herds. They had to move because they depleted resources like game and firewood. They didn't move on for any noble reason; they moved on because the game moved on, or because they had used up things they needed. And they wouldn't return until those resources were available again. They moved because the winters were more survivable to the south, or at lower elevations. Were they good stewards? Hanna thought that they were really only stewards by coincidence. They were simply nomads, going where they had to, to fill their bellies, to stay clear of their enemies, to survive.

She sat with the Clovis in her lap and looked around her

at the tiny flakes and pieces of shattered stone, chert, which was most available along any of the limestone formations. The obsidian came from far away to the north, only occurring in areas of volcanic activity.

There was nothing more significant; it was all just the detritus of chipping and flaking. But it filled her with awe, and she felt that feeling of sliding into the past. She sat where they had sat, probably generations of hunters, young men and boys, maybe women, getting out of the wind or finding shade from the heat. It was just a nice place to sit and talk with busy hands.

It was hot, even in the shade. She wiped at a thin film of sweat with the waist of her T-shirt and looked out at the buttes half-expecting that they had moved. But there they were, covered with a crusty layer of capstone, angled up like volcanic cones layered in the mud and fossils of ancient sea beds. She could find fossils there if she looked for them. There were more sea turtle fossils in this basin than any other place on the Earth. She had seen the fossil of a sea turtle from this area when she was a child, where it was displayed at the Peabody Museum. It was big enough to fill the room. At the time, she was filled with dread at the huge, sharp jaws that could have snapped her in half like scissors. She knew that it could swallow her whole, and she'd be stuck under the huge carapace. She remembered that shudder vividly, because she was very fond of turtles at the time, but not the horror show before her. And it came from here. This was the vast inland sea where it had come from. Perhaps The Great Turtle myth that had circulated among the tribes, had begun here as the Clovis culture found the shells of the huge turtles rising out of the mudstone.

I'll go there, to the buttes, tomorrow. She looked to the west and saw how low the sun had dropped. She wondered how that had happened, and she realized that it was only a day since she awoke after her run. A day since she had stabbed Wade with a barbeque fork. The ache of her body reminded her of what had happened. The ache in her face reminded her of a conflict that now seemed so inconsequential. Hanna got up to leave and took the Clovis with her, promising to return it. She scrambled down to the base of the moraine and then followed it to her truck, where she looked through her cooler and food box. Though acutely hungry, nothing seemed appealing. She got out her camp chair and sat for a moment, looking around, thinking how vulnerable she would be if men showed up.

"I need a gun," she said aloud. "If they find me, they'll rape me and kill me."

She thought of the ignominy of being raped in the dust and then shot like a dog. She fingered the Mace under her shirt and then knew that she couldn't rely on it forever. There was little chance of anyone venturing out here, but if someone did, it would be a man or men. She put it out of her head—no point in worrying about it now. Where could she drive to this late in the day?

Although still starving from the day before and from the depletion of energy caused by her run, she decided to skip dinner. I'll take this day and tomorrow to fast. I'll fast and sweat away that foulness with Wade and Claire. I'll search for Paul. I'll consider things, everything. She decided that she would drink nothing but water, mixed with apple juice from her cooler. The idea seemed so brilliant to her that she jumped up, took three bottles and filled each a third full with juice, then filled them the rest of the way with water from her larger jug. Tomorrow she would take them with her and explore the buttes.

She slept well for the first half of the night, but then her hunger awoke her. She thought that she had perhaps heard a motor, but then knew that there was nothing. She lay there in her sleeping bag still fearing Wade's massive paws. She drank some juice, moved to the center of the truck and willed herself back to sleep.

* * *

She felt elated as she drove away in the morning in search of the roads that would take her to the buttes. She consulted the large BLM map and its spider web of roads. There were many secondary dirt roads that could not be trusted. But then there were the larger roads, which appeared in solid black on the map. These were well maintained gravel roads and more reliable. She found the most logical route to the closest point and memorized it, saying the directions aloud. Two miles from the base of the buttes she turned off the main road and it was all guesswork from there, following two tracks to the base of the saddle between the two buttes, threading her truck amid huge jumbled boulders, and twisted desert junipers. She chose a campsite among the stubby mud towers and stunted, desert trees, where her truck would be well concealed.

She felt good about the camp, and the whole idea of her trip. She liked the idea of fasting. It sounded meaningful as she said it in her head, 'fasting'. She drank a liter of diluted apple juice and decided to climb the taller butte, to the north and west. At the saddle, she looked around and found a single set of old boot tracks frozen in the sun-baked mud. She immediately found flakes and shattered chert at the saddle. She hunted more carefully and found tiny flakes of black obsidian. Of course, they had come up here out of curiosity just as she had, and of course it was a place of cultural and religious significance. It was visible for scores of miles, or even a hundred miles, in many directions. How could it not be significant? How could young men not have climbed the buttes? That's what young men do.

Tim had said that these buttes were some of the first summits he had ever climbed. He had seen them from the interstate when he was 20 years old. He took a likely exit and drove off on dirt roads until he found his way to climb them, with his old dog Babe. Hanna imagined the youthful Tim up here in Levis, a red flannel shirt and heavy work-boots, with long, unruly hair. She smiled at this idea and then leapt as she heard the buzz of a rattler in the brush beside her. She carefully stepped back toward the brush and saw its drab green skin entwined in the woody stalks

"You're lucky Dog isn't here. He'd cut off your rattle."

The snake didn't like that idea at all, wriggling its way deeper into the thicket, it disappeared from sight.

Hanna found a trail winding to the top of the butte. There were mule deer tracks cut into the trail both coming and going, as if they often climbed up here. She followed the tracks, and they led to the tricky last few feet through the capstone. It looked like an unlikely rotten chimney, but it was really an easy, irregular set of steps to the summit. She took one more step, and there she was on the summit, immediately spinning around 360 degrees. It was dizzying, not the height, but the endlessness of the surrounding terrain, like standing on a tower out in the middle of the Pacific. To the north she saw the distant moraines where she had been the day before. They seemed so obvious, as if they were geologically connected to where she stood now, but they were two entirely different geological events.

Her eyes dropped to the smooth reddish capstone, hunting for flakes, finding them in the lee of irregularities where the wind had not swept them away. They were there, the ubiquitous grey and red chert, and there were also clear quartzite flakes and small blades. Then there were the black obsidian flakes—tiny, as if they were chipped with the greatest of care. After hundreds or thousands of years, these flakes were still as sharp as freshly shattered glass. Hanna could see that obsidian flakes no bigger than her thumbnail were reworked to use as blades.

After an hour on the summit, she went down to the saddle and then climbed the lower butte. It was much the same, but there was more cultural material scattered on top. Surveyors, geologists, cowboys and rock hounds had carried off anything prehistoric, but left items of their own, a beer can in a crack, a penny, a plastic button. It was all cultural material, the penny was from 1971. The beer can was from the sixties, as it had been opened with a can opener rather than a pull-tab. The button could be easily traced by style and material.

The sun was unbearable, and Hanna went back to her truck to find some shade. As she turned to leave she swooned a bit from the lack of food and felt her lips tingle with the headiness of a near fainting spell. How many hours since she had eaten, more than 30?

She found some shade in the shelter of the hoodoo village of eroded boulders. It was hard for her to be idle. But that was her plan. She would sit through the night on top of the taller butte. She wanted to be in a sacred place and feel something holy. It had been so warm the night before that she had hardly needed her sleeping bag. With a jacket and long pants, she would be fine to last the night.

As evening came on, she packed her daypack with water, extra clothes, her foam sleeping pad, and headed up to the top of the higher butte. She passed the night there, watching the emptiness and the distant, winking lights crawling along slowly across the desert, following the endless dirt roads. The interstate was barely visible at this distance, and then only at night, like a luminescent stream, the lights crawled along with their missions.

She meditated well a few times, attaining a pleasurable state, as bats and nighthawks hunted insects. Moths bumped against her head now and then, and a couple of mice pattered across her sleeping pad. There was a cricket or cicada that chirped to a nice rhythm. She could follow its cadence with her breathing, and her head buzzing from lack of food.

Somewhere in the middle of the night, she fell asleep and awoke curled in her jacket in the middle of her pad, with the sun just below the horizon. After standing and stretching, she was a little disappointed to be no closer to any kind of holiness. In a word, raunchy was how she felt.

Although it was now 48 hours without food, she was surprised that she no longer felt hungry, just depleted and spaced out. She sat until the sun was high and drank some

diluted juice. She took off her jacket and then her pants and
then the rest of her clothes. She sun bathed for a while, and
then she stood naked to the world, spread her arms wide and
circled three times.

She exposed herself to the world, to the interstate, to a
distant vehicle throwing up a rooster tail of dust miles away.
Mid morning she went down to her truck. She looked
through the cooler and saw that the last of the ice was gone.
She would have to take the greatest care in saving the food
she had, which at this moment all seemed unappetizing. It
wasn't time to eat yet. She covered the cooler with her
sleeping bag. There was hunger in her stomach, but it was
too sharp and anxious to sate. She washed the dust from her
face and hands. There was still something more to see here.
It would be worth it to spend one more night. She went off
to wander down along the base of the buttes and the broken
badlands. As she walked, she began to have thoughts that
were not normal. Her mind wandered easily, and at times,
she wondered how long she had been walking. There were
antelope that barked at her, and she ran after them, but she
had no stamina. Several times she thought that she might be
getting lost, but she simply looked over her shoulder and saw
the towering geology behind her.

Hanna walked out in the flats until the ground was
searing and the sun cooked her skin. She squatted in the
shade of some tall sage and wondered what it would be like
if this was her existence and this was what she did every day.
She listened to the buzz of insects, and the chirping of desert
sparrows. A shrike flew by with its fast wing beats, a large
grasshopper in its beak. She could eat grasshoppers. The
Indians did. She was about to stand up and go back to her
truck when a scrawny coyote with its scruffy summer coat
came into a break in the sage a hundred yards away. It had a
limp ground squirrel its jaws. 'What are you doing out in the
middle of the day?' she asked in her mind. It stopped at that
moment and turned to look at her. It considered her and
turned, loping away at an easy gait, but then it stopped and

spun its head, looked to the east, pulled its tail tighter between its legs and left at a full run. Hanna turned her head and listened, and then she could hear it too. The low rumble of an engine, she knelt with her head flush with the tops of the sage, and then she could see it—two hundred yards away heading toward the main dirt road. It was a white company truck with a black logo on the door. She couldn't recognize it from that distance, but she guessed that they were either geologists or petroleum people. Whoever they were, she was sure it wasn't a truck full of friendly women. She crouched down a little lower, and watched as it bounced toward the main road, and then it was gone.

She was dazed and toasted by the sun. Her nose was burned and flaking, and her lips were split. She staggered with an intense rubbery weakness in her limbs. If she were running, she would call this 'bonking'. It appeared that with fasting this became the norm. She trudged up the final hill to the saddle one step at a time, as if she was at very high elevation. Once at her truck, she pulled the chair into the shade and sat in a stupor, with her feet up on a rock, not moving, thinking that tomorrow morning she would have go back and wash her dust-caked body. The crew would begin to wonder where she was. She wondered what she must look like as her stomach squirmed and growled. The vehicle that had passed by fed her anxiety which gnawed at her, and she climbed to the top of the squat stone tower and watched and listened. There was nothing. Satisfied she was alone, she lay in her truck and pulled a light cotton blanket across her torso. She couldn't believe the luxury of such a simple comfort. The sun was already past its zenith, and it would only be a few hours before the evening came on.

After dropping into a deep, sweaty sleep, she awoke with a start, listening for signs of danger, peeking through her windows. It was evening, and though the sun was still up, it had lost its brutal edge. She got up and filled her pack with the same things from the night before, making sure the Clovis was still there in the top.

She rummaged through the truck for anything else she might need. She opened a gym bag, searching for a headlamp with better batteries and found some clothes she had been looking for. She realized that she hadn't opened the bag since her trip to Averoso with Tim. In the bag with the missing headlamp, she happened across the tiny box that Dean, the dying man, had given her. She opened the box and took out a small, lined index card. Her scalp tingled as she read the note.

Hanna,

Sorry to burden you with this, and I know I am assuming a lot, but I have enclosed the broken Clovis point that I found with my father. Now that he is gone, I feel that it was never really his, and it definitely isn't mine. I assume that you and Tim are often down in the desert, and I am hoping that one day you could return the point to an appropriate location, as close to the buttes as possible. My only clear instruction is that it never ends up cataloged in a museum.

Sincerely,
Dean

Hanna looked around to see if anything could bear witness to such a coincidence. Her eyes hunted the brambles of junipers suspiciously, expecting to see the chickadees. Unfolding the tissue, she saw the two halves of the broken Clovis, and picked them up, delicately fitting the two parts perfectly together, which pleased her greatly and made her smile. She re-wrapped the point snugly back into the box and stashed it away in her truck, took one last drink from the big water jug, and started up the path as the sun dropped behind the horizon.

On top of the butte, she had to breathe deeply to steady her wobbly knees. She surveyed the distant plains for danger and saw nothing. There was an hour of light, and then there would be a long twilight after that. Hanna rolled out her sleeping pad and arranged her extra clothes and ski cap against the possible chill of a desert night, and set out her headlamp, and her bottles of juice and water where she could find them in the dark.

She relaxed and watched the world get ready for a long night. After a while, she sat in her meditation pose, putting her jacket under her butt to ease the pressure on her crossed ankles. She settled in and noticed that the calmness was coming much more quickly now as She fell into her breathing rhythm. A gust of wind buffeted her, and she opened her eyes noticing it had grown darker. There was a distant thunderstorm moving slowly above the desert, sending down spears of lightening and dragging nets of rain across the earth. She thought that the wind must have been from that disturbance. She closed her eyes again and soon she felt the skin of her scalp begin to crawl. Then her lips began to tingle as if she were about to faint. A rush of wellbeing spread across her body, and then moved deep into her stomach and spread up into her chest. Her skin tingled and rippled with chills. She continued to think of nothing and soon seemed to be floating alone in a wide, wide sea with rolling waves rocking her as she sat undisturbed on her sleeping pad. The vision was so real and vivid that she was jolted back to a wakeful state.

Now the darkness had a subtle sparkle to it, like the grain on an old television. She rubbed her hand across her face, feeling that perhaps she was wearing thick rubber gloves, and she was scared of the odd sensation. A few tendrils of golden light reached out to her from below the clouds on the western horizon and then died away. She stared off toward the distant oil patch, wondering if she would be able hear the ceaseless clang and roar of its equipment churning in the night, and see the flare of toxic gases and the glare of floodlights lighting the insomniant commotion.

She stood to stretch as the darkness settled heavily upon her. She could see the difference between the earth and the sky, and then, in a blinking, there were stars! She gasped at

not having noticed them. How could it be? The stars! Hadn't
there been a moon last night? She remembered sitting in the
moonlight. It was a half-moon.

She sat back down and tried to blot out her thoughts.
She felt around her one last time for her stuff and then
settled down. Her brain flitted from subject to subject
quickly. She wondered where Tim might be, and then if Paul
was with her, and then thought of Dog and Hugh. She
wondered if they were in a girlie bar or around the fire in
front of Hugh's teepee. She thought of them on barstools
with large-breasted women dancing before them. And then
there were Catherine's eyes; they sparked before her. She had
held Catherine at Tim's party. Hanna swooned for a moment
and hiccupped a breath.

Any form of deep concentration derailed, and she
reached over for her pack unzipping the top to retrieve the
Clovis. She resettled the jacket under her butt and held the
point in both hands in her lap, focusing on her breathing.
The crickets began to fall into cadence with her breath.
Other insects sang in the night. She focused on their songs
and let them resonate through her head. The music seemed
to align with her breathing and form a chorus. Hanna let the
song become her mantra, and words to the cadence were
filling her head. Oddly enough the words were, 'It doesn't
really matter.' Her mind sang the song in a deep, spiritual
way, until she questioned aloud, "It doesn't really matter?"
She disagreed, and her voice came out like shattering mirrors
and resounded through the night, silencing the bugs. Even in
the clamor of disruption she laughed, "You can't just say it
doesn't matter!"

The insects seemed to stop and reconsider, falling silent,
and Hanna re-evaluated her breathing rhythm, but she was
unable to re-catch the wave, and her mind bumped among
many negative things, like being discovered out here. What if
that Wade guy had gone to the police? What if the police
were after her? Her hand went to her Mace, but then she
wondered about money, and car insurance, and bank

accounts that she had lost the information to. "I should look after that," she said anxiously.

She saw Paul's face, and it was happy, he was lecturing on something, but she couldn't hear the words. A vision of his Norsemen came to her, and she could see their gleaming copper spearheads and armbands as they marched across the desert, so far from the sea. "You were such a liar, Paul!" He blushed and smiled like a child caught in a fib. Paul became the night sky and the stars, looking down omnisciently from above, and his susurrations filled her skull.

The insects' song fell into time with her breathing again as her mind went blank. The song seemed to hum in resonance with the hum of the sweep of the stars. She began to breathe easy as they sang their mantra; at first Hanna associated no words with it, but then words began to swim in her brain, rising to the surface. 'It does-n't really mat-ter.'

When she was wakeful again, she said with disgust, "Of course it matters!" and the insects fell silent. The moon was up and blasting the earth with sharp intensity. How had it snuck up that way? How did the stars sneak out that way? She stood and raised her arms to greet the moon and pointed at it with the Clovis. She could feel it return its rays, warm on her face like sunshine. Her vision was acute, and she could see all the irregularities on its surface, and she could see its dark side. The moon was so boisterous in the clear desert night. The blue light upon her face made her blissful. She could see everything passing below, like thieves caught out in searchlights.

Hanna looked down, and she was shocked to see her body was dark brown. It was beyond any range of tan, it was brown, nut brown. She wondered if it could just be the darkness. But her feet were wide and broad, hard and cracked. Her legs were lean and knotted with muscle. She gripped the Clovis tightly.

Listening to the night, she thought she could hear the endless bustle from the patch, the reverberation of that distant engine, pounding with one giant galloping piston. She thought she could see the fiery glow of the toxic, flaming derricks, over the horizon to the southwest. She carefully lowered herself to her pad, to stay clear of any searching eyes. She felt her condition spinning away, out of control, and she focused on her breathing. She closed her eyes and she felt the presence she felt while she ran, the sentient being of the brown girl.

She dozed momentarily and then awoke to reach for water and found herself paralyzed. Her eyes wouldn't fully open and her tongue flopped around in her mouth, unable to utter anything more than a moan. She felt as she was buried in sand and nothing would budge. She panicked for a moment and then focused on her breathing to calm herself. She felt her face tingle, and her body relaxed, sinking into the pad. And then she was, free of it all, sitting upright beside her unconscious self.

She saw the brown skinned girl next to her unconscious body, the same presence she often felt while running. The girl sat watching all the creatures traversing the desert below. Hanna didn't recognize the enormous beasts grazing and walking until she realized that they were Pleistocene bison, and the elk were not elk at all, but giant red deer. Swift, stealthy carnivores wove through the sage, hunting huge rodents below the moon, and bats flew past her head like fighter jets.

It was peaceful, and Hanna was calm again. The two of them sat watching, and Hanna knew the brown girl would like to catch and eat some of those animals. Hanna's hand sought the Clovis, and she found it there between her knees. She held it tightly, and a jittery mood passed through the movement of the animals below. They continually looked up from their grazing, and hunting. The game began to walk more than graze. Some loped a few steps and then looked behind them, over their backs. Soon they were gone, and Hanna sighed at their passing.

Then, there was more movement, and she saw them gliding amongst the sage. A small band of hunters moved deftly along game trails. The men loped in front and the women followed, continually searching for food in the brush beside the trails, tasting grasses as they passed, pulling up plants by their roots and signing to the others what they found. They did all this while herding the children along and without falling too far behind the men. They were followed by a surly group of adolescent boys, who carried their atlatls lazily but with a dart notched to the throwing stick and ready, held by a pinch of the thumb and forefinger. The people made no noise. Their passing was the opposite of sound, a vacuum.

Hanna picked up a small whisper behind them, and the tribe heard it too. There was a frantic pause and backward glance from the women, which was picked up by the boys; the men felt the vibe and signaled for all to hurry, and they hastened their strides across the basin.

Following behind them, she saw a second band of men, covering ground swiftly, many more than the first group. They were intent on their mission; it was obvious in the way they held their darts and throwing sticks ready. Hanna felt panicked, she wanted to shout down to them but had no voice, and the brown girl held up her hand for silence. Hanna sensed that to shout would bring their death.

What followed was obvious from the shouts and screams, the grunts of men colliding at full force, the ululations of victory and the grunting of rape. She could see the scattering of children running to hide in the sage.

Hanna sobbed, and the brown girl held her with one hand across her shoulders and the other across her mouth. The brown girl tightened her grip in terror as another group passed along the trail. They were leaner and taller and held bows, arrows, and long lances. They passed at a jog, hardly glancing to read the trail. As soon and they were gone there was a new succession of warriors, now on horseback. The ground trembled and then there were waves of a new kind of men, white, pink, angry men, swarming through the sage, tearing it from the ground, searching, shaking out its clotted

roots, searching, searching for anything of value, tossing all
aside. They were followed by their women, clutching pink
babies to their large breasts, kicking aside what their men
had churned up, occasionally picking at something they had
missed—some dead, unpleasant booty.

Their adolescent boys followed, pink and cherubic,
sinister and insidious, clutching long, thick-tubed guns low
to their crotches, firing them at the sky, roaring in rage, so
that even the stars shuddered and the moon shushed the
calamitous roar. The brown girl flinched with every volley,
and when the echo of the shots abated, she heard the
apocalyptic madness as the distant groups found one
another, the children rippling through the sage, the sobbing
of plundered women.

Hanna held her head in her hands, crying silently as the
brown girl held her by the shoulder and stroked her back. In
time, it had become silent again except for the humming
dynamo of the arching night sky, or was it the clatter of
distant machines?

The brown girl shook Hanna and pointed down below.
Hanna could see that the land was restored but different, and
there was timid movement winking among the vegetation.
There they were, a swarthy band, moving through the sage
on foot, venturing back out, the men were mixed with the
women, and they were hunting and gathering quietly. The
children scurried nervously between their legs, running to
the forefront and peering ahead, then running back to their
clan. The men cuffed them lovingly, and the women rubbed
their heads. They moved quietly until they came to a cluster
of rocks where they rested. The women handed out dried
food and tubers, and the men sat with the children at their
feet, playing games with sticks and showing them slight-of-
hand tricks.

The brown girl communicated to Hanna in silent signs,
'That part down there, that is what matters.' They sat quietly
as the group of hunters and gatherers stood up and wandered
off. After a long moment the brown skinned girl

communicated again. 'You can search all you want, but you live here now, and they are gone.'

Hanna took a deep, quiet breath, like the sigh at the end of a good, long cry. The night seemed to have lifted slightly. She could hear the cicadas again, and she let her breathing follow their rhythm. Then the lines of their song returned to her head. 'It does-n't really mat-terrrrr.' She shushed them, angry at their song, but she let this be her mantra and good feelings again welled in her chest. She held up her hands to the stars and the moon, and looked further into the west where the sun had gone so long ago. There, at the horizon, one last stubborn storm flashed its lightening silently. Fear shook Hanna as she noticed that the brown skinned girl was gone. Hanna looked at her skin, and it was still brown, but the girl was no longer with her. She looked down at her own self, catatonic on the sleeping pad, and combed her fingers through that inert person's hair, feeling herself pulled down into the warm waters of her own being. She could no longer sit up, and thought that maybe it it'd be OK to lie down and just stare at the stars for a while.

* * *

Hanna awoke in dim light and sat bolt upright to see that the night had passed. She looked at her stuff and saw that it was all there, though mostly unused. She had her jacket wrapped around her. She looked about for the brown skinned girl. A shiver shuddered through her. She pushed her arms through the sleeves of the jacket. Her hands were covered in dust, her nails dirty and chipped. She ran her fingers through her hair, and felt the sand and grit on her scalp. She walked around the butte and tried to locate where everything had happened. "And what do I take away from all that?" she asked. "When they finally speak to you, it is mostly gibberish."

There was movement at the corner of her vision, and a

chickadee stared at her from the rock slab. "Did you see all that?" she asked.

The chickadee hopped in tight arcs and gave its 'fee-bee, fee-bee' song. It hopped a little closer and looked at Hanna with its black, bird eye.

"You shouldn't even be here. And I don't think you know anything at all!"

"Fee-bee, fee-bee, chick-a-dee dee dee."

"Should I go now?"

The chickadee hopped back and forth in an arcing dance, right, right, right, left, left, left, and then it flew down where her truck was hidden.

She rolled up her sleeping pad and put the empty bottles into her pack. She felt vacant and sad, but intact, as if walking away from a terrible wreck. The unassuming, slick rock summit showed no sign of all that had passed the night before. The Clovis was there at her feet, and she rolled it in her ski cap and zipped it in the top of her pack.

At camp, she tossed her pack into the back of the truck, folded her camp chair and tossed that in the back also. She opened the cooler and could tell that things were quickly going south. Hanna gave two apples and some carrots the sniff test, and determined that Dog would definitely eat them—if he ate fruit. She refilled two bottles from the last of the water from the large jug, and said good-bye to the rocks and desert junipers. She bowed to the butte and said, "Thank you." She bowed to the expanse of desert to the west, to the souls scattered in the sage and said, "I'm sorry."

She ate an apple as she drove away and nothing had never tasted so delicious. Everything about it was exquisite, the snap of the skin and texture of the firm pulp, the sweetness, the juice that sluiced through her teeth. It was manna. She ate the next apple and then the carrots. She felt sated, driving into the sun just rising from behind the clouds on the horizon.

She had to stop at the moraines to return the Clovis to its place, covering it with sand, and she replaced the rock on top of it. In front of the boulders, she raised her hands to acknowledge the distant buttes. The wind found her for a moment and raged about her, whipping sand in her face and then moved on, leaving the air still. "Did you see that last night, Paul?" she asked, looking at the sky. "You should consider *that* story for a while."

On her way back to the truck, at a wide, level spot on the moraine, Hanna buried Dean's Clovis. She placed the two pieces carefully together, pointing it at the buttes, covering it a few inches deep in sand and crushed stone. The sun was half hidden in a passing cloud, and it felt momentarily cool. Two ravens circled just out beyond the ridge and one rested on the tallest boulder, watching her.

Home

Hanna drove carefully to the highway and headed east, stopping when she passed the first large creek. She parked there and walked upstream to a thicket of trees and willows and immersed herself in the clear, icy waters, scrubbing her skin and her hair. She dried off with her old, dirty clothes, and put on a clean set. Feeling revitalized, rejuvenated and reborn, she drove back for many hours without the radio on. She thought about the night and Paul, or she thought about nothing. It was easy to let the beautiful world go by, and appreciate it for what it was.

Tim's truck was where it should be when she returned to camp to claim her spot under the cottonwood. She could see that the cook tent was open for business. Tim was not there, but Bob the dog came and greeted her exuberantly. He was all awag, and kept leaping straight up in the air while trying to press himself against her at the same time.

She rubbed him and patted him and pulled his ears, which made him groan in ecstasy. She went to the cook tent to see what there was to eat. Martha was behind the serving table. "Good Lord, girl, what happened to you?" Martha shook her head. "You look like a goddamn scarecrow! Jesus! A fat lip, scratches? You look like you've been in a cat fight!" Martha frowned with her fists on her hips. "Here, I got some bean soup for you. There's no meat in it yet. I'm gonna put some pork in it later for the rest—and bread, look, take lots of bread," she said, pushing a bowl of soup at her in a huff.

Hanna carried the huge bowl and bread to a table and fell on it like a hungry dog. It was so delicious she wanted to cry, but she didn't want to make a scene. She wanted to thank Martha, but that would have brought on tears, so she let her enthusiastic eating be her thanks. She mopped the bowl with her bread, and her stomach was as full as it could be. Martha came out and put her hand on Hanna's shoulder. "You want more, honey?"

"I do, but I couldn't fit anymore right now."

"You know, starving yourself won't bring anyone back. What the hell did you do to your cheek?" Martha took Hanna's chin with two thick fingers

"Oh, I took a bad tumble in some rough terrain."

"Lord, you like you've been in a bar fight."

"I know that. I just had to wrestle with some things, but I'll be OK now." Hanna had to quit talking as her throat constricted.

"I'll put aside some soup before I put the meat in it. I'll have a good salad for you tonight."

"Thanks, Martha."

"You look like shit, you know. Whatever you been up to isn't doing you any good."

Hanna didn't know why, but tears began rolling down her cheeks, "I'll be OK now." Her breath started heaving, and Martha pulled her close into her hip and ran her free hand through Hanna's hair.

"The boys won't be back for hours, and the rest of the crew aren't even here yet. Why don't you wash up and try to nap?"

"I will, thank you for the soup."

Martha laughed, shook her head and waved the words away, "The way you talk."

Hanna was weepy as she walked back to her truck, and she was glad no one was around. She cried hard at not seeing Paul's car. She knew that she would never see that little sedan again. She would never see him again. She would never drive back quietly from the field with Paul sitting on his hands in the back seat. She began to cry huge hard sobs, her chest aching and tears blinding her, running down her cheeks. She sat on a stump beside her truck and cried until her tears ran dry, while Bob leaned hard against her.

When she was done, she hoisted the hot, black shower bag onto its hook in the new shower stall. She used soap and shampoo and scrubbed herself with a bath sponge and

rinsed until all the water was gone. She dried and put on
clean shorts and a T-shirt, crawled into the back of her truck
and called to Bob. He jumped up to his spot on the tailgate.
"You keep an eye out, Bob!"

Bob grumbled a short growl, and Hanna fell into a deep
sleep.

She didn't wake until evening. A light rain was falling, and
it was cool. In her sleep, she had heard the thunder and then
the quick, hard rain, but now a light mist followed, which
was odd for this time of year.

Everyone was in the mess tent, and they gave her a small
cheer when she walked in. She took their shoulders in her
hand as she walked past them, as if they were holding her up.
She took Dog's shoulder, too, and patted his back as she
moved by him. To her surprise Alise stood and gave her a
brief hug. Tim was sitting out of reach, but he gazed at her
and gave her an impish wink, and then a troubled look as he
noticed her face. The tent was warm with all the bodies and
cooking. Martha had water boiling for the dishes, and it
seemed like everyone had a hot drink. Hanna took a bowl of
soup with bread and sat with Tim and Brad, who asked,
"Hanna, where ya been?"

"I am starving," she said, "so why doesn't everyone just
shut the hell up until I'm done!" The others laughed and
raised their cups, asking obnoxious questions to disrupt her.

"What the hell d'ya do to your face?"

"Goddamn it!" Hanna shouted, "Can't a girl take a
tumble without an investigation?"

They laughed, but continued to heckle her, "Hanna, what
do you think of the new route the line has gotta take?"

"Hanna, you want some tea?"

She laughed, shook her head, and turned her attention to
her soup. She ate ravenously, soaking her bread in it every
few spoonfuls.

Hugh came back with a bottle of whiskey, and a bottle of
rum, and all agreed that it would be good to have a hot
toddy on such a night. It was nice to have a cool evening and

hear the rain on the tent. Martha made a pot of coffee for Irish coffees and a pot of hot water for those who wanted a spiked sweet tea. Hanna didn't need any liquor in her state, but she had a mug of sweet tea, and watched the faces flush with alcohol, and listened to the voices get louder. Martha joined them when Hugh demanded that she drink on the job or be fired! And Fat-Assed Brad forced his way into the kitchen to help with the dishes.

They were laughing at the fit that CanAm had thrown over their route dead-ending at the huge site, with all the cultural material that Paul and Hanna had discovered. There was no solution yet. CanAm had made some offers to adjacent landowners for a right-of-way, but that option was just as complicated as excavating the entire site. "Anyway we go is going to cost them a lot of money, and now the Crow Agency is asking questions," Hugh said, giving the final word.

The crew was still digging test pits for a few more days, because their responsibility was to the original route, and there was a chance that they would hit the edge of all the artifacts and then the original route could squeeze around it. "That is what we call pure bullshit!" Dog laughed.

Tim said, "Now that we've walked around and looked at it from the hill and cut some of the brush, you can see where stuff's going to be. Just about every rock poking up through the ground is either part of a hearth or a teepee ring." When Martha asked if she could come out and observe, everyone insisted she do so and raised their cups to toast to her.

She blushed and accepted another small snort from Hugh's rum bottle in her cup of tea.

Hanna left as some of crew forgot about the tea and coffee, sipping straight out of the bottles.

With Brad in the kitchen, Hanna whispered to Tim as she got up to leave, "I have to sleep. We can talk tomorrow."

"Yeah, I didn't want to make an issue about anything...."

"Don't worry, we'll talk in the morning," she said, and then walked out into the steady, subtle rain.

It was nice to have the soft rain and not to have to wait for the evening to cool. She brushed her teeth and crawled into her truck with a sigh, closing the back against the chill, and was asleep long before dark. Bob the dog stood guard, irked that he wouldn't be allowed to sleep on her tailgate. In disgust he walked back to settle in on his patch of carpet under Tim's truck.

Tim was persistent, whispering Hanna's name until she raised the door of the shell on her truck. "Do you know how tired I am?" she grunted.

"I do, but you have to tell me what happened, because I know you didn't fall on a trail," Tim said resolutely.

She motioned him in quietly, while looking through the window at the figures hulking around the fire. He filled up the tiny shell like a fat man in a bathtub. "This doesn't work too well," Hanna grumbled as she tried to make space for him. "OK, listen and I'll tell you, but then you have to go," Hanna took a big breath and sighed. "When you left, and nobody was around, I had nowhere to go. So, I went to run a loop down in the Glacier Lake drainage."

"That's pretty ambitious."

"Well, I guess it was, but that's where I went, and things went really well. I did the whole Glacier Lake, Black Lakes loop in a day, running most of the way."

"Wow, that's huge! That's really a feat. A tiny bit reckless, but truly a feat!"

"Thanks, I was as careful as I could be."

"And you didn't fall during the run?"

"No, I came out unscathed."

"I am sensing a, 'but then'…."

"Right. So, I was at camp recovering, the next day or evening, and this woman invited me over to have dinner and drinks with her friends. It was fine, except that all there was for me were potatoes and salad."

"Why does everyone assume that that's all a vegetarian needs?"

"I know. Other than the food, everything was great,

except for this huge mountain of a guy, who was getting drunk and doing this whole passive-aggressive routine on me about being an archeologist, and on the environmental side of things."

"And you couldn't just let it go."

"No, I am done with that," Hanna said, shaking her head, moving her pillows to the corner of the truck so she could sit more comfortably. "We had some words, and I threw a drink in his face and the next thing I knew he had me by the hair and he was shaking me like a rag doll."

"Oh, my God, Hanna, I had no idea that anything like this would happen. I made that commitment to go climbing so long before, that I had to go. I had no way…"

Hanna held up her hands to stop his apology. "I know. I do. It's like you said. We can't foresee things. We can't be responsible for everyone all the time. But let me finish. Let me just tell you!"

Hanna paused for a moment and then continued, "So, he was shaking me by the hair and we crashed into the table and went to the ground."

"Holy shit!"

"And when he lifted me up, I had a barbeque fork and I stabbed him."

Tim stared and blinked for a long moment. "You stabbed him, like, really stabbed him?"

"Well, not in the heart. It was his thigh, which was the only thing I could see—you know, the way he had me by the hair."

"Only in the thigh? So did his friends all jump you?"

"No, they were too stunned, and one girl looked like she was going to laugh. They didn't know what to do."

"Well no, what would you do?"

"But he did toss me through the air, and that is when I got so messed up."

"So how did it end?"

"I got the hell out of there. How do you think it ended?"

"And all that took six days?"

Hanna stopped and looked at Tim, and tears came to her eyes, as she wondered how she could relate all the rest. She blinked back the tears. "No, but I can't tell you the rest right now. I am just too tired. Really. I'll tell you the rest tomorrow or whenever." She leaned forward and awkwardly kissed him.

"I'm sorry, I didn't think…" Tim began to explain.

"Shush, Tim! It's like you say. We can't see what's gonna happen. We can't keep people safe from themselves. Now you have to go…really. But let Bob stay on the tailgate, I feel warm now." Tim awkwardly clambered out of the truck shell, standing and stretching.

"By the way," Hanna said, "not one word to Karl or Hugh. They'll call the police, and I am not going to do that." She thought for a moment. "But we're gonna have to find out if the police know. You'll have to help me do that."

Tim tried to speak, but Hanna held up her hand, and then lay back with a heavy sigh.

Deceit

They stood and stared in disbelief. The little valley of artifacts had been plowed down the middle, two bulldozer blades wide, just enough for a pipeline.

"And this means?" Hanna asked.

"It means CanAm says, 'Fuck you'," Dog said.

"That's about it," Hugh said. "It means they know more rich white men than we know. It means there are friendly state senators, or a judge or two, who will refuse to hear a complaint. It means that the landowner was pissed off that he might lose the cash from the right-of-way."

"So what do we do?"

"Treat the bulldozed ground as compromised terrain and refuse to sign off on the paperwork. Then we'll pick up the survey where the 'dozer scar stops, I guess."

"Are you going to call Karl?"

"Yeah, but with all the people he knows around here, I'd say he's heard about it already."

"Well, are we just going to ignore it?"

"For now, I'd say we are. I'll call Karl, but my guess is that CanAm is belligerently unconcerned. The only other option is to walk off the job. Which means that CanAm would probably come in with a more compliant crew of archeologists to finish the survey."

"And they're Canadians!" Dog muttered. "It's bad enough when Americans do this shit, but now they're letting a bunch of foreigners do it."

Hugh and Hanna stared at Dog for a moment, then Hanna said, "I know. You think they would use a little respect and diplomacy."

"Well it was an American 'dozer that did it. It was probably even the guy that owns the place. All they have to do is whine about how many jobs it's gonna cost and the prairie parts like the Red Sea," Tim said, waving his arms at the dusty scar.

Hugh shook his head and kicked the ground. "Well, I gotta go call Karl. I'll catch up at the camp."

* * *

From that point, surveying got sloppy, and any artifacts found brought the whole crew to a standstill. They would break out the shovels to dig test pits for the most minor artifacts, even fire-cracked rock, which could be caused by anything, including wildfires. When any of the crew mentioned calling Karl, Hugh would snort, "That's a great idea, if you want your head torn off."

Hugh had lost his jovial demeanor and was often red-faced after dealing with administrative issues. He ran Leon and other CanAm officials off the job under a hail of locker room expletives.

Karl and CanAm couldn't reach a settlement on how the bulldozed camp could be rectified, and the situation had come to the full attention of the reservation elders. The crew noticed that a car sat near the bulldozed cut, with two Crow men and a white guy with a telephoto lens taking pictures from the edge of the fence.

The older Crow man crossed the fence and walked to Hugh, who wore the friendliest smile.

Hugh shook his hand, and the man asked, "What happened here?"

"We're not sure," Hugh said, "Someone got impatient."

"That's too bad," the man said kicking at the dusty scar. "Now they'll really need to be patient." The old man looked at the scar with an inscrutable gaze. "We always knew that this camp was here. This land went over to private ownership in the sixties."

"I don't mean to be nosy, but is that guy your lawyer?"

"Are you with CanAm?"

"Not really, we're just the archeologists." Hugh smiled.

"Well then, yeah, he's the lawyer, an expensive one, but

he says he'll do this for free."

"Ahh, pro bono?"

"Ahh, no, he says his name's Anderson," the Crow man winked and smirked.

Hugh laughed, and the Crow man gave the smallest of smiles.

"So, what are you thinking?" Hugh asked.

"The easement of the right-of-way is a joint agreement between the rez lands and private lands. I'd say that this violates the agreement." The man looked at Hugh for a long time. "But that's just my opinion."

* * *

"All we're doing is facilitating it," Hanna said, nursing a beer that night, staring into the fire outside Hugh's teepee.

Tim smiled philosophically, "Did you really, honestly, think any different? Those guys would plow the entire state from one end to the other, and sow it with salt if it would net them another million dollars."

Dog grumbled, "If it was an early cavalry fort we found, the state would declare it a historical landmark, and they'd all be here singing 'God Bless America' by tomorrow morning."

Even sweet Sarah grumbled, "What's the sense in any of this? The pipeline would have gone through. All we wanted to do was catalog what was here. Give it some recognition and maybe some respect. But the money people would never let that happen. We may as well be out here playing Frisbee."

Work got slower and more careless, as they now tried to go as slowly as absolutely possible, which was even more maddening. The crew's only advantage was that the paperwork for every surveyed section had to be done, and Karl couldn't fake it. The stacks of forms from the field had to corroborate the final computer forms, and it would be a herculean effort to fake them.

Bulldozing the right-of-way affected Dog the most, and he smoldered about it for days. He made more racist and misogynistic comments than usual. He left gates open, left the vehicles blocking roadways. He would ignore landowners who came out to check on the crew surveying across their ranches. Hanna had been making her way with Dog, but now he had soured and she was ignoring him again. The meaning of the work had evaporated; not that they were saving anyone or anything, but they had been doing work that was important to them. Everyone had been adhering to the rules. Hanna could see Dog's point. Even if the people from these sites were not his tribe, they were still his people. There were rules in place to protect what little was left. He was doing this; he was complying, making sure that all sides got their share, but then some whiteman made a phone call for CanAm, and the 'dozers ran right through teepee rings and fire hearths.

* * *

The outrageous affront from CanAm cast a shadow on camp life too, and the crew members seemed to go their own ways in the evenings. Hugh and Dog drove off to the bars, and Alise and Sarah went hunting men. Hanna stepped up her running regime, knocking off 30 miles a week. This left her at the edge of a comfortable exhaustion, and she rose past her funk. She was getting over her episode down South, but the one thing that gnawed at her was whether or not the law was involved.

Work was busy, and it took a while for Hanna to find enough time alone with Tim, to relate all the events that took place in the desert.

"Hmm," he said scratching his chin, "so when the gods finally talk, they're speaking in tongues?" Tim asked.

"I guess I am now something of an authority, so I would have to say it's mostly gibberish."

Hanna recounted her version of the brawl to Tim several times, until he knew it by heart. As soon as they had a free evening, they drove to Covet, to phone that county's sheriff's office. Tim spoke to the dispatcher, reporting the incident as something he had 'witnessed' at a trailhead campground. Hanna listened intently to his side of the conversation as he gave the dispatcher a fake name and address, and then started an interview of the facts.

"No Ma'am, I was not involved. All I am telling you is what I saw from my camp."

"The Glacier Lake Trailhead."

"Yes, the one in your county."

"Yes Ma'am, there was physical abuse against a female."

Hanna nodded her head in agreement. She was impressed with his 'Ma'ams'. They were so sincere.

"No, I don't know her or what her relationship was."

"It was almost dark, I couldn't see so well."

"The day? That would have been…" Hanna flashed a ten and a three with her fingers, "the thirteenth of this month. It was approximately…" Hanna was flashing numbers with her fingers.

"I don't know," Tim said, "just before dark."

"I don't know exactly what happened; there was some sort of physical assault upon a woman and she seemed to hurt the guy pretty good, in order to free herself, and then she ran off into the night."

"No Ma'am, I chose not to get involved. There was only me, and several of them."

Hanna nodded her head and smiled in agreement with his statement.

"I couldn't contact anyone. I was meeting a larger group, and we left first thing in the morning on a backpacking trip. I just got back, and it was bothering me…. Yes, the woman appeared to be out of danger. But the man was hurt."

"No, I called to see if I would be needed as a witness."

"No report, no? Nothing reported on the fourteenth either?"

"No, I don't choose to make a report. They must have worked it out on their own."

"No, thank you, you have been more than helpful. I

appreciate it."

Tim smiled and held up his empty hands to her, and Hanna nearly collapsed with relief, and then jumped up and down, clapping.

"Hanna, you're really lucky. You know that I'm sorry I wasn't there, but you can't keep doing stuff like that. You could get killed!"

"Don't lecture, Tim. You're the one who was beaten in a bar."

He held up his hand to argue but Hanna stopped him. "Don't try to tell me that was different. I didn't do anything to precipitate this event. The whole thing just had a life of its own. He was trying to intimidate me, and threaten me, like his friends from the desert."

"And you won't go to the law with this one either?"

"No, especially not this time. He has three witnesses against my word. Plus there was alcohol involved. No, it would be a mess."

"I hate to admit it, but I agree with you. You did throw a drink in his face."

"You think I'll have to worry about bumping into them every time we're down South?"

"We're more or less done down there. And God knows what job that guy's been sent to next. If we have to go back to finish up anything, just tell Karl you don't feel safe down there, and he won't force you to go."

"You're right."

"You'll have to keep an eye out, though.... You did stab him with a barbeque fork."

"He had me by the hair, and I thought he'd break my neck."

"Keeping your mouth shut wasn't an option?"

"Not at that point in time."

"They're going to have to start a support group down there to help the guys you've been...savaging. There'll be rumors circulating about the crazy little bitch with Mace and cooking utensils."

Hanna snorted a quick laugh. "Why do you think he didn't report anything?"

"Well, he's a big macho guy, and he'd have to admit that a woman got the best of him. Plus it'd look just as bad for him, because no matter what you say about them, the cops know that a skinny thing like you doesn't attack a huge guy like that for no reason."

As the survey moved farther north, the mornings and evenings commutes were eating up too much time. They began to look for a new camp. Karl and Martha knew people who knew people, and they were sure that they could find a new base camp. This would be the last move of the summer. The days were growing shorter, and the job was on schedule to reach the final point of the contract in a month. It was hard to find a good place for so many to camp. It couldn't be just any place, it needed to be shaded and sheltered, close to a road, yet quiet. Karl was offering pretty good money, and Martha came up with a spot after a week of hunting around. "My ex's cousin has a small place that the family's been wondering what to do with. The cows were in there this spring, but now it's pretty good. We'll have to flip some dried turds away to set up tents, but all in all, it might even be better than it is around here. It's a nice place and Little Goose Creek runs through it. If you woke up there tomorrow, you'd think you were right around here."

Their slowdown had caused Karl and CanAm a headache, and now the CanAm digging crews were laying pipe only 40 miles behind them. CanAm had taken over a big lot north of Covet where they cached pickups, cargo trucks, and earth-moving equipment. Their vehicles were more apparent now, and they would show up every few days, checking on the survey's northward progress.

Sensing the pressure from behind, the crew picked up speed. It wasn't Karl's fault, and a work slow down was not the solution. They all knew that it was tedious as hell to work so slowly. As they racked up more miles, even Dog cheered up, regained some energy, and quit cussing like Satan.

The day before their move, Hugh and Dog set about helping Martha tear down the kitchen and pack it off to the new spot. Moving camp would take a whole day, and everyone would have to fend for themselves, which was no big deal. They were all practiced at living out of a cooler.

Alise and Sarah had become spoiled with Martha's cooking and drove to Gluttons. This left Tim and Hanna alone in camp, and they sat in the chairs outside Tim's truck and talked as the evening fell. Tim had anticipated the evening and prepared a large chilled bowl of tabbouleh and chopped vegetables with hummus for dinner.

Hanna blushed as he laid out dinner on the tailgate of the truck. She was speechless, and confused by her emotions. But then she remembered that some things just don't matter, and she was comfortable with the love that she felt for this man. She was done with '-isms' and she refused to be an '-ist', an '-ian', or a '-ual'.

She put her fork down, looked at him and said, "I am what I am, Tim. I want to be honest with you, because I never told Paul how I felt, and now I can't…. I think that would have meant a lot to him."

"We never say those things…and people kind of freak out when we try to."

"You know how I feel about you?"

"I can guess," Tim said. "It's hard to tell sometimes, but I think I know."

"Do you want to walk Bob all over the hills after dinner?"

"I know where he can chase some wild turkeys."

"These turkeys are actually a feral, invasive species. Did you know that?"

"You stupid turkeys!" he shouted, shaking his fist.

Hanna laughed and took his hand in hers. "I'm happy with you, and that matters."

He squeezed her hand and looked at her. "I am as happy with you as I've ever been with anyone."

"Tell me about one of those anyones," Hanna said,

sitting back in her chair.

Tim thought for a moment, meaning he had many anyones to consider. "OK, well I lived with a woman in California once."

"Wow, California. That's far away."

"Yeah, it is."

"So, go on."

"That was when I was in my twenties, and I still had Babe and the Volkswagen."

"Don't stop, just tell me the story."

"OK, well, I was traveling, you know, and I had been to Yosemite and climbed a lot, until a huge storm came in and shut it down in late fall. I met some people who were going to a Dead concert in the Bay Area. They had a scam on tickets. So I went with them; I went to a Dead concert in Candlestick Park! And that was a total trip. Let me tell you. There were freaks there that weren't even from this earth— have you ever been to a Dead concert?"

"No, but I can see you there very clearly."

"So it was an amazing event, and then I went and stayed with these guys who had a place in the Berkeley Hills. That was crazy also. You know, they had this tree house, and a tight rope, and they all juggled, and one guy was a talented magician and a hotel flew him to Vegas once a month."

"And there were girls, of course."

"Yes, but not for me."

"Ohhh," she said sympathetically.

"Well, yeah," he frowned dramatically and nodded, "so, one day I was out on an errand, and my car broke down. I was trying to fix it on this busy street, and a cop started hassling me about moving the car, and asking if Babe had had her shots.

"Then, this car pulls into the driveway right in front of my car, and a woman steps out, obviously interested in what's going on. She carried her groceries to the house, and then comes back and asks the officer what's going on. In the end, she talks the cop into helping me push my Bug into her driveway, and then tells me I have until the end of the day to get it running. I couldn't, so I had to push it onto her lawn so she could get to her next class."

"She was a student?"

"No, she was sociology professor."

"She was a professor? How old was she?"

"In her thirties."

"And you were in your twenties?"

"I thought you wanted me to tell the story without stopping." He glared at her, and then smiled. "So I couldn't get it running, and she comes home from work like she's pissed off, and then she tells me that dinner would be ready in one hour. So I ate there, and she let me sleep on the couch, but made me shower first. Then she came out of her room an hour later, and told me I didn't have to sleep on the sofa."

"Of course. What else would a single 30-something say when there's a young man in the house?"

"So, anyway…" he scowled at her, "the next morning I go out, and the car starts first try, and she was mad and accused me of staging the whole thing. It was pretty awkward, and I went back to the place where I was staying, but more friends of theirs had arrived. It was crowded, and obvious that I would be intruding if I stayed any longer. So, I decided to leave town. I stopped for gas and some groceries and bought wine and good bread to leave at Carol's house— that was her name—because she really didn't need to do everything that she had done. I left a bag for her on her porch just as she pulled into the driveway. At first, she thought I was up to no good, but then she saw the bread and wine, which she looked over, and said, 'Nice try, but I think you owe me lunch.'

"She was funny. She had that pushy way that some Californians have. She more or less interviewed me while she ate this really expensive lunch that I was paying for.

"She had a fenced backyard and loved Babe. I stayed for a while and found a job with some guys that did her yard work. Her ex still had tools in her garage, and I repaired things that were wrong with her house. When she wasn't working, we went to Point Reyes and other places along the coast. When she had a few days, we went up to Tuolumne Meadows. That was really different, because I was all ready to sleep in the dirt, but she would have nothing to do with it, and rented us a cabin. And that was pure luxury for me.

"Carol was an easy person to be with, once I got past her defenses, and I was still there a month later. I had never really had a girlfriend that had a place we could share. You know? I'd had girlfriends, but it was always like at 'my place' or 'their place'. There was never an 'our place' where we would be day after day. That was new for me.

"I was young and never even questioned what was going on. It seemed like she didn't either. Then one night we were out having dinner, and a woman from her department came by our table. She was obviously amused with the situation. And that was it. It took one nosy person to ruin everything. I never completely understood, but Carol started to question everything about us and about me. I had no education, I had no money, no address, and this was too much, even for a woman from Berkeley Hills."

"Ah, convention got the better of her."

"Maybe women feel time differently than men. Maybe 30-year-olds feel time differently than 20-somethings. At some point, maybe we all get older and feel like it's time to quit screwing around and get down to business."

"If only we could find out what that business is."

"Of course, the whole time I suppose I knew that it would fail. How often does a relationship with a 15-year difference succeed? And I knew that, but I was happy at that point in time, with that person. When I left, I was later surprised at how lonely I was without her. How other women failed to measure up to her. I wrote a couple of times, but she never responded. She offered to keep Babe for a while until I found a place. And I was like, 'Find a place? I have a place.' I didn't even really know what she was talking about. I thought I was supposed to be wherever I was."

"I guess we're not far from there are we?"

"I don't know. Sometimes I am, and sometimes I'm not."

They walked into the Pine Hills with Bob. The flycatchers were already migrating through and Hanna took out her field glasses. The flycatchers and pewees and phoebes drove her crazy, they were all a bunch of small green birds that looked exactly the same, acted the same, inhabited the same environment and fed on insects on the wing. They seemed to start migrating in August, and were usually gone with the first cold storm of fall.

August flycatchers filled her with anxiety because it marked the end of summer. They reminded her of what she had left undone. They marked change, and Hanna feared change. The end of summer meant hard choices. She had spent some bleak winters in university libraries, in dead-end jobs, in poor relationships. She tried to put all that out of her mind and just be there with Tim and Bob.

Bob hunted mice and ground squirrels in the tall grass. He stepped gingerly, avoiding the plentiful prickly pear growing up through the tall grass. He leapt into the air, and Hanna and Tim heard the following buzz of a prairie rattler, Bob kept going as if nothing had happened. Tim stopped for a moment and watched him, but he could see that there had been no contact. He shook his head, "It's pretty amazing he's never been bitten."

"I know. He's good with those things."

They followed cow trails to the top of a hill. There was prickly pear everywhere and they carefully chose a flat sandstone rimrock to sit on and watch the evening drop. Bob grew tired of avoiding cactus and found a flat rock also. They were looking down on the camp, when they saw the Bronco with Hugh and Dog arrive down below. After while, they saw the leaping tongues of flame and knew that Dog had started the fire with gas.

"Dog sure is a reckless one, isn't he?"

"I'm sure we don't even know the half of it. You should see him in the bars. He's the most ornery dickhead you've ever seen. He's so bad that everyone leaves him the hell alone."

"According to Hugh and Dog, you're the one the bouncers rough up."

Tim blushed brightly. "Well, that was just once."

"Maybe."

"No really, I had this great idea that the dancer would think it was funny if I danced with her."

"Spare me."

"Don't worry, I paid for that one. But listen! Really, I wasn't trying to be crude, or mean, I just thought it would be funny. You know, the whole absurdity of a filthy field worker taking off his grubby clothes beside such a dolled-up stripper."

"The bouncers didn't get it, though."

"No, they don't do absurdist irony."

"Bouncers can be so dense!"

They laughed for a while and sat quietly together. The air was calm and the rocks were warm from the day's sun.

"How long do you think it'll be before we're done?" Tim asked.

"Oh, a month. Hugh and I drove it and measured everything, and we calculated it out to be a month, if we don't find any more difficult sections."

"I'm still pissed about that last section they fixed with the 'dozer," Tim growled.

"Me too, but it's past now—let's let it go. I get the feeling that CanAm isn't going to walk away from all that too easily. The lawyers are circling and the Crow elders seem pretty smug about it."

"I know. I get that feeling, too. And Karl has never signed the papers on that section."

Hanna sat quietly for a moment before she spoke. "Dog can't seem to get past it. It's seems more like a personal attack for him. He grumbles about excavating because of his arm, but you can see a reverence in him when he's doing it."

"I don't know about reverence, but he's pretty involved with those kinds of digs."

"Think about what he said. If it were an insignificant old cavalry fort, it would be hallowed ground."

"I know." Tim nodded, "He should be pissed off. More than I am."

They walked back as the evening cooled. Bob caught a thirteen-lined ground squirrel.

"That's too bad." Tim shrugged, "I like those things."

"Me too. They seem kind of rare. Bad, Bob, bad!" Hanna scolded.

Bob ran off smugly, to look for something else. They hadn't gone very far when they heard a heinous howling. Bob was on his hind legs swinging his head back and forth. They could see a ground squirrel clinging to the side of his cheek. Finally it went flying off in one direction, and Bob ran off in another with his tail between his legs, looking back suspiciously as if the rodent might still be after him. Tim and Hanna laughed, and Bob scowled at them and then ran off down the trail as if he couldn't care less.

"Don't be a bad sport, Bob," Tim shouted.

An hour after she had gone to bed, Hanna got up to pee. There was a quarter moon, and she saw someone walking off down the road. She could tell from the limping stride that it was Dog. It was a quick, unlikely pace for him, and she watched him go for some time, until she was sure he wouldn't be back. She wondered if Dog and Hugh had gotten into it over something, but that was unlikely. Where would he go?

She slept well and awoke early to brew her coffee on the tailgate. She felt generous and took a cup to Tim's truck and left it on a small shelf just inside the door. He was still asleep but she knew he would quickly catch a whiff.

Bob was waiting for her on the small patch of carpet in front of the tailgate of her truck. He was impatient. He wanted her to sit and have her coffee, so he could be at her feet. He was alert to motion down the road, and Hanna looked up to see Dog returning to camp. He ambled with a fatigued gait, as if he had walked far. The legs of his pants were wet with dew. He had to pass close to Hanna to get to his droopy tent. The look on his face said he had been caught at something, and he avoided her eyes. Bob thumped his tail nervously. Finally, Dog turned as he passed and gave an uncertain glare, and with his good hand he held up his finger to his lips for silence.

Bob watched him go, knowing that it was odd. He turned to look at Hanna to see what she thought, and she pushed her toe against his ribcage. He thumped the ground with his tail and gave his canine smile. Hanna watched Dog disappear into his tent.

The crew was eating lunch under the shade of a cottonwood when a sheriff pulled up. Hanna jumped. She was wrestling with either running or playing dumb, when both Tim's and Hugh's eyes fell on her, and they casually shook their heads.

The officer asked for the supervisor, and took Hugh to his truck for a while. Hanna watched Hugh talking, shaking his head and exchanging a few words now and then. She noticed that their eyes never even glanced in her direction. Then, in sudden understanding, Hanna shot Dog the most furtive of looks, as he sat, emotionless, with an old McDonald's bag in his lap, munching down stale fries one after another. The cop and Hugh shook hands in front of the truck and laughed a bit, shaking their heads. Hugh was schmoozing, playing up his jolly, good-ole-boy routine, and he and the sheriff parted ways amiably. He was smiling as he came back to the crew. "Well you're not going to believe this, but someone set two of CanAm's trucks on fire over at their equipment yard last night."

"Where?" Tim asked.

"You know, their new equipment lot, over on the highway by Covet."

"Two trucks?" Hanna asked.

"Yeah, two brand-new pickups."

"Probably kids," Alise said, shaking her head, wondering what'd gone wrong with the world.

"Or goddamned Canadians," Dog said dryly.

"OK, listen you guys, they are no more Canadians than I am," Hugh said in a huff. "It's a mongrel multinational corporation."

Everyone laughed for a minute, muttering, "Goddamned mongrel multinationals."

"How far do you think that is from camp?" Hanna asked.

"Farther than I can waddle," Hugh said, holding up his hands in innocence. "Twenty miles on roads, eight or ten as the crow flies." Hugh eyed Hanna smiling. "Did you run over there last night and set those trucks on fire."

Hanna shook her head, "It wasn't me! I was shaggin' Dog all night. Wasn't I, Dog?"

The crew erupted in laughter, and Dog choked on his fries. Hanna caught his eye, and he smiled slyly at her.

"Ah well, karma works in mysterious ways," Tim said sagely, packing up his little cooler.

"Amen," Hugh shouted, holding up his hands like a preacher. He farted loudly, chuckled and said, "Couldn't a happened to nicer folks."

Sarah giggled loudly and pushed Hugh roughly as if he had crossed a line.

Hanna got her things together and shook the dried grass from her flannel shirt. She waited a moment for the crew to wander away and stared at Dog until he met her eyes. She winked at him, and he smiled like a naughty boy.

"You're lucky you didn't set yourself on fire."

"You got that right."

Catherine

Fall came with its initial cold rains only days after they reached the end of the line. Then, it cleared and a long Indian summer followed. Hanna returned to the office, or ventured out with Hugh and Dog, following up on various sections of the survey. The rumor around the office was that Donna, Karl's secretary, divorced her husband and appeared to be openly pursuing a relationship with Karl. Her bottom swung even more defiantly than it had in the past, like a plucky church bell it swayed—ding-dong, ding-dong—in her sleek skirt, all around the shabby office.

Tim wasn't one for office work. He left on a long rock-climbing trip with Andy, Catherine's partner. They went to try some longer routes in the mountains where Paul had died. Hanna was jealous of Tim's trip and wondered why he hadn't chosen her. When out of the mountains, Tim was dutiful and called the office now and then to catch up with her. The calls were sweet, but he was terrible on the phone, as if he didn't quite know how to use it. In his conversations, he would often mention Andy, and then in the same sentence, he would find a way to mention Catherine. "You know, Catherine is his partner?" or, "Remember, you danced with Catherine?" or more obviously, "What do you think of Catherine?" Hanna came to hate the name Catherine, and the way he pushed it at her.

Hanna's interest in office work was waning, and she felt odd, there with just Karl and Donna. Hugh and Dog were out in the field, but traveling every day or two, staying in hotels, and Hanna knew she wouldn't be comfortable as the third person. Alise and Sarah were still up North, but they were on very small excavations. So, Hanna chose the office. The house that Karl rented had an acre of land, and some good shade trees. That was where she parked and lived in her truck. She had known better times.

Hanna had just finished, and filed a report on a section of the CanAm line that crossed state land when she thought that she heard someone knock lightly at the door, which was odd because everyone seemed to barge in. She opened the door cautiously. There was Catherine, standing on the sad, dark, paint-chipped landing of the second floor, like a princess in a dreary tower. They looked awkwardly into each other's eyes. "Yeah," Catherine said shyly, "I wasn't sure that this was the place."

"If you're looking for me, it must be," Hanna said as she hugged her briefly and pulled her into the office. Catherine was nervous and blushing in Hanna's presence, avoiding eye contact for a moment. "Is this crazy?" Catherine asked. "Am I crazy? I hope you don't think I'm dangerous?"

"No, but I'm jealous of how nervy you are."

"All I did was ask Tim how you were doing—and he laid out your whole routine to me."

"No doubt. He is shrewd that way."

"I called the office phone, but no one ever answered, and leaving a message seemed so... desperate."

"And this isn't?" Hanna laughed.

Catherine looked around the room, and Hanna could see all that she saw, a dingy office, a coffeepot ringed with bitter, scalded residue, stacks of papers leaning precariously, a white copy machine morphing to yellow, a low ceiling missing a few acoustic tiles, the tired linoleum floor tramped over by hundreds of muddy, dusty boots. In contrast, Catherine stood there in her tanned, lovely skin—with her ginger hair, her slender frame—in her expensive, casual, athletic clothes, the juxtaposition glaring.

Hanna motioned to the coffee bar in jest. "Coffee?"

Catherine grabbed the scalded pot and a chipped cup, and poured the bitter brew. She added some Cremora and took a sip, "Just the way I like it."

"I don't know if my estimation of you just went up or down."

"I like the lack of pretention. I can hardly wait to see your motel."

Hanna laughed hard and saw a bit of confusion in Catherine's green eyes. "Actually, I'm living in my truck, behind Karl's house."

Catherine looked at Hanna with raised eyebrows, holding her dirty cup elegantly. She made to say something conciliatory, but then snorted a quick chuckle. "Oh, well, it's not like I didn't know."

"Don't worry, we can move over to the motel. It might be a little too crowded in the truck."

"Tim told me to take you climbing. He said that today was the last day of the session...." Catherine suddenly lost her confidence. "This is crazy. You don't have to go anywhere with me."

"Don't be a baby!" Hanna said, happy to see Catherine's defeat. "Of course we'll go climbing. But I don't know where you want to go."

Catherine's eyes rekindled. "Don't worry—I know."

"I know you know."

Hanna ushered Catherine out of the office, locking the door, and down to the main street where it was baking hot. They both squinted and put on sunglasses. There was a block or two of old, brick buildings, but that quickly changed to steel warehouses and then in a quarter mile there was nothing but the weedy desert and bright green alfalfa, and beet fields shining in the sun.

Catherine walked to a sporty little van parked at the curb. "I thought we could take this and go down to the Shell River Canyon." She opened the door, and Hanna was impressed with the tidy and compact interior, with a tiny stove atop a tiny fridge, and a cupboard beside it.

"Wow, I think this could be classified as Freudian anal."

"Yeah, that's my Andy all the way. You should see how long it takes him to get it ready for a trip—oh, my God, and then you should see him clean it after a trip. I don't get it."

"And he's off with Tim?"

"I know. It makes Andy crazy, but Tim's good for him."

Catherine wheeled the van around the back of Karl's house, and they loaded Hanna's gear and cooler in just a few minutes.

"That's it?"

"That's all I need."

Catherine whistled, staring into the back of the truck, "You are one gnarly bitch!"

"Maybe clueless is a better word."

"Yes, but I see a Zen-like ideal here that few have."

"Well, when your reality is a Zen-like ideal then it's nothing special."

They headed down the blistering highway in the cool air conditioning with music on the radio, they were quiet and nervous in each other's company. They drove across the huge, hot basin with craggy mountains to the west and the uplifted shield of the Lost Horse Peaks to the east. The hills climbed first as desert, and then as grass and sage, until they met the forested plateau.

Catherine pretended to be sure of herself, chatting about things she was doing and how she had been climbing a lot again. She mentioned some of the people Hanna had met, and some she had not. Hanna could feel the pregnant topic of Paul's death hanging heavily. She knew that Tim would have told Catherine all about it.

Hanna looked across at Catherine and saw someone who was a couple of years older than her, economically established and slightly more conventional. Hanna wondered what she was doing. How could she let people walk into her work and take her away like this? She didn't even leave a note for Karl. She had imagined running off with Catherine as something wild and adventurous, but now it seemed like it might be sordid and slutty. Hanna folded her arms and thought. 'All I really know about her is how it felt holding her hand for five minutes at a backcountry bacchanal.'

Catherine stopped at a junction and looked at a map, and then turned onto a dirt road marked Fossil Beds.

"Have you ever been here?" she asked.

"I'm embarrassed to say I haven't. I was always in too much of a hurry."

They drove down the road for longer than Hanna thought they should and then came to a dry wash with a parking area and an outhouse.

"For me, this is mind blowing," Catherine said. "I saw it the first time with my dad, when I was 12. It stunned me."

They walked 50 yards up the sandy wash, until the riverbed turned to sandstone slabs, and everywhere were huge chicken-like tracks, walking every which way. Some were the size of turkey tracks, and others where ten or 20 inches long.

"My dad was a geologist. He said that these were probably fast, wicked, birdlike carnivores that hunted in packs."

Hanna wasn't ready for that. She spun to look at Catherine.

"I know," Catherine said. "It is hard to imagine wolf-like chickens prowling around. It gave me nightmares."

Hanna put her hand down into a fossilized track so that her fingers fit the mold, and she shivered in the dry desert air.

Catherine smiled down at her, "Even the smaller ones' heads would've come up to your waist—wolfish two legged carnivores—sound familiar?"

* * *

Up in the Big Shell Canyon, the highway climbed through the scrubby juniper and mountain mahogany foothills, through the blonde and red sandstone walls; then the road began to climb along the river. This was a popular tourist route, and they passed camping rigs by the side of the road. Grown men in baggy shorts stood amazed at the scenery, with zoom-lensed cameras perched upon their bellies. The traffic fell in behind a long line of tractor-trailers, and Catherine shifted to a lower gear.

They drove into an established campground and paid the fee. Hanna left a water jug on the picnic table to mark their territory, and they went back down the canyon to find some climbing, which appeared to be everywhere. There was a pullout crowded with climber vans and efficient, little station wagons. Catherine's climbing pack was tidy and trim and ready to go, but Hanna had to move things around to pack food and water bottles. It didn't take long to leave the van, and Hanna could see Catherine's efficient drive; she had dismissed her as soft, but she had forgotten that she had been doing this for a lot longer than Hanna had.

They navigated the trail of steep switchbacks up past a hillside of yellow flowering balsamroot daisies and purple lupine. Passing into the forest, they continued steeply upward. Hanna's tank top clung limply to her sweaty torso. A small drip of sweat dangled from the tip of her nose. The pines grew larger as they climbed the hill and then bumped right up against a band of sheer limestone walls. The serpentine trail followed the wall closely for a while, though Catherine showed no interest in the rock. Then it leveled out after another short hill, and the earth was obviously pounded out at this point. Catherine dropped her pack at the base of a large limber pine. Her top was dark with sweat and she took all of her fine, straight hair and pulled it up into a topknot. She smiled at Hanna. "It's not running, but it can really get you going."

Hanna was glad to see how much Catherine enjoyed the workout. "I don't think I'm gonna have to run during our downtime."

"No, don't do that! It'd just be so…Nazi bitch."

Hanna laughed and Catherine joined her, but she was already pulling gear out of her pack. In a flash, Catherine had her harness on and a guidebook in her hand. Hanna was looking up at the blank-looking wall, following the lines of bolts that climbed through the bands of pocketed roofs, ending at pairs of chains. They walked down the cliffs, and Catherine pointed out various routes that she would like to try. She was polite and asked several times what Hanna would like, and then they settled on a few routes that would be suited to their ability.

The day was getting on and Catherine was anxious to climb, so she set off up a blank-looking wall with ample pockets and edges along the way. She climbed it swiftly, past the bolts to the chains, and Hanna lowered her down. Hanna followed it and retrieved the gear, surprised at how steep and hard it was. She didn't want to be seen struggling and did her best to move smoothly. At the anchor, she ran the rope through the chains and rappelled down.

Catherine congratulated her on her effort and then offered her the next lead. This climbing was new to Hanna. It had nothing to do with climbing mountains, and it was physically harder in a steep, gymnastic way. She didn't want to be a wet blanket, so she took the draws and carabiners, tied into the rope and set off once she was on belay. It was immediately evident that this route was more difficult than the last, but the bolts seemed close together, which she liked, and she quickly clipped them and moved past, onto some good pockets, until she got to a vertical edge that she could layback off of for a few moves, keeping her feet up high to her right. Her forearms were pumping, and sweat was rolling down her back. She continued on past another bolt, and then she was back into good pockets. The rock laid back a few degrees until she came to the anchor, clipped it, and Catherine hooted with joy for her. Hanna smiled and lowered to the ground like a sack of potatoes. All the veins in her arms and legs were standing out, full of blood, and she was breathing like she did during speed workouts.

Catherine slapped Hanna's back when she hit the ground. "What a little bulldog! You just went right after that thing!"

Hanna pretended to be mad, "You didn't tell me it was that hard."

"Well, I implied it, but you weren't listening."

She felt good about the climb and put her arm around Catherine's shoulder. "Thanks for the belay. You kept the rope just the way I like it."

"Well, you led it just the way I like it…fast!"

They drank some water and talked a bit. Hanna was loosening up in Catherine's company, and she was feeling happy to be out climbing with a woman. Catherine launched up a harder route for the last climb of the day, as the shadows lengthened. She did the route well, but took two short leader falls while passing over a roof. With each fall, she pulled Hanna a foot or two off the ground. Catherine hung there for a minute in her harness, with her toes touching the rock just enough to push off and get a swing going, so she could lunge in and grab a good pocket to pull herself back onto the wall.

Hanna was impressed with Catherine's nerve and gumption. She hung tough with the route and finished it in good form, up a final steep headwall. Hanna yelled and cheered as she clipped the chains and lowered to the ground. Hanna followed it and had to hang at the roof, and then once more on the head wall, but felt good about her attempt.

They packed up their gear and headed back down the trail, arriving at the car with the sun shining on just the tops of the highest ridges. It was only a few minutes up to the campground, and they drove back drinking water and flexing their sore hands.

Catherine backed the van precisely onto a level piece of ground, and Hanna set up the table for cooking and eating. There was a stove in the van, but Catherine said it was too much of a bother, and it was only good for morning coffee or really crappy weather. "But in crappy weather, I just drive the hell away!" she laughed, thinking her statement hilarious.

Hanna stood staring at her tent bag while Catherine folded out the van bed and made it up with cotton sheets. Hanna grabbed a towel to avoid any awkwardness and walked down to the creek to find a spot to wash off the salt, dust and climbing chalk. The creek ran through a heavy forest, and it was easy finding a private pool. The icy water refreshed her and cleared her head.

Back at the van, Catherine was still fiddling about inside, so Hanna went about making quesadillas, and called out, "Beer or wine?"

"I think I'll have a real drink. I have a kit," Catherine called from the van.

Hanna wondered what Catherine had in mind, but shrugged and poured herself a coffee cup of white wine.

Catherine was behind her in a moment and put her hand on Hanna's shoulder, grabbed a folded quesadilla and took a huge bite. "Oh, yeah, that's the ticket." She set her food down on a paper towel and fished a bottle of gin out of a milk crate. She took out a large, plastic cup filled with cooler ice and prepared a hefty gin and tonic, with a slice of lime. Hanna raised her eyebrows, and Catherine winked at her. "Mother's milk," Catherine said with a Scottish accent. And she toasted Hanna's cup of wine.

"Look at you, all cleaned up already," Catherine said.

"Well, Tim taught me well. You just can't be too clean!"

"I'm surprised you camp as civilly as you do after traveling with that guy. I've found him just sleeping in the dirt some mornings."

"But he looks so cute when he's like that." Hanna laughed.

"You can have that kind of cute! I like my men tidy and anal retentive."

"Eww, nope; I don't think I even like men, but definitely not Freudian anal."

"Have you ever noticed how manly men can't stand Tim?"

"I know. Hugh and Dog are always setting Tim up to deal with macho guys. It's really funny."

"It sounds like those guys came close to getting him beaten to death?"

"Well, our friend Tim had his share of the blame in all that. He apparently thought dancing with the strippers would be...ironically absurd."

Catherine laughed long and hard at that, and Hanna

giggled.

Catherine wiped her eyes, "Did he tell you that?"

"Yes, he did."

"You'd think he'd be too embarrassed."

"I don't think he's seriously embarrassed very often." Hanna finished the end of her quesadilla and licked her fingers. "So were you and he ever...?"

"Oddly enough, we never were. Not that Andy really would have minded, not back in those days...."

"But...am I feeling more here?"

"You are, and it's pretty bad."

"And of course you have to tell me now!"

Catherine smiled but avoided her eyes, and then began talking carefully. "At one point in time, Tim had the sweetest hippy girl in the whole valley. I mean men used to wreck their cars when she walked around the town square in Averoso. Her name was Rose, and she was from Sausalito, California. She had everything, the look, the body, an ethereal personality, her laugh was like falling water. Honestly, she was amazing."

"So what happened?"

"Well, she was between places, and Andy and Tim were off working on some condos down South, so she stayed at our place while the boys were gone."

"So?"

"So we slept together...and ran off back to the Bay Area to stay at one of her folks' places."

Hanna stared at her for a few minutes. "Wow, you ran away from Andy, with Tim's trophy girlfriend?"

"It gets worse. The reason why she had left California was because her father was one of those super-conservative, self-made Californian millionaires, all that. And I guess I wasn't her first female affair. So, he caught wind that Rose was back at their townhouse and he shows up with the Jaguar, and fastidious clothes, and they have it out right there in front of the condo, like you have never seen a father and daughter have it out."

"Wow, it might have been better to mind your manners and stay in Averoso."

"No kidding, he was originally from Mexico and he was calling me a 'fucking *marimacha puta*'!"

"That's no good."

"Well that wasn't the worst of it."

"That wasn't the worst?"

"Nope! Rose became clinically depressed over it all until she couldn't even get out of bed. I finally got in touch with her mom, who had her committed to a clinic for a while. I guess it wasn't the first time."

"Are you lying? Rose went insane?"

"Well not insane. She was, 'acutely clinically depressed'."

"Wow, what did you do?"

"Good question. I didn't really have much money. And I was pretty sure that Daddy was coming after me, so I took buses and bummed rides all the way back to Averoso, and that was no easy feat."

"And Andy took you back?"

"Oh yeah! He felt bad for Rose, but he really wasn't too surprised. He always thought that Rose was crazy, and always suspected my crush on her."

"And Tim?"

"He was pretty bummed out for a while. But he never really blamed me. It's not like I maliciously drove her insane. Rose had always told him what a beast her dad was. She just freaked out, and I happened to be with her."

"Is this a lie? Why wasn't anyone jealous or hurt, other than poor, crazy Rose."

"Believe me, I wish it weren't true. But that was just Averoso in those days. Someone was always running off with somebody else. People were more concerned over who *was* or *wasn't* a local, than they were over tainted love. You could write an encyclopedia of the affairs from those days."

"You know, I always think that I have done some crazy things—but you guys seem like a Barnum and Bailey for the certifiably insane."

Catherine winced at that one, and they both took a long sip of their drinks. Hanna asked, "Did Tim ever try to get in touch with her?"

"Yeah, but Daddy told Tim that he would be really sorry if he came to California. And then Rose never even called—who knows?"

Hanna took Catherine's hand across the table and laughed. "Wow, all I really wanted was a 'yes' or 'no' if you had slept with Tim."

"Well, there you go, you got the long version of no."

"Why did she decide to run back home?"

"I have never figured that out, unless she had wanted what was coming in a twisted way."

The last few minutes of light smoldered as they swished the dishes and frying pan clean and put things away.

Hanna picked up her tent, which was still in its bag, and Catherine took it away from her and stowed it in the van. "Don't be silly. I won't bite you, and I have clean cotton sheets and a four-inch foam mattress."

"Luxury."

"Why don't you get ready for bed, and I'll go splash off in the creek."

Hanna dressed in baggy shorts and a T-shirt and spread her bag over the tiny van bed. It was pure luxury to her. She had been living in her truck, or sleeping on the ground forever. She hadn't even had an indoor shower in over a week. The bed felt great.

Catherine came back and crawled into the bed, under the sheets, and they were quiet for a moment.

Hanna spoke first, "I hope you don't think I was rude about the Barnum and Bailey thing. I know how things happen; we can't control them."

"No, I am not offended. That's a pretty odd story by any measure."

"And who am I to talk, now that I've been sleeping with Tim. Did you know?

Catherine laughed, "Oh, please, it was written all over

your faces the second I saw you. Don't forget that I've known Tim since he was a scruffy, 20-year-old hippy."

They were quiet for a moment, and Catherine squeezed her hand. "I'm sorry about you losing Paul that way.... Tim told me...."

Hanna hadn't been thinking about Paul, and now Catherine caught her unaware; tears immediately welled in her eyes before she could control them, and they ran down her cheeks.

Hanna was silent for a moment, and then Catherine heard a sniffle in the dark. She rose up on her elbows, and then sat up to reach for some tissues. She put a couple in Hanna's hands and lay down behind her and took her in her arms. "You can cry.... I'm sorry...I just wanted you to know that I knew, so it wouldn't be an odd, weighty thing. I'm sorry."

In the morning, Catherine was up first and made tea on the van stove. She put a hot cup on the shelf beside Hanna and watched her sleep. She was reading the climbing guidebook in the shadowed light when Hanna stirred and looked around, not knowing where she was. She looked up at Catherine in her funky reading glasses and smiled. "Your tea is right beside you. Don't knock it over."

Hanna took a sip and let the warmth run through her body. The van was cool and dark, and there was a dewy fog clinging to the windows. Hanna arranged her pillows so she could sit up, propped against them. Catherine had real pillows; not just hard, old, couch pillows. Hanna remembered what happened the night before and felt embarrassed.

"Sorry about last night. That was odd. It was like the dam burst."

Catherine patted her knee. "Don't even apologize. There was nothing to it. You were sad, and you cried. I feel stupid for bringing it up. I know what losing someone is about. Especially out of the blue like that. It's stunning...and haunting."

"It is. It's like this nagging, 'where's Paul?' I look around for him, like I'm waiting for him."

"I know, and it takes a long time. But eventually that feeling makes you glad. It's like they're there with you."

They sat quietly for a moment. "Is it late? Do we have to get up?"

"No, it's seven. Just relax."

"What, it's seven?" Hanna laughed. "Tim would be pacing back and forth with his pack on by now."

"No lie, my Andy is the same way. But then he's totally trashed by two in the afternoon."

Hanna hung onto the 'my Andy' for a moment; she could hear the love and affection in it. But she could hear that it was there for Hanna, too.

"They just can't pace themselves," Hanna said, pulling on a fleece jacket, opening the sliding door to step outside. The campground was cool and deep in shadow. A grey jay stood on the picnic table, eyeing Hanna coolly before it continued to look for scraps. "At least there aren't any chickadees," she said aloud.

"There aren't any what?"

"Never mind," Hanna said in a hushed voice. No one was moving yet and heavy dew clung to the grass. She grabbed her coffee kit from her food box and returned to the van.

While Hanna was gone, Catherine turned the front seats around so they faced backward, and the water was boiling nicely. Catherine watched intently as Hanna went through her whole coffee routine. She clicked her tongue, "What a bother. You should just make tea."

Hanna harrumphed to let her know that she had no idea what she was even saying and settled into the passenger seat, zipped in a fleece jacket with her feet tucked under her butt. They sat quietly until Hanna asked about Andy.

"Oh, you know, we get along just fine. And Andy, he's busy all the time, a very busy guy, and as soon as he's done with one thing, he's right off to the next. I think he's truly who I should be with. But you know, it's been 20 years; things have cooled off quite a bit." She drank some tea. "We've been together a long time," Catherine repeated. "We're definitely a couple, but at some point it becomes more of a partnership."

"He still wants you to travel and climb with him, doesn't he?"

"Oh, he practically begs me. The problem is that I don't like big mountains anymore. Too much bother, too much toil and too little climbing. But that's what he wants to do, climb mountains and walls, and this is what I want to do. I like climbing hard, bolted routes. There are a few places where our interests overlap, and we have a great time when we are in a place like that, but there just aren't a lot of places for both pursuits."

"I never realized it was so complicated," Hanna said facetiously.

"You wait, it's hard to stay engaged with one person no matter what you do together. You should see him when he is engaged with one of his electronics' projects. He will literally work until midnight, and he comes home and wonders why the house is dark, as if it's five o'clock."

"Well, I guess he's not interested in what you made him for dinner, is he?"

Catherine laughed heartily and kicked Hanna's foot, and she had to balance her coffee not to spill it.

"Hey! If you spill that I'll have to tell Andy you did it."

Hanna laughed and licked a drip off the side of her cup.

Catherine caught her in her green eyes and asked seriously, "How long is the longest you've ever been in a relationship with someone?"

"What, you mean like full time—like, 'Hi honey, I'm home'?"

"Yeah, like that."

"A few months," Hanna said trying to sound experienced.

Catherine smiled her broad, sly smile. "How long is the

longest you've ever lived in the same house—after you left home?"

"Oh, like a year."

"A year? And you're what—30?"

"Twenty-nine."

"Catherine guffawed. Oh my God! Do you know that you're practically feral?"

Hanna was offended for a moment, "That's a harsh word."

Catherine took her hand and held it for a moment. "No offense, it is just that you're such a tiny minority. I'm a little jealous. You see, I know exactly when Andy is going to wake up, and I know how he is going to make his coffee, and I know what he'll say when he kisses me good-bye. I know how he'll cup my bottom in his right hand when he kisses me hello, I don't know what I'll cook for him, but I know exactly what he'll cook for me, and he'll try to please me with it, and he'll watch my face as I eat it. I know how we'll sit in small talk, and then begin reading—we don't do TV."

"Of course not."

"He tries so hard, but after 20 years?" Catherine looked at her for a moment. "Can I just go with you?"

"In my truck?" Hanna asked with exaggerated surprise.

"We'd have to do better than the truck."

"Well, let's see how we do this trip. We might not even like each other."

Catherine hiccupped her surprise for a fleeting moment, and confidence fled her green eyes. Her smiled drooped, just at the corners. Her voice was bold but Hanna could hear the possibility of what she'd said echo in her reply. "That could never happen," she huffed theatrically.

Hanna made up to her as she prepared breakfast and packed food and water for the day. She was surprised how sensitive Catherine was to jibing humor. That was the type of barb she traded with Tim all the time.

Catherine carried the rope and all the quickdraws, while Hanna carried everything else.

They walked up to a wall that was smooth and grey, shady and wonderfully cool. Again, Catherine was all business. She spread out the rope and draws under a likely-looking line of bolts and got out the guidebook.

"This is good here, it starts easier on this end and then generally gets harder as you move to the left. "Do you like it?"

"I like shade," Hanna said, "and I like climbing."

She laughed, "You gnarly girls are so hard to please."

Catherine pulled on her harness, and Hanna studied her, thinking how natty she looked in her Capri tights, and clean, bright tank top. The only contradiction to it was her hair, which she had pulled straight up and tied off. She was svelte, strong, and this was her element. Hanna watched her freckled skin as she stretched and wondered why she wasn't cold in the chilly shade.

When Hanna had her harness on, she stepped forward, picked up the rope and put Catherine on belay. Catherine climbed smoothly and quickly. The route was steep but easy with obvious deep pockets, and she moved from one set to the next with a simian ease.

"It almost bothers me to clip the bolts. I just want to climb the whole thing without stopping."

Catherine pulled the rope, and Hanna led the route, taking the draws on her way down. It felt good, and Hanna was warm and ready for the next route down the line. They fell into a good cadence and were patient about climbing anything too hard. Two guys came along and went out in front of them for a route farther down the cliff.

Hanna and Catherine completed four routes, and packed up their gear to walk down to a line Catherine had tried but failed on previously. They came around the corner, and the two men were there. One guy was lowering to the ground. He smiled, obviously happy that two women had happened along. "Are you looking for a route?" he asked.

Catherine was on to the routine and immediately began indulging him. "Yeah, I think I'm looking for the route you're on. Is it very hard?" she asked demurely.

"Oh a little. There are two hard parts, one down low, and one up high. Do you want me to leave the rope on it?" he asked, assuming that she would.

Catherine smiled slyly, and Hanna knew what was coming.

"I don't know," she said, taking a step toward him. "I was thinking I'd like to try to lead it, but I'm just not sure." She was now standing right next to him looking up at the route, and he was looking down into her cleavage. Hanna could hear the 'babe alarm' going off riotously in his head.

Hanna said hello to his partner and asked if he had done the route yet.

He smiled at her sincerely, a pleasant looking man, very clean-shaven, with nice brown eyes. "Oh no," he said to Hanna, "not yet. I'm going to follow it and clean the gear. It's probably more than I am looking for today."

Hanna reached out her hand, "Hanna."

"Les," he said smiling without any pretense.

"What's your friend's name?"

"Brian."

Brian heard his name and said, "Brian," holding out his hand to Catherine.

Catherine took his hand and held it just a moment too long. "Catherine," she said, looking into his eyes, "and that's Hanna, with your friend."

"Les," Hanna chimed to her, enjoying the show, pointing at the guy beside her.

Catherine and Brian looked above them and moved their hands and feet, miming the moves of the route. Catherine laughed at Brian's jokes, humoring him.

The two women sat eating energy bars and drinking water. They talked as Les followed the route, falling and hanging here and there at the harder sections. When he made it to the anchors, he ran the rope through the rings and rappelled down. The boys talked for a moment about the nuances of the route, and Les congratulated Brian on his lead.

Catherine stood and counted out the draws she'd need. Hanna could feel her cool anxiety. Brian encouraged her just a bit too much. Hanna knew Catherine was wishing he'd go away. "Did you have any trouble on it?" she asked smiling, catching him with her eyes.

He paused for a moment, and then Hanna saw him choose a jovial honesty, "Well, I fell at the first crux and then hung at the second." He considered defending himself for a second, but then offered, "But don't worry, you'll get up it even if you hang a bit. All the moves are good and the bolts are close together."

Les caught Hanna's eye, and she could see that he regretted his partner's hubris.

Hanna threaded the rope in her belay device, patted Catherine on the butt and whispered, "I'll keep you tight, just don't be a PUSSY."

Catherine guffawed a snort of laughter and chalked her hands. Starting up, she was jerky through the first moves, but calmed down after the first two bolts put her out of danger of hitting the ground. There was a series of horizontal edges with long reaches, but she passed these quickly, clipping two more bolts as she went. Then she was at the first crux, with a short blank section that she had to pass, with a tiny layback to the right while high stepping to the left. She trembled here, and her right foot skidded a bit as she pulled onto the lonely left foot. Then she was at good pockets for her hands and clipped another bolt. She moved quickly through a vertical section with good holds, up to the crux, which was a steep, shallow corner with no crack. She stemmed through this with a foot and a hand desperately working each side. Her calves seemed huge, and all the muscles in her back and shoulders stood out. She made two difficult, trembling clips, another long move, and then she was at the anchors.

Hanna hooted, laughed and turned to look at Brian, who was looking dejected, and Les was blushing with a huge smile. He winked at Hanna, acknowledging that they'd been gamed.

"Nice…nice," Brian shouted up hollowly.

She lowered to the ground with her chest heaving, and all the veins in her arms standing out.

"Good job," Brian said, gathering his stuff. "Good job."

Catherine sat in a glow of her euphoria, drinking water, and Hanna waited until the guys left before she started up, knowing that it was much, much harder than Catherine made it look. She climbed quickly and had to hang several times. She didn't try too hard, hanging often on the rope, because she didn't want to completely wear herself out for the afternoon. At the anchors she ran the rope through the rings, and rappelled down.

Catherine was laughing when Hanna touched the ground.

"You're a shameless bitch," Hanna hissed, making sure the guys were out of earshot.

"Listen, it's better this way. If I didn't do that, they would have clung to us all afternoon, and the way you sleep around—who knows what would've happened."

"Ha, you're the one that crawls into random tents in the middle of the night." Hanna pushed her, laughing. She looked into her eyes, batted her lashes, and said in a throaty, whispered voice, "Oh gosh, is it really that hard…?"

Catherine blushed and they stared into each other's eyes.

They took a long siesta, swatting at horseflies, as the sun pounded through the hot, hazy, midday. They roused themselves begrudgingly, feeling the hard climbing they had done in the morning. There was a nice section of wall with a lot of moderately hard routes, which they climbed until they were sated, and the shadows were reaching east.

They drove back to camp in the bliss of physical exhaustion, with their forearms throbbing and their hands hurting. At camp they grabbed towels and cold beers, and hiked down to the river to wash away the dust, and soak their hands and tired muscles.

It was funny to see Catherine with her wet hair clinging to her head, and no masquerade of clothing, sitting on a rock with a beer. She was smiling broadly, as if she knew the only joke in the whole world worth knowing. If an ancient Greek shepherd had seen her like this, he would have surely mistaken her for Aphrodite.

They didn't stay long; thinking some of the boys from the campground might discover them. Hanna took Catherine's hand for a few minutes to see her blush on the walk back.

"Do you remember when I took your hand at the party?"

"Do I? I thought I'd have a heart attack. I had such a crush on you at that moment, but I was thinking of how useless it all was—and then you did that. You were spot on."

"Really? I thought it was one of the most awkward things I had ever done in my life. I thought you were just putting on your gay face to be hip or something. I was actually trying to be a funny bitch."

"No, I knew before I even saw you. It's crazy, but I knew when Andy told me you were coming, that it was going to be meaningful. I knew it when I heard your name, and I wouldn't have missed meeting you for anything."

"Well, now I'm blushing," Hanna said as the trail narrowed, and they passed some boulders.

"Good!" Catherine said as she let Hanna pass. "Did you really Mace two men and leave them for dead in the desert?"

"Is that the way Tim's telling it now?"

"I'm just asking about what I heard."

"Yeah, that did happen."

"And you stabbed somebody with a barbeque fork!"

Hanna spun around. "He told you that? He wasn't supposed to tell anyone!"

"Well, it was only me. He didn't even tell Andy. I swear! And it was only because I could tell he had something on the tip of his tongue, and I wouldn't let it go."

"OK, I did do that, but I was being assaulted."

"So, it's true? You really stabbed somebody?"

"Well, I did something similar to that," Hanna said, turning around to look at her hard. "So maybe you should be careful, and do exactly as I say...."

Catherine laughed, but then stopped when she noticed

that Hanna didn't.

For dinner Catherine made a great pasta dish. She had the sauce precooked in the cooler so all she had to do was stir it around and serve it once the noodles were done. Hanna got out a bottle of white wine as they sat side-by-side in their camp chairs talking and laughing until it was twilight.

"What will Andy think about all this?" Hanna asked.

"About the same as Tim. We've both had our affairs. We're really just partners at this point, you know, we still have sex now and then, and I love him—I do—but we're really just partners."

"So, what did Tim tell you? Did he put you up to this?"

"Don't be silly, but Tim knows me better than Andy does. He knew how I felt about you, and he told me I should go find you. He told me you'd be moping around the office and would go off climbing in a second."

"But he knew that this is what we'd do?"

Catherine laughed, "Oh, he'd be surprised that it took this long." Catherine was quiet for a moment; she reached over and stroked Hanna's hair. "Tim just doesn't believe in conventional assumptions. And he's not just saying it. He really believes that people should do what they feel compelled to do."

"Well, that could be a total disaster with a lot of things. And people would take advantage of each other because of things they feel compelled to do," Hanna said seriously.

"Oh, I agree, but what good would come out of Tim trying to control you?"

"Nothing."

"I think that that's his point, that the control is what undermines a lot of the good things that people find in each other." Catherine looked earnestly at her. "You know that I'm going back to Andy, right? And I want to go back to Andy. But I want to go climbing with you. And I want you to sleep with me, rather than you sleeping on the ground in a tiny tent. Why should we not sleep together because it might offend someone else's sense of decency?"

"Well, I guess you guys have it all figured out." Hanna smiled. "Is this the general philosophy of the Meadows."

"No," Catherine laughed. "Most of the relationships in the Meadows are a mess. But where aren't they a mess?" Catherine was quiet for a moment. "Let's not analyze."

"No, I'm not analyzing. But you have to admit that it's not a normal situation by any standard."

"No it's not. But Tim is not normal. Nowhere close to normal."

"You have a sense of normalcy about this?"

"Really, Hanna, why worry? Who's to judge? I don't even know why these issues are still part of anyone's conversation. If you love Tim, maybe you do maybe you don't, and he loves you, why wouldn't you just get along however it worked best? And if you have a woman friend, he won't care. And I don't mean that in a thoughtless way."

"I know. I understand all that, but most of the time I feel this huge gulf between myself and the rest of the world. Because of one flaw, because I don't believe in the accepted rules about who one should love and how one should love. So I feel I'm unacceptable to most of the population, and my only response to that is that I cannot be bothered. I can't be bothered by the fact that I'm worse than...*Everybody*. I'm worse than the companies trying to drill the desert into a wasteland. I'm worse than all the money people bankrolling these projects, and worse than all the circling vultures who cheat the people working out there, worse than politicians who embezzle the money." Hanna took a sip of her wine. "I say that I can't be bothered, that I shouldn't be bothered, but I am bothered. It seriously bothers me."

Hanna looked at a Winnebago parked next to them and saw the windows glowing blue from the TV, and looked at the satellite dish up on the roof, and the SUV they had carefully towed behind them.

Catherine took her hand, and they sat quietly for a moment. "Do you know what my job really is?"

"No idea."

"I am basically a slut who charms old white men out of their money."

"OK, but you'll have to clarify a bit."

"Well, basically, I stay busy around the office doing whatever I feel like, until there's a hard sell going on with a house or piece of property, usually involving an older guy, either married or not. Then I start showing up at meetings, or I'm the one sent to the airport for a pick-up, or I attend functions where the clients are drinking, and I flirt with them in a socially acceptable manner. I sit next to the client at dinners, and in river dories on private fishing trips, but I have to make sure I don't catch as many fish as him, and that is actually really hard to do. So, I'm the tramp who disappears just before bedtime."

"Are you ever propositioned?"

"That's the whole point, but my job is to seal the deal without giving up any tail."

"So does it ever go all wrong?"

"Oh, sure, but they only swing the sales to me when it's already difficult, so I really don't get the blame." She pushed a few strands of hair back away from her face. "But it does get pretty weird. These guys are very rich, and very white, and they want what they want, and they get really bizarre when I start my evasive actions."

"I bet!" Hanna said impressed with her guile. "I guess I'll stay with my poor, hot, dusty existence. Do they pay you for your skills?"

"Hell yes! The office and I have fought about it over and over, and they didn't want to pay me any more because I barely have a realtor's license, and I don't even have a degree, but the guys can't do what I do, and I told them to go ahead and try. One guy got so pissed off that he quit, but why should I care? If I had all the experience, and a degree, and I played the exact same game they did, I could tell you I wouldn't make the same money they do."

"Seventy percent!" Hanna agreed, "That's what we make."

"But that's not my point," her eyes flashed with anger. "My point is…is that it's OK for me, for us, me and the boys, to make money that way. It's even admirable and *clever* to take that money, to swing that deal by whatever means we can. But if you and I sleep together, that's wrong and immoral, and then if we go back to our men, that's even worse?"

Hanna smiled, "You seem so angry?"

Catherine harrumphed and squirmed in her seat, allowing her anger to pass.

The Winnebago still glowed blue, but its generator had stopped its annoying din. Around the campground, fires burned brightly, distant laughter and animated voices wafted to them in bits and snatches. There was a bat flying past every few minutes, and down the canyon, a thunderstorm flashed dully.

Hanna got up and put the last of the food away in the cooler. She rinsed their cups and turned them upside down on the table. It was dark now. She stood at the open door of the van, using it as a screen, took off her clothes and folded them, placing them neatly behind the passenger seat. Except for her T-shirt. She threw that at Catherine, who watched dreamily from her camp chair. She caught it deftly out of the air, held it to her nose, closed her eyes, and inhaled deeply, and then followed her into the van.

They were almost too sore to move in the morning. Stretching was painful, but slowly they regained a little flexibility. It was hot by the time they got moving. They were too late to catch the morning shade at the crags, so they drove up into the higher peaks and hiked for a few hours in the cooler air. Hanna insisted that they wear running shoes. There were still patches of snow, and it felt wonderful to hold its iciness in their sore, chaffed hands. The distant mountains were higher and craggy, but mostly the trail followed a long massif of meadows and low domes. They walked for a while and stretched and walked some more. When they came to a long flat plain, they broke into a slow jog. Hanna tried to pick up the pace a few times, but

Catherine resisted, and she walked whenever the trail climbed. She took Hanna's hand, "Chill my little filly, we could barely walk an hour ago, remember?"

Hanna was watching the sky, "Maybe those clouds might get you to run."

They made it back by the time a brief storm cut loose, and sat for a while snacking in the dry comfort of the van as the rain drummed on the roof. Later, they drove down to check the weather at the crags. The storm lost its intensity as they descended, but the cloud cover remained.

"This will be perfect, with the clouds we can climb on any exposure."

Hanna harrumphed grumpily as she flexed her hands.

"C'mon princess, don't be pouty," Catherine said.

"Don't princess me! Let's run hard every day, and see how you do!"

"I just ran all the way back to the van!"

"That wasn't running. I jogged and you waddled!"

Catherine laughed loudly, and some guys a few cars away looked over as Catherine put her arm around Hanna's shoulder and kissed her on the cheek. "That was pretty pathetic."

"Just don't be too ambitious today. I don't have to follow everything you do."

Catherine held up three fingers in a pledge, "Cross my heart. Today is the last day anyway. After that, I won't be doing any good."

Hanna wilted a bit at the news. She hadn't thought about their time together ending yet. "I know," she said, "I'm really too tired to even run, and that doesn't happen very often."

"I can't believe you're as tired as me. I thought you were a super-heroine."

"Well, I guess you must be my kryptonite," Hanna said.

"And you must be my spinach, so I should eat you every day."

Hanna laughed and pushed her, which made her stumble with the weight of her climbing pack.

Requiem

In the middle of September, Hugh agreed to meet Leon Filmore one last time at Paul's site. Hugh made Hanna come along to distract Leon and dampen his whining. Try as they might, they simply couldn't reach it. The Crow had set up multiple gates that Hanna had to open, close and latch as they approached the site. The agency had also tightly lined the road through the communal tribal lands with shiny new barbwire fences. Multiple vehicles lined the narrow road and there was a stalled earthmover blocking a gate between the tribal and the private lands, and multiple baffled Crow dignitaries were wondering how such a thing had happened. There were two Bureau of Indian Affairs' trucks with their emergency lights flashing and a sheriff's SUV, and Leon's gleaming white CanAm truck. A faint sense of urgency glimmered, but no one was moving too fast, except Lyin' Leon Filmore, who was racing red-faced and exasperated from official to official.

Hugh stopped at the last gate that had a turnaround after which those who followed would hem him in.

He turned to Hanna. "I think if you looked up SNAFU in the dictionary, there would be a picture of this situation right here," he said looking in the rear-view mirror. "I don't want to get stuck here, and I don't think there's really anything that we can do."

"You don't need my permission," Hanna said. "I never wanted Leon leering at me in the first place, and I'd say he appears to be screwing things up better than we ever could." She punched Hugh on the shoulder with a snort of laughter. "I'd say our work is done here Tonto."

By the end of September Karl was reluctant to enter into any new contracts with CanAm as they were rumored to be going under, and about to abandon the line. Global gas prices plummeted and had not yet reached the bottom.

Hanna was floored by the idea of abandoning a project of that magnitude.

"It's all about timing and gambling." Karl explained, unconcerned. "A boom is always gonna bust. It's about hype and scamming and schmoozing and speed. You make your money, and you get the hell out, and you don't let anyone catch you holding the bag. We're lucky; we had a good run and got all our money." He shrugged his shoulders philosophically. "There'll be another project in the spring."

"So, it was all for nothing? The entire survey, the digging, and trenching—the land?" Hanna's mouth hung open. "It was all for nothing?"

Karl furrowed his brows for a moment and tried to find a better answer, but then sighed a bit. "Other than the money? Yes."

"And what about all the money? What about CanAm and the other companies? What about the investments and the employees, the trucks and equipment?"

"They'll just dissolve the corporation, change their name and wait for a new gig to come along. The little guys will lose their jobs, and probably everything they have mortgaged. But the big guys never lose much. The investors will lose, but all they ever wanted was money for nothing anyway."

They stood in silence for a moment, and then Karl continued—"I think I see what you're thinking, and you shouldn't. There are a lot of miles of pipe that were never laid because of us.

There are large sections of the line that were never dug because of us. The pipeline was for nothing. So what? We did our jobs: we re-routed the line in culturally sensitive areas." Karl looked at her and smiled. "Listen, this was more or less about gas, but it was even more about establishing a right-of-way and a precedent. What CanAm really wanted was a foot in the door, and a way to bring that toxic Tar Sands treacle down out of Alberta. Now, without this pipeline, they can't come along and lay the second, larger pipe right next to it."

* * *

Without work or anywhere special to go, Hanna spent most her time in Tim's orbit. They went back into the mountains where Paul died and continued up onto the high plateaus to the south, the area that Paul had talked about so often. They went for a week and passed his creek on the way in and the way out. Hanna needed to see if she could feel him there anymore, but he was gone. There was nothing left of him anywhere.

After that long trip in the mountains, Hanna drove a day and a half to Paul's home. His parents' farm was in a small town in a flat basin with distant mountains and bright green potato and beet fields sprouting from every irrigated patch of ground. Mormon, redbrick churches appeared every few miles. Hanna found the place from the address without even asking directions. She drove up the long driveway to the tidy farmhouse beside an enormous barn and steel outbuildings. A longhaired, red cow-dog ran out barking steadily as Hanna came to a stop under a huge spreading cottonwood.

Hanna had put on her best work clothes and combed out her hair. She knew Paul's mom well from his stories and wanted to make her more comfortable. A slender woman came to the door and held it timidly as if she might withdraw and slam it shut all of a sudden. Hanna stopped under the tree and stood out from the truck, knowing that a scrawny woman like herself could never be a threat. She waved as she stood away from her truck. "I'm Hanna. Paul's friend."

The woman's hand came up to the throat of her simple buttoned dress. Her face didn't understand for a moment, and Hanna could see that she wondered who could speak that name? Who could say that syllable?

"Of course you're Paul's friend, Hanna—you look more like her than I ever imagined." She came down the stairs uncertainly, timidly, putting a knuckle to her mouth. The dog stopped her at the bottom step, and barked in a more vicious manner with the stranger so close.

"That's enough, Rudy! Just shush!" she chided, giving him a slight kick on his rump.

Rudy was obviously happy to be relieved of guard duty, and he switched over to a tentative wag, but hung close to Paul's mom.

Hanna came closer, uncertain if she should hold out a hand, or both arms, or nothing at all. She knew from Paul's demeanor that they probably weren't big huggers.

The final five yards between them hung like a yawning gulf, but Hanna swallowed and crossed it, taking the woman's hand and then reached out to hug her. The woman ceded reluctantly but then returned the gesture with her strong housewife arms.

"Paul always said I'd meet you someday," Paul's mother said. "I just thought he'd be here when it happened." She laughed to show her strength, but there was no depth to it. Her hands were busy, one minute flattening her dress, and the next pulling on a button, then running her fingers through her sandy, grey-flecked hair. She was young to have had a child as old as Paul.

Hanna didn't know what to say to that. She was too uncomfortable to return a joke. She never knew that Paul had spoken of her. "We were always planning on coming, but one job leads to another." The statement ended hollowly.

They stood quiet for a moment, but then Hanna continued. "I have a few boxes of things in my truck. They're small things, mostly books and clothes, but there are photos and papers; I thought you should look through them."

"Oh, you didn't have to do that. You drove them all the way?"

"Well, I thought we should meet. Paul spoke of you often. He talked about your farm so much and how he worked as a kid. He talked about driving a tractor when he was only twelve."

"Oh yeah, he was a worker. Always was, not crazy like some boys. You know, his dad would tell him to keep the tractor straight, and no craziness, and that was the way he'd do it. He was a good boy. He never gave us any trouble. Never trouble." She looked around for another word. "Oh, I'm Beth. I forgot to tell you, it's because I feel as if I know you so."

"Thank you Beth. I can see Paul in your face."

"Oh yeah, the boy always looked so much like me. Drove his dad crazy."

"Is his dad around?"

"No," she said pulling in a long breath. "He's been gone for a month. His heart had been bad for a long time. Paul's death finished him. After a life of working hard, he never cared for sitting around. He wouldn't change his diet or watch his meds. Of course, he never agreed with the way the leasing farm took care of his land. Drove him nuts. He'd go do work he shouldn't be doing. He never listened to anyone."

"Oh my God, Beth. I had no idea," she put her hand on Beth's shoulder. "Do you have family? How will you run an entire farm by yourself?"

"Well, let's go inside and sit down. I guess all this is going to take some talking. We'd be standing in the driveway all night."

They sat at a wooden table in a tidy kitchen. It was hot inside, as there was no air conditioning. Beth poured tall glasses of ice tea.

"Well, you know, everything is leased out now. And it's good land. I'll head to my sister's in Washington State soon. I'm really just waiting for Rudy, to pass. He's the last of 'em, last of my boys. He really has no idea. He still waits by Rob's pickup to go to town. Still sits by Rob's chair. He's cheerful as ever; he doesn't get it." Beth looked out the window at the red shaggy dog looking down the driveway. "My sister says I'm crazy, but how could I just leave him here? I'm not putting him down." She was quiet for a moment, and Hanna thought that she heard a slight catch in her voice.

"But he's the last thing. When he is gone, I can go, you know?" Her voice was trembling now. "As long as he's around, I still feel like they might be back. Like Rob might come back from town, or Paul will be back to visit in the fall. I can still feel them here, but I don't think I will feel that way without Rudy."

"That sounds right."

"He won't be long, he can't see anything as it is, but he loves me, and he loves this place, and I won't abandon him. He is still waiting on Rob, and I'm not gonna tell him he's not coming back."

Beth took Hanna on a tour of the house, all intensely tidy, no feet on the coffee tables here. Upstairs was a nice family room, a bath, and Paul's room, looking like he'd be home any moment. The bed was made military crisp. Along all the walls there were books on every topic: fiction, biology, ethics, history, anthropology, and, of course, archeology. Paul had mounted some nice points he found on the farm in picture-frames with felt beds. Hanna went to the closet and recognized some of the coats and jackets that he had worn on previous jobs. Beth wasn't in the room so she held them to her nose and inhaled, but all she got was the scent of fabric softener.

Hanna went over to his bureau to look at a small, framed photo. She was shocked to see herself; it was a photo of her with Paul. They were standing in a trench, both leaning on shovels. Paul's face was full of wary hope and expectation while Hanna smirked, exasperated with heat and dust. One of Paul's hands held the shovel and the other floated just above Hanna's shoulder as if he might really touch her. It was only from a few years ago, but she could see that they had been so much younger then. She wore her hair a bit longer then, and that was when Paul kept his hair fastidiously short. He would drive 30 miles just to go get a trim. He looked like a lovely, high school boy, who you would trust to do anything. She saw how it was right in the center of the bureau by itself, so important. She picked it up, and tears ran down her cheeks.

"He thought the world of you," Beth said, coming into the room. "He could barely stand waiting for the next session, and I knew it was because of you. I thank you for that. Lord knows he had his problems; you looked after him, and he loved you." Beth had been stoic until this point, but now a tear found its way alongside her nose.

"I never looked after him!" Hanna said. "He was a good worker and fun company, and he was with me all the time. We made a good team."

"Well you can pooh-pooh it if you like, but I know how you looked after him." Beth's eyes swept the room, and her chest heaved with a huge sigh. She picked up a small animal skull from a bookshelf and considered it for a moment. And then set it back down.

"Did Paul ever tell you what happened? What really happened?"

Hanna lifted her head slowly, hearing the gravity of Beth's voice. "He told me a lot of stories, I never knew which were true and which weren't."

"Oh, you would have known that this one was true. It was the one he never told you."

"Then I guess I've never heard it."

Well you should pull up that chair because this will take a few minutes."

Hanna sat in a wooden kitchen chair from Paul's desk.

Beth smoothed her dress as she sat on the corner of Paul's bed and then smoothed out the wrinkles that radiated out from the weight of her bottom. "It was the summer before his senior year.... It was a good summer for him...he was just having fun, and working, and he had friends, some of his friends were girls. You could just see that he was happy with who he was. It was a good time for him—but he got arrested for some marijuana."

"Paul got arrested? He never told me that. He never smoked it around me."

"No, I think it was an isolated thing, but he had it in his car. There was a little fender bender and the police found it. It was nothing, and the police really didn't even want to deal with it. But my Rob—he was a man who believed in right and wrong, and consequences. And he thought that Paul should spend the night in jail. So they took him in, and that was the last we ever saw of my boy."

Hanna's mouth hung open, her brain buzzed, and she knew how it was going to end. She could see Paul in the back seat, sitting on his hands and jerking in retraction whenever she touched him.

"There were two deviant monsters waiting for him."

Hanna saw Paul survey each bar and restaurant he entered, as if his life might depend on it.

"They burned him with cigarettes."

Hanna could see him with his long-sleeve shirts buttoned at the wrist—never swimming at hotel pools or in mountain rivers. Tears ran down her cheeks.

"Of course, they sodomized him, and who knows what else…."

Hanna saw him blush distastefully at sexual jokes around camp. She saw him walk across the street to avoid dangerous-looking men.

"They hit him so hard they broke his orbital socket—can you imagine? He couldn't see straight for a month."

Hanna remembered how he had to wear his sunglasses and drink so much water to avoid migraines. Hanna's chest heaved as she sobbed for Paul.

"But the worst was how they shamed him and us. Our boy. Our Paul never came back. We betrayed him. Rob couldn't live with himself. His last day of good health was that day they arrested Paul. But, the irony was that he was trying to be the good father. He believed in consequences. He believed in lessons. At that point in time the world was unraveling. There were pornographic movies playing at the theater, and we wanted our boy to be a good moral man…. We didn't want any saint, but we wanted him to be a good man."

"And he was," Hanna interrupted, "he was one of the most honorable men I ever knew. He was honest and hardworking, and he would always follow through on what was expected of him. I would have trusted him with anything." Hanna paused for a moment and let a short silence pass. "I miss him all the time. Every time I climb into one of the work trucks, I wait just a moment for him, or I wonder where he is."

"I know. That's how it was when he went away to school. Rob watched and waited for him all the time."

She sat on the bed beside Beth and put her arm around her, resting her head against Beth's. "I often thought that if the world were full of more people like Paul, it would be a much better place. We don't need heroes; We just need people like Paul."

Beth nodded her head and thought about that statement, as if she had never considered anything like it before. She sat pulling on one of her buttons, but then she spoke, "You know, when I was a young girl, my grandmother wanted me to go to a private school for my junior year, so she sent me to Washington, DC to be among all kinds of people and be cultured. We weren't a 'monied' family, so I only went for one year. That was where I saw my first black person. I went to school with girls from Europe and Africa. There were some girls that struggled with English. I loved to spend time with them and tutor them. I actually got credits for being a tutor, and I loved talking and laughing with those girls." She looked at Hanna, and she was smiling with some memory. "One girl was as black as black can be, and she had the biggest, whitest teeth you ever saw, and when she threw her head back to laugh, every person in the room just had to laugh along with her."

"We went to all the monuments and speeches, and we paid homage to the heroes. Then, one day we went out to Arlington, to the cemetery, and one of the pastors went with us to say a mass out there. It was a foggy spring morning, and we walked up and down those misty hills in that forest of white stones until I had no idea where we were. It seemed like we were just repeating the same route over and over in a labyrinth. And then we came to the grave of a simple private in the Army. Private Joseph Hemple. I remember his name. The pastor knew his name and repeated it several times so we would know him—we stopped at this soldier's grave and the pastor gave a sermon right there. And when it was done, we said the Lord's Prayer, and it was like I had never heard those words before, but they echoed and hung in that fog like ivy on an arbor. I looked at all those soldiers' graves, and I wondered how all those mothers and wives and lovers had said good-bye to their boys, to their husbands and sons? What were the last words they said to them? How had they let them go? I prayed right there that I would never lose my boys. I cried, and one of the women comforted me, thinking I was having a religious or patriotic moment, but all I was doing was selfishly praying that I shouldn't outlive my future husband and sons, that they would never be soldiers and would never leave me behind. Maybe that was a fateful premonition?" Beth asked. "But now I know how women say good-bye to their men, and I relive those last words to my boys every day. Both of them were meaningful partings. Paul's was good because he was my boy, he was heading off again, to work with you, and my last words to Rob were good because he was failing."

It was growing darker in the slow evening. Hanna looked out the upstairs bedroom window and saw that a dusty haze hung over the potato fields and large black flies occasionally dinged against the screen in the warm autumn night.

"I'm sorry I went on like that, I thought I had a larger point to make," Beth said.

"No, I understand what you meant."

"Well, they're gone now—and I'm hungry," she said with a huff that signified the end. "Paul told me that you only eat good food, and you won't find any of that within 50 miles of here, so I guess you have to stay for dinner."

"That'd be good, if you don't mind. I'd like to."

"Well, you have to help, we can just throw some stuff together. I've been keeping the garden going, so you can pick just about any vegetables you want to eat."

"Wow, that sounds great. I've been living on Don Pancho's bean burritos for two days."

"Maybe you should just take a chair out to the garden and eat your way through," she laughed in a sincere way. "But really, pick whatever you want. I give most of it away. When I planted it, I thought Rob would still be here and Paul would be visiting."

Beth handed Hanna a large wire basket. "You know, I don't eat much meat anymore either. My stomach just doesn't deal with it very well. I only eat small portions if I eat it at all. God knows meat didn't do Rob any favors. He had the gout so bad. But all he wanted was meat, gravy, and bacon. Doc told him to cut it out, but he wouldn't do it. I don't think he was very rational by the end—he was perfectly lucid, but not rational anymore. Well, let's go before it's dark—anything you want, and take anything you think you can eat in the car. I'll make some noodles."

After dinner, Beth insisted Hanna stay the night because the hotels would also be terrible. They spoke through dinner, and Hanna could see that Beth was healing and looking ahead to living with her sister and getting away from the farm. Beth went off to bed early, and Hanna sat out on the porch with Rudy and watched bats chase the last of the autumn moths through the floodlight up high on the barn.

She went into Paul's room and sat on his bed until she was sure he was not there. She snooped around, looking at the stone points he had mounted. They were very good, mostly older, larger, Paleolithic spear points.

On one of the lower bookshelves there was a heavy, cardboard box of flakes and broken points from the farm, and Hanna sifted through it for a moment. Next to it was a small wooden box with a sliding top. She lifted it, sliding back the lid back and was jolted from the top of her head to the soles of her feet. She jerked so hard and so fast that she hurt her neck. There, resting on a bed of folded paper towels was an encrusted bronze horseshoe cloak brooch, with curled ends, and a swiveling pin. "Paul," she whispered, "you stole it? You stole the brooch?" It was corroded so she held it carefully and laid it on the bed. She lifted the paper towels from the box and found the carefully folded field cards underneath them. She read the cards and recognized his script. She could take these cards and find the exact location of the dig. Although now that the entire site had been dug up and reburied, it would be compromised.

She noticed that the box had been sitting on a thin purple binder. She set the cards down beside the brooch and opened the binder, knowing what it was before she saw the first page. It was a complete report on the dig. The first photo showed the brooch in situ, barely recognizable, embedded in the wall of an excavated trench. There was a meter stick marking the depth of the trench, and to the right she could see darker, carbonized material, which would be the edge of a fire pit; there was fire-cracked rock among burnt debris. Then there was a second photo of Paul beaming, smiling proudly, as she had never seen him smile. His finest moment, waist deep in a trench with a meter stick and trowel. "Paul, you crazy son of a bitch." She quietly forced some air through her lips and whispered. "Well, I guess you finally showed me, but what the hell am I supposed to do with it?"

It was very late when she went down to the small guest room Beth had set up for her. She lay there in the dark and listened to the house settle and creak, feeling the past. She could feel a generation of Christmases, Thanksgivings, and birthdays. She could smell the smoke of the Fourth of July. Hot, hot summer days and cold winter nights. Waves of sadness washed over her from time to time, and tears came suddenly to her eyes, but then they dried as she thought of him out in the yard with Rudy, shooting baskets against the barn, or riding a tractor in the heat of the day...this is how we say good-bye.   .

Accord

It was November, and cold, but still dry. There was snow slowly inching down from up high but nothing very big yet. Tim had agreed to take care of one of Dean's—the dying man's—properties, out at the foot of the mountains and the edge of the desert. They stayed in the old main house surrounded by barns, sheds, and two old bunkhouses. They had a lot to look after, but mostly they were there to prevent vandalism from hunters and the four-wheel crowd, who get curious when properties look abandoned.

Hanna agreed to spend the winter with Tim, with the disclaimer that she could come and go as needed, which was fine with Tim, who claimed to need a good break after his stressful summer.

Hanna told him about her affair with Catherine, and Tim smiled. "I always regretted never having a relationship with her," he said nodding his head.

"Well, I bet you do, but that's an odd thing to say."

"Well I think we would have gotten along really well. But Andy swooped right in, and I never had the chance."

"So you don't mind?"

"No, I don't mind. What if I did mind? Would I demand that you stop? Could I change how you feel? If you started bringing big, ugly guys back to the ranch, sure, I would mind, but if you go off climbing with Catherine for a little while, why would I mind?"

"Because that would just be a normal reaction."

"If you're looking for a normal reaction, you're talking to the wrong person. I have so much to do and worry about here, why would I worry about you and my good friend Catherine?"

Hanna wondered if he really believed that his life was stressful. They had just spent an entire month climbing, and living in a truck. They had climbed hard and mostly he had been relaxed about it, even on the longer routes they did. He said that this was because the weather was more predictable down South. He said that it was the huge summer storms he feared the most. Hanna led more of the pitches they climbed, and her comfort level continued to soar. She could move on vertical terrain and then anchor in on tiny ledges to belay Tim up. It never ceased to make her giddy when she anchored in and leaned back, even after pitches that scared her to the core.

Hanna knew that the ranch was perfect for Tim. He had already retrieved and unloaded the tools he stored in Karl's garage. He would tinker and hammer and drink coffee all day and then get up the next day and do it all again, which was the way he liked to operate. He spent the early mornings and evenings looking for a good deer to shoot, and sometimes caught a few trout for dinner. Bob was uncertain with the unexpected stability of their move, and he hung close to the trucks in case they should leave at a moment's notice. He patrolled the ranch faithfully, running off the raccoons and fighting uncertainly with the badgers that came looking for mice. There were lots of mountain chickadees, which hunted flies among loose boards and stacked firewood. Hanna thought of hanging up a bird feeder for them, but chose not to, so she wouldn't be trying to read the signs of an animal that hangs blissfully upside down while gorging on flies and moths hidden among the shingles of the eaves.

Dean and the estate hired Tim and Hanna as caretakers and for maintenance, but a lot of they did went far beyond maintaining things. A lot of things had to be rebuilt.

After all the digging and dirt moving and sifting she had done as an archeologist, Hanna was used to hard labor, so the work on the ranch was nothing new. She liked the way Tim worked, and could anticipate what he would do next when they were fixing fences or doing manual labor. Sometimes there were jobs that took real skill and knowledge, and she let him lead.

They tore the old, shake roofs off the bunkhouses, and

screwed down new, shiny tin roofs. They also had to replace one of the rotting bottom logs on a bunkhouse cabin. This involved jacking up the entire building, taking out the old log, rebuilding the foundation wall, replacing the new log, and then lowering everything back into place. Hanna was engrossed and involved in seeing how all these things worked. It was logical enough, but she was awed by how these things functioned.

Tim was easy to work with, and explained and taught as he went. Hanna understood why people hired him. He knew a bit of everything, and he could always figure out what he didn't know. He loved to work, not obsessively, but he loved to be busy in a composed and comfortable way.

Autumn was Hanna's favorite running season. She could run in the icy morning air, or in the warmth of the middle of the day. Often, she would run in the evening if she hadn't labored too hard.

Sometimes there were hunters, but mostly she ran alone, down empty dirt roads, or along stony cow trails through an ocean of waist-high sage. She ran a marathon, by herself, which Tim had mapped, measured and timed. He shot off his rifle at the start, and tied a string across the road at the end. She was happy with her time, and smothered Tim with affection for helping her.

They were happy as a couple, and she knew that it was much more than just the company of two freaks seeking refuge with each other. She loved him as she could, and slept with him as his partner, she held him as a man when they made love. "I love this person," she said aloud more than once, although not to his face. She could lie in bed and stare into his eyes and see him for all that he was and all that he was not, and there was nothing disagreeable.

She still thought of Catherine though. They were planning another weekend climbing together. As Hanna backed her truck away from the cabin to go meet Catherine, Tim stood there grinning like a blushing idiot, his smile saying, "That's my gal."

"What a goddamned freak," she muttered to herself. She rolled down the window and hung her head out, "You should go drink some whiskey with someone."

He looked down for a moment playing the role of the indolent child. "No Ma'am—no one to do it with."

She felt an acute pang of empathy for him there all alone. "Well be safe, and don't do anything dangerous." She worried about him working with chainsaws and sledgehammers and the quirky old tractor.

"No Ma'am," he said now smiling like the faithful servant. Hanna laughed at how swiftly he could change roles. "You're an ass."

"I know," he said proudly.

As she drove away, Hanna looked at him in the rear-view mirror, watching her faithfully until her truck went over the hump in the long driveway. She wondered how he could be so devoted to her, even though she treated him so indifferently. She wondered how he would be, if she never made love to him. Was that all you needed to do to make these bad boys good? Give them the password to the venerable vagina and there they were, goose-stepping to your every need like erect Prussian soldiers.

But her feelings for him were not the same as the ones she harbored for Catherine, or Meg. Even in the middle of the day, busy with hard labor, a whimsical vision of Meg or Catherine would fill her with sweet butterflies and make her stomach muscles flex. She'd look at Tim and say, "I guess I'm as bad as you are."

"I know," he'd say with a wink.

She thought of him and the scenarios that might play out that winter, once they started to get snowed in, and there was no real work left to do. Tim had assured her that they would start skiing, which was fine except that Hanna really wasn't a skier, and she didn't understand all the terms and gear that Tim and Catherine had described to her. She had a vision of herself hiking down to the highway, digging out her truck and driving south as fast as she could go, but where to?

What tribe would take her in? Tim was her tribe, and there was Catherine and Andy, Old Dean, Dog and Hugh. Meg— Meg had written. "Perhaps that is enough," She said.

"So what will it be, Tim?" She asked herself aloud outside the ranch house one night, staring at the cold November stars. "Will we break our hearts, or are we even incapable of that?" Cynicism and pragmatism are terrible things, she thought. Our minds and imagined justifications are all we have for explanation and consolation. We have no dogma to cling to. She giggled at her momentary lapse into philosophical reverie, and chanted the cicada's mantra, "It doesn't really matter."

She imagined asking Catherine what she thought about all this heavy love and relationship baggage, but she knew Catherine would thoughtfully take a sip of whatever she was drinking, "I don't know," she'd say. "Do you want noodles in miso broth, or a tabbouleh salad for dinner?"

* * *

Snow began falling in earnest on Thanksgiving weekend. It snowed from the mountains all the way to the desert. There was so much wind that some snow spun and whirled beneath the boulders on top of the lonely, desert moraine, but it was only a dusting that made it below the boulder— not enough to begin to cover the stone that hid the Clovis.

Back at the office, Karl was locking up for the rest of the winter. He wouldn't return until tax time brought him around to dig through the books. He was leaving to take Donna to Mexico in celebration of her recent divorce and their engagement. He carried a stack of ledgers to a closet he used as a vault. Tim, Hugh and Dog had installed a steel door, reinforced the jambs and trimmed it with metal. He set the ledgers down on top of a box that was carefully taped and labeled: 'Hanna's Stuff. Fragile! Do Not Open!' He turned off the light, closed and locked the metal door, hiding the key on top of the trim.

More books from
Harvard Square Editions

People and Peppers, Kelvin Christopher James

Gates of Eden, Charles Degelman

Love's Affliction, Fidelis Mkparu

Transoceanic Lights, S. Li

Close, Erika Raskin

Anomie, Jeff Lockwood

Living Treasures, Yang Huang

Leaving Kent State, Sabrina Fedel

Dark Lady of Hollywood, Diane Haithman

How Fast Can You Run, Harriet Levin Millan

A Cat Came Back, Simone Martel

Nature's Confession, J.L. Morin

No Worse Sin, Kyla Bennett

Stained, Abda Khan

Reader, I would love to hear your thoughts
on my book. If you enjoyed this book,
please leave a review!

CPSIA information can be obtained
at www.ICGtesting.com
Printed in the USA
FSHW04n1230150318
45500FS